Bradshaw, Gillian. **Horses of Heaven.**
Doubleday. Apr. 1991. c.464p. LC 90-
43095. ISBN 0-385-41466-8. $19.95. F

Bradshaw continues the tradition of excellence begun in her earlier historical
novels (*Imperial Purple, LJ* 11/15/88).
Here she takes us to the kingdoms of Ferghana and Bactria (present-day Afghanistan) about 140 B.C. The widowed King
Mauakes seeks a wife to assuage his loneliness and to create political alliances.
Beautiful young Heliokleia of rival Bactria is selected to be the old man's queen.
Unfortunately, the young woman, who
has studied meditation with Buddhist
monks and who prefers prayerful solitude
to royal fanfare, seeks escape and sereni-
ty through meditation. Mauakes, in his in-
security, refuses to let her function as the
queen she was trained to be, and she emo-
tionally slips away from him. This so infu-
riates the king that he abuses her. Of
course, there is an admirable younger son
to soothe her, plus ambitious and corrupt
council members. Ultimately, the gods reward the just in this satisfying contempo-
rary story about an ancient land. For most
fiction collections.—*Joan Hinkemeyer,
Englewood P.L., Col.*

This is an uncorrected proof of a review scheduled for Library Journal, Mar. 1, 1991

Other Books by Gillian Bradshaw

Hawk of May
Kingdom of Summer
In Winter's Shadow
The Bearkeeper's Daughter
The Beacon at Alexandria
Imperial Purple

HORSES
OF
HEAVEN

CENTRAL ASIA
In the Second Century B.C.
(Modern place-names are shown in parentheses)

SAKARAUKAI
NOMADS

MOUNTAINS
OF
HEAVEN

Jaxartes River

Naryn River

KHOTAN

N

Oxus River

FERGHANA

Terek River

SOGDIA

Maracanda
(Samarkand)

Alexandria
Eschate
(Leninabad)

Polytimetos River

MOUNTAINS
OF THE SUN
(PAMIRS)

PARTHIA

Antiochia
Margiana
(Merv)

Tarmita
(Termez)

Alexandria
on the Oxus
(Aikhanum)

BACTRIA

Margus River

Bactra
(Balkh)

HINDU KUSH

Alexandria
(Kapisa)

Alexandria
in Aria

To India

©C. Carlson

HORSES OF HEAVEN

GILLIAN BRADSHAW

NAN A. TALESE
DOUBLEDAY
New York   London   Toronto   Sydney   Auckland

PUBLISHED BY DOUBLEDAY
a division of Bantam Doubleday Dell Publishing Group, Inc.
666 Fifth Avenue, New York, New York 10103

DOUBLEDAY and the portrayal of an anchor
with a dolphin are trademarks of Doubleday,
a division of Bantam Doubleday Dell
Publishing Group, Inc.

All of the characters in this book are fictitious,
and any resemblance to actual persons, living or
dead, is purely coincidental.

Book design by Anne Ling

Library of Congress Cataloging-in-Publication Data

Bradshaw, Gillian, 1956–
    Horses of heaven / by Gillian Bradshaw. — 1st ed.
       p. cm.
      1. Bactria—History—Fiction. 2. Afghanistan—History—
Fiction.
    I. Title.
    PS3552.R235H6   1991
    813'.54—dc20   90-43095
                                              CIP

ISBN 0-385-41466-8

Printed in the United States of America

May 1991

1 3 5 7 9 10 8 6 4 2

First Edition

PREFACE

This is a fantasy set in a real time and place. The time, 172 of the Seleucid Era, is the nice round date of 140 B.C.; the place is Central Asia. The Hellenistic Greek kingdom of Bactria flourished in what is now Afghanistan from the conquest of Alexander the Great until approximately that date. Its history, however, is a patchwork of ignorance and controversy, and very often all that is known of a Bactrian ruler is his name. Antimachos the God, Heliokles the Just, Demetrios the Invincible—we know they existed because they struck coins, but what they did that was godlike, just, or invincible, no one can say. I am not a historian, and this book owes more to imagination than to learning. I could even have set this story in an imaginary world—but I find real worlds more surprising and more interesting.

I've been asked to provide a guide to the pronunciation of the characters' names. This is a bit awkward. If I were reading a passage in Greek and I came across the name Eukleides, for example, I would do my best to pronounce it in the way modern scholarship has taught me, which involves at least two sounds with no good English equivalent. But to use that pronunciation in English speech would be irritating and pretentious, and I'd content myself by saying something like "You-*clay*-dees"—unless I were discussing the most famous bearer of that name, in which case I'd call him Euclid. As for the non-Greek names, I'm not really sure how their owners would have pronounced them. They are all genuine names, borrowed from the sources, but the Greeks, Indians and Chinese who wrote some of my sources probably couldn't pronounce Iranian names either. As for the Zoroastrian holy book, the *Avesta,* which I used for most of the Iranian women's names, as far as I can make out it's a Gordian knot of linguistic difficulties—and I'm a classicist, not an orientalist. Here, however, is a quick, *very* rough guide to pronunciation, using the Anglicized pronunciation mentioned above.

There are no silent vowels: Inisme and Amage are approximately "Ee-niz-mee" and "A-maggee," Choriene is "Khoree-aynee." (If you can't aspirate the *ch,* pronounce it as in "character," never as in "charge.")

Au, ai, oi and *ei* are pronounced, respectively, "ow," "eye," "oi" (as in "coin") and "ei" (as in "vein"). Mauakes is "Mow-akes"; Armaiti, "Ar-mighty"; Heliokleia, "He-li-o-klay-a." *Eu* is also a diphthong. The English pronunciation as "you" (as in "eucharist" and "euthanasia") is inaccurate, but too well established to differ with. In any other combination of vowels, each should be pronounced separately—Theodota, Anti-ochis, Go-ar.

Itaz is "Ee-taz," not "Eye-taz," and that goes for all other words with *i* in them. *Y* ought properly to sound like long French *u,* but "eye" will do for it—Tomyris, Tistrya.

There is really nothing more to add, except my thanks to the Department of Coins and Medals of the Fitzwilliam Museum in Cambridge for permitting me to examine their collection of Bactrian coins for so frivolous a purpose as this novel.

HORSES
OF
HEAVEN

CHAPTER

I

I first heard of Queen Heliokleia when I was eighteen: my father returned from Eskati that spring and told me that he had proposed me as one of her attendants.

Father had gone down to Eskati, the king's city on the Jaxartes, which is ten or twelve days' ride from our family estates by the Terek River, very early in the spring. Our family is noble, one of the seventy great families of the kingdom of Ferghana, and Father had gone to take his rightful part in the spring meeting of the tribal council. After the council meeting, he stayed in Eskati to keep an eye on events there and to do some business, and sent my two elder brothers back and forth in relays carrying news, orders, and requests for money or things to trade. It wasn't until late in the season that he rode through the gate in the mud brick wall of our village and dismounted in the yard before our house.

I heard the noise of his arrival—the dogs barking, the horses whinnying, and people shouting and laughing—but I didn't go to greet him

1

immediately; I was helping in the foaling sheds, and, as Father himself
always said, you should look after horses first, and men afterward, or
you and the men will both regret it. It was late in the season for a
foaling, but the little colt was born without trouble, and the groom
and I were standing about grinning as we watched the mare lick it
clean when my brother Havani dashed into the shed.

"Tomyris!" he bellowed. "Father wants you!"

The mare snorted and laid her ears back, and I grabbed Havani's
arm and hauled him out of the shed. "Don't you know better than to
shout like that in a foaling shed?" I yelled at him. "Merciful Anahita!"
Then I hugged him, because he'd been down at Eskati with Father and
I hadn't seen him since his last errand home. Of my two brothers, he
was the nearest to me in age, and we'd always been very fond of each
other.

"Watch out!" he said indignantly. "You've got mare's blood on
my coat now. Come on, stop worrying about livestock and hurry up;
there's big news from the city."

At that I looked at Havani in some alarm. This was in the spring of
the thirty-second year of King Mauakes' Era—the hundred and sev-
enty-second of the Seleucid Era to you, Greek readers—the year after
the Tochari first invaded, and the whole kingdom of Ferghana was as
restless as a horse herd with a tiger prowling just upwind. My father
and brothers had joined in the war the summer before to turn back the
invasion; two of my cousins and half a dozen of my family's tenants
had died in that battle, and we were all horribly aware that it was only
the beginning. We had met only one tribe, the smallest tribe, of a great
confederacy of the nomads. They had all lost their grazing lands in the
north to another confederacy, and now they were all looking for new
lands to replace them. The council meeting my father had attended had
been largely concerned with how we could defend ourselves against
the rest of the invaders.

"Have the Tochari come back already?" I asked Havani.

"Not yet," he said impatiently. "Father will tell you the news. But
hurry up!"

I washed off my hands at the cistern in the yard, then hurried with
Havani into the house.

Father was sitting on a leather cushion in the reception room, washing the dust out of his throat with a cup of wine, while my mother stood at the door giving orders to the servants. Father grinned and beckoned me over when I came in, and when I knelt down beside him, he gave me a rough hug. "Tomyris," he said, giving my braid a tug, "we may have made your fortune."

My mother left the door, came over, and settled gracefully opposite my father, giving me a particular, gratified, expectant smile. I gulped. This didn't have the look of a piece of news about affairs of state. I wondered if they'd arranged a marriage for me. I wondered, with a nervous thrill, who it could be.

"You know that our king decided to make an alliance with the Yavanas of Bactria, to protect us against the Tochari," my father said briskly, beginning to explain. (In my native tongue we always use "Yavana," the old eastern word, for the people who call themselves "Hellenes" or "Greeks.")

I nodded. That had been the chief result of the council meeting, and my father had sent us news of it weeks before. Like most people in the valley, I hated the idea of the Bactrian alliance, though I reluctantly accepted the necessity of it. "Never trust a sunny day in winter or the oath of a Yavana," goes the saying, but we would have to trust Yavana oaths now. The Greeks of Bactria, I know, find our suspicion unreasonable and ridiculous. "After all," they say, "King Alexander the Great, who founded our kingdom, founded your capital city as well. We ruled you for generations; some of us still make our homes in Ferghana. We built canals and irrigation systems which enriched your land, and paved roads to help you travel; we taught you how to raise the vine, how to use money, how to write. Before us you were just a confederacy of warring clans, scarcely more civilized than the nomads of the steppes. Your king uses a Greek system of administration to this day, uses Ferghanan Greeks to run it, and your coins bear counterfeited images of our kings. Since we were willing to do you the favor of agreeing to an alliance, why should you be stupid enough to oppose it?"

Yes, the Greeks ruled us for some forty years, and we did benefit by it. But they also drove all our nobility into exile and treated the rest of us like slaves. Think a moment, Yavanas of Bactria: think about your own subjects, the native Bactrians. Do you treat them like equals?

Of course you don't: you hold them as tenants on your estates and slaves in your houses, to till the land for you and serve you. Would you be content if the positions were reversed? I know, you'll say, "The Bactrians are used to it; they had the same treatment from the Persians before us, and they know nothing else. They don't complain." That's true enough. But when you conquered us, you treated us, the Sakas of Ferghana, as though we were Bactrians—and we were a free people, who had no master on earth, not even a king. It was bitter to us to be subjected suddenly to foreign overlords, forbidden to bear arms and required to pay taxes. If the first Yavana king had been an ordinary man, we might have rebeled again and again, until all the valley was watered with blood. And even though he was touched by the gods, and knew how to make the yoke easy, still, all the while the Greeks ruled us, we longed for freedom. It was our king, King Mauakes, who regained it for us, and he only kept it by his own strength and cunning. The Yavanas of Bactria, and their rival dynasty in India, tried to overthrow him by force, and they suborned the Yavanas who lived in Ferghana to try by treachery. The Bactrian Eukratid dynasty was particularly well versed in treachery: they owed their royalty to it. Most families in the valley had sons or fathers, uncles or cousins, dead in Yavana wars. Naturally we were afraid to make peace with enemies so powerful and so treacherous. When King Mauakes summoned the tribal council and announced what he meant to do, one councillor after another rose to speak against the plan. No one spoke for it but the king. But when the king blandly rejected all their arguments and asked them to vote, they all voted in favor—so great was the king's authority. Envoys had duly been sent south to the city of Bactra, where the Bactrian king Heliokles resided, and we had all waited to hear his terms.

"King Heliokles has agreed to the alliance," my father went on, matter-of-factly. Well, that was no surprise: the Tochari threatened him as much as they did us. "What's more, to bind the kingdoms together more closely, he has offered our king his sister Heliokleia in marriage. King Mauakes has accepted the proposal, and because of the threat of invasion, the marriage is to take place as soon as possible; the new queen may already be on her way from Bactra."

I stared at my father, appalled. I hadn't liked the idea of the

Bactrian alliance, and I liked the thought of a Bactrian queen even less. We Sakas are not like the Persians or the Parthians, who keep their women locked up at home: Saka women ride about the land like men, and our queens are accustomed to holding real power. No one in the valley would want a Bactrian Yavana woman as queen.

"The king *agreed* to this?" I exclaimed. "What about his grandson? I thought his grandson was his heir!" King Mauakes had designated his eldest son Goar as his heir long before. When Goar died in the battle against the Tochari, Mauakes had accepted Goar's son instead. The little boy was then seven, and had been named Mauakes after his grandfather.

My father shrugged. "So he is. The Yavanas have agreed that our king may make whatever arrangements he wishes about the succession, and this marriage won't affect that. But I haven't come to the point yet, Tomyris. King Mauakes wishes to appoint four young women, virgins chosen from the noblest families of the kingdom, to attend on the new queen when she arrives. Your uncle Kanit and I managed to suggest you as one of them, and the king has asked us to present you to him so that he can see if you're suitable. Think, girl!" My father grew warm. "Think what it means if he appoints you! Honor, riches—and, when it comes to that, a splendid marriage as well, since at the court you'll have the finest young noblemen in the kingdom coming and going all around you! So I've come home in a great hurry to fetch you, and if you like we can set out for Eskati tomorrow."

I was first horrified, then terrified, then furious. I glared at my father, outraged that he should think attending a Yavana queen conferred honor on anyone. Unreasonable, I know: whatever else they were, the kings of Bactria were favored by the gods with glory and splendor far greater than the rulers of our own kingdom. Our king would feel flattered to marry a Bactrian princess, and I should have felt flattered at the thought of attending her. The only way I can explain what I felt instead is to say that I was afraid for my own honor, which sounds unnatural now that I write it, as I must, in Greek. (How I wish that Sakan were a written language! The thoughts of the Greeks are mapped out with royal roads, but our own beliefs are like the paths taken by birds across the sky, and leave no tracks.) The Yavanas are never much concerned with honor; and the Parthians and Persians, who adore it, don't admit that women have it, except in the matter of not sleeping with any man but their lawful husband. My own people view things differently. If you take service with a lord or lady, your honor is bound up to theirs, as you must be faithful and obedient. What would a Eukratid queen expect me to do? What if she commanded me to do something wrong? I wouldn't obey; I would certainly be faithful to my own people and my own customs—and that would make me a traitor to her. But I couldn't put this fear into cold words, not immediately. Instead my anger centered on another side of the prospect which, in my youth and inexperience, I disliked almost as much. Was I supposed to mince about a palace, worrying about my lady's clothes and the style of her hair, scolding slave girls if the bath water was cold? My parents named me Tomyris after the famous queen of the Massagetai who led her people to victory against the King of Persia: that was my kind of queen.

"How could you suggest me for a royal attendant?" I demanded. "What sort of company would I be for a Bactrian queen? This Yavana woman probably doesn't even know how to ride a horse! Yavana girls wear dresses all the time, and paint their faces, and giggle, and read poetry, and cover their heads in public. I'd go out of my mind, locked up in a palace trying to please a queen like that!"

My father looked hurt, and my mother was annoyed. "It wouldn't hurt you to wear a dress occasionally," she said, looking pointedly at my trousers. I was wearing some of my brother's castoffs, very worn, muddy and bloodstained from the foaling, with only a short man's tunic instead of the long feminine one I was supposed to have.

"I was working," I told her sullenly.

"But you should have changed to greet your father on his return home. You're eighteen now, and a noblewoman: you should have more care for your dignity. As for this Yavana giggling—the lady will be a queen, not a merchant's daughter."

"Well, that's worse, isn't it?" I said sharply, coming to the real problem. "Yavana queens do nothing but plot and poison people."

"This one won't have any chance to do that here," said my father confidently. "The king will see to that."

"Then she won't be a proper queen at all: she'll be a prisoner and I'll be one of her keepers. No thank you!"

"Tomyris," said my father, in his no-nonsense-now tone, "you've no business refusing the arrangements your mother and I make for your benefit. Your mother is right: we've let you run wild here for too long. You need to spend more time with girls of your own class, and learn something of the world. In a few years it will be time for you to marry, and you need to know how a lady should behave."

"What have I done that's unladylike?" I protested. "Most men prefer a wife who can manage a farm, and are delighted if she's skilled with livestock. They can be sure their estates are well looked after if they have to go off and fight."

"There's more to being a lady than handling livestock," said my mother drily. "If you attended a council meeting, looking and talking as you do, you'd disgrace the whole family. A bit of experience in a palace would be good for you. And it's a great honor to be a royal attendant. If the king accepts you, it will benefit us all."

Of course, it would do the whole family good to have a royal attendant at the court, someone with access to the rulers, who could put in a good word for the rest of us if there were any offices going vacant or honors about to be disposed. I could see that, but still, I was appalled at the thought of living in a palace waiting on a Yavana queen.

"I'm not the right sort of person," I said.

"You speak Greek," my mother replied at once. "And you can read."

So I could; so, obviously, I can. The ability is rare in a Saka, and needs some explaining. My family was related to Lord Kanit, who was the high priest of the Sun and King Mauakes' favorite cousin. It wasn't a close relationship—he married my mother's father's sister—but it was enough for Uncle Kanit to take an interest in us, and to visit us whenever he was up our end of the valley. Once, when I was twelve, Kanit brought his Yavana secretary along with him on a visit. I was always a curious child, and was intrigued by the mysterious marks the secretary made on his wax tablets, so I asked him to explain them to me. The secretary was a nice old man, amused by the attention of this gawky girl, and he showed me the letters and taught me to write my name. As soon as I'd scrawled it out I rushed off to show it to the adults and be admired for my cleverness. They admired it too much: to my horror, I found Kanit suggesting that I come down to his own estates during the winter, when there was time for study, and there continue to learn how to read and write. "We don't have enough Sakas who can read," he said. "It's not good that we have to depend on the Yavanas for it: a Yavana will cheat whenever he can. If Tomyris learns she can supervise her husband's men when she's married."

My father was delighted. He agreed to Uncle Kanit's proposal at once. So late every autumn for the next five years, he dropped me off at Kanit's estates, which were two days' ride from Eskati, and there I stayed until the spring, huddled with Kanit's secretary over a pile of wax tablets. My fellow students were three of Kanit's own grand-daughters. He thought they would benefit from the same treatment, and his grandsons were all too busy learning more important things like how to repair an irrigation gate or fletch an arrow. I got on with Kanit's girls at first, but when I learned more quickly than they did, they turned against me—whenever one of them made a mistake, her grandfather would ask her why she couldn't be like Tomyris; I think I'd have taken a dislike to myself in the circumstances. Later on again we grew older and became friends once more, but by that time I'd learned to hate everything about Kanit's, including the Greek, and though I liked the old secretary, I was relieved when he died and the lessons were discontinued. But he lasted long enough to take me from alpha beta gamma to Book I of the *Iliad*. So when my mother said, "You can speak Greek," all I could do was scowl.

"If you were a royal attendant," said my father cunningly, "you'd be allowed to ride the royal horses. You might even be given some royal mares when you came to marry."

That made me waver. The royal horses are unrivaled, sacred, price-less. They are the reason that we inhabit Ferghana, and are a settled people while our cousins, the nomad Sakas, still roam the steppes. Our Lord the Sun pastures his horses in the mountains to the south and east of the valley, mountains which the Greeks call the Imaos range, but which we Sakas call the Mountains of the Sun. Sometimes travelers wandering among the high peaks have seen, in the unreachable dis-tance, a valley among the snows where the crystals of ice become flowers, and the air is warm and smells sweeter than jasmine. There the Sun's horses graze, immortal animals winged with light, resting from their task of drawing the god's chariot across the peak of heaven. But once one of these horses, a stallion, the proudest and swiftest of them all, ran from the mountains westward across the sky, until he came to Ferghana. A band of nomads, Sakas related to the Massagetai, were pasturing their own herds on the rich grass beside the river. The immortal stallion descended to them, and mounted the earthly mares. Then the Sun, looking down, saw his horse flashing like lightning in the valley, and descended to claim him. The earth was scorched by the wheels of his chariot, and the nomads covered their eyes against his brightness. Quickly they ran to offer sacrifice to the god, and they flung themselves on the ground before him. He was pleased with their piety, and before he took his horse and departed, he blessed them and told them that if they remained in the valley, they would prosper and grow strong. They honored his words, settled in Ferghana, and prospered as he'd promised, and from their mares sprang horses finer than any in the world, heaven-descended horses that sweat blood. Only the king's servants are allowed to ride them, and only the king's own family can keep the stallions. Royal guardsmen and attendants are sometimes allowed to keep the mares, though, and these may be bred to ordinary bloodstock, and their half-royal offspring still excel the common breed as mountain eagles excel blunt-winged hawks. I'm like all my people: I'd suffer a great deal to get possession of some royal mares, and my parents knew it.

"Well," I said, after a silence, "I suppose we could go down to Eskati and see if the king likes me." And chances are he won't, I reassured myself, as my parents expressed their satisfaction. There never was anyone less of a courtier than I am myself.

I went to bed that night very anxious and unsettled, not sure what to hope for. When at last I managed to get to sleep, I had a dream.

In my dream I was scrambling up a dry riverbed in a country of barren rock. I was panting and drenched with sweat, but couldn't stop: I was searching for something, searching desperately. I came to a dry pool and paused, looking up: beyond me to my right the sky came down like a sheet of blue ice, a wall between a gap in the mountains. Suddenly, with the mysterious certainty of a dream, I knew that I had come to the mountain pass by the Terek River, which leads eastward through the Mountains of the Sun—the closed pass, haunted by some nameless terror out of the darkness, from which no one ever returned. I stood there, frozen in terror, looking up into that place of death. It was very quiet, with only the bare rock around me, and it was very cold. Then behind me a voice said, "Sister, you must move; the water will drown you!" I turned and saw my little sister Tistrya standing there at the edge of the dry pool. She died before she was two, little Tistrya; died of fever when I was seven years old, though I threw my favorite toys into the river as an offering to the goddess Anahita, praying for her to live. I ran toward her, jumped out of the pool, and dropped to my knees to hug her. Tistrya was warm and alive in my arms, and her hair smelled of river water and balsam. She laughed, and behind me came a rushing noise, and the pool and dry river were full of loud blue-green water. There was a great light, and I woke up laughing painfully for joy.

Not all dreams come from the gods. But this dream, so vivid and so powerful, seemed to me a window opened by Heaven. It alarmed me, and when I told it to my parents it alarmed them too. It is unlucky to dream of the dead, and to dream of that place where no one goes is worse.

"But to dream of water coming to a dry place must be a sign of wealth and good fortune," said my father, puzzling over it. "And Tistrya appeared to you to save you. She always loved you. Perhaps it's a good omen."

"We will ask your uncle Kanit about it," my mother declared, deciding the matter. "And we will have him check the omens. We will make sacrifices to Anahita, too: water is her concern. If the omens are bad, we will find some reason why Tomyris can't be a royal attendant. Now we must go."

We started for Eskati that morning—my father, my mother, my two elder brothers, two of my father's archers, and me. I'd never been to the capital before—when I'd been to Uncle Kanit's, the weather had always been too bad to do the two-day ride just to sight-see. It was spring, and in the fields by the river, people were planting rice, backs stooped under a sky like lapis lazuli; beyond them the mountains were a soft blue, their peaks still glittering with the melting snow. For eleven days we rode west along the Jaxartes, and the towns clustered more and more thickly: it seemed that we would hardly leave behind the mud brick walls that ringed one when the next loomed up on the horizon. When we came to the lakes at the far end of the valley, the blue water was bright with cranes and the shallows full of lotus flowers.

By the Lesser Lake, which is close to the city, we stopped at an ancient shrine of the goddess of water, Anahita, the pure and full-flowing. We made offerings of flowers to win her favor for our mission. The statue of the goddess behind the main altar was the most beautiful sculpture I had ever seen: baked clay, shaped and painted so delicately that you could have sworn that Anahita herself stood there, her black hair braided behind her, but curving in crescent moon wisps upon her wide forehead, and her white hands cupping a water lily. It almost seemed she might step out and speak. It was Yavana workmanship, put there during the days of Greek rule. I found the statue disconcerting: I was used to Sakan statues of the goddess, stiff and clumsy dolls with big black eyes. I didn't know what to say to this foreign divinity, and stood mute while my parents made the offering. When we were outside the temple again, my parents handed me the ring dove that was also to be offered to the goddess. We Sakas do not kill animals in sacrifice to Anahita; she prefers living offerings, and birds set free. I held the dove a moment, feeling the softness of its feathers against my hands, and the quick beat of its heart. I remembered holding my toys over the river when Tistrya was ill: my little clay doll with her dappled horse; the gold bracelet my father had given me for my birthday; the little wooden tiger painted with yellow ochre and charcoal. Gone into the quick noisy water, and Tistrya died anyway. "Lady Anahita," I said aloud, as I had said then, "merciful, pure, full-flowing, hear me! Show us if you favor our mission!" and I tossed the bird into the air.

With a burst of wings it climbed upward toward the sun, then flew to the right, going higher and higher until it was lost in the light. Gone, like the toys, like Tistrya. I found that I was smiling. I had no cause for bitterness.

My father gave a whoop and slapped me on the back. The bird had flown to the right and directly toward the sun: the omen couldn't have been better. We all felt much happier when we continued toward Eskati.

The valley of Ferghana is shaped like a pear, the narrow end pointing toward the west, and Eskati is sited where its stem would be. Alexander the Great himself laid out its foundations by the Jaxartes River, and he called it Alexandria after himself, and adding Eschate, "the Farthest," to the name to distinguish it from all the other Alexandrias he'd founded already. The Yavanas here in the valley call it simply Eschate, Farthest, and we Sakas call it Eskati. The first I saw of it was a cliff in the distance, which seemed to rise white and sheer out of the middle of the lake; but as the road turned, I saw that the cliff was not in the lake, but on the plain beyond it. Then, as we drew closer, I saw that it was not a cliff, but a wall, and what I had taken for a steep crag beyond it was a building, a white building that glowed in the afternoon sun like a tower of light.

The walls were all of great blocks of stone, piled up thirty feet high, guarded by round towers. We often give the walls of our Saka towns foundations of stone, but to build high walls is difficult: the stones slip over one another and fall; mud brick, roofed against the rain, is safer. But stonework is nothing to a Greek; aqueducts such as we saw striding across the fields are nothing; all ingenious works of cunning come easily to them. When we arrived at the gates, I gaped while my father greeted the guards. The doors were half again as high as a man, and plated with iron. One of the guardsmen grinned at me and tapped one of the massive things with one hand. It swung back as lightly as a window shutter. How did they do it? I wondered—a wonder that ran in my head like the refrain of a song the more I saw of the city.

Eskati is laid out four-square and four-gated, like all Yavana cities. The houses are of brick or stone, and stand two or even three stories high, so that the overshadowed streets are like defiles in the mountains. All the streets run east-west or north-south, taking no account of the lie of the land but going perfectly straight, climbing up and down any hill with stone-paved steps. Most of the streets are narrow, barely wide enough for two horsemen to pass each other, but the four main streets are wide and flanked with porticoes—long rows of columns fluted and carved like acanthus leaves, all alike, supporting red tile roofs that give shade against the summer sun and shelter from the winter snows. Most of the buildings behind the porticoes are shops. Of these, most were selling common goods like the ones I'd find at home on market day—

fruits and vegetables, fresh bread, buckets and spades and ploughshares, bridles and leatherwork—but some of them had things I'd scarcely seen before, and I kept turning in my saddle to gape as I rode past. There was a shop that you smelled before you saw, which sold herbs and incense in boxes of polished wood, and oil in vessels of shining glass; there was a shop that was ablaze with more gold than I'd ever seen in my life; there was one glittering with the white edges of swords and armor fit for a hero; another was a rainbow of Indian cottons; another was full of gods, big and little, modeled in clay. I was quite dizzy by the time we arrived in the center of the town. This is a marketplace, with more porticoes of shops on the east and west sides; a huge public council house, round and domed, stands on the north, surrounded by a crowd of statues, inscriptions and notice boards. On the south side of the market, next to the river, is a temple. The Sun's disk is set in gold on the temple pediment, above a Greek carving of the gods so lifelike they almost seem to move. In the middle is set a divinity on a throne, a man whose gilded hair and beard flow back in an unseen wind, who looks down on the tiny mortals below him with solemn majesty and justice. His face is at once ancient and ageless, and wonderfully beautiful. There, I thought, is the face of the Sun himself. I dismounted and bowed to him, and my legs were shaking with awe.

I learned afterward that really the god was the Greek Zeus Olympios, to whom Alexander the Great had dedicated the temple. When the Yavanas depict the Sun, they always show him as a young man, beardless, crowned, and driving his chariot—and far prettier, to my mind, than suits the all-seeing Lord of the world. But our king Mauakes had rededicated the shrine to our own chief god, so here Zeus had his hair gilded and sat under the sun disk. The Greeks of the city didn't mind the change in dedication: they identify all their gods with other gods any way, and the Sun worshipped in the temple of Zeus became Zeus Helios, Zeus the Sun, without a murmur from the citizens. I felt uncomfortable when I first found out my mistake, but afterward I thought it very appropriate.

Behind the temple steps mounted the towering building I'd seen from the distance—it wasn't all stone, I saw now, but a hill covered with stables and barracks, armories and storehouses, and, at the top, the royal palace, white and shining in the gold evening. I swallowed sev-

eral times, staring at it, and my mother, who had dismounted beside
me, patted my arm.

We stayed that night with Uncle Kanit, who had the priest's house
beside the temple for his own, and who welcomed us hospitably. He
told us that the king had chosen three of the attendants already, and
was only waiting to see me before picking the last. "He's waiting as a
courtesy to me," he told us. "He's told me that he'd like to choose
some relation of mine, and he's turned down my granddaughter
Ardvisura already."

"Why?" I asked nervously. Ardvisura was one of my fellow Greek
pupils. The other two were married and engaged to be, and so not
available as royal attendants.

"He didn't say," replied Kanit innocently. "If he doesn't say, it's no
use asking him. But I think"—with a smile full of good-natured rue-
fulness—"I think it was because of her spots. Poor girl, she looks like
she slept in a flea pit. I hope you do better, my dear."

It was impossible to dislike Uncle Kanit. He never had a mean or
envious thought in his life.

I told him my dream, and he frowned over it, then smiled and said
it was not a warning, but a portent of good fortune, as I dreamed of an
escape from peril and of water coming to dry places. "And we are all
in peril," he said, frowning again. "The Tochari are a terrible danger to
us all. But I will consult our Lord the Sun for you."

We rose next morning before dawn and went to the temple. There
was a terrace in front of it, with a fire altar, and there we sacrificed a
white ewe lamb to the Sun as it came up, praying for good fortune for
our house and for Kanit's. Afterward Kanit counted out the divining
rods for me. The Yavanas, I believe, don't use this method of divina-
tion, but we Sakas always check the omens this way before any important undertaking. The rods are about as long as a man's forearm and are
made of willow wood marked with charcoal and chalk; a priest counts
them out of a bundle and can predict the future from the patterns they
make. I watched as Kanit counted them out, one by one, black and
white onto the pale stone of the terrace, while the new sun cast their
shadows long and black to the right as they descended. The joy I had
felt at the end of the dream seemed misty now, together with the relief
I'd felt at Anahita's shrine, and I remembered most vividly the silence

and cold among the barren rocks; I felt heavy with dread. But the omens for me were good: the signs for "long life" came up, and "wealth," and, lastly, the combination that means "kingship." "You will have long life and good fortune in the royal house," said Kanit, with real pleasure, and he swept the rods back into the bundle and escorted us up to the palace.

I was afraid. My mouth was dry and my palms were wet as we passed the guards and climbed the hill toward the marble-columned front of the king's house. King Mauakes had ruled since my parents were children. He was the first, the only Saka king. He had never been loved, but people spoke of him as though he were a god. I had been raised on stories about him—how he had led a small band of Ferghanan exiles into Eskati as a young man, and tricked the Yavana garrison into allowing them into the citadel, and overcome them, and held citadel and city against all comers. How he had made himself king, tricking his own followers, who had expected that the tribal council would rule the valley as it had before the Yavanas came. How he had fought the Yavanas, and defeated even Demetrios the Invincible, the conquerer of India, when that lord came to Ferghana hoping to reclaim his father's territory. And all who had plotted against him— Sakas to restore the council's power, Yavanas to restore Greek rule— had been outwitted, and discovered, and destroyed. In short, he didn't seem to me like a living man at all, but like a king in a hero tale: I imagined him as nine cubits tall and eagle-faced with a long white beard, and dressed in gold. Now I was going to meet him, what should I say? It didn't help that the palace had been built for one of the Yavana kings, and was the most magnificent building I'd ever set foot in, its walls painted and floors polished, and everywhere carpets so rich and beautiful I didn't know where to put my feet. I'd never felt so awk-ward and stupid in all my life.

The king was finishing his breakfast when we were admitted to him. The dining room was a large, high-ceilinged one which looked out on a colonnaded courtyard with a fountain; the king was sitting at a citron wood table with a bread roll in one hand, listening to his secretary read a list. He wasn't nine cubits tall, of course, but he was wearing a lot of gold—fragments of it were stitched all over his tunic, and the thick fingers that held the roll shone with rings. He swallowed the mouthful of bread he was eating and greeted Kanit warmly. Kanit bowed to him and clasped his free hand, then introduced us.

Mauakes looked at me a minute carefully. I saw he was not a large man and he had grown stout with age; he had a flat face and cut his gray beard short and round, so that his face was moonlike, hard to read. His eyes were like agates. I was dressed in my best clothes—loose trousers of white wool, boots stitched with red, and a long red and white dress fastened with a gold brooch; my mother had woven a red ribbon into my braid and painted my eyelids blue. I'd felt very splendid that morning. But I felt now as though I were wearing my brother's castoffs again, filthy from the foaling. I found myself scrunching my shoulders up to make myself look less tall. Being a tall girl is awful: there's more of you for everyone to stare at.

"Tomyris," said the king thoughtfully, "your uncle says you can speak and read Greek."

"Yes, my lord," I said.

"Then we will speak it," he said, switching to that language. "Do you like the Greeks, Tomyris?"

"I don't know any Greeks to talk to, O King," I replied after a moment. "I learned Greek from my uncle's secretary, but he's dead now."

"Ah yes, and you come from the east of the valley, don't you? From the lands by the Terek. Not many Yavanas there. Why did you learn Greek?"

I explained that Kanit and my parents had thought it might be useful. The king nodded and asked, "And you can read? If my new queen were to write a letter, could you read it?"

"Yes, my lord."

"Can you read this?" He took the list from his secretary and held it out to me; I wiped my sweating hand on my tunic and took it. It was a list of contributions to the wedding celebrations: So-and-so offered to give so many oxen; so-and-so else volunteered so many piculs of wine. I stumbled down it a little, until the king nodded and took it back. "Are you my loyal subject, Tomyris?" he asked, his eyes sharpening.

"I should hope so, sir!" I exclaimed, surprised. "Everyone in the valley knows how much we owe to you, and we'd be fools to be anything but loyal to a king who's ruled us so well."

He smiled at that. "Would you be pleased to serve a Yavana queen?"

I hesitated again. "I'd be pleased to serve you, my lord," I said at last. "If you want me as an attendant to your wife. That is . . . I mean . . ." I didn't know what I did mean, but it seemed to please the king, because he smiled again.

"Excellent," he said, and proceeded to ask me a few more questions about myself and what I knew about councils and palaces. This didn't amount to much, and I felt clumsier and sillier every minute. When he dismissed us, I walked back down the steps from the palace with a little disappointment and a lot of relief, sure that he'd choose someone more accomplished. I was astonished when he sent a slave down that afternoon to say that the position was mine.

Because of the time Father and I had spent traveling up and down the valley, the other attendants, who all lived nearer Eskati, had been chosen some time before. Messengers had come from Bactra to say that the new queen had set out, and there were now only seven days or so before she was expected to arrive. I was required to go up to the palace that same afternoon, so that the queen's household should have some idea what it was about before she appeared to command it. My parents stayed at Kanit's. There was no need to leave until after the wedding, and in fact people from all over the valley were beginning to pour into Eskati for the festivities. I was glad my mother and father were close at hand during the first weeks. The palace took a lot of getting used to.

The queen's apartments consisted of four rooms in the middle of the palace, on the second floor overlooking the courtyard and just above the king's rooms. One room at the back was for the four slaves to sleep in; two rooms at the sides were for royal attendants; and a big room in the middle was for the queen. It seemed a waste, as she wouldn't actually be sleeping there, since the king expected her to share his bed. "But she'll need space for her clothes, of course," said Inisme. "I expect she'll have lots of lovely things. The Yavanas do such beautiful weaving."

Inisme seemed to be the leader of the attendants. She was the daughter of the steward of one of the king's estates, and knew much more about royalty than the rest of us. She was born in the same month as me, but we had nothing else in common. Inisme was small and pale, with a face like a white rose and little neat hands with fingernails like onyx. Her clothes were always immaculate and every gleaming hair on her head stayed in its place. She knew all about who was related to whom, and what one should wear with what, and how to keep perfume sweet and eyeshadow in place, and what was the correct thing to do or say to anyone, in any circumstance, in a palace. When I first unpacked my clothes into the chest in my room, she cooed over my coat with its lining of snow leopard fur, then exclaimed in horror when she learned I'd shot the leopard myself on a hunting expedition. "How *could* you?" she asked.

"Well, they're a pest, up my end of the valley," I said. "It would have killed our sheep if we hadn't shot it."

"But to ride out on a hunting expedition!" exclaimed Inisme in disgust. "Up in the wilds of some mountain, eating dried goat's meat with a pack of dirty shepherds! And shooting! That's unladylike."

"Couldn't your brothers have done it?" said Jahika, one of the other attendants, who was the niece of the captain of the king's guard.

"I like hunting," I said: and Jahika and Inisme looked at each other in amazement and dismissed me once and for all as a wild mountain woman.

The fourth attendant, Armaiti, was more sympathetic. She was related to the king's son-in-law, and had been brought up on an estate not far from Kanit's; she knew Ardvisura and the others and we were friends the instant we discovered this.

To my surprise, I found that none of the others could read. Armaiti spoke reasonable Greek, but Jahika and Inisme knew only enough of the language to buy clothes with. Everyone knows that Yavanas think it beneath them to learn foreign languages. Many of the citizens of Eskati, Greeks born in the valley, didn't know more Sakan than would buy them vegetables in the market, so how likely was a Bactrian princess to speak a word of our language? And what sort of attendant are you if you can't understand your mistress' orders? Then I had an uncomfortable feeling that I could answer that question: a jailer doesn't need to understand a prisoner's complaints. I looked at myself and my fellow attendants, all of us of families that were in some way dependent on the king's, and I remembered the king's questions ("Are you my loyal subject?"), and I felt acutely uncomfortable. I was a loyal subject. But I wanted nothing to do with keeping any prison.

But the arrangements for the queen's reception seemed royal enough, and probably, I told myself, the king had merely chosen his bride's attendants as a precaution. I hoped so. I could already tell that the work was going to be bad enough without guard duty added to it.

My duties seemed to consist mainly of sitting still and standing still. The four slaves—two old women and two young ones, all born in the palace—were to keep the rooms clean, fetch wood and water, and wash clothes. We royal attendants were supposed to fetch things for the queen, sit with her, spin with her, and stand about looking decorative when she spoke to people. I was bored with it even before she arrived, and spent a lot of time wondering what the woman would be like. I looked at the Bactrian silver coins I'd been given as an advance salary: most of them had Heliokles' face on them, though some had his father Eukratides'. Both kings had a large nose, an indulgent, fleshy chin, and sharp, dangerous eyes: strikingly ugly faces and unpleasant ones.

"Do you suppose she'll look as much like a pig as her father?" I asked Armaiti, showing her the coins.

Armaiti giggled, then whispered confidentially, "She might and she might not. She's only a Eukratid on her father's side, you know."

"Who was her mother?" I asked.

Armaiti's face lit up as she realized I hadn't heard this juicy piece of news. "Her mother was the sister of King Menander of India, the daughter of Demetrios the Invincible."

"What?" I said, shocked. "She's a descendant of Antimachos?"

Armaiti nodded. "No one realized that before the king agreed to marry her," she said, explaining why I hadn't heard before, "but it's been all over the city just in the last week."

When Ferghana was first ruled by a king, that king was Antimachos: before him there were only priests and the tribal council. As I said before, he ruled the valley wisely, and reconciled the Sakas to kingship as perhaps no other man on earth could have done. He was the one who commissioned the irrigation systems which doubled the amount of arable land in the valley; he built the roads; he introduced the cultivation of the vine, apple and pear trees, almonds and pome-granates; the use of money: all Yavana civilization we learned from him. He was revered, despite the fact that he was foreign and our master. I said just now that people spoke of Mauakes as though he were a god, but when they spoke that way about Antimachos, they believed it—and he had used that. Antimachos the God, he called himself, and in many parts of Ferghana he's still worshipped as one. Never by my family—as my father said, we could hardly give divine honors to a man who'd sent our own ancestors into exile—but on our own lands there are peasants who burn incense to him whenever they repair the dikes. There had been no rebellions in his reign; none. It was his son, Demetrios the Invincible, who lost Ferghana to Mauakes, and even so, Demetrios only lost it in his absence. He had been confident of the people's loyalty to his house, and left the valley under a light garrison while he set out to conquer a vast kingdom in India. When Mauakes reclaimed the valley for the Sakas, Demetrios made one attempt to retrieve it, and very nearly succeeded in doing so, since there were Sakas as well as Yavanas willing to fight for him. If he'd fought harder, Demetrios might have been king of Ferghana again. But his attempt had been halfhearted: India required his full attention. The Antimachid dynasty had since had little to do with us. But we still listened, half against our wills, to their fame, which had a brightness that exceeded any ordinary repute of power or military glory. Demetrios' son Me-nander was said by his Indian subjects to be "a king of the wheel," whose enemies are subdued by the mere power of his gaze; he was, they said, an arhat, a saint who has overcome all worldly conditions, and is like a rock that cannot be shaken by any wind. The Eukratids, as I've said, were our familiar enemies, our neighbors across the Oxus, an arrogant and treacherous dynasty that we hated comfortably with a touch of contempt. The Antimachids were another matter altogether. The prospect of an Antimachid ruler, Menander's niece, was at once less distasteful, less depressing, and much more frightening than a Eukratid. I thought of the face I'd seen on an old coin—delicate, with a long nose and fine eyes, and a peculiar smile as though it were laughing at itself, amused to be on a coin at all. King Antimachos the God, it had said beneath the face. On the reverse of the coin was a winged thunderbolt. I remembered the irrigation canal that crossed the heights of our own land, and the inscription cut into the stone that marked a division in it: "Antimachos made me," clear proud letters, half-masked, usually, by the wildflowers the farmers would leave there in gratitude for the life-giving water.

"Probably she'll take after her father," I said, to reassure myself.

"Her mother died when she was little," agreed Armaiti. "She was brought up at the Eukratid court."

"Well, there you are," I said. But I still felt more uncomfortable than ever, and wished that I hadn't come to Eskati, and that the king hadn't accepted me when I did.

I must pause here. I began this account because it seemed to me that the events of the first year after the queen arrived needed a memorial, a paved, fixed Greek account, since the winged words of my own people have already transformed them into legend. Ever since Queen Heliokleia's death, people have been saying that she was a goddess. I've visited her tomb myself to find old country women placing flowers on it and mumbling prayers for a good lambing season or a cure for their granddaughter's colic. Now the present king and queen have ordered a bowl altar full of continually smoking coals to be put there as well, and visitors can burn a pinch of incense too. She would have found that ridiculous—slightly distasteful, totally pointless, but principally just ridiculous. She wasn't a goddess; she wasn't even pious, in any ordinary sense of the word. What she was, though, is harder to say. I decided to write because, as everyone points out to me, I know more about what happened than anyone else who's still living. Much of it I saw for myself, and what I didn't see firsthand I learned secondhand— sometimes from the queen herself, sometimes from her family and the palace servants, or from my brother and his friends in the army and the royal guards. Philomela told me quite a lot. Long ago I worked out in my own mind how it must have been, guessing, imagining what I didn't know—not because I'm a lover of gossiping stories, but because I felt a mystery in much that I saw which I needed to understand. But I'm no artist, and the more I think of it, the harder it is to make the words match the image in my mind. What will it look like to those who don't have my memories behind it—the heat of that summer, and the flies, with the scent of nard and jasmine in the women's quarters of the palace; or the loud rush of the streams in the mountains, and the smell of snow and horses? Up to now I have spoken straightforwardly, saying what I did and thought myself—and I've found that even so it is hard to speak the truth, hard to remember clearly what it was like *then,* when I was a raw country girl and knew nothing of the court; hard not to let all the years between that girl and the old woman I am now color my words. And now I must do more, and say what others did, and how they felt, things I didn't know for certain even at the time. Should I repeat only bare facts? That would be like arranging a collection of bones, and saying, "Here is a tiger"—which would be a lie. The bones might be a tiger's, but a tiger is a living creature of flesh and blood, sun-colored and terrible—not a pile of sticks. I must concentrate on telling the story as I understood it, as simply as I can, and hope that truth will make all things clear.

King Mauakes' only remaining son, Itaz, wasn't in Eskati when I arrived there. He was the youngest of the king's children—the king's daughter Amage was ten years older, and the two elder princes were both dead, the eldest, as I have said, in battle against the Tochari, and the second years before in a Yavana war. Itaz was, in a way, a stranger to Ferghana. Early in his reign King Mauakes had made an alliance with the Parthian kingdom to the west, who were traditional enemies of the Bactrians. When his youngest son was eight years old, Mauakes had sent him to be fostered by a noble Parthian family to strengthen the alliance; he had only recalled him to Ferghana when he was preparing for the Tochari invasion. Itaz had returned from Parthia at the age of twenty-two, half a Parthian himself. He shaved his chin, carried the short sword, and spoke with the tripping accent of the Parthians, saying *d* for *l* and so on. He had also embraced the Mazdayist religion, and swore by the Wise Lord, Ahura Mazda, instead of by the all-seeing Sun like most of the people in the valley. In spite of this, he was popular among the younger noblemen: he was a good horseman, an excellent archer, a brave warrior, and accomplished in every art that we Sakas admire, and had a generous and open nature that made friends readily. He was a tall, slim young man with a dark, thin, eager face and clear eyes, and he was as transparent as water: alight with enthusiasm, dark with anger, totally incapable of deceit. He admired his father enormously—Mauakes, after all, was the founder of a kingdom, a man the Parthians spoke of with awe and the Yavanas with hatred and respect, a father any young warrior would be proud of. Since his return, Itaz had done his utmost to please the king. Nonetheless, after the council had first voted its agreement to the king's Bactrian alliance, and the messenger had been sent to King Heliokles, Itaz went to his father in his private room of the palace, closed the door behind him, and said, "I know we must have allies against the Tochari, but why make a treaty with evil spirits? Make a treaty with the Parthians instead!"

Mauakes looked at his son affectionately. The king was a cunning man, subtle and indirect by nature, and made suspicious by long scheming and many betrayals. His son's transparent honesty enchanted him. Still, faced with opposition, he gave Itaz the bland forgiving look he used to visit on his opponents, the one which always set their teeth on edge. "We already have an alliance with the Parthians," he said mildly.

Itaz nodded impatiently. "I meant you should strengthen the alliance," he said.

Mauakes sighed, still with the forgiving look, and shook his head. "Do you think that would help?" he asked. "They've already agreed to send a troop of cavalry when we ask—though whether they'll do that when it's not the Yavanas we want to fight, who can say? When the Tochari come they may want to keep their cavalry for themselves."

"They would do no such thing!" declared Itaz hotly. "Lord Suren's lifeblood is honor, and he'd sooner sell his wives and children into slavery than break an oath. When we ask them for help, they will give it." The Surens were the family with whom he had been fostered.

"Selling wives and children doesn't mean much to a Parthian," Mauakes said drily. "No Parthian noble has much regard for wives, or he wouldn't try to keep a dozen ladies in the one house. If your Lord Suren were willing to give up some of his lands rather than break an oath, I'd feel happier. No, no, I won't insult him; I'll grant him an honorable man. But it's not to the point. The Parthians are delighted to help us against the Yavanas, their old enemies. But the Tochari don't threaten them at all—not unless they cross the Oxus. And if they did cross the Oxus, the Parthians would be pleased: it would mean that the Yavanas would be destroyed once and for all. Why would the Parthians help us, if it meant preventing that? And if Lord Suren would keep faith, would the Arsaces?" The Arsaces is what the Parthians call their king. "But leave that aside, assume they'll send the cavalry if I ask. If we strengthened the alliance, they might send two troops of cavalry. But I couldn't keep all that cavalry here; I've only food and fodder enough for my own army."

"You could raise more," interrupted Itaz.

Mauakes raised his eyebrows. "I began raising more when I first heard of the Tochari. Now the council lords are raising more, too—for their own men. The land can feed only so many horses, Itaz, my dear, and the people grow only so much food. No, I couldn't feed an army of Parthians. So I'd have to send off for it when the Tochari arrived; and the Parthians would have to collect it; and it would have to come here—not too fast, or the horses wouldn't be fit for fighting—and in the meantime we'd have lost the war. And besides, what use is cavalry? We have plenty of cavalry already; better cavalry than the Parthians. But so do the Tochari, and they have more of it. What I need are elephants. Elephants, and some Yavana catapults. That would stop the Tochari."

"But a treaty with the Yavanas!" exclaimed Itaz. "And not even with the King of India, who's an honorable man, but with Heliokles of Bactria, the son of a murderer and the brother of a patricide! How can we trust him?"

Mauakes smiled at that. He had never trusted anyone in his life. "If I need a fire, and I can't find any wood, I'll burn dung," he said. "Heliokles wants us to weaken the Tochari and keep them away from his own lands; we can trust *that* absolutely. India is too far away to be any help to us. No, no, we must now take our ally Heliokles at his own word, and call him an honorable man. His father Eukratides murdered his master to avenge his grandfather's death. And as for the patricide—well, Heliokles had him put to death, didn't he?"

"He did indeed. He had his own brother, his father's murderer, put to death—and he gained a kingdom by it."

"There you are," said Mauakes. "He put filial loyalty above his feelings as a brother. Heliokles Dikaios, he calls himself; Heliokles the Just."

"He's filth," said Itaz. "A son of Angra Mainyu and an adherent of the Lie. I wouldn't touch him." Angra Mainyu, say the worshippers of

Ahura Mazda, is the prince of demons, the spirit of the Lie, which fights against Rectitude and the Light, and has done so ever since the world was made.

"Tch," said Mauakes, "I didn't send you to Parthia to make you a priest. An alliance with the Yavanas is the best chance we have of keeping our kingdom safe, and that, if you ask me, is the best way to please the gods. We don't have to love King Heliokles to do it. Chances are we won't even see him. He may not even want an alliance with us—though if he doesn't, he's a stupider man than I took him for. But whatever happens, I expect you to obey me, like a good son, and say nothing about this to tribal council, or the councillors will think of using you to replace me." Mauakes gave Itaz a straight look, no longer so forgiving. He adored his son—but his nature merely made him more suspicious of those he loved.

"May the gods forbid it!" Itaz exclaimed, shocked enough to convince even his father. "But . . ."

"But?"

Itaz sighed and shrugged. "But I prefer the Parthians," he said ruefully. "Though I suppose you're right. If we play our part of the alliance honorably, there's no disgrace possible to us."

"There's my son," said Mauakes warmly; and the young man went off, still with a nagging feeling that the alliance was dishonorable, but determined to be loyal to his father and say nothing in public. But, as I said, he had an open nature and a crowd of friends, mostly young noblemen in the king's guard, and he'd already spoken against the alliance to them and announced his intention of discussing the matter with his father, and they naturally asked him how it went. He didn't know how to evade a question, so he told them, in strict confidence, what his father had said, and of course it was all over the valley within a week. I'd heard about it myself long before I left home; peasants in the fields were chuckling over the king's blunt "If I can't find wood, I'll burn dung," and the lords of the tribal council whispered among themselves, pleased. Itaz was horribly embarrassed. The king said nothing about the matter, but he made delicate inquiries among his guardsmen, and had his son watched. A popular young prince in public opposition to his father's highly unpopular new alliance was a potential danger no aging king could afford to overlook.

Of course, King Heliokles had accepted the offer of an alliance gladly, and at once sent envoys to Ferghana to draw up a treaty of peace and friendship. These were the actual terms as the Bactrian envoys proposed them: that Heliokles and Mauakes should undertake to stop raiding each other's lands and subverting each other's subjects; that neither should make any alliances with the other's enemies—the old Saka alliance with the Parthians excluded; and that Mauakes, who was a widower, should marry Heliokles' sister Heliokleia. She would be sent north to Ferghana with a dowry of five elephants and their drivers, and some twenty catapults with an engineer to manage them.

This last proposal was a surprise, and Mauakes regarded it with some suspicion. The additional bond that such a marriage would give the alliance was not something to be thrown away lightly. But Mauakes was an astute man, and was keenly aware of how unpopular such a marriage would be. Moreover, he had no intention of disinheriting his grandson for any child he might have by Heliokles' sister, and this, he reckoned, would certainly be unacceptable to the arrogance of the Yavana king. So he smiled at the envoys and made a gesture of helplessness. "King Heliokles flatters me," he told them. "And I thank him for his royal and generous offer. And yet, good sirs, I must hesitate to accept. You know, perhaps, that my son Goar died last summer in the battle against the Tochari. But though he is dead, his son lives, and both I and all the people of Ferghana expect that he will be my heir. How could I disappoint the hopes that are placed in him? Even if I wished to do so, all the people of the valley would rise up to deny me, pointing, with justice, to his father's merits and his sacrifice."

He expected that this would settle the matter, but, after some whispering, the envoys swallowed their disappointment in one gulp and told him, "King Heliokles has the greatest respect for you, O King, and he is eager that, in this crisis, he may rely on you as a kinsman. Questions of the succession belong to an uncertain future: the Tochari threaten all of us now. We understand that you wish your grandson to succeed you, but why should that be a bar to a match that will unite our kingdoms and end the long wars between us?"

Mauakes watched them a minute with a bland smile and expressionless eyes, trying to puzzle out their motives. He knew that Heliokles considered him a formidable enemy, but he had a surer knowledge of the Bactrians than most people in the valley, and he doubted that he was considered formidable enough to be worth Heliokles' sister if she wasn't to inherit from him. Was Heliokles planning a new war against Parthia or India, and trying to enlist Mauakes' support? That seemed improbably rash, with the Tochari invasion threatening them both. Did the king of Bactria have some reason to fear a domestic threat, then, and was he trying to make sure this new alliance was made exclusively to himself, and not to the Bactrian state? Or was there something wrong with the sister? She wasn't old: Heliokles himself was barely thirty, and the girl, thought Mauakes, must be much younger. Was she hideously ugly, half-witted, pregnant? Had she made enemies at court? There was no use asking the envoys: they'd no doubt assure him that she was beautiful, virtuous and wise, like all marriageable princesses.

Mauakes told the envoys that he must give serious thought to this solemn proposal, and went off to order inquiries among their slaves, and among Yavana traders who'd recently returned from Bactria. The following morning he resumed the meeting, and graciously accepted the proposals for the alliance.

The move caused only grumbling among the nobles who had stood by the king in the negotiations: it was, after all, a mark of great respect that Heliokles was willing to offer Mauakes, a barbarian, his sister's hand. Itaz, however, was horrified. Again he went to his father's room in the palace and closed the door. "How can you do this?" he asked, struggling to keep his voice level.

Mauakes shrugged. He had agreed to the marriage, but now he felt embarrassed and ashamed at his son's reproach. Being himself, however, he showed none of this, and instead continued in his work, counting out tallies of taxes. "Hmm? Do what?" he asked.

"You know what!" said Itaz angrily, not deceived by the casual air. "Marry Eukratides' daughter and make Heliokles your brother. That!"

Mauakes shrugged, still counting tallies. "We need the elephants. I thought you'd agreed to that before."

"Elephants!" exclaimed Itaz in disgust. "How can you take a Eukratid, a Yavana whore, into my mother's bed? What would my brothers say if they were alive to see it? Five elephants!"

"She's a Yavana queen!" shouted Mauakes, jumping to his feet, tipping over the table, losing his temper, as he always did, suddenly and without warning. "And why do you object so much to that? Don't you come whining to me about your brothers: you're glad they're dead! With them out of the way you had your hopes up, didn't you? You've been peddling your opposition to the alliance to get the councillors' support. You know that if I died tomorrow they'd make you king instead of the boy, and now you're afraid that the Yavana woman will have sons to supplant you, sons with powerful allies. You'd prefer it if I were dead as Goar!"

Itaz said nothing for a moment, merely looked at his father. He was not shocked so much this time. He had been home longer, and was growing used to the king's sudden suspicions. But they still hurt him, and the pain showed. "I loved my brothers," he said at last. "And I pray to all the gods that you have no successor until your grandson is old. And Father, I'm sorry that I didn't keep my opposition quiet last time: I was clumsy and stupid and spoke when I shouldn't. But I wasn't treacherous; I'd never betray you of my own free will. Please believe me."

"Well," said Mauakes, after a moment. "Well." He sat down again. "I was wrong to say that to you," he said, after another minute. "But you shouldn't try to tell your own father who to marry."

"But Father," said Itaz, going to him and catching his shoulder, "if I love you, how can you expect me to say nothing when I see you doing something that will disgrace you and cause you grief?"

Mauakes sighed: the hand on his shoulder, the evidence of love, was terribly sweet; it weakened him. He never knew how to ask for love or acknowledge it, but he wanted it, the more desperately because of his wariness. "Why do you think this woman will disgrace me?" he asked, anxiously, his suspicions at once whirling in another direction. "I was told she was young, quiet and retiring, and a virgin. Are there stories that say otherwise? Do you know anything about her?"

"Only the names of her father and her brother. That ought to be enough," Itaz said fiercely. "She comes from a people who have always been our enemies, and from a family without honor or natural loyalty."

Mauakes snorted. He had no great faith in honor or natural loyalty in any family. "If the woman betrays me, I can have her put to death," he said. "But I've never heard of any Yavana queen playing the whore. The tyrant, yes, but not the whore—and she'll have no chance to play tyrant here, even if she's old enough to want to. I'd be a sorry king if I couldn't manage one little Yavana girl."

"How old is she?" asked Itaz suspiciously.

Mauakes shrugged, tossing off the arm. "Nineteen, twenty? Younger than you are. Heliokles himself is only thirty, and the girl was Eukratides' youngest child. I was told she was religious and bookish."

"Twenty isn't a child," said Itaz. "And the Yavanas know nothing about the gods; even when they think they're religious they're full of blasphemies. And their books are full of impious ideas. If she's scholarly, she'll despise us for being illiterate. If she can she'll take advantage of us, and plot with the Yavanas of the city behind our backs to betray us to her brother."

Mauakes again snorted. "Has anyone, Saka or Yavana, ever got the better of me by plotting?"

Itaz hesitated. No one ever had. "But a young wife . . ." he said. "If she's beautiful . . ."

Mauakes laughed at this. "Do you think a member of Heliokles' family is likely to be beautiful?" he asked. "I didn't even ask about that side of things: leave the bad news until she arrives, I thought to myself. But even if she were, do you think I'm such an old man that I'd dote on her, like a silly old lecher, resting my aging head and trusting her to run my affairs for me? Do you think I'm a stupid old man, eh?"

Itaz met his father's eyes, and saw, sadly, that the penetrating look was back in them; the hint of another suspicion, not quite formed.

"No," he said. "No, I'm young, but not that foolish."

Mauakes leaned back, contented. "Well then, what harm is there in a young virgin?"

"Plenty," said Itaz shortly, "if she makes Heliokles your brother."

"But I want him to be my brother; I want him tied to me, and obliged to keep his word even if the Tochari don't invade again."

"He had his real brother killed!"

"Tch." The king was again withdrawing into the bland look. "He's tried to have me killed, too, and failed. But now he'll want me alive, to protect him from the Tochari. And the girl is a queen: it's an honorable match. It will be valuable for all of us."

"Worth five elephants," said Itaz bitterly. "Don't do it, Father. Send to Bactra and say that you've checked the omens and they predict disaster if it goes through. Won't Heliokles send the elephants anyway, if he's afraid of the Tochari?"

"Not if I insult him that way," snapped Mauakes, losing patience. "I will marry the woman, and I won't be ordered about by you. You may go—and this time don't say to anyone else what you've said to me; I'll have enough trouble with the council over the marriage without you dredging up the memory of your mother. She's ten years dead, and I'm free to marry whoever I want to."

Itaz paled, opened and shut his mouth, and finally stalked angrily from the room.

This time he obeyed his father and said nothing to anyone about the marriage. He was too honest, however, to pretend that he liked it, so he took some of his friends in the royal guard off on a lengthy hunting trip into the mountains, and only returned, reluctantly, the day before the bride was expected in Eskati.

It was late in the spring by then and the nights were warm; the bride's party had camped, with the elephants, a little way outside the city, ready to enter by the west gate in the morning and celebrate the wedding. To the east along the lakeshore camped the Sakas, too many now to fit inside the walls, overflowing the city for miles. Itaz rode in by the south gate and found all Eskati bustling and bubbling with holiday excitement. Mauakes had made the city more magnificent than ever for his wedding, planning to win over the common people by their love of a show. The citizens of Eskati itself, as I'd already learned, had needed no such persuasion. Despite more than thirty years of Saka rule, they remained Greek to their fingertips, and did their utmost to welcome a queen of their own blood. The statues were garlanded with flowers, the porticoes were hung with banners, the temples were newly painted, and when Itaz rode in, the fountains were just being filled with wine. Fires were being built to roast goats and oxen for the next day's feast, and the air was full of the scent of baking bread and honey cakes. The king's son sent a servant to the palace to announce that he'd obeyed his father's summons and returned, sent some of the guards home with the horses, and went directly to a brothel.

There's an establishment in Eskati where all the young noblemen go. It's so famous that even I had heard of it—well, overheard of it: my brothers talked about it once. The house has floors of fine mosaic, gold-worked awnings, carpets patterned with scenes of the loves of the gods. The beds have sheets of fine linen, scented with flowers, and bedspreads dyed with purple, indigo, and crimson. The whores wear tunics of Indian cotton, spun so fine that through it you can see the color of their nipples; they can dance with the cymbals or play the kithara and the flute, and sing songs of love in Greek and in Sakan. It's a Yavana establishment, as you might expect: only the Yavanas have such brilliance and such ingenuity even in depravity. Though Itaz was ordinarily a devout enough Mazdayist to avoid brothels, he went straight there.

He shoved the door open and came in, still in his hunting clothes, together with five or six of his friends, young noblemen of the royal guard, all calling for drink. It was still only the middle of the after-noon and the brothel was supposed to be closed, but for the king's son the madam came running in her slippers, shouting for the servants and shouting for the girls. She settled Itaz and his friends in the bathhouse with a jug of wine and a girl each. They finished the wine and went to dinner. They don't sit up to eat, in this establishment; they lounge in the Yavana fashion on couches. Itaz drank three or four more cups of wine, then ate something, then drank some more, then lay back with his head in the lap of one of the girls, listening while another girl played the kithara and sang.

"Give me a kiss," he told the girl when she'd finished her song; and she came over and gave him one. "This is what my father's doing tomorrow," he said, taking her hand. "Finding himself a Yavana whore. But instead of him paying her, she has to pay him five ele-phants."

His friends sniggered at this. "Well, she's not as pretty as Philo-mela," said one of them, a fellow named Azilises, whose family still holds the lands up to the northwest of the valley. He was a good-looking young man, clever, witty and irreverent, and one of Itaz' favorite companions.

They might have contented themselves with abusing the Yavanas to each other, but it happened that the singing girl, Philomela, was disappointed to think that the new queen might be ugly. She loved the city in holiday, and she was a true Yavana and delighted at the thought of a queen of her own race. "Oh," she said, "people were saying that she was as beautiful as golden Aphrodite. What does she look like, then?"

"There's her brother," said Azilises, spinning a Bactrian copper coin at her.

"And there's her father," added Itaz, handing her another coin, a silver drachma like the ones I'd been studying myself, with the portrait of Eukratides.

"But her grandfather was Antimachos," said Philomela, "and her uncle is King Menander of India. They're handsome men."

Itaz, of course, had been away on his hunting trip when this news came out. He stared at the girl, then rummaged in his purse and found a coin, a gold tetradrachm of Menander, king of India. He turned it under the lamp, looking at that delicate, mocking, dangerous face. Then he looked up at the whore again and said impatiently, "How can she be a descendant of Antimachos? They've been at war with the Eukratids for years."

"But they made a truce at the end of one of their wars," said Philomela, "and Menander's sister married Eukratides. Didn't you know that, sir?"

"I'd heard that. But I'd heard the lady died without heirs, a few years after her marriage, and on Eukratides' death the war broke out again. I'm sure Eukratides' children were by an earlier marriage."

"His sons were," said the whore, "but his daughter, Heliokleia, was from the second marriage."

"Are you sure?" demanded Itaz.

"Of course," said Philomela. "We were talking about it all day— how exciting it is that a descendant of Antimachos is coming back to rule Ferghana."

Itaz stared at her for a long minute, then laughed, loudly and drunkenly. "By the Sun!" he said. "It's worse than I thought. A descendant of Antimachos the God! There won't be a Yavana in the valley who'll obey my father's orders if she chooses to contradict them. I wonder if my father knows."

And then he realized that of course his father knew; his father was counting on it to finally reconcile the Yavanas to his rule, so that he

could face the Tochari with the country united behind him. But
Mauakes had not mentioned it to him, even to explain. The young
man suddenly saw how little he was trusted, how far he was kept from
any real power in the country. He'd noticed, of course, that he'd been
given no real rank or position since he'd returned from Parthia the year
before, but he'd thought it was because he was young, because he
needed time to get used to the ways of his own country again. He
loved and admired his father immensely; he knew that Mauakes loved
him: he had trusted his father to do what was best for him. He'd
thought, as we all had, that his father had recalled him from Parthia to
have him at his side, to help in the time of danger. He had never
understood the suspicions, never really believed that they were serious.
Now, like a roof falling on him, he saw that they were, and with a
flash of insight knew he had been recalled because he was not trusted at
large in Parthia while the king was threatened. Mauakes feared that he
might enlist Parthian help against his own clan to gain the succession,
and wished to keep him at hand and under surveillance. He was told
nothing of his father's plans because he had no part in them.

If he'd been ambitious, it would have made him angry. But he was
a loyal, warm-natured man, devoted to all his family. He was hurt and
bewildered; he remembered his bold attempts to argue with the king
and was ashamed at his own naive simplicity. But at the same time, he
was strangely sorry for his father, so suspicious, so much alone. He fell
suddenly silent, fumbling drunkenly with the confusion of his own
feelings.

"Probably the king hopes to satisfy the local Yavanas with it," said
one of the young nobles sourly, not noticing his friend's abrupt silence.
"He's always trying to please them."

Azilises grunted. "A Yavana treasurer gets caught with his hand in
the privy purse," he said, "and the king says, 'Now, now, don't do it
again.' But if a Saka lord keeps some of the king's taxes for his own
men, it's a steep fine and 'Next time you'll die for it.'"

He was drunk, or he wouldn't have spoken so plainly in front of
the king's son. His friends shifted uneasily. "The Yavanas are all thieves
and whores," one of them agreed, as though nothing more than that
had been said.

The Yavana whore was still watching Itaz and the gold tetra-

drachm. "May I see the coin?" she asked shyly. Absently, Itaz handed it
to her. "Oooh," she said, smiling at King Menander's face, "the new
queen will be pretty, if she looks like him."

"She won't look like an uncle," said Azilises harshly. "She'll look
like her father, with jowls like a frog and a stork's beak for a nose, and
the king will put out the lights and pray before he beds her." He
laughed and took another gulp of wine.

"You want her to be ugly so that you can laugh at the Yavanas,"
said Philomela angrily.

"If she's ugly, she might be honest," returned Azilises. "A pretty
Yavana woman is probably a thieving whore, like you. Here, give
Lord Itaz his coin back. Gold tetradrachms are worth more than a little
slut like you, even in this place: one bit of silver a night, that's what
you cost, songbird. It's what you've got already—and a copper from
me. Say thank you for it."

The girl was used to abuse. She merely flushed, blinked, and held
the gold coin out to Itaz. "Thank you," she whispered. His fingers
brushed hers as he reached to take his money, and he saw that the blink
had been at tears. He suddenly forgot his confusion in a stab of feeling
for her. He dropped his hand.

"Keep it," he said. "Azilises doesn't know value when he sees it.
Gold for a night with you, nightingale, is cheap at the price. Come on,
sing me another song, and we'll go to bed."

CHAPTER

II

The next morning saw the start of the king's wedding day, the day the new queen was to enter the city for the first time. I slept very little that night; I lay awake, listening to the noises. In my home the night sounds were mostly of animals—the tentative bark of a dog at a scent caught on the wind; an owl's hoot; the stamp of a horse in the stable just the other side of the house wall. The palace was different: there was only the lap of the fountain below in the court-yard, the chanting of the crickets, and, remote, the thump of boot and spear when the guard shift changed at the palace gates. Even the soft sound of the wind was different, hissing past stone and tile instead of rustling in thatch and wattle. How long would it be, I wondered, before I could go home again?

At last, distantly, came a sound that's the same anywhere: the first hoarse, uncertain crow of a cockerel calling on the invisible dawn. At once there was a stirring throughout the palace, the muffled thumps and rustles of people rising and dressing. I rolled off my sleeping mat

and got up, trailing my blanket, to feel in the dark for my clothes. By
the time the youngest of the four slaves came in with a taper to light
the lamps, I was dressed.

All over the palace slaves anxiously polished, and swept, and baked
and garlanded the rooms with flowers; the king's guards groomed their
horses, put on their freshly polished armor, and rubbed scented oil into
their beards. In the queen's apartments we burned incense to perfume
the air while we washed and dressed and painted our faces ready for the
royal reception. The king had given all the queen's household new
clothes, even the slaves. The things were all similar, I suppose to mark
us clearly as the queen's, which didn't please me. The four slaves had
gowns of blue and white cotton, with belts of embossed leather:
Parendi, the oldest, a tired gray woman, went pink as a girl when she
received hers, and clutched it as though she was afraid someone would
take it away again. We four attendants had similar gowns, but much
more magnificent: they were ankle-length, of blue and white cotton
like the slaves', but the sleeves and hems were embroidered with purple
silk, and all down the front they were spangled with gold that danced
and glittered when we moved; we had gold-studded belts, too. Inisme
fastened her gown with two brooches and added three necklaces on
top, as well as earrings long enough to brush her shoulders, and she
stared at her reflection in her Yavana silver mirror with satisfaction.

"Don't you have any more jewelry?" she asked me pityingly. I had
only one brooch and one necklace and a pair of simple gold hoop
earrings. "You really ought to wear it all: the queen is sure to have
splendid jewels, and we don't want to look poor."

"I never wanted much jewelry," I said, remembering how I'd once
used a gold necklace my father had given me to buy a horse. "I'll be
standing at the back anyway, and no one will notice." That's the
advantage to being a tall girl: you always stand at the back.

I wished we were riding out to greet the queen, with the king and
the royal guard, but it had been decided that we should wait beside the
temple terrace, where the wedding ceremony would take place. Standing and sitting still. What happened outside the city I only learned
afterward.

Itaz arrived back at the palace when the late stars were still bright
in the paling sky. The streets of the city were empty, their bright

decorations drab in the gray predawn: the hush was so deep that even the wind's sound could be heard in the roof tiles, and the fountains were still. But at the palace he found the lamps lit, the servants busy, and his father, fresh from his bath, having a haircut. The king disliked bathing, did so very seldom, and was irritable when he did. In the old days the Sakas never washed in water, only in tents of steam, as the nomads do to this day; bathing in water is a custom we learned from the Yavanas, and some of the old men and women still swear that it's bad for you.

"There you are," said Mauakes angrily, when his son appeared, disheveled from the night's drinking, in his well-worn hunting clothes. "So you decided to come after all, did you? Where were you last night —and for that matter, last week?"

The king was dressed only in a towel. Naked, his arms and legs looked thin and his body bloated; his age showed as it never did when he was clothed. Even his face seemed to have lost its disguises, showing tiredness, anxiety, doubt, as though he had only just realized what the years had done to him. Itaz felt his confusion resolve itself into a sudden rush of tenderness, surprising him by its protectiveness of one who had always been so strong. He knelt by his father's stool and kissed his hand.

"I was hunting last week," he said. "I didn't know what else to do. You'd told me not to talk to the councillors. As for last night, well, I'm sorry. I went out and got drunk. But I'm here now."

Mauakes snorted and snatched the hand away. "You couldn't have made your opposition plainer if you'd made a speech against the marriage in the council! There've been whispers about it for weeks: the king's own son gone off hunting because he couldn't bear to have anything to do with his father's marriage to the Yavana queen! Now they'll add to it: Lord Itaz drank himself insensible with grief the night before his father's wedding. What are you here for? Still wanting me to send the girl home?"

Itaz leaned back on his heels, looking at his father. "I'm sorry," he said again, at last. "I wish for all our sakes you hadn't arranged this marriage, I'm afraid what may come of it, and I don't know how to lie about it—but it's done now, isn't it? We can't back out with the bride encamped before our gates, I'm not such a fool that I can't see that. I've

come to help—to stand behind you, if you'll allow it, and show
everyone that if they thought I would oppose my father, they were
mistaken. And I want the woman and all the Yavanas of Bactria to see
that she's marrying a great king, the only lord of a great kingdom, and
she should be proud."

Mauakes stared at his son for a moment in surprise, suspicious of
some double meaning. Then, slowly, uncertainly, he smiled a peculiar
nervous smile, quite unlike his usual bland confident one. He was
immensely touched, more so than he could admit. He caught and
squeezed Itaz' hand. "Well then," he said, almost savagely. "Well. You
can stand on my left."

"What should I call the woman when I meet her?" asked Itaz.
"Not 'Mother'!"

"You should call her 'Queen,'" said Mauakes. And indeed, the
daughter of a Yavana king is called queen in her own right: if we Sakas
are free with gifts of authority to women, the Yavanas aren't far
behind us. "Queen Heliokleia, daughter of King Eukratides of Bactria."

"And granddaughter of Antimachos the God."

Mauakes gave his son another stare of suspicious surprise. Itaz met
it levelly. "Great-granddaughter," the king corrected. "Go and get
dressed for the wedding."

Mauakes had tallied up the risks and the benefits and made his
decision in solitude, and would admit no company even after the fact.
Itaz bowed his head, then kissed his father's hand again before leaving.

A few hours later he was waiting beside his father in front of the
west gate of the city. Behind them, fanned out along the wall in a
wing five-deep, were the three hundred men of the royal guard, their
scale armor polished till it glittered in the sun like glass, mounted on
armored horses of the royal breed, with pennants fluttering, red and
white and gold, from their long lances. Maybe we do have fewer men
and horses than the Tochari or the Parthians, but those we have are
unmatched in all the world. The royal guard is unmatched among
unmatchables, a force almost invincible in battle, and it held itself
proudly. Usually when the king rode at its head he wore the same gear,
but not today, when he welcomed to his kingdom a peaceful alliance
and a young bride. He wore trousers of purple linen, stitched with

gold, and a tunic of gold-worked silk, the purple cloak of the Yavana kings and the gold tiara of the Parthians. His horse, Griffin, a bay, had been brushed and oiled till his coat shone like bronze, and instead of the blanket of armor his harness was heavy with gold. To Itaz, who sat his own horse just behind him and to his left, Mauakes appeared god-like in his royalty. He listened to the excited shouts from the people of the city, pointing at his father from the walls, and felt his heart hot with pride.

The bride's party appeared descending the hill opposite: first a party of Bactrian cavalry, more lightly armored than the Sakas; then some wagons carrying, plain to see, the promised catapults; and then the elephants, with a few supply wagons behind them. The great beasts looked like huge boulders as they rolled down the slope, only their backs visible behind the rocks that flanked the road. But as they drew nearer, one could see the heavy treading of their red-painted feet, their tusks bound with iron and gold, and the red and white patterns painted boldly on their flanks and foreheads. The last three were loaded with supplies, but the first two carried howdahs—the second gilded, so that it blazed on the animal's back like the sun.

As they came nearer, the Bactrians touched their horses to a canter and fanned out opposite the Sakas, the ones who had been on the right of the column going left, and the ones from the left, right, so that the troop wove about itself like a line dance, a very pretty maneuver. There were a hundred of them, and they turned neatly into a single line facing the Sakas and about a stone's throw away, leaving a gap in the middle. All at once they touched their horses so that they suddenly reared up, snorting and curvetting, then plunged down again and were still. Into the gap strode the elephants. They stopped, shifting backward and forward restlessly, the drivers calling to them and tapping them upon the neck. Then all at once all five set their trunks to their fore-heads and trumpeted.

It was a fearful, a terrible noise, like a hundred iron horns all blowing together. Even the horses of the Bactrians, who were used to it, stirred and snorted. The Saka horses, though royal and experienced in battle, reared up, kicked, shied into one another; a few bolted. In a moment the whole royal guard was a confused turmoil of struggling men and frightened horses, the king, like all the rest, reduced to fighting to control his own mount. Even when the trumpeting at last stopped he had to dismount to calm his horse. He swore to it under his breath, holding its head and stroking its neck. "They did that to make fools of us in front of the whole city," he muttered. "Damn Heliokles; damn the woman!"

Itaz also dismounted, though he could have managed without doing so. "Well," he said to his father, "the whole reason we wanted elephants was to terrify cavalry."

Mauakes snorted, but smiled. "And they're *my* elephants, now," he said. "There's a thought."

When the horses were calm again, the king remounted and rode toward the Yavanas. His horse refused to go near the elephants, so he stopped, lifting his hand as a signal to the guard to stop as well. The Yavana cavalry captain rode over to him.

"Rejoice, O King," he said in Greek, bowing from the saddle. The Yavanas say "Rejoice" as a greeting, or sometimes "Much health." "We have brought you your bride, Queen Heliokleia, the daughter of Eukratides. May we enter with her into the city?"

Mauakes smiled politely. "Many thanks," he said in Sakan. "You are most welcome, you and Queen Heliokleia—and the elephants. I thank you for demonstrating them to us. I ask only that you and your men surrender your weapons at the gate."

The captain stared blankly. "I do not speak barbarian languages," he said.

Mauakes looked at him without expression, then gestured to Itaz. "Translate," he ordered.

"But you speak Greek better than I do!" protested his son in a whisper.

"If he's too fine to speak foreign languages, so am I," whispered Mauakes impatiently.

Clumsily, Itaz translated. The conditions for the entry of the Yavanas had in fact been arranged by messengers the previous evening, and though the captain was unhappy with them, he accepted now as gracefully as he could, with another bow.

"But where is Queen Heliokleia?" Mauakes asked, looking expectantly at the gilded howdah. It was covered and had red curtains worked with gold; he could see that one of them was being held slightly open by a watcher inside. Itaz, again, translated.

The captain gestured, as expected, at the howdah. "She rides, as is fitting for a king's daughter, upon an elephant."

Mauakes scanned the height of the beast. He had meant to ride into Eskati beside his new bride, preceded and followed by his guard, thus demonstrating to his people both the magnificent fact of the new alliance, and his dominance within it. To his annoyance, he realized that he had not taken into account the problems raised by an elephant. Even if he could persuade his horse to go near it, it would still dwarf him and make him look ridiculous. He could always ride in front, and let the elephants follow—but then everyone would be craning their necks to get a glimpse of the elephants, and he and his guards would become insignificant. They'd already been made fools of in front the whole city; any more and people would start to laugh at him. "Let her come down," he ordered, making a quick decision; and, to provide a reasonable pretext for it, "the streets are decorated, and the elephants will be too big to go under the banners. You may bring them in by the north gate. One of my men will give the queen his horse."

"The queen is a Greek noblewoman, and cannot ride," said the captain, frowning, when Itaz had translated.

"She can ride a little, with someone to steady her," insisted Mauakes. "Let her come down. My men will show you where to bring the elephants."

The captain had begun to protest when there was a call from the howdah. He went over to it; there was a brief discussion, and then the elephant knelt. The driver jumped from its neck and pulled a small rope ladder from the base of the howdah; the captain reached up his hand, and the queen took it and stepped carefully down, holding up her long skirts with one hand. The watchers noticed that the long, sleeveless tunic and the draped shawl-like cloak she wore, the common clothing of Yavana women, were dyed orange-gold with saffron—the color they wear for their weddings, but which the Indian Buddhists take to renounce the world. She walked over to Mauakes with a steady, unhurried step and as she came they slowly realized that she was beautiful—beautiful enough to stop a man in the street. She wore no jewelry, and her hair was piled simply on top of her head, bound with a band of purple linen tied with the ends trailing behind her—an ornament the richest citizen in the kingdoms of the Yavanas cannot afford, as the diadem is the mark of kings. Itaz suddenly felt how gaudy and savage the Sakas must look beside her regal simplicity, and hated the Yavana subtlety that had chosen the contrast. Mauakes just stared at her with his mouth open.

She stopped a few paces away, tilting her head back to look up at him on his tall horse. "Rejoice, O King," she said in Greek. Her voice was low, clear, and carrying. She went on, in Sakan, "They say that the streets are decorated and are too low for the elephants."

Mauakes closed his mouth. "Rejoice, O Queen," he replied. "That is so. My son will lend you his horse."

"No!" protested Itaz loudly, with a sense of sudden and inexplicable terror.

Mauakes looked at him. It is not usual for us to allow anyone else to ride our war horses, but a king may do what he likes. He had offered his son's horse on the spur of the moment, and what business had his son to refuse it? In fact, it was the best horse he could have offered; it would be the finest gesture of support Itaz could make, the conclusive proof to all that he was indeed loyal to his father. If he was indeed loyal. "No?" the king asked softly.

"I . . . I mean, the horse is a war horse, a stallion," stammered Itaz, aware of the suspicion falling on him again, not able to explain his own intense dread at the thought of the queen sitting in his own saddle, steadied by his own hands. "And if the queen is unaccustomed to riding, surely she'd be happier with a gentler animal . . ."

"Do not concern yourself," said Queen Heliokleia politely, with a glance at him; he noticed the sweep of the lashes across the deep blue-green of her eyes. "I do not know how to ride. Captain"—switching to Greek—"if your men can move the thirty-pounder, I will ride on the wagon."

"Indeed, you must not," interrupted Mauakes quickly. "It would not be fitting to your rank and dignity. You may ride on my son's horse. It is a well-trained animal, and will be perfectly gentle if its master holds its head."

Itaz flushed bright crimson and said nothing. He patted the neck of the horse, a jet black stallion of the royal breed. Queen Heliokleia looked up at him again, at the height of the horse and the crimson flare of its nostrils, and at the angry young man who rode it. Itaz was in his finest clothes, and they were Parthian in style—the gold-stamped leather leggings over the dark red trousers, the embroidery on the tunic, the red and gold cap with the rounded peak, and the gold-hilted short sword. She looked back at the king. She did not smile, not quite, but suddenly her face looked like her uncle's on the gold coin, not in its shape but in the expression of delicate mockery. "Is it worth so much discussion," she asked, "whether I enter the city on a horse, an elephant, a wagon . . . or on foot? I will do the same things when I arrive no matter how I get there. I have heard, O King, that your people—and the Parthians—attach great value to their horses, and are unwilling to let strangers sit upon them. Please do not argue with your son about it for my sake."

Itaz flushed still hotter and jumped down from his horse. Now the woman had made him seem childish and ridiculous. "It was only that I thought a war horse like mine might frighten you, O Queen," he said. "If you aren't frightened, I'm perfectly happy for you to ride him." He clicked his tongue to the horse and tapped its knees; it was a well-trained beast, and knelt. The queen looked at the saddle, then at her own long skirts.

Mauakes jumped down from his own horse. "I will help you," he said, and caught her round the waist, lifted her, and set her down sideways in the saddle, the saffron fringe of her cloak trailing across the horse's rump. Unlike the Yavanas, we use tall saddles with a wooden frame, since a man in heavy armor requires plenty of support. There was little danger of the queen falling off, particularly as she at once grabbed hold of the pommel and cantle. But Mauakes remained a moment with his hands about her waist, then ran a hand down her legs, pulling the skirts straight. She turned her face away. He grinned and went back to his own horse; Itaz pulled at his charger's bridle and brought it to its feet.

"Will you be safe there, O Queen?" asked the Bactrian captain anxiously.

"At worst, I'll fall off," she replied. "Demetrios, see that my women . . . that is . . ." She stopped, turned to Mauakes, and said, "I have two women, sir, my personal attendants, on the other elephant.

They are freeborn and noble, and they will wish to be with me. Since your son is walking, may they walk beside me?"

"Of course," said Mauakes; and the captain went to the second howdah and helped out the two ladies-in-waiting. They were both of middle age, both splendidly and elegantly dressed with an abundance of jewelry; one was a brown-haired Yavana, the other a very dark Indian. Both looked furious at being asked to walk behind a horse, instead of riding in on the elephant as expected. They looked at the dusty road and turned their feet to inspect the state of the soles of their embroidered slippers, and they cast venomous glances at the Sakas. But they said nothing, and moved to stand on either side of the queen as smoothly as if they had rehearsed it. At a signal from the king the whole party set off into Eskati.

The people cheered madly when the queen came in through the gate, and showered her with flowers of rose, tulip, and rhododendron. She sat very straight, clasping the saddle so that her knuckles were white, nodding occasionally at the acclamations. Itaz, leading the horse, was also very straight, stiff with anger. First the woman had had her elephants make fools of the best of the Sakan cavalry; then she had made him look suspect and stupid before his father; and now she sat calmly bowing to the adoration of her people, the Yavana ruler returned triumphant. And she was so beautiful. He had been afraid that she might be beautiful, but he hadn't seriously expected it. Already his father was grinning with pleasure whenever he looked at her, and the people were shouting with delight. Itaz glanced back at her again and again, taking in the curve of her neck; her arms, white and straight, clasping the saddle; the slim body braced stiffly against the unfamiliar movement of the horse; the foot curled up in its sandal of saffron-dyed leather, pressed tightly against the patterned saddle blanket for balance. How old was she? Older than the nineteen his father had suggested. But not too much older, though that calm, mocking assurance made her seem so. She was accustomed to her royalty; accustomed to command. She had had to check herself from giving orders about her women and their place in the procession; courtesy had made her refer to the king, not indecision. And intelligent, quick to size up a situation. And learned, as well, they'd said. Dangerous, ten, a hundred times more dangerous than he had feared. And so *beautiful* it hurt him. Like an ache from his back teeth into his heart, he longed to touch even the tensed feet with their delicate, rose pink nails; even the white-knuckled hand that gripped the ornamented cantle of his saddle. He did not see the crowds or the banners or the flowers, he did not hear the cheers or the music; he walked, stiffly holding his horse, and saw only his father's bride.

I was waiting with the other attendants on the terrace in front of the temple of the Sun; we were grouped opposite Uncle Kanit and the priests. The marketplace was a solid mass of people. Everyone who could—Saka visitor or Yavana citizen—had packed into it to watch the wedding, and you could smell the crowd even over the incense that smoldered on the sacred fire. The streets were crowded, too: we heard the cheering begin as the queen entered the city, but it seemed weeks before the bridal party entered the marketplace; the king's guard had to clear the way, one of them stopping every few yards to keep the people back, until the whole square was crossed by a line of men and horses in bright armor, making an aisle in the crowd. Down it rode the king on his golden bay, with Itaz beside him leading the black horse with its saffron-gowned rider. A choir of girls and boys from among the Yavana citizens, positioned on the temple steps, began to welcome the approaching party with a marriage hymn. As the new queen drew nearer we realized, slowly, that she was improbably beautiful, and that we were all overdressed. I noticed how Inisme in front of me went stiff with embarrassment, and I was young and silly enough to feel pleased.

Mauakes reined in before the altar terrace and waited until the song was finished, then dismounted, handing his horse to a palace attendant who was waiting there for the purpose. Itaz stood stiffly, looking at the ground, still furious; he forgot to give his horse the signal to kneel, and his father had to remind him sharply. The king came forward to lift the queen down as he had lifted her up, but she slid off by herself before he reached her, and Mauakes had to stand back and pretend he had meant to wait. The queen's two women rearranged the drapery of her cloak, and the king gave the bride his hand and led her up to the altar.

We Sakas swear oaths at our weddings, promising before the all-seeing Sun to honor and be faithful to one another. The Yavanas have no such custom; they merely carry off their brides willy-nilly to the groom's house in a mock rape, with much singing of loud songs and drinking of wine. I think our custom is better—and this was a Saka wedding. The king and queen stood before the altar, their hands joined before the sacred fire, and swore the oaths. Mauakes swore the usual form, which goes, "I"—and one's name—"son of"—whomever— "swear before all people, by the Sun our Lord, to take this woman as my sole wife, to keep in honor and guard in faith; and if I prove false, may the Sun who sees all punish me."

Heliokleia, though she must have been instructed in the usual form, swore differently: "I, Heliokleia, daughter of Eukratides, swear by the Sun, by Zeus Olympios, Artemis-Anahita, and by all the gods, to bind myself to this man as my sole husband, to keep in honor and guard in faith; and if I prove false, may I never obtain release." All the people in the marketplace heard it, understood that she had sworn by her own gods, and approved with a cheer. "Release"—no one asked what she meant by that. Even Mauakes took no notice of it. Only Itaz understood it, and he stared at her in shocked suspicion, suddenly guessing the ambiguity in those saffron robes, worn so plainly without the gold and jewelry that should have adorned a queen at her wedding. He had met a Buddhist monk once in Parthia, a missionary. He and his Mazdayist friends had found the man's teaching impious and ordered him to leave the region. "Release" is the Buddhist goal. They say that death is not release, but only the beginning of rebirth to another life, and that the soul is bound to the world as though to a wheel of torture, and must be liberated by meditation and austerity. The Mazdayists, however, believe that the world is good, though invaded by evil, and to reject it is wicked. Itaz looked away from the queen, still more appalled by what his father had done. It was too late now even to protest; the oaths were sworn, and there was only the sacrifice to the god left before the ceremonies were completed and the feasting began.

We offer horses to the Sun—the swiftest of beasts to the swiftest of the gods—though sometimes we make do with lesser cattle. This, however, was not an occasion for making do. Mauakes himself had chosen the sacrificial victim: a pure white mare of the royal breed, a true-descended daughter of the Sun, two years old and unmated. When Heliokleia had finished swearing the oath, he nodded to Kanit, and the horse was led up onto the terrace. She seemed to burn in the sunlight with a light of her own. Her steps were as delicate as a heron's by a stream; her hooves were gilded, her halter hung with gold, and she held her head high, nervously rolling her brilliant eyes at the crowds. She was a beautiful creature, and I felt a stab of grief that so wonderful an animal should be destroyed—though for a horse that came from the Sun, to be sent back to him should be no hardship. Kanit fastened the lasso about her forelegs and stood back, holding the end of it, and Mauakes picked up the sacrificial knife from the altar beside the fire. He cut off the mare's forelock and tossed it on the fire, which was burning almost invisibly in the bright sunshine, then dipped his thumb in the dish of ochre and drew the sun disk on her head. He turned to the east and lifted his hands, praying in a loud voice so that all the people could hear. "Master of the world, all-seeing and swift, look on us favorably, Lord Sun! See and bless the alliance we have made, uniting in peace Saka and Yavana, as I unite in marriage with this woman. Lord, accept our offering!"

At this Kanit jerked tight the lasso and the horse should have fallen, leaving Mauakes to seize her head and cut her throat as she tried to rise. But the mare, moved by some impulse from Heaven, chose that moment to shy. One foreleg slipped from the noose; the other, caught, left her staggering and frightened but not fallen. Mauakes had already seized her head as she staggered and, not realizing what had happened, leaned down and struck quickly with the knife. But the victim was not helpless on her knees; she shied again, and the blow missed the throat and tore down the side of the neck. The knife caught on the shoulder bone and broke in half. The mare screamed in pain and reared up, lashing out with her hooves and catching the king a glancing blow on the head. He fell, and the hooves of the terrified horse plunged down on top of him.

Kanit yelled wordlessly; someone nearby screamed. On our side of the terrace, I started forward with some vague notion of helping, and, at the same moment, Jahika spun round and started back, covering her eyes: we fell down in a tangle onto the hard stone. I heard Itaz give a shout of horror and I looked up to see him leaping onto the terrace, drawing his sword. The horse staggered again as the still-taut lasso dragged at her leg, then lurched violently away, pulling the rope from Kanit's hands; she turned toward the edge of the terrace, trailing blood, then wheeled from the drop. She turned back toward the temple—and found Itaz kneeling over the king directly in her path. He rose in one quick movement; at the glint of his sword, the mare reared again, screaming. Itaz ducked past the wild hooves and thrust his sword into the animal's heart.

The mare fell to her knees, then collapsed on her side; her flanks heaved once—then her straining, blood-streaked neck relaxed, and she lay dead beside the altar, the sun's rays glowing in her mane. Itaz stared at her a moment with intense, bewildered grief, then turned back to his father.

Mauakes was sitting up, staring at the horse; he looked quickly at Itaz, then looked away without saying anything. He was covered in blood. Itaz went over to him and caught his arm. "Are you hurt?" he asked anxiously.

Mauakes shook his head, and used his son's arm to draw himself up. He felt the side of his head with one hand, rubbed his ribs, then drew his fingers across his eyes. "No," he said. "Just bruised." He leaned heavily against the altar. The whole square was very quiet. I picked myself up. Jahika stayed crouching in front of me, panting; Inisme had her hands over her mouth. I felt sick, too. I had never heard of a royal sacrifice going so disastrously wrong before: it was an omen—but of what? What nightmare was going to jump on us out of the blind future?

Itaz felt the crowd's eyes on him, pushing like a strong wind, and hunched his shoulders in confusion. The marriage, controversial to begin with, had been inaugurated with omens unspeakably disastrous. And his own place in them was a murky one. He had saved his father, perhaps—but he had taken his father's place at the sacrifice. And yet what else, he wondered, could he have done?

There was a movement beside the altar, a flutter of orange-gold. Itaz looked up and met the queen's eyes across the fire. Her face was unreadable through the shimmer of heat, but the gaze was fixed on him. They stared at each other for a moment—then Heliokleia moved quickly round the altar to the king's side. "The people are frightened," she whispered to him. "We must do something to calm them at once. Can we say that the priests will offer special sacrifices tomorrow, to avert the omen?"

He stared at her, then nodded and straightened, turning to face the crowds. "My people," he called, raising his arms to them. "Do not be alarmed. I am unharmed. The priests and priestesses will study the meaning of what has happened, and see what it portends; if it threatens disaster, they will offer sacrifices to avert it. But I think it may be a good omen, for death and ruin passed over me and did not touch me— as I hope the Tochari will now pass by us all. Take note that the ceremonies are complete, and our lord the Sun has the victim we offered him—and our lord is like any Saka nobleman, and likes a horse with spirit." The crowd stirred, still too shocked to laugh, but beginning to relax from its frozen silence. "Now I invite you to a feast to celebrate my wedding," the king went on, raising his voice. "You, here in the marketplace, and my nobles in the palace. Eat and drink freely, make music and be glad, for you have a new queen, who will bring us safety."

He took Heliokleia's hand and began walking toward the palace. The queen gave Itaz another unreadable glance and followed her new husband quietly, her two foreign attendants fell in behind her, and Inisme suddenly dropped her hands, grabbed Jahika, and pulled the rest of us after them. Behind us in the marketplace the fountains began to flow with wine, and the city officials started to distribute the feast the king had provided.

Itaz remained frozen beside the altar for a long time, waiting until the flutter of the saffron robe had disappeared up the steps of the citadel. Then, slowly, stiffly, he followed, praying in his heart to Ahura Mazda to avert disaster. He was very much afraid.

CHAPTER

III

It had been before noon when the king began the sacrifice to the Sun; the festivities were due to go on all the afternoon and into the night, and to continue over three days. Immediately after the sacrifice there was to be a free distribution of food in the marketplace, while the principal nobles of the kingdom came to a banquet in the courtyard of the palace—the palace dining room could never hold all the nobility of the Sakas. When we stepped into the palace, however, the king told the captain of his guards to welcome the guests, while he himself went to change his bloodstained clothes. "And you, my queen," he said, turning to Heliokleia politely. "Perhaps you could go to your own rooms to refresh yourself, and I will send to you when I'm ready, so that we can join the banqueters together?"

She nodded graciously. "As you will, sir."

Mauakes turned to go, then remembered that the queen had no idea where her own rooms were, and turned back. "These are your attendants," he told her, indicating us. "Inisme, Jahika, Armaiti and

Tomyris. They are all nobly born girls suitable for your service. They will show you to your apartments."

"I thank you, sir," said the queen, sweeping us with a glance, then again nodding graciously to the king. He nodded back and strode off, his hands held stiffly clear of his bloodied clothes.

The queen looked back at us. The entrance hall was momentarily still, since the guests were still sorting themselves out of the crowd below and climbing the hill. It was the first chance I had to get more than a general impression of the woman. She might have posed for the image of Anahita in the lakeside shrine—tall, though not as tall as me, she had the same slim, deep-waisted build, the same wide forehead and pointed chin. She stood as still as though she were posing for a statue, too, as composed and self-possessed as if the ominous shambles of the sacrifice had happened only in a dream. Her skin was very fair, and her hair was a strange and wonderful color, a kind of golden bay, which I'd seen on a horse before but never a human being: all Sakas, and most Yavanas, are dark. Her eyes were blue-green like a mountain lake, and when she looked at me, it was as though she were looking down from the sky; the eyes were deep as Heaven and made me dizzy, and after meeting them a moment I had to look away. A few loose flowers, rose and wild tulip from the handfuls she'd been showered with, clung to her hair and the folds of the saffron tunic and cloak. She was so calmly beautiful that you had no idea what, if anything, was going on inside her head. It was impossible to believe that a woman that lovely ever needed or wanted anything. "Inisme, Jahika, Armaiti and Tomyris," she repeated, getting all our names right, though she'd scarcely seemed to listen when the king said them. "For your offered service, I thank you all. But we have no time to talk here. Could you kindly show me to my rooms?" She had a low, clear voice and spoke Sakan carefully, with a Bactrian accent rather than a Greek one, hesitating before the s sound, which the native Bactrians pronounce *kh*.

We could hear the first guests climbing up the stairs in the sunlight behind us, so we whisked her off to the rooms. She looked about them with a kind of mild interest and sat down on the couch, folding her hands in her lap. Beside her, the two attendants she'd brought from Bactria looked doubtful. We'd heard that she was bringing the two, of course: it had been stated that they were coming for the first year, to

help her settle in. But we'd expected girls our own age. These women
were as old as my mother, and one of them, the dark one, looked at my
legs just as disapprovingly. I followed her stare and saw that I'd scraped
my knee when I fell on the terrace, and the new gown was smeared
with blood and crushed flowers. "Oh," I said, and rubbed at the stain
rather stupidly.

"Who are these people?" asked the dark woman in Greek. It was
only at this that I thought to be astonished that the queen had spoken
in Sakan.

"These are attendants King Mauakes has chosen for me," replied
the queen, in Greek now. "He said they are all noble virgins." And she
introduced us all, finishing by introducing the new ladies to us: the
dark one was called Padmini, and the brown-haired one was Antiochis.

"Oh," said Antiochis, reassured. "Do you speak Greek?" asked
Padmini.

For a moment nobody said anything, and then I blurted out, "I do.
And Armaiti does. Inisme and Jahika only a little."

I could tell that Padmini thought this odd, but she made no comment on it. "Well, you are all pretty girls," she said, still in Greek,
"and I'm sure it was very thoughtful of the king to appoint you.
Antiochis and I do not speak your tongue, but it seems we have
translators enough to get by."

Heliokleia smiled at that: it was the first time I saw that smile on
her, the delicate mocking smile of the Antimachids, and I found it
almost as disturbing as her eyes. But Inisme smiled too, bowed to
Padmini and to the queen, then went over to the niche in the back wall
of the room, where a pitcher of water had been placed out of the sun
to keep cool. She filled a cup and offered it somewhere between the
queen and Padmini. Padmini raised her eyebrows, nodded in apprecia-
tion of this deference to herself, took the cup, and gave it to her
mistress.

Heliokleia drank a little, then pulled her legs up and sat cross-
legged. I went over to the pitcher and tipped some of the water onto
my stained gown, while Inisme filled other cups for the rest of us. The
brown-haired woman, Antiochis, went over to the queen and straightened the saffron folds of her cloak, brushing off the flowers. "Don't
worry about the omen, darling," she said—pointlessly, I thought, be-

cause her mistress looked far less worried about it than she did herself. "Probably it meant what the king said it did."

"I am not frightened of omens," said Heliokleia. "If they are good, fine; if they're bad, there's nothing to be done about it. 'Against Necessity not even the gods can contend.' Oh, but I am sorry about the elephants. I thought . . ."

Antiochis hugged her. "Darling, don't worry," she said. "The people adored you, couldn't you see? You looked like golden Aphrodite. Everything will be fine, you'll see."

Padmini had been looking about the room again. "Hmm," she said, as though she didn't think much of it, "we have some luggage that should be delivered here soon: where is the queen's bedroom?"

When I told her that this was it, she compressed her lips in disapproval. "Where's the bed, then?" she asked.

"There's the couch," I told her, pointing to it. "The king didn't think we needed a separate bed here, since the queen will be sleeping downstairs."

"Ah, then she has a bedroom downstairs!" said Padmini, brightening. "The books can go in there, then."

"N-no," I said. "It's the king's room."

"But surely the king doesn't expect my lady to sleep with him *every* night. That would hardly be proper, after all!"

"What's improper about a wife sleeping with her husband?" I asked, surprised.

"My dear girl, a queen can hardly go slipping down the stairs like a country girl off to meet a lover. Is she to dress there, in front of the king's slaves? Or is she to traipse downstairs undressed? Really! A niece of Menander and daughter of Eukratides is a person of more importance than that! She must have her own rooms, her own loyal servants, her own place where she is supreme. Her husband comes to her and she receives him with dignity and grace: others may not enter her domain without her permission. That is how it should be done."

"Not in Ferghana," I said.

Padmini gave me a scalding look. She began to say something more, but stopped herself, deciding that it would be inappropriate to make an issue of this now. "Well then," she said, "someone will have to find a case for my lady's books, and a table for her to write at. This room is very bare." She looked disapprovingly around at the tiled floors, the sumptuous carpets, the painted walls that I had found so luxurious.

"There will be time for all of that later," said the queen, with another slight smile.

One of the king's guards knocked on the door and announced that the king had changed and was ready to accompany the queen to the banquet. Heliokleia took a deep breath, let it out slowly, then rose and walked unhurriedly to the door. The rest of us shuffled into places behind her and went down to join the banquet.

Heliokleia was seated next to the king at a table beside the fountain, and we were put to work serving the guests. I found my mother and father sitting with Uncle Kanit, and felt better at that, though I had no time to talk to them. The queen sat smiling assurance while the guests were introduced to her, greeting them all graciously. First came the king's family—his daughter and her husband; the widow of his second son; Itaz; Kanit and the king's other cousins. With the king's daughter Amage was his seven-year-old grandson, his appointed heir, who was being brought up by his aunt since his own parents were both dead. The whole courtyard went still and watched when he was presented to the new queen. How would she treat this boy who would thrust her own children from the line of succession?

She smiled into the sullen face above the stiff, uncomfortable gold-worked tunic, and reached out her hand to the boy. "So you are Mauakes, grandson of Mauakes!" she said. "I heard about you even in Bactra. I am very pleased to meet my new lord's heir."

The boy scowled and didn't move; the aunt, unsmiling, gave him a shove forward. Still scowling, Mauakes the grandson bowed to her and reluctantly took her hand. "Do they call you Mauakes?" the queen asked him.

He shook his head. "No," he said shortly, then, after an awkward silence, realizing this wasn't enough, added, "They call me Moki."

"They call me Heliokleia," she replied.

"I know," he said. "Doesn't that mean 'ambition'?" There was a moment of shocked stillness all around, and he went on, mumbling, aware that he must have said something he shouldn't, "I heard that

Yavana names all mean something. My un . . . that is, somebody told me yours meant 'ambition'; isn't it true?"

"No," said Heliokleia, smiling as though the slur meant nothing to her, "'Philotimia' would mean 'ambition.' My name means 'sun-fame.'"

"Oh," said Moki, and suddenly smiled at her. "That's good, isn't it? The Sun is our lord, the good lord of the world."

"Of course," she said, "and I'm not ambitious, Moki."

"That's good," he said, with a relieved sigh. He kissed her hand and went back with his aunt to another table; as he went I overheard him commenting, "*I* don't think she's horrible at all; *I* think she's pretty."

His grandfather grinned at her. "Well done," he whispered contentedly, and turned to summon another notable.

There were over two hundred guests at the banquet—all the lords of the tribal council and their wives, as well as an assortment of royal guardsmen and officers. The queen smiled and greeted them all, said appropriate things to them, and asked the right questions. Gradually, people began to forget the fear and doubt that the ominous sacrifice had engendered. They murmured to each other that probably the king's interpretation of the omen was right; probably it meant we would escape unscathed from the danger of invasion, thanks to this alliance; no harm, surely, would come of a queen so young and lovely, and so courteous; why, she'd even learned Sakan! Who would have believed it! And she'd accepted the king's grandson as heir already, when she could have just greeted him politely and said nothing. They sat nibbling at the endless succession of courses; they drank the wine, and began to laugh and clap happily for the countless musicians, minstrels and poets, jugglers and acrobats, dancing bears and trained birds who performed for them. The king laughed louder than anyone, and looked frequently at the new queen, who smiled graciously at all.

When dusk began to fall the young men of the guard did a dance with swords and torches, whirling the spitting flames and bright iron about their heads while the courtyard grew darker and darker, until nothing could be seen but the red sparks trailing and the glitter of leaping metal. The close of the dance was the agreed signal for the queen's attendants to escort her to the royal bedroom; the four of us made our way through the soft blackness, scented with pine smoke, and

took up places at the queen's elbow. She understood at once. When the
dance ended she bowed her head politely to those of her neighbors
close enough to see her, rose unhurriedly, and let us show her back into
the palace. Antiochis and Padmini joined us before we reached the
door.

The king's room was larger and more lavish than the queen's. It
had a wide wooden bed with a heavy frame, not an ordinary sleeping
mat or box bed; the head and foot boards were high, carved with
griffins and horses and inlaid with gold. It was covered with a magnificent bedspread that glowed purple and gold, indigo and red in the light
of the jeweled lamps that hung from the ceiling. Heliokleia sat down
heavily and took another deep breath. I looked for the incense I'd been
told would be there and, when I found it, put a pinch in each of the
lamps. "Bring a basin of warm water," Padmini ordered us, then sat
down beside her mistress and gently began to unfasten her hair as
Inisme and Jahika ran to fetch the water.

It was only then that the queen's self-possession cracked a little.
Her face, if anything, became more rigidly calm than ever, but she
began to tremble.

"It's all right," said Padmini soothingly, holding her head with
both slim brown hands.

"I'm frightened," Heliokleia said in astonishment, half choking on
the words.

"It happens to all of us," said the Indian. "Be still, darling. You're a
queen, the daughter of Antimachos and Alexander; you will be brave."

"I'm sorry about the jewels," Heliokleia said hurriedly. "And the
elephants, I thought . . ."

"Never mind, child! Do you think we care about that now? Be
still and don't worry about anything."

Heliokleia said nothing, but she was still trembling. Antiochis
knelt, unfastened the saffron-dyed sandals, took them off and put them
aside; she pulled the cloak from her mistress' shoulders, folded it, then,
after a moment's hesitation, draped it across the clothes chest for the
queen to wear when she went up the stairs next morning. Padmini
brushed out the long bay hair, then as Inisme and Jahika came back
with a steaming basin of scented water, stepped aside to allow her to
wash. Heliokleia fumbled in the water a moment, splashed her face,

dried herself on the towel Armaiti had brought, then sat very still upon the bed. Padmini kissed her. "We must go now," she said. "Your husband will come soon."

The queen nodded.

"Good night, and may the gods bless you, and grant you children," said Antiochis.

Heliokleia nodded again and, as we all filed from the room, watched us with a masklike face and liquid, terrified eyes.

I have written this account trying to remember clearly how I saw the queen then, not imposing on the first disturbing meeting all the thousand memories that follow. I thought that to write with the benefit of hindsight would be to confuse and falsify what took place—but now I see that I have falsified in another way. I have said plainly how I felt, and what I know of how Itaz felt, and a little of the king, but nothing about how things appeared to Heliokleia, and surely that, too, confuses and distorts the truth? Because, as I learned later, she was not nearly so calm as she seemed. I will try again, and write the things which before I left out.

Heliokleia was born and raised in Bactra, the capital city of her father's kingdom of Bactria. She was the result of a truce that wasn't kept. Her mother died while Heliokleia was still a child, and no one else in her family was interested in her. Her father was almost constantly away on campaigns, her two brothers were much older than her, lived in another part of the palace, and saw her only on festivals. She had a nurse who looked after her for a time—but the woman died. Then there were Padmini and Antiochis. They were both noblewomen from the Indian kingdom who had come to Bactria with her mother, and remained there as her own attendants, staying professional court ladies even when they married and had families of their own. They were fond of her, but scolded her frequently—for being clumsy at weaving and spinning; for losing her bracelets; for getting her clothes dusty; for forever pulling her hair out of its braids; for not listening when they spoke to her. They found her exasperating and couldn't understand her at all.

She was educated, of course. Greek education is no bad thing. I found reading useful enough to have my children educated in the Greek fashion here in Eskati—at least, I had them given a primary education. (I don't hold with the secondary schools, the gymnasia, where the Greek boys run about naked. That's pointless and indecent.) My daughter won her school's contest in lyric poetry, and was given a crown of ivy, which hung on the wall until the leaves fell off, and even then I wasn't allowed to throw the thing out and had to put it in the bottom of her clothes chest: she certainly enjoyed her school years. But Heliokleia didn't go to school. A king's daughter has a private tutor, a distinguished old scholar who's impatient with the fumbling attempts of children, and gives no prizes, not recognizing excellence when it comes in a girl's first try and not a grown man's five hundredth. I learned to stumble through the first book of the *Iliad* when I was seventeen; she'd finished the poem when she was eight. She learned what they all learn—to read, to write, to recite poetry, to sing and to play the kithara and the lyre. And she learned a few things more—history, geography, mathematics, philosophy. She learned quickly and easily, because she was brilliant—but she didn't realize that, since there was no one to tell her so, no one to compare herself to; it seemed hard work to her, and she thought she was slow.

She was twelve when her father Eukratides died, murdered by his second son Platon for the sake of a headband of purple linen. For two years there was civil war, Platon against the elder brother, Heliokles, though her life went on as before, and neither brother paid any more attention than usual to their neglected sister. When the war was over, with Platon executed and the diadem on Heliokles' head, the new king decided to make peace with his old rivals, and envoys went back and forth between Bactra and the capital of the Indian Yavana kingdom, Sakala. Among the envoys from Sakala was the Buddhist monk Nagasena. He was a favorite of King Menander, who had asked him to visit his niece Heliokleia if he had any time to spare from his political duties.

Nagasena was already famous over the whole of India for his learning and eloquence. Besides knowing by heart the writings of the Buddhists, he was familiar with the teachings of the Hindus, and had read many of the Greek philosophers as well. They say he was the only man who could beat King Menander in debate, and the king admired him immensely and showered gifts upon his order. He did not usually undertake secular missions, but the Buddhists consider it meritorious to make peace, and he had agreed to mediate between his patron and King Heliokles. He undertook the private mission as well, for the Buddhists value conscientiousness and charity. So he left the king and the councils and took time to talk to a fifteen-year-old girl whom no one had bothered with before. Surprised, at first, ashamed of her tangled hair and ink-stained fingers, awed, she could not understand why he had come; and in answer to her shy questions he explained Buddhism. Is it surprising that she was converted? She was soon fired with enthusiasm for the eightfold way; she wanted to shave her head and put on the saffron robes of an ascetic at once. Nagasena, however, who was wise in the ways of kings and had no wish to offend her brother, gently told her that a different destiny—what they call karma—is allotted to each, and that hers was to be a queen. If she fulfilled it well, in her next life she might become a great monk, a teacher and ascetic, but by neglecting her duty she would harm her soul. She wept at this, but accepted it; she wept more bitterly when he returned to Sakala, and begged him to allow her to write to him, begged that he would write back giving her advice on the eightfold way. He agreed.

It was after this that the shy child, who thought of herself as clumsy and slow, who had allowed her ladies and her tutors and even the servants to order her about, began to be a queen. It started in small things. Even though she could not shave her head and become a nun, she still longed to renounce the world. She refused to wear the bracelets and the earrings, the necklaces and rings, the silk veils and gold-worked cloaks which her ladies used to dress her in. They were shocked; they scolded; they complained to her brother. He was annoyed that they should bother him about such a trivial matter, but he sent for his sister and told her that she must try to look like a queen or the common people would hold the whole family in contempt. "But the common people don't see me," she replied reasonably. "It would be improper for me to go about in public much, at my age, and when I do go out I have to dress modestly and cover myself with a cloak. So why can't I dress modestly at home, too? No one would know, and it would take less of my time and less of your gold as well."

Heliokles was amused at this answer, and he told the ladies to respect his sister's wishes, though he warned her not to adopt the Indian philosophy so completely that she offended the ways of her own people. He was not concerned about the Buddhism in itself. There were plenty of other Bactrian Greeks who were Buddhists: as I said, the Yavanas adopt foreign gods and philosophies easily. So Heliokleia went back to the palace women's quarters and told her women what her brother had said. A week later, looking at the chest full of neglected dresses, she ordered her ladies to sell the jewels and silks and give the money to the poor—and though they protested, exclaimed at the waste, lamented the loss of such lovely things, they did as she said. So she made that discovery: she could order and others would obey. That was not a small thing. It troubled her. Clumsy and stupid, she thought herself, yet she could give commands even to Padmini and Antiochis, who still scolded her for getting tangles in her hair. She wrote to Nagasena about it.

The monk's reply was that to hold power was her karma, the karma of kings, and that she must not use her authority to gratify her desires, but to promote equity. Equity, benefaction, benevolence: those are the virtues the Greeks, too, call royal. Heliokleia took this answer very seriously, and began to look about for ways to be equitable. She decided it was unjust that she, a Greek, was born to rule over Bactrians when she couldn't even speak their language, and she engaged a tutor to teach it to her—which was why she arrived in Ferghana speaking Sakan so fluently; the two languages are closely related. Not satisfied with this, she studied the laws and the courts and the systems of taxation, and wrote earnest letters to her brother's officials, asking them to explain their tasks and their decisions to her, as she wished to understand justice. They were unsettled by the queries, as you can imagine. Some were honest and some weren't, but they all suspected that her brother was using her to spy on them—he himself was by then out on campaign, fighting against the Parthians. They were afraid to put her off, however, in case she thought they had something to hide, so they came and told her some truths, some lies, and many generalizations and specious justifications, and she listened seriously to them all and thanked them. It took her some time to grasp the true position, but she was an intelligent girl and understood in the end: they were afraid and suspicious; she was privileged and interfering. Ashamed of herself, she would have backed out of public affairs again—but by then her fluency in Bactrian had brought her news of some of her brothers' ministers that the Greek-speaking court had missed: rumors of corruption. Her duty was plain: she must find out the truth of the rumors, and stop the injustices. She didn't like the task, had no confidence in her ability to perform it well, and it made her unhappy—but to the Buddhists, unhappiness is the fundamental fact of life. That was probably one of the things that made her adopt the philosophy. She accepted her karma and began to study what she could do.

So she gradually became a threat to her brother's ministers. Most of them had once hoped to marry her and become brother to the king, but in the end even the honest ones felt that she would be better married to some foreigner, in a land far away. When Mauakes' messenger arrived, he was welcomed gladly. King Heliokles was inclined toward a straightforward military alliance, but his ministers convinced him that the additional bond of a marriage would be profitable to them all, providing a tie that could hold after the old king's death into the next generation.

When Heliokles told his sister that she was to marry the king of Ferghana, she accepted it quietly. Of course she was frightened. Ferghana had been an enemy nation to her as much as Bactria had been to us, and Mauakes, the man who had stolen the province from the Greeks and raided the cities on the Oxus, had been discussed in Bactra with anger and hatred for years before she was even born. She also thought, as most Bactrians do, that the Sakas were nomads, savages, though she knew there was one Greek city in the land. Still, as a Buddhist she believed in the value of making peace, and she hoped that by reconciling Greek and Saka she would obtain merit. She took the idea of marriage as she took everything, seriously. When she set out that spring, with the elephants and the artillery, she did so firmly and calmly, without looking back. She had no particular ambition to be a great queen, but she was resigned to doing her utmost to become one. She certainly did not expect love and happiness—but never having known much of either, she was sure she could do without.

She had found a Saka slave in a private house in Bactra, purchased her, and engaged the woman to teach her the language and customs of the Sakas, promising her that if she taught well, she would be given her freedom and ten pieces of gold when they arrived in the valley. The slave rode with her on the elephant, and she studied all the way to

Eskati. It seemed a very long way. One day's ride through the fertile lands of Bactria to the Oxus River; five days more across the ridge to Maracanda; then another five days going due east through the wilderness, along the slopes of the mountains—and then there it was below them, Farthest Alexandria, its walls in the afternoon sun looking as though they were carved from light, with the valley of Ferghana like a lake behind it. The great river shone in the level rays, the lakes were blue as indigo, the road stretched pale up and up out of sight, and the mountains rose sunward on each side, their peaks gleaming with ice. I've seen that sight a hundred times and it always takes my breath away. Heliokleia came knowing that this land would be her home, and she would be its queen. She stared at it a long time, then ordered her attendants to make camp for the night on the spot, and sent a messenger ahead to announce her arrival to the king. Then she freed her Saka slave and dismissed her with thanks, so as to begin her stay in the valley with an auspicious act of kindness.

She spent most of the night in prayer and meditation, trying to achieve the detachment from desire that leads to justice, and eventually, so the Buddhists say, to release. In the morning, light-headed with fatigue, she bathed, anointed herself, and was dressed for her wedding in the saffron tunic and cloak. When the clothes were packed in Bactra, it had seemed an irritating joke that they were the same shade as a monk's robes; on the mountainside above Eskati, it seemed deeply appropriate. She was entering a marriage to a foreign enemy in an alien land, undertaking it to ensure peace: could a monk taking vows renounce the self more completely? She put the clothes on gladly and proudly. Then her two ladies brought out the jewelry her brother had given her to wear. She'd meant to put it on before, but now she refused it. "No," she told them, "just the diadem."

The two ladies looked at each other. "Child," said Padmini, "it's your wedding day. You must look like a queen for that, at least."

"I'll look like a queen if I wear the diadem," replied Heliokleia. "No jewelry."

"Oh!" exclaimed Antiochis. "Don't be impossible, not today! All the city will be looking at you; don't make us and all Bactria ashamed in front of the Sakas!"

"If I go into the city in a bride's cloak and a queen's diadem, with nothing else but modesty and purity of intention, how will that make anyone ashamed?" Heliokleia asked fiercely. "If all the city wants to look, let them see *me*, and not a pile of gold hats and necklaces. I want to go in with complete simplicity, and keep my heart free of desire."

"Don't be ridiculous," said Padmini sharply. "Your mother went into Bactra with modesty and purity of intention, but she wasn't too proud to dress like a queen. Put the things on."

Padmini's authority had disappeared long before, blown away like a drawing in the dust by the wind of conversion. Heliokleia simply shook her head. "You may dress my hair," she said, and sat down, very straight, on the stool in the center of the tent. After a moment Padmini began to comb and fasten the thick bronze hair, her lips compressed angrily. Antiochis sat down mournfully on the ground, shaking her head.

"You've disgraced us," she told Heliokleia. "I knew you'd do this!" She began to rock back and forth. "Everyone will see you without a single piece of gold, and think your brother hates you, and only sent you here to get rid of you. They won't be impressed by your 'sincerity'; they'll just despise you. And they'll despise me, too, and Padmini, because we're your attendants. Please, please, put on the jewels for our sake, if you won't do it for your own!"

"No one will despise us," Heliokleia said, gently now. "People don't notice gold nearly as much as they notice elephants, and we'll be riding on them."

"You won't be on the elephant at the altar," Antiochis retorted. "And the king will certainly be covered with gold; they stitch gold all over their clothes, these Sakas. I warn you, darling, you won't look modest next to him, you'll look poor and shabby."

"Well, then," said Heliokleia, "you wear all your jewels, and some of mine as well, and stand near me, and everyone will see how important you are, and understand that I might have dressed the same, but chose instead to come to them in simplicity."

Padmini sighed. "It's just shocking enough it might work," she said. "But I don't see the point." She pinned in the last gleaming strands. "At least you haven't shaved your head," she observed, assessing her work. "Antiochis, dear, don't quarrel with the girl on her wedding morning. Let her have her way, since she'll take it whatever we say." She picked up the diadem, smoothed it between her fingers, and tied it carefully about the young queen's head; critically, she straightened the ends. Then, unexpectedly, she leaned forward to kiss Heliokleia on the forehead. "Darling, you always were a strange girl, and we never have been the servants you wanted, have we? You always wanted monks and scholars to form your soul, and all you had was us to do your hair. Well, we were your mother's servants; we did what we thought was best. We saw her married, and now it's your turn: may the gods bless you and grant you more happiness than they gave to her!"

Heliokleia turned her face up to the other's, then stood and hugged Padmini. "I'm glad you're here," she said thickly. "You and Antiochis both."

"Where else would we be?" asked Antiochis, getting up at last and coming over to give a hug as well. "But I wish you could have married a Bactrian. Then we could have stayed with you for more than this year, and watched your own children grow up."

Of course, they were not allowed to ride into the city upon the elephants. It had been the queen's suggestion that the elephants trumpet to greet the Saka king when he rode out to meet her—not to alarm him, but to show respect; the elephants always trumpeted to greet kings. But when the Saka cavalry scattered, Heliokleia realized that it had been a mistake. She was not surprised, after that, to see that there was going to be trouble over the entry of the elephants, and she was watching closely as the king rode up and talked to the captain of her bodyguard. She called the captain over as soon as he began arguing with the king.

"What's the matter?" she asked him.

The captain, Demetrios, flushed angrily. He was a young man, unmarried, and admired her enormously; he thought it a great shame that so beautiful a woman, so purely Greek, should be sent to marry a barbarian. "The king's annoyed with us because his men can't control their horses in front of an elephant," he said angrily. "He's invented some excuse about the banners on the streets being too low to allow the elephants in, and he's insisting that you get down and ride in on horseback. I told him it was out of the question. It's complete nonsense about the banners; I rode into the city yesterday evening to check the route, and there wouldn't be any problem."

She looked at him thoughtfully for a moment. She had never sat on a horse's back in all her life, and in Bactra it would have been considered a scandalous suggestion that she should. "Are you sure that's what he said?" she asked.

The captain shrugged. "It's what his son said, anyway. He's pretending he doesn't speak Greek and is making the son translate. That's nonsense too; everyone knows he's fluent in it, the old devil."

"I'll speak to him myself," said Heliokleia. "Perhaps he'll relent if I ask him in Sakan."

So she descended from the elephant and walked over to where the Sakas waited on their tall horses. She could feel the whole royal guard watching her, and beyond them the eyes of the city, and she struggled again to detach herself from fear and desire, to remain calm, correct, watchful. Two men in tunics, the others in armor; the old one was the king. She noticed, with a sense of dread, that he was indeed completely covered with gold; that he had a round face, with a short thick gray beard that masked his mouth; that he was watching her with an expression of astonishment. She stopped. "Rejoice, O King," she said in Greek, and went on, in Sakan, "They say that the streets are decorated and are too low for the elephants."

She had hoped that when he saw her coming humbly to consult him, and in his own language, he would pretend there had been a misunderstanding—but he kept to his excuse without batting an eye, and agreed, yes, the banners were too low for the elephants and she would have to ride in on horseback. And he watched her, watched her in a way that made her feel uncomfortable, as though she were immodestly dressed. She had been stared at before, of course, and told by ministers that she was beautiful, but she had not paid much attention to anything so trivial and frivolous. A queen is untouchable in the ordinary way of things, and more so when she views protests of love as pointless and childish. She had been told what to expect in the marriage bed, and had been told that it would hurt, "but not too much," and had not worried about what had seemed the least interesting part of being queen of Ferghana. She was a virgin not just in body but in mind and imagination as well, and standing there in front of an old man who would deflower her that night she couldn't even understand why his look made her feel ashamed.

The idea that she ride into Eskati, which the Sakas made so casually, was deeply shocking to the Greeks, and Itaz' protests that the horse was a war horse didn't help. The horses of Bactria are smaller than the sun-descended horses of Ferghana: the height of the beast offered as her mount would have frightened her even if it had come without the obvious hostility of its owner in his Parthian finery. But she had dressed that morning to renounce the world, and she felt absurd to be standing there arguing about how to get into a city. So she quietly accepted the offer, and got on the horse. As soon as she was sitting in the tall saddle she remembered Padmini and Antiochis with a wave of guilt, and hurriedly tried to arrange some other obviously important position for them—but when they took their places just behind her she was afraid to look at them. She was bringing them into a strange city, scandalously riding like a soldier, without the jewels and without the elephants as well. They had been right, and she had been wrong: she had simply been clumsy again, and lost something more than a bracelet—honor, perhaps, or at least respect. When they entered the city and the people threw flowers at her and cheered madly, she was completely bewildered.

I've said what happened at the temple. But I didn't say what it must have been like for her, the bride, when the white mare bolted from the sacred knife, knocking the groom down and trampling him, covering him with blood. She had been afraid of the tall horse she had ridden on; the frenzied mare terrified her. She felt that her duty was to run to protect Mauakes, but she stood, clutching the side of the altar and staring in horror while the horse wheeled about before her like a white dragon, bared teeth and burning eyes, the gilded hooves striking like fire.

Then Itaz appeared out of the crowd again as from Heaven, stepped between his father and the furious animal, and killed it with one quick blow. All that fire and fury was gone, vanished in an instant into a bloody carcass lying beside the altar. Heliokleia stood watching silently while the son helped the father up. Itaz' dark, narrow face was sharp with concern and grief, the strong young arms gentle. How he loves his father, she thought, wonderingly; how quickly, how bravely, he stepped in to save him—while I did nothing. She did not consider that there was nothing she could have done; she was bitterly ashamed. And she had already understood that Itaz was her enemy.

The people were staring at her in a crushing silence. She had studied political matters painstakingly, and her numbed memory at once told her that something must be done to reassure them. She came round the altar, still clinging to it with one hand, and stopped at her husband's side. "The people are frightened," she whispered to him. "We must do something to calm them at once. Can we say that the priests will offer special sacrifices tomorrow, to avert the omen?"

As soon as she had spoken she realized that she should first have asked him how he was. How callous she'd been! Itaz was staring at her again and she stared back miserably. She could see that he found the chaos of the sacrifice ominous, that he was afraid that she would bring down some disaster. And perhaps he was right; the omens for the wedding could hardly have been worse. But it was already too late to do anything about it. Inadequate as she was, she was still bound to do her best as queen and wife, and if the omens predicted sudden death, for her or the king, well, she must accept her karma. She stood still and tried to calm herself and clear the passion from her mind while the king spoke to the crowds, then followed him quietly into the palace.

She spent the rest of the day like a Greek actor in a tragedy, wearing the mask of a queen and playing her allotted role, saying and doing the things her study of the part had suggested were the best. It was only in the evening, sitting on the bed, feeling Padmini's quick hands loosening her hair, that she finally realized that what happened in the marriage bed would happen to her, not to some other person called "the queen," and bit her tongue and began to shake. She'd married a man older than her father would be, if he were alive; a foreigner, a barbarian, and a traditional enemy of her people, and she was bound to him for the rest of her life. As the women left the room, leaving her alone, she had to fight with herself not to call them back and beg them to stay with her. Be brave, she reminded herself desperately, every woman has to face this; most come to enjoy it. She crossed her legs, folded her hands, and tried to lose herself in meditation. Detachment from sense in thought: that is the first of the four trances recognized by the Buddhists. Detachment eluded her; she remained sick and unsteady, continually distracted by the lamps, the patterns in the Indian cotton of the bedspread, the buzz of a fly against the window. After what seemed an age she heard voices coming toward her, and loud singing. She closed her eyes, gave up meditation, and prayed frantically, "Merciful Anahita, don't let me make a fool of myself and cry!"

The door burst open and the king came in, followed by a mass of friends and relatives carrying torches, high spirited, more-or-less drunk, and laughing enthusiastically at the traditional crude jokes. There was a smell of wine. Heliokleia wished she'd drunk more herself.

Mauakes stopped just inside the door, grinning at the young woman who sat cross-legged on the bed, dressed only in the saffron tunic. His friends peered at her over his shoulder and whistled. "Is that what you get for a Yavana alliance?" asked one. "If so, I'll send to Bactra myself!"

"I'll send to Bactra and Sakala as well!" said another. He got a laugh and a box on the ear from his neighbor.

"Don't just stand there," said a cousin whom Heliokleia vaguely recognized as the priest of the Sun. "Let us in, Mauakes; we have to sing our song. It's according to your Yavana custom, Queen, to make you feel at home!"

The king strode over to the bed and sat down beside her, putting an arm about her shoulders. The rest of the men poured into the room and stood about the bed in a close hot mob. They shuffled their feet, then stamped all together and roared out a cheerfully vulgar marriage song; at the conclusion they threw handfuls of nuts and sweetmeats over the newlyweds and cheered loudly.

"Very good," yelled the king, over the cheers and hoots, "thank you, thank you, and get out, out, out! I've private business here and I don't need all of you!"

They laughed again, made a few more jokes about the private business, and filed out, tossing a few more handfuls of nuts behind them. Like a vision, Heliokleia glimpsed Itaz' dark face, serious and angry, in the corridor outside. Then the door closed. Mauakes crossed to it quickly and bolted it, then returned to the bed. He brushed the nuts off it with his hand, then sat down with one leg folded under him and matter-of-factly began to unfasten her belt. "That's done with," he said briskly. "It seemed a long afternoon. I never thought you would be beautiful. I wasn't looking forward to tonight—until this morning." He grinned at her, pulling the belt away. "Then I couldn't wait." He slid his hands up her thighs, pushing the saffron folds of the tunic about her waist.

She had managed to compose herself in front of the others, but now she began to tremble again. "We . . . Were you hurt at all?" she asked.

"What?" he asked, glancing up at her face again in surprise, though his hands played gently where they were, stroking the pubis, which was smooth shaven in the Greek fashion.

"That horse . . . it kicked you . . ."

"Oh, that. I take worse knocks on the practice field all the time. I'm not such an old man as they may have told you; I'm not going to collapse because of a few bruises." He let go of her, slipping his hands back out of the saffron tunic, only to put them back on her breasts. He fondled them a moment, then tugged at the folds of cloth. "Here, stand up and let me take that off."

Slowly, she stood up. He drew the tunic in folds over her head, blocking off the light, catching heavily in her hair. Then he had tossed it aside and she was standing naked in the lamplight, with the king regarding her with great happiness. No man had ever seen her naked before, and she felt herself going hot all over. He grinned at the blush and put his arms round her, one hand digging into her buttocks and the other rubbing the nipple of her right breast, and began to kiss her ardently, pushing his tongue into her mouth. She felt sick, wanted to scream, hit him, run; she wondered if she would faint. But she was, as Padmini had said, a daughter of Antimachos and of Alexander, and she stood perfectly still, dry-eyed and unresisting, while the old king kissed her and mouthed her and mauled her with increasing eagerness, thrusting his hands into parts of her so private she herself had barely brushed them. She even wondered if she ought to say or do something to help him, offer to take his clothes off. She couldn't, didn't want to, dreaded even the thought of his nakedness next to hers. She could smell the mare's blood on him, and see the faint sticky film of it in the crevices of his body which his hurried wash after the sacrifice had failed to reach, and it turned her stomach. "I . . . I'm sorry," she stammered faintly.

"Eh?"

"I'm not used to this," she whispered.

He laughed uproariously and slapped her bottom. "I should hope not!" he exclaimed. "I'd have something to say to your brother if you were! 'I'm not used to this'! That's good!" He laughed again, then leaned over with one arm about her hips and pulled back the bedspread. He pushed her down on the sheets, then, kneeling over her, began to unfasten his trousers. Heliokleia closed her eyes, struggling against the tears, and tried in the darkness to find the path to the first trance, the detachment from sense.

CHAPTER

IV

It would have been much better for the queen, then and certainly in the months that followed, if she had cried. The king would have understood that. He was not a tyrant: if he was autocratic and suspicious, he was never gratuitously cruel, and his worst enemies admitted that he was fair. In his personal life he was chaste and moderate: while his first wife had lived he was faithful to her, and even after her death he had not touched so much as a palace slave girl, let alone the wife or daughter of any of his nobles. (He had, it was said, occasionally sent quietly to the Yavana brothel for a girl to come to him at the palace, but everyone agreed that this was entirely pardonable in a man who was not yet sixty, a widower still strong and hot-blooded.) He had made his Yavana marriage alliance for the advantages it offered, but he had been prepared to be a faithful husband; unlike the Yavanas, our people condemn a husband's adultery as strongly as a wife's. He had waited, then, with resignation, expecting either a jowlly hook-nosed gawk or a hot young harlot, who would have to be coaxed into

learning Sakan and cajoled away from the complacent superiority of
the Yavanas, and possibly threatened with death for adultery. He received Heliokleia. She seemed the more stunning and admirable for
being wholly unexpected. And even by the end of her first day in
Eskati he had other reasons to admire her. She kept her head even in
the shambles of the sacrifice, and instantly reminded him of the need to
reassure the people; she was dignified and gracious to the nobility, and,
best of all, she openly and publicly accepted his grandson as his heir
and abjured ambition.

He took her into his bed eagerly, with affection, delight, and an
immense gratitude, to her and to the gods. If she had cried and resisted,
however, he would have checked himself, gone very gently, excused
her—he wasn't unreasonable, he would have granted a young virgin's
right to be frightened, finding herself in a strange man's bed in an alien
land. But she seemed to accept him as calmly as she had accepted
everything else, and so he gave free rein to all the ardor and possessiveness he felt. Even so, he was not deliberately rough, and when he saw,
as he could not help seeing, that he had not pleased her, he was not
overly concerned. She had been a virgin and it would be easier for her
the next time, and he trusted his own affection to wake affection in her.
He went to sleep, in a contentment simpler and deeper than he'd
known for years, with one hand upon her breast.

When the king woke up, he found his new wife curled up on the
far side of the bed, her long hair in tangles over her face. He looked at
her for a moment with a great sense of peace and well-being, then
gently stroked the hair away. She did not wake. She was frowning
slightly in her sleep, and her eyelashes were wet. Her eyelids were red
and swollen, as well, but again, he was not concerned: when a woman
marries, she leaves her family behind, and she's entitled to cry. He ran
his hand lightly down her body from the hunched shoulder to the
curved bone of the hip, and even before the eyes flew open he felt how
she woke shuddering. She started up, met his eyes, then lay down
again, biting her lip. He was surprised. He hadn't thought he'd hurt her
that much.

He made love to her again, very gently this time, then left her
lying motionless in the bed and got up to unbolt the door and shout
for the servants. "Your things will have been delivered to your room

upstairs by now," he told her. "I'll have your attendants called, and they can escort you up to dress."

"Oh!" she said, some life coming back into the still face. "Thank you. Sir, according to my people's custom, I should sleep there as well, once my things have been properly arranged."

The king snorted and shook his head, then grinned. "I expect you to sleep with me," he told her. "Your rooms upstairs are for the day only; at night you belong to me." She looked down and blushed and he was satisfied.

Armaiti was the first one to answer the summons to escort the queen, and she proudly walked with her up the stairs and into the women's apartments. Heliokleia came in, draped in the saffron cloak and looking as composed as ever, but when the door closed behind her she stumbled over to the couch, pulled the cloak over her head, and sat there shaking. Antiochis went over and put her arm around her, but the queen hunched her shoulders away from the touch. "Leave me alone a little, please," she said, in Greek, and there was a force to the words that made them an order. Antiochis drew back with a look of concern on her face, and stood a moment staring at her mistress, but Heliokleia did not uncover her head, merely crossed her legs, clutching the saffron linen against her face. After a moment she let go of the cloth and lowered her hands, slowly and painfully, down onto her knees; the clenched fingers uncurled to leave the palms upturned and open, helpless and suppliant as a beggar's. The cloak drooped over her face, concealing it, leaving one white arm and side bare.

"Very well, then: meditate," said Antiochis resignedly, and turned back to arranging the room. She caught our fascinated stare and told us, in a low voice, "You don't need to stand there looking at her like that, girls. She won't pay any attention to us till she's finished. The queen spends some time in meditation every day; it's best to get on with your work while she does, but quietly, so as not to disturb her."

"She's praying to the gods?" asked Armaiti, impressed.

"She's meditating," corrected Padmini. "Our queen is a Buddhist laywoman, a follower of the philosophy of the prince Gautama Siddartha, the descendant of the royal house of Sakya. She's striving to discipline herself, which is a task worthy of any person, and especially of a noblewoman. Come, we must clear this room."

The queen's luggage had been deposited there the previous afternoon; we had come upstairs from the king's room, after leaving the
queen, to find the place submerged in chests and boxes we were too
tired to unpack. It had been all we could do, then, to sort out our own
sleeping arrangements, and decide that Padmini and Antiochis should
share one of the attendants' rooms, while the two who'd been there
before packed their clothes chests and mattresses into the other room
and bickered over space with the other two. Despite my tiredness, I'd
had trouble going to sleep that night. When we woke up—and we all
woke up early, despite ourselves, because of the unfamiliar sleeping
arrangements—we had had to start unpacking right away simply to be
able to get out the door.

"The green case is clothes," said Padmini, taking charge again.
"We'll need to open that now. And there should be a locked pinewood
chest with a bathtub, somewhere: we'd better unpack that, too, as my
lady will want to wash."

"It's in the corridor," said Armaiti.

"Well, someone should fetch it in! Where are those slaves?"

She'd already sent the four slaves down to the kitchen to warm
some water for the queen's bath. I pointed this out to her, and she gave
me an exasperated look. "They don't all four of them need to stand
about watching the kettle! They should have come back; you'll have to
admonish them for me, since they don't speak a civilized tongue. Well,
you and Jahika bring in the chest from the corridor; Armaiti, you and
Inisme stack those boxes on the teak chest there, to get them out of the
way."

We dragged in the chest from the corridor—and by the Sun it was
heavy!—and opened it. It was full of small leather boxes, with the rim
of the bathtub just showing pale in gaps round the edge. "What are
these?" I asked.

"Money," said Padmini shortly, glancing at them. "Put them over
there under the window for now; they can go down to the treasury
later on. I suppose your king has a treasury?"

I swallowed, told her he did, and started lifting the boxes. There
were a dozen of them, ten full of Bactrian silver coins, and two smaller
ones of Indian gold tetradrachms. I know that because there was an
inventory with them. It wasn't a dowry, it was simply a supply of

spending money. I'd heard about the wealth of Bactria but, till that minute, never quite believed it. When they put it in the treasury it more than doubled the amount of coin there—but then, we Sakas don't coin silver or gold ourselves, and even for bronze we rely on imitations of Bactrian coins.

We got the bathtub out just before the slaves came back with the heavy water jugs. It was a small tub by Greek standards, just big enough to crouch in, but it was made entirely of silver. (I discovered afterward they'd brought it because they weren't sure whether Sakas ever washed.) The slaves poured in the hot water first, and Antiochis added a handful of balsam, which filled the whole room with its scent, before adding the cold. Then Padmini went to the queen, who had sat completely motionless through all of this.

"Child," said the Indian, gently, touching the bare shoulder, "do you want to bathe?"

For a moment there was no response; then Heliokleia drew a deep breath, released it slowly, and lifted her head. "Yes," she said quietly, and pulled the saffron cloak off her tangled hair. Her face was tear-streaked but calm. She left the cloak on the couch and knelt down in the bath, with the complete unconcern about her nakedness that Greek women have in their own apartments. They're used to bathing together —and she was used to servants; she'd probably never dressed herself in her life. But I had to stop myself from staring. Her thighs were covered with blood, and it somehow looked much worse on the shaven, childlike hairlessness than it would have on me. I'd been told that loss of maidenhead was a sweet pain, but there was nothing sweet in the look of this.

The queen washed, dried herself, and allowed herself to be dressed from the green chest, and have her hair combed and arranged, all as though she'd never wept or bled in her life. Then it was time to go down for breakfast. We Sakas have a custom that the groom must give a gift to his bride on the morning after the wedding, and usually he does so at a breakfast party which he gives for his immediate family; we stretch out the stained marriage sheets in the breakfast room, so everyone can be sure that the bride was an honorable virgin, but it's not true, as some say, that we use them for a tablecloth: we're not savages. The king had told us to bring the gifts in to the queen at his order. We decided that Inisme and Jahika should bring them, and Armaiti and I continue unpacking, since we knew Greek and could follow Padmini's instructions. So they escorted her downstairs to the breakfast room and went off to fetch the gifts from the treasury, and brought them in when commanded. They looked a bit perplexed when they at last came back.

"Where's my lady?" asked Padmini, looking behind them.

Even Inisme could understand that much Greek. "She went down to the stables with King Mauakes, to inspect the horses he gave her," she said; I translated.

"Is anything the matter?" demanded Padmini, frowning at the doubtful look on their faces.

"She had an argument with Lord Itaz," Inisme said, "about that philosophy, Buddhism. He thinks it's wicked."

"That Parthianized young man?" said Antiochis, alarmed, when this had been relayed to her. "Is he very powerful here? My lady will never give up that philosophy, not for anyone; the king mustn't even try to ask her that."

"Oh, Itaz isn't powerful," said Inisme, when I'd translated. "The king told him to be quiet and not mention the matter again, as the queen had a perfect right to practice a philosophy common among her own people."

Padmini and Antiochis were reassured, and we went on unpacking. It was only later that Jahika told Armaiti and me the real reason she and Inisme had looked so perplexed. "When we came down to the dining room," she told us, "we overheard the king laughing over something the queen said last night. Nothing shameful, just the sort of silly thing one might say: 'I'm not used to this,' I think it was. When the queen heard him she stopped dead in the doorway and backed up the corridor, and then she burst into tears. It was so sudden I didn't know what to make of it. She just leaned against the wall and stood there with her mouth working, not making a sound, crying. After a moment she wiped her face and looked as cool as ever and went on in. She's a very strange woman, isn't she? And Lord Itaz was saying that the reason she wasn't wearing any jewels was because the Buddhists hate the adornments of the world, and think life is evil."

"She has enough jewels, though," I said. We'd unpacked them. "And dresses."

"But they're all new, aren't they? Look at the nap on the cloth—it's never been washed. And there are no pin holes. Most of the things have never been worn. I think her brother gave them to her to come here, to impress us. I think she must have dressed like an ascetic at home."

It seemed strange, and rather unsettling, to me, too. I remembered my dream of the dry river. But because it was Inisme standing there looking nervous and a bit disgusted I said, "Well, she means to dress like a queen here, clearly, so what does it matter?"

"I don't like it," Inisme snapped. "And I don't like the sound of this Buddhism; it sounds impious to me. She's a very strange woman."

She was. So Itaz felt, as he found himself sitting beside his sister Amage in the palace dining room that morning, waiting for his father and stepmother to finish dressing. The servants had already brought the sheets in and hung them against the wall. They were of fine muslin from India, and the bloodstains on them were raw red, as though the light fabric had been torn. Itaz hated to look at them.

He was in a foul mood. He had obediently done everything required to show his loyalty in front of the people and nobility on the previous day. He had ridden with his father to meet the bride; he had given the woman his horse and led it by the bridle; he had even gone with the groomsmen to the bridal chamber. But he hadn't been able to force himself to go in and join the singing and joking. He'd meant to. But when the door opened he had glimpsed her sitting cross-legged on the bed in her saffron tunic like a monk, so beautiful the sight of her hurt him again. He stood outside, furious with her, with himself, and, mysteriously, with someone else he didn't want to name, even in his thoughts. When his father threw the others out and shut the door, Itaz went off hurriedly into the darkness, unwilling to stand about with his father's supporters in comfortable drunkenness, laughing.

He left the palace and went down the path from the citadel two steps at a time, past the temple of the Sun, through the marketplace—where the people were still feasting and dancing—past the theater and the concert hall to the Yavana brothel. It was busy, as you can imagine; the men waiting had spilled out its doors onto the pavement, dancing a line dance by torchlight in the street, singing drunkenly. Itaz pushed past them and looked about inside for the madam. She was in the central room, the dining hall, which was almost deserted, smilingly counting the evening's takings. When she looked up and saw Itaz, however, she put the money down and hurried over. The king's son was too important a client to be kept waiting.

"Where's Philomela?" Itaz demanded.

"She's busy," said the madam, simpering. "All the girls are busy, with more men waiting; such a festival! But she should be finished very soon, and then you may have her, for the whole night if you like, though there's two or three others who came asking for her before you."

Itaz grunted and sat down to wait. He felt disgusted with himself, waiting in a brothel for another man to finish with a sweaty whore. He told himself that he ought to go back to the palace and finish the feast decently with his cousins and the other nobles—but he didn't move. The madam smiled at him and solicitously fetched him wine, then went out to check on how the girls were doing.

Presently she came back and told him that Philomela was free now, and fussily escorted him through the courtyard and up the stairs to the girl's room, where she left him. It was dark on the landing; from the neighboring rooms came grunts and stifled shrieks. Again Itaz felt tempted to turn and go back to the palace, but he knocked on the door and it opened.

Philomela stood in the light of the single oil lamp, wearing nothing but a gold necklace and a thigh band; her makeup was smeared. She was young, not more than seventeen, and the gold light shone on the sweat between her high breasts and along her sides. Her pretty face was flushed and smiling—not the grinning grimace of the harlot, but a real smile, sweet and delighted: the disgust Itaz had felt was suddenly swamped in desire. She flung her arms about him, kissing him ardently. "You came back, and tonight!" she said. "I'm so glad! I'd much rather spend tonight with you than with anyone."

Itaz only grunted and swept her up, into the room, and over to the bed. He felt swollen inside and hot and somehow hurt as well, and when the girl touched him he wanted nothing except to forget and escape from himself in her. He tore off his clothes, fumbling with haste; the girl, surprised but compliant, did her best to help him, then yielded easily as he pushed himself on top of her. He took her very quickly and passionately—then lay on the narrow mattress beside her wondering why he didn't feel any better.

Philomela propped herself up on an elbow and stroked her lover's back. "I'm so glad you came," she repeated happily. "I saw you this morning, leading the queen's horse, and you looked so magnificent I thought I would burst with pride. And then you saved your father's life! I was so proud!"

"I did what?" asked Itaz in astonishment.

"You saved your father's life. The horse was going to trample him again."

"Well, yes, but . . ." He remembered again his desperate leap onto the terrace, the mare's gilded hooves flashing, her weight falling, pulling the sword from his hand, the blood. He had jumped into her path to protect his father, it was true. "But all the horse wanted to do was get away," he said. "It would simply have jumped off the terrace beside the temple and galloped away."

"Yes, but it would have gone right over him, again, to do that! And it might well have killed him, trampling on him again. It was a miracle he wasn't hurt the first time. He really *wasn't* hurt, was he?"

He remembered how he had seen his father just an hour before, going into the bedroom, grinning. He felt another stab of pain and fury and hauled himself up on his elbows. "He wasn't hurt," he muttered at the pillow.

"That's wonderful," said Philomela with a contented sigh. "We were all so frightened. But we decided afterward that probably the king was right, and what happened was really a good omen, and means that the Tochari will be defeated and we'll come through unscathed. Maybe it means that you'll defeat them, since you killed the horse! And I'm sure it means that the queen will bring us luck. Isn't she lovely? I thought she'd be lovely, in spite of what Azilises said, but she's even more beautiful than I thought she'd be. And so modest! She wasn't wearing any jewels at all, even though she comes from a long line of kings."

"She did it to make the rest of us look like a pack of gaudy savages," said Itaz sharply. "And she succeeded."

Philomela stared at him in surprise. "But you looked magnificent," she said.

Itaz thought again of his father and Heliokleia standing together before the altar of the Sun: the graying, short, stout man in his gold crown and gold-spangled clothes, and the tall slim young woman in her perfect simplicity. It seemed to him that nobody could have failed to see how ridiculous his father looked beside the Yavana. "She made a fool of my father, and of me!" he said hotly. "First she had her elephants trumpet to frighten our cavalry; then she laughed at me because I was slow to lend her my horse; and finally she made the rest of us look overdressed by that ostentatious modesty. When my father was trampled the first thing she worried about was what the crowd thought; she didn't even ask him how he was. She's a cunning, arrogant vixen."

"You don't like her," said Philomela in disappointment, after a shocked silence.

"No. And probably she's a . . . an adherent of the Lie, a Buddhist, as well." He put his head down on the pillow, finally feeling some relief of the swollen heat inside. He went on, "My father won't see any of that, though. He's already in love with her. He grinned all over his fat face whenever he looked at her, itching for the night to come, the stupid old man."

He recoiled in shock from his own words. He had never spoken, or even thought, of his father as a "stupid old man" before, hadn't believed he could. He was horrified, and at the same time, immensely relieved. The hard surge of anger he had felt when he watched his father go into the bedroom where the young queen sat waiting was finally named. He had taken his father's place at the sacrifice, and he longed to take it in the marriage bed as well. He imagined the woman, flushed and naked in his father's arms, and he went rigid with anguish, blinking at tears. It was not right or fair that she should be so beautiful, that he should feel such an agony of longing for her, when he had never wanted a woman that badly before and didn't even like this one. And he had just had Philomela; his flesh was tired, but the desire was still hard, as though it had dug itself into his bones.

How could he, loyal, devoted to his father, a follower of the good religion, possibly do such a monstrous and unnatural thing as to desire his father's wife? He suspected suddenly that it was the work of some evil spirit, one that had followed the scent of the queen's impiety like a dog on the scent of meat, and which now tormented him with lust, hoping to bring ruin on him and the whole country. He should not have come to the brothel. He should have stayed awake and prayed for relief. He sat up quickly.

The whore beside him was staring in dismay. "I should not have said that," he told her in a low voice. "Of course I respect my father. For his sake, I'll respect the queen as well. I'm just tired. I had better go." He stood up.

"Now?" she cried, her face folding with disappointment. "Gyllis said you would stay with me the whole night." Gyllis was the madam.

He looked down at her in confusion. He should not have come; he should tell her that, and tell her that fornication was wicked, and he would not come back. But she was young, pretty, and tired, and watching him wide-eyed with tears on the smeared paint of her eyelashes. He suddenly realized that she thought he was in love with her, and she had been clutching the thought to herself all day with delighted excitement: the king's son in love with *her!* And it wasn't unreasonable for her to think that. He'd given her a lavish payment and an extravagant compliment the previous evening, and he'd come down from the palace on his father's wedding night to be with her again. He could tell her that he'd given her gold out of pity, and come tonight because he couldn't have the woman he wanted and so had taken her instead—but why be cruel to her? She wasn't demanding anything. Even the money he'd given her had probably ended up in Gyllis' money chest; the girls in the brothel were all slaves. She couldn't have much to delight her, and she'd seized on such harmless things—a royal wedding, a festival, a nobleman briefly infatuated. Why take those few things away from her?

It was stupid, to worry about hurting the feelings of a whore. But he sat down beside her on the bed and kissed her. "Gyllis should have realized I couldn't stay the night," he said. "I have to be at the palace for the morning gift, and I shouldn't have come here at all. I must go. But I don't want you sleeping with anyone else tonight, and I'll pay Gyllis for it, and tell her so."

Philomela looked at him earnestly. "You'll come back, then? To-morrow?"

"I'll come back as soon as I can," he replied, and kissed her again.

Trudging back up the steps to the citadel, he cursed himself for saying he'd come back. He meant to cling very firmly to the path of Rectitude, rejecting the solicitations of the evil spirit that had put the unnatural lust into his heart. He meant to pray to Ahura Mazda, the lord of infinite light, and force himself back to purity. " 'Purity is the best good,' " he muttered, quoting the favorite prayer of his faith under his breath. " 'Happiness, happiness is to him, who is purest in purity.' " Visiting seventeen-year-old whores had no part in that. But he hadn't been able to check the impulse to make her happy. Weak and vacillating, he told himself, with contempt. If I'm to keep my own soul I will have to be stronger.

He spent much of the night praying, falling asleep in the early dawn, when the last of the feasting was finally over and the whole city still. He had only an hour or so of sleep before a slave woke him, telling him that his sister and her husband had arrived for the morning party and were already waiting in the dining room. Itaz washed his face, dressed, and stumbled across the courtyard to the dining room, feeling dirty, clumsy, and angry with everyone and everything. He almost bumped into the servants who were bringing the bridal sheets to hang up in the dining room. He looked at the bloodstains, then looked away again quickly.

His sister Amage and her husband Tasius were already seated at the breakfast table, nibbling preserved grapes from a silver fruit dish. Amage was her father's oldest child, ten years older than Itaz, a thick-set, round-faced powerful woman very like her father, but more open and affectionate. She grinned at her little brother when he came in looking like a storm cloud. "Sleep well?" she asked.

"No," he said shortly, and sat down, scowling at the table.

"By the Sun, what a face!" said Amage. "I know you don't like the idea of a Yavana stepmother, but try and cheer up and make the best of it; she won't go away for scowling. We don't need to start off by quarreling with her."

Itaz grunted. "You've changed your song. Last month you were as suspicious of the woman as I was."

"And I'm still suspicious—but we might as well make the best of it. Besides, most of my suspicions were for Moki. I love that child as if he were my own, and I didn't like to think of him losing his rightful place to some half-Yavana. But she's recognized him as the heir now without even being pushed."

"Words don't cost her anything. She could easily change her mind when she has children of her own."

"We can worry about that if she does. And words can cost, if they're said publicly and everyone remembers them. She didn't need to acknowledge Moki as the heir, especially not with all the nobility of the Sakas listening to her—but she did. I thought she acted very graciously. And I never thought she'd have learned to speak our language; I thought we'd have to sit here this morning trying to talk Greek, and you know I can't. We may even be friends after all."

Itaz scowled still more. "Who told Moki that Heliokleia means 'ambition'?" he asked.

Tasius looked embarrassed. He was a lean, angular man with a sharply pointed beard, a descendant of a family that had been the traditional rivals of Mauakes' own. The king had reconciled them by means of Amage. "It was a joke," he muttered. "He wasn't supposed to repeat it in front of everyone."

Itaz snorted and helped himself to a grape. He was sure that Tasius hadn't meant the boy to repeat the slur in front of everyone, but equally sure that it hadn't been a joke. But it seemed that now everyone was prepared to bow to the king and pretend that all would be well. He supposed he was bound to do the same.

Kanit came in, followed by Choriene, the widow of the king's second son, who had been made a priestess of the Sun on her husband's death. That completed the family party, as the king had no parents or brothers living, hadn't invited his other cousins, and his eldest son's wife was dead; the morning party was considered too tedious for the grandchildren. Kanit slapped shoulders all round and sat down next to Itaz. "Where did you slip off to last night?" he asked.

Itaz shrugged and didn't answer. "Did you inquire of the gods about the sacrifice?" he asked instead. It was part of Kanit's duty as high priest to count out the divining rods for the royal house. Itaz was not such a strict Mazdayist that he rejected this practice; he worshipped

the Sun as well as Ahura Mazda—or perhaps it would be better to say
he worshipped Ahura Mazda in the Sun, as the Greeks worship Zeus,
identifying the two. Kanit was not an exceptionally good diviner, and
not really overly devout, but everybody liked him, and the king
trusted him as nearly as he trusted anyone.

"We counted on the rods," he said to Itaz, "and the omens are not
good, but they don't seem to predict disaster for the whole land."

"Only sorrow for the royal house," put in the Sun's priestess, the
widow Choriene.

"Possibly," said Kanit, with a deprecating smile.

"The rods were quite clear," said Choriene stubbornly. "They
spelled out death, and some great misfortune, to some member of this
house."

"There's a war ahead," said Itaz. "You don't need the divining rods
to know that."

Everyone nowadays believes that King Mauakes, and the rest of us,
must have been either perversely stupid or deluded by some demon, to
misinterpret the omen so badly. But at the time it was far from clear.
We were afraid of the Tochari, and we had hopes that the marriage
alliance would save us. Just as a girl in love can convince herself that
the man she wants loves her or hates her from something he does
indifferently, so we misread the will of Heaven, interpreting the signs
according to our own fears or desires. Only with hindsight can we
look down at an omen as the Sun does, and see it clearly.

The door opened and the king came in. He looked well rested,
more relaxed than Itaz could ever remember seeing him, and immensely pleased with himself. Everyone stood up and he went round
to each of them, giving a hug or a kiss on the cheek, then sat down at
the head of the table. "Well," he said with satisfaction, "the queen
should be down presently." He looked at the stained sheet and grinned
to himself.

"You're a lucky man," said Kanit, joining in with the grin. "It's
plain your wife is honorable as well as beautiful."

"Indeed she is," replied the king. He snapped off a bunch of grapes
and popped one in his mouth, then started laughing as he chewed it.
"You know what she said last night?" he asked, spluttering grape seeds.

" 'I'm sorry,' she said, 'I'm not used to this,' blushing like a baker at a furnace, too!"

Kanit laughed; Amage laughed; even Tasius managed a smile. Choriene sniffed and looked out the window. Itaz imagined the queen blushing and stammering her apology for virgin modesty and felt sick. He looked away from the others just in time to see Heliokleia come soundlessly into the doorway and pause a moment in silence, watching them. Kanit and Choriene were seated with their backs to her, Amage and Tasius were as intent on the king's story as the king himself, and didn't notice her. Heliokleia did not see Itaz at the corner of the table, screened by the bulk of his sister, and he watched her breathlessly. During the night he had called her a cunning, arrogant vixen, and prayed against her as a bait for evil; he had built another picture of her in his mind, the picture of a cool, proud, devious Yavana devil worshipper, and he had, he thought, got the better of his lust. But before the real Heliokleia the devil picture melted away. She had put off the monkish saffron bridal robes and wore a plain tunic of undyed cotton under the royal purple cloak, and she stood with one hand on the door frame, listening. Her eyes fell on the stained sheet hung up on the wall behind her husband, and, as Itaz himself had done, she looked quickly away.

"I told her that if she had been used to it, I would have had something to say to her brother," the king was saying happily.

The queen flinched, glanced over her shoulder.

"She'll get used to it, I think," said Kanit slyly.

"I think she may," agreed Mauakes.

Heliokleia backed out of the room and disappeared.

"Have you inquired of the gods?" Mauakes asked Kanit and Choriene.

Kanit repeated what he had already told Itaz, and this time Choriene sniffed and did not add to it.

"I would expect the omens to be bad," said the king, "given the presence of the Tochari. If they don't predict disaster, that's good. We can tell everyone that the gods have confirmed what I said yesterday— that we're threatened with disaster, but we'll escape."

Itaz heard footsteps, deliberately loud this time, approaching the doorway, and the queen appeared again. This time the others saw her, and they all got up. "Good morning," said Mauakes, going to her and kissing her. "Good morning," chorused the others, smiling. "Good morning," muttered Itaz, between his teeth.

"Much health," said the queen softly. "I mean, good morning."

The king escorted her to the place at the head of the table, seated her, and sat down beside her. Heliokleia sat very straight and still, looking perfectly calm and assured. Why on earth, wondered Itaz, had she found it necessary to pretend she hadn't heard the king laughing over her modesty? Too proud to acknowledge her silly apology? But as he asked it he had a horrible sense that he understood exactly: the memory was painful and bitterly shaming, the king's laughing retelling wholly intolerable, and she hadn't wanted them to witness her struggle not to cry.

"Are your apartments in good order?" Mauakes asked Heliokleia expectantly.

She nodded. "They're lovely rooms, sir. Thank you. My women are busy unpacking even now. Lady Padmini and Lady Antiochis wish me to express their gratitude to you for giving them such pleasant accommodation, so fitted to their rank." She wasn't exactly lying when she said that—merely making the correct noises, as Padmini and Antiochis would have wished.

"Good," said Mauakes. "And now, as you know, it's our custom for a husband to console his bride for the loss of her virginity with some gift. I took time over this matter, trying to decide what would be proper for my queen to have, and in the end I determined on two gifts, a lesser and a greater." He clapped his hands, and after a moment Inisme and Jahika, who'd been waiting in the corridor, came in, each carrying a box of carved sandalwood, which they set on the table before him. "Which will you have first?" asked Mauakes.

"The lesser, sir," said Heliokleia, looking at the two boxes with polite interest rather than excitement. "Then there's no danger of the gratitude due to it being lost in the gratitude due the other."

Mauakes smiled. "And there's never any danger of you Yavanas being at a loss for clever reasons, is there? Here." He handed her the larger of the two boxes, which was decorated with flowers.

She rested her fingers a moment on the lid. "Thank you for your favor in making the gift," she said, looking at him with the box still unopened. "And now"—opening the box—"thank you again for the gift itself."

She looked into the box a moment, her face solemn and intent, then lifted from it a crown of gold. It was Yavana workmanship, but Saka in taste; it was made from the gold of the north, the griffin gold, set with rubies from Badakshan, turquoise of Khorasan, and lapis lazuli and carnelian from Sogdia. The present queen still wears it. The circlet is worked with griffins stooping upon gazelles, and in the center, modeled exquisitely small and seeming almost to fly off the crown, there is a chariot, the four-horse chariot of the Sun. Heliokleia touched the delicate gold heads of the Sun's horses, then set the crown cautiously down onto the lid of the box before her and stared at it. "It is very beautiful," she said at last. "I've never seen anything like it before. Where was it made?"

"Here in Eskati," replied Mauakes complacently. "We have good craftsmen here. The goldsmith is a Yavana, of course, and he did his best for the descendant of Antimachos the God. It was his idea to decorate it with the Sun's chariot, to honor our god and your name both together. But you haven't emptied the box yet; go on."

Heliokleia looked back into the box, then pulled out a gold necklace and some earrings and set them down beside the crown. "And this is the lesser gift?" she said. "I thank you, and send the warmest of compliments to the goldsmith, who must have the skill of Daedalus."

Mauakes grinned. "Well then, put them on!"

Very slowly she picked up the jewels and put them on; first the earrings, then the necklace, and last the crown, sliding it awkwardly back and forth to get it over her hair, which was fastened in a mass behind her head. To Itaz, the gold cheapened her, glittering gaudily around her neck and jamming the sides of her face into a clumsy box. But Mauakes was pleased. "Now you look like a queen!" he told her. "It was good that you dressed so modestly yesterday, and left off all your Bactrian jewels; the people will notice it all the more when you reappear like that! They'll see and understand that in this kingdom, your royalty comes from me."

"If she wears them!" said Itaz, suddenly and impatiently. He found he disliked the sight of the queen entangled in the gold, disliked his father's complacent claim to her through it. "She's a Buddhist and doesn't like wearing jewelry. Adornments are wicked in your faith, isn't that right?"

Heliokleia looked over at him with a quick flash of the eyes. "I know what's due my position," she said sharply. "I am content to wear jewels to honor my husband and display his power."

Mauakes looked at her in confusion. "What's this?" he asked.

"She's a Buddhist," repeated Itaz. "That's right, isn't it? It's what you are, isn't it, Queen?"

She gave him a straight, serious look, almost a triumphant look, then turned her eyes back to the king. "Yes, it's what I am," she said. "If the eightfold way is viewed with distaste here, I am very sorry. I didn't know; if I had, I would have warned you to choose some more suitable queen, as I am deeply devoted to this philosophy and cannot give it up."

"Don't be ridiculous," said the king. "Nobody in Ferghana cares much about this philosophy. Except perhaps my son, nobody even knows much about it. But no one had told me you were a Buddhist. Your brother just said you were devout. What's involved? You swore yesterday by the Sun; you do still honor the gods, don't you?"

"Of course," replied Heliokleia earnestly. "I honor all the divinities as you do. The Buddha taught nothing about the gods: his concern was how to end suffering. How could that knowledge offend the gods?"

"That philosophy is impious and perverse!" said Itaz hotly. "It teaches that the enlightened man is superior to the gods, and that the world God made is evil, a thing to be escaped from as quickly as possible! Instead of calling on us to fight against evil and destroy it, it says we should endure it patiently."

"There is no impiety possible in the way," returned Heliokleia passionately. "Who did you learn about it from? Or did you read about it?"

Itaz flushed. He was like most Sakas, particularly in those days, and couldn't read at all. "I heard a Buddhist missionary in Parthia," he said. "He had much to say about the evil and misery of the world; you can't say that's not a part of your faith."

"In Parthia, of course!" said the queen, sarcastically now. "In Parthia they didn't allow the missionary to finish, but drove him off with violence, as they always do, and refused to hear the whole of what he had to say. If they had, they might—God forbid!—have seen how true it was, and been converted."

"We heard quite enough to know that what he had to say was wicked!" snapped Itaz.

"You Mazdayists are very eager to fight against evil, aren't you?" asked Heliokleia, her eyes shining with anger. "So eager you declare things to be wicked on a moment's acquaintance, without waiting to get to know them first! To me that seems absurd. If I were hasty, I'd dismiss the whole teaching of your prophet Zoroaster as a comical invention—but *I* won't condemn something on hearsay!"

"Blasphemy!" shouted Itaz furiously, starting to climb to his feet. "Zarathushtra was the holiest man who ever lived! What's absurd and comical about saying that the world is partly good and partly evil? Isn't it obvious that—"

"Silence!" shouted the king. Itaz subsided into his place; Heliokleia sat looking at him, her eyes still shining in her flushed face.

Mauakes looked at Kanit. "Buddhism is common in Bactria," said the priest, trotting out his little knowledge of it with some embarrassment. "As it is in India, particularly popular among the nobility of both kingdoms. It's a philosophy more than a religion, from all I've heard. And I've never heard of any unpleasantness associated with the practice of it; in fact, I believe it's very strict in its morality. The monks won't even marry, and refuse to eat meat, though the laypeople have more freedom. They say that King Menander . . ." He coughed.

"We've all heard of King Menander," said the king sourly. "King Menander, they say, is a saint. Better that than a god, like his grandfather. We'll leave him out of it." He looked at his new wife for a moment, then at Itaz. "Well, it seems to me there's no harm in this . . . philosophy—whatever your Mazdayist friends think, Itaz. A bit of piety and moral strictness is a fine thing in a queen. And how could I forbid you to hold a philosophy common and respected among your own people? You may keep to this faith all you like, my dear." Itaz sat very stiff, glaring. Heliokleia, he remembered bitterly, had already announced she would keep to that faith whether Mauakes liked it or not. But she bowed her head gracefully to this grant of permission, politely pretending that she'd needed it.

"But is it true you don't like jewelry?" the king asked, after a moment's silence.

She sat very still. "I know what is due my position as a queen," she said at last. "I do not like to wear jewels privately, and adorn myself for nothing but my own vanity. I am content, as I said, to wear them to honor you."

Mauakes gave her an unreadable look. He had expected any young woman to be delighted with the jewels, and had thought she was. He hadn't known before that her face was capable of lighting as it had when she defended her faith; he had believed the calm assurances of pleasure. He saw now that she had taken his gift dutifully, not happily, and his own pleasure in giving it was gone. He glanced quickly at Itaz, who sat glaring at the queen, still visibly smoldering with righteous Mazdayist anger. It was best, thought the king, to know about the queen's philosophy. Though Buddhists were virtually unknown in Ferghana, Mazdayists were not uncommon, and could be assumed to hate the Indian philosophy as much as Itaz did. Of course, it could also be assumed that they were all of the anti-Greek party and hated the Yavana alliance anyway, so it was not of much significance; still, it was best to be aware of the problem.

But Mauakes couldn't help feeling a sense of loss. For once he had allowed his habitual wariness to be swallowed up in an unguarded, uncomplicated pleasure. Now he saw that he had misjudged: for some personal or political reason she had been wearing a mask, and who could say what the face beneath was like? He had his first small premonition now that life with her might not be entirely sweet, after all. Though the heart of the problem, he told himself, was not the new queen, but his own son. The queen, after all, had a perfect right to follow a philosophy adopted by her famous uncle and popular among the nobility of her own people. Itaz had no right to make her feel unwelcome because of a Parthian religion, a faith foreign to the worship of his own people. The king gave his son a dark look; Itaz caught it and abruptly bowed his head.

Amage coughed. "Well," she said, "what about the greater gift, Father? Perhaps nobody else is curious to know what it is, but I am."

"Hmm," said Mauakes, trying to recover some of the pleasure he'd felt a few minutes before. He picked up the smaller wooden box and placed it before his wife, pushing the jewel case out of the way. This one was carved with griffins and horses.

Heliokleia looked at it expressionlessly, as though she too were trying to recover herself. Silently, she fumbled with the lid, found the catch, and opened it. Inside was another mass of bright gold. She picked up the top strand, then stared in bewilderment as the rest dangled from her hand, the gold merely the decoration for straps of dark leather. Picking up the gold bit, she finally recognized the contraption. "Oh," she said blankly, "a bridle."

Mauakes laughed, looking at the confusion on her face and beginning to enjoy himself again. "Well," he told her, "I couldn't bring the whole horse into the breakfast room, could I?"

"A horse?" she asked, blinking, still bewildered.

"Horses, then," said the king, relishing it. "Forty mares of the royal breed, with four stallions and thirty geldings; and another two hundred of the common breed, together with the farms and fields, stables and slaves to care for them; and, as well, as much arable land as a hundred teams can plough. A queen needs land and income of her own, and a Saka queen needs horses."

"Oh," she said, in quite a different voice, one of recognition. Itaz felt that she understood perfectly the need to possess land, to have money to make gifts and reward service. And he could see that, even though she was afraid of the royal horses, she had some idea that they were important among the Sakas, and that therefore she should own some. She had expected to be given all the symbols of authority at some time, and she would have felt herself wronged if she didn't get them—and perhaps it was a queen's right, but he disliked it, that instant comprehension of the sources of power. "This is a kingly gift," she told Mauakes. "Worthy of you and of all the Sakas. Thank you."

He beamed.

"These horses of the royal breed," she went on, looking at the golden bridle, "they're the ones you say are descended from the horses of the Sun, who came down from heaven?"

Kanit cleared his throat and solemnly assured her that this was so.

"In Bactria they said that the horses of Ferghana are descended from Pegasus," she told him, "a winged stallion, an immortal, the possession of the gods."

At this Kanit beamed as well, genially. "So the Yavanas agree with us about that, at least."

"At least, sir! And on another thing we agree as well: that the royal horses of Ferghana are the finest in all the world. My brother was . . . disappointed . . . that you refused to sell him some." King Heliokles had, in fact, been extremely angry; he had wanted some of the royal horses for his own stable.

"In the old days," said Kanit, "only the priests and priestesses could keep and breed the royal horses. Now they are all entrusted to the king, in the keeping of the glory of his house. But it's still sacrilege to sell them."

"And worse sacrilege to send them out of the valley," put in Mauakes quickly. "We could not allow your brother to keep them and breed them."

"No," said Heliokleia, catching the undertone of warning, "so I shall own some of these horses and my brother . . . won't." She looked down at the bridle in her hands and again her face had that not-quite-smiling expression of mockery, as though she found the Saka admiration of the horses faintly ridiculous, and her own position as the owner of some absurd. She looked up again. "I think, sir, it must be a disgraceful thing for a Saka queen to be unable to ride."

"I could teach you to ride, if you like," Amage offered suddenly. "I'm teaching my daughter now anyway, every morning. You're right; you will have to learn, and it would be better for you to learn from me than from some servant."

"Thank you," said Heliokleia, meeting her eyes directly in honesty and surprise. "You are most kind to offer it, and I am grateful."

Mauakes and Amage took the queen down to the palace stables after the breakfast, to show her the horses she'd been given. Choriene and Kanit went back to the temple, arguing about the divining rods; Itaz got up to go as well, but Tasius caught his arm. "Are you in a hurry?" he asked. "There was something I wanted to talk to you about."

Itaz looked at him suspiciously. He had never liked Tasius. But he felt bound to treat his sister's husband politely. "I'm not in a hurry," he said, sitting down again. "Talk away."

Tasius didn't talk, at first. He sat with his elbows on the table, looking at Itaz in silence for so long that Itaz grew impatient. "Well?" he said. "I'm listening."

"The new queen is a very dangerous woman," Tasius said bluntly. "I wanted to know if you'd be willing to help with some kind of defense against her."

Itaz stared at him darkly. "If you think the queen is dangerous, you should say so to my father, not to me," he said. "I can hardly be expected to scheme in secret against my father's wife."

"I'm not asking you to scheme against her," replied Tasius, with a calming gesture. "Everyone knows your loyalty to your father; everyone's seen how you stifled your own feelings about his new wife, and even brought the woman into the city on your own horse. I'm not proposing anything treasonous; you ought to know me better than that. But I don't dare say anything to the king. You know I spoke against the alliance when it was first proposed; I know you argued with him as well. And we both know how he regards opposition. He's never forgotten that my family's as good as his own, and he'd sooner suspect Amage than trust me. And I can tell you something that perhaps you've discovered for yourself already: he'll never trust you, whatever you do. You have a claim on the succession and could be dangerous."

Itaz' cheeks darkened. "I have no claim," he said. "Moki is Goar's son, and I'd sooner die than insult my brother's memory and profit by his death. My father knows how much I loved my brother; he ought to understand that."

"That's irrelevant," said Tasius. "In the eyes of the people you might have a claim, and that will be enough for Mauakes. He doesn't trust you, or me, or any of us. He trusts elephants and siege machines and his Yavana alliance. He prefers them to our own cavalry and our faithful allies in Parthia."

"You've never been pro-Parthian before," Itaz broke in. "You're bringing them in to impress me, aren't you?"

"I'd sooner a Parthian alliance than a Yavana one!" snapped Tasius. "We both argued against that, and I—"

"You made a speech in council, but you voted for it," Itaz interrupted again. "You've pretended to support him ever since."

"Well, what else could I do? He disregarded me and you and

everyone else. And now that this Yavana woman is here, it's perfectly clear, to me anyway, that she's a hundred times more dangerous than I feared. To begin with, she's beautiful. Didn't you see the mob yesterday, showering her with flowers? It wasn't just the Yavanas from Eskati; the Sakas were joining in, just because she looked so lovely. She's bewitched you, too, even though you hate her. Don't think I didn't notice the way you kept staring at her through breakfast, as though your eyes were on strings! I thought before that only the Yavanas would support her, but you add her looks and her knowledge of our language to her wealth and ancestry, and you'll soon see that she's going to win over Sakas as well, and plenty of them. And that's the second point: she's clever. I sent a man to Bactra to find out what they say about her, and he came back with some gossip that might interest you. It seems that she's been interfering with her brother's officials, digging into their account ledgers and interviewing their native subordinates, and all the ministers were in a sweat to get her out of the country before she discovered enough evidence against them to cost them their heads. If she can do that in Bactra, in a court where she was merely an unimportant little sister, what do you think she could do here, where she's queen, and more than that, the descendant of a god? And already the king's in love with her. You must have seen that."

Itaz was silent for a moment. "Did you tell my father what your man found out in Bactra?" he said at last.

"I didn't dare," replied Tasius. "If he'd sent anyone, he'd have heard for himself. But he didn't send anyone; he had to say yes or no while the envoys were here in Eskati."

"You shouldn't have sent a spy behind his back."

"He'd hardly allow me to send one openly! Listen. Don't you understand what this means for *us?* The queen can say she's not ambitious, but when she has a son of her own she'll change her mind. They have an evil reputation, these Yavana queens; there's more than one of them that's murdered her husband's children by a first marriage, or plotted against his brothers and his friends. It's Moki she'll want out of her way, and you, and me."

"We don't yet know that she's like that," protested Itaz. "I don't like Buddhism, but it's true that it's very strict in its morality, and condemns killing of any kind."

"You just said that it was perverse and impious."

"Yes, of course! And it is. But not impious in that particular way!"

"You were sure of that from hearing one monk for an hour or two in Parthia?"

"It was more than an hour or two. We listened to him, on and off, for a few days, and we questioned him carefully, before we decided to tell him to leave. We weren't as hasty as that . . . woman . . . implied. But perhaps she was right, and I am too quick to say something's wicked, without getting to know it first. Certainly I'd be wrong to condemn *her,* my father's wife, on the day after she arrives."

"Who said anything about *condemning* her? I told you, I'm not proposing anything treasonous."

"What are you proposing, then? And why are you so eager to have me party to it?"

Tasius laughed with a patently false attempt at ease. "You're the king's son," he said, "and everyone knows how loyal you are. And you're everything a warrior prince should be, and admired for it—oh, I suppose you've paid no attention to it, but your example carries a lot of weight, particularly among the younger men. If you joined us you'd settle a lot of men on our side, and carry a lot more over with you."

"Who's 'us'?" demanded Itaz. "And join you in what?"

"Join us on the council, of course," replied Tasius. "You're entitled to a place, you know, though you've never taken it. You see, there's a number of us that are unhappy with this alliance, and we've been coming together to decide what to do to counterbalance the power of this Yavana queen. Nothing treasonous, I've told you that twice now! Council lords are entitled to take their own view of matters, even if it does disagree with that of the king. But people are nervous of opposing the king in any concrete way, and we need support if we're to do anything."

"What sort of thing are you hoping to do?" asked Itaz, still deeply suspicious.

Tasius shrugged. "Get some of our own people put in charge of the elephants or the siege machines. Take some of the important offices away from the Eskati Yavanas, and give them to Sakas instead. Put some kind of check on the Yavanas throughout the valley, so they can't surprise us. And get some of our own people appointed to the queen's guard, so that, whatever she does, she can't do it secretly. I'm not proposing that we harm her in any way, or interfere with her in anything she's entitled to do! If she's honest, we'll be no bother to her at all. But we'd be fools to blindly hand her the reins of the state and let her do whatever she wants."

"That's reasonable," said Itaz, after a long silence. "I think even my father will understand that. Yes, I'm with you. But listen"—he slapped the table, meeting Tasius' eyes—"whatever I do is going to be done openly and honestly, with my father's full knowledge. I'm not going to scheme behind his back. I'll tell him what we intend. He knows I've opposed this alliance all along, so it won't surprise him; the thing I mustn't, and won't, do is make plots in secret. I'm still his loyal son and subject, and obedient even if I disagree with him. If you don't like that, you can leave me off the council."

Tasius hesitated, weighing Itaz up, then nodded. "Very well," he said, "that's fair. If you want to meet the others, we're having a meeting on the exercise field by the river this evening, while the Yavanas are putting on their play in the theater."

"I'll be there."

CHAPTER

V

The wedding celebrations went on for another two days, and by the end of them I'd had enough of being a royal attendant and was ready to go home. It was life in the palace that I minded, of course, not the celebrations themselves. To begin with, Padmini and Antiochis, who were firmly in charge of the household from the evening they arrived, didn't like me. Or perhaps that's not quite fair: it wasn't so much that they disliked me, as that they thought I wasn't a right and proper person to wait upon a queen. I was too big and clumsy: I dropped things and spilled things, had no idea what to do with Yavana drapery, and couldn't do my own hair right, let alone anyone else's; I laughed too loud and walked too fast, couldn't sing, and was no use at weaving. Padmini and Antiochis liked Inisme, who did everything properly, and deferred to them as well. They weren't actually unpleasant to me, but I got very tired of lips compressed in disapproval, motherly admonitions to look at my dress!, and rolled eyes or sidelong glances and muters behind my back. Besides, I'd always been useful and admired on the estates; I hated being made to feel a clumsy idiot all the time. I did my best to behave quietly and with dignity, to maintain the honor of my house—but I was so homesick I cried every night.

But that wasn't the worst of it. No, the thing that made me feel as though I were sitting on an anthill was the ambiguity of the queen's position, which led to an ambiguity in my own. Ordinarily a queen would expect to have her own steward to manage her estates for her, and perhaps a secretary or an accountant to handle her money. But King Mauakes coolly announced that his own steward and treasurer would manage the queen's lands and funds. He put it as though he were relieving her of an irritating burden, but it was perfectly clear that what he really wanted was to make sure she couldn't get up to any mischief without him finding out about it. The queen didn't try to refuse, but didn't completely accept: instead, she quietly agreed that it would be a needless waste of effort to tinker with the administration—*while we were threatened with invasion.* What, I wondered, did she mean to do afterward? However the invasion turned out, there was almost certain to be an afterward: even if we lost, the Tochari were unlikely to do more this time than plunder us. And if there was a clash between the king and the queen, afterward, what was I supposed to do?

The worst thing of all was that I knew what I was supposed to do: the king told me. On the third day of the wedding celebrations he summoned me to his study in the evening while the queen was bathing, and asked me if she had written any letters.

"No," I said, surprised. "She hasn't had time." (The king and the celebrations had between them accounted for every minute of the three days and nights.)

"I thought she might have written a note to her brother," said King Mauakes, watching me with a mild, gentle expression. "The escort which accompanied her from Bactra returns there tomorrow, and she may yet wish to send back a message to her family. You can offer to bring it to Captain Demetrios if she does."

"Oh," I said. "Yes, I'll do that, sir."

"And if she does," he went on, very smoothly, "bring it here first and read it to me. If she won't trust you to carry it, you should still have some chance to read it before she sends it, and you can come tell me what was in it."

I stared at him with my mouth open. Spying, like Yavana drapery, is not something I was brought up to. The king noticed my shocked face and went on gently, "I don't mean to treat the queen dishonorably, Tomyris, and I'm already confident that she's an honest and noble lady—but her family have been our bitter enemies, and it's not to be expected that she'd abandon all her loyalty to them overnight; she'd hardly be an honorable woman if she did. Her brother may have asked her to send him information—not necessarily information that he means to use against us, not now—but still, information that could be used to hurt us at a later date. If that's the case, I need to know about it; and if it's not the case, I need to know that, too. If I'm ever to trust the queen I must know what's in her mind. I wish to treat her decently, but my first task as a king is to safeguard my own people. You understand that, don't you?"

"Yes, sir," I said unhappily. "Everyone in the valley knows that you can't trust the Yavanas of Bactria, and everyone in the valley opposed this marriage for just that reason. I wouldn't want you to trust them myself. But . . ."

"But?"

"I'm not much good, sir, at . . . at pretending."

He smiled. He knew I meant, "At worming my way into people's confidence so as to betray them." "You are a loyal and honest Saka, aren't you?" he said drily. "And does the queen expect you to be anything else?" I didn't say anything, and he went on, "For my part, I considered myself lucky when I found you: there aren't many presentable young noblewomen who can read Greek. You're ideally placed to discover how things stand between Queen Heliokleia and King Heliokles. That will be a great service to your people, Tomyris. And if the queen is honest, as I expect, it can only help her, too. If she writes, or if she receives letters, I'm sure I can rely on you."

"Yes, sir," I said at last, "you can rely on me." And I stomped unhappily off to the women's apartments.

But the more I thought about it, the less I liked it. I didn't doubt that the king was right, and that we should keep an eye on our Yavana allies and our Yavana queen. It was perfectly true as well that Heliokleia didn't show much sign of trusting me or any of her Saka attendants and probably expected us to spy—but still . . . spying wasn't something I could do. I was brought up on the idea that lying was despicable, and I'd never been able to manage it convincingly. Even if it had to be done, somebody else should do it.

I was spared the effort, though, for a while anyway. The queen wrote no letters, merely sent for Captain Demetrios, thanked him for his journey on her behalf, and told him to convey her respectful greetings to her brother. The Bactrian escort set out next morning, leaving behind only the things they had come here to bring: the elephants, the catapults, and the queen.

My mother came up to the palace that same next morning, accompanied by Kanit. My father was staying in Eskati for the tribal council meeting, which had been arranged for that afternoon, while all the nobles were still in the capital, but my mother was going home. The council lords might have to remain with the king for some time, making preparations for the Tochari invasion, and somebody had to go home to the estates to manage the sheep shearing: with such a long journey, my mother would barely be in time as it was. The queen had gone down to the palace stables that morning for her first riding lesson with Amage, but I was stuck in the women's apartments, translating for Padmini. She didn't really even need me for that: she was arguing with the king's steward about the arrangements for administering the queen's estates, and the steward, like most administrators, was an Eskati Yavana, chosen for his ability to read and keep accounts—which were of course in Greek.

"It is not right or proper that the property should be administered by you!" Padmini was saying, for about the fifth time, when Kanit knocked. "She ought to have her own steward, accountable to her, not to your master—Armaiti, get the door—who will manage things on her behalf, not the king's!"

"But I will manage things honestly on her behalf!" the steward protested. "How could I think of cheating her, a descendant of Antimachos? The king simply wants me to manage her estates together with his own; it's more efficient and cheaper."

"You think she can't afford her own steward?" demanded Padmini contemptuously—then my mother strode in, calling "Tomyris!," and the argument stopped while I ran over and hugged her.

"I just came to say goodbye," my mother told me; then, looking around, "ehh, what magnificence!" She caught Padmini's icy glare and bowed to her gracefully. "Forgive me, lady: I have come to say farewell to my daughter."

Padmini understood the gesture, if not the words, and allowed herself to be pacified. At least, I thought, Mother looks ladylike enough to please even Padmini and Antiochis.

After introductions, I took my mother off to my room, leaving Kanit to join in the argument about the administration of the queen's estates.

"So," said my mother, after kissing me, "how do you like it?"

"I hate it," I answered. "I have all the problems I was afraid of, but worse."

"I'm sure the queen doesn't giggle," Mother said disapprovingly. "She seems a most charming young woman, and she's obviously put a great deal of effort into learning our ways." Mother, and most of the rest of the Saka nobility, had had a good look at the queen during the celebrations, and, I had to admit, nobody could have asked for a more courteous ruler. She had watched even the polo match put on for her by the king's guard with an expression of alert interest plastered onto her face—and it had looked like nothing so much as a cattle stampede. Two hundred men tussling over a goat's head down the other end of a drill field is hard even for a Saka to follow.

"Oh, the queen!" I exclaimed, trying to remember what I'd thought she'd be like. "No, she doesn't giggle. I can't make her out at all, but she certainly doesn't giggle. No, it's the others. Nothing but clothes and jewels and hairstyles, and I can't do anything right for them. And I haven't even had a chance to look at the queen's horses, let alone been given one."

"Give it time," said my mother complacently. "She only arrived three days ago."

"But I've only told you half!" I protested. "You hear them arguing in there?"

We listened for a moment: Padmini's sharp voice was saying, "The money Queen Heliokleia brought is hers: why should she apply to the king's treasurer to be allowed to spend it?" And the steward soothingly replied that the treasurer would keep it safe, it was still the queen's, it wasn't going into the king's own fund.

"All the queen's money, and all her estates, are going to be managed through the king's men," I told my mother in a whisper. "That's the king's orders. Is that the way things should be done?"

"No," said my mother, unruffled. "No, but . . . she is a Yavana, and a daughter of Eukratides. I can understand it if the king doesn't trust her immediately."

"Oh, well, I can understand it, too," I said. "I wouldn't trust the Bactrians myself, and the Eskati Yavanas are as contrary as donkeys. But I don't like sitting in the middle, obliged to take the queen's part in name and the king's in fact. And I don't like spying on her." And I told my mother what the king had asked me to do.

"What did you say to that?" asked my mother, frowning hard now. She knew me; she knew that vices I may have, but deceitfulness isn't one of them.

"I said she hadn't written any letters. She hasn't. I suppose I would tell him about them if she had—but I don't like it. Mother, I don't belong here. This isn't the place or the job for me. I want to go home. Can't you get me out?"

"Darling," said my mother, after a silence, "it's only been three days. That's too soon to tell what things will be like."

"Some things you can tell right away!" I objected; but my mother raised her hand and stopped me.

"Even if I thought you were right," she said, "it would be disastrous for you to go now. No matter what we said, people would believe you'd been rejected by the queen because you'd done something wrong. People would talk, and imagine what it was. Darling, it would ruin your chances of a good marriage; it might well ruin your life. You must stay—for now, anyway. And it may well happen that the new queen is completely trustworthy, and you'll find you have no conflict of duties at all. Wait until the autumn meeting of the tribal council at least: if things haven't improved by then, we'll tell Kanit that we need you at home, and take you back. Until then you must simply be patient. I agree, spying . . . is not the job for you. I wish

the king had told us that he expected it. I would have told him myself
that you weren't the one to do it."

I could see the truth of what she said, so I agreed, heavily, and she
kissed me and went back out. Kanit greeted her with relief—he didn't
like facing Padmini, who was a formidable woman—and escorted her
out of the palace. The steward made an excuse to withdraw as well,
leaving Padmini to prowl about the queen's apartments—now
crowded with clothes chests, jewel cases, tables, and book racks—
before finally settling at her loom and the ladylike task of weaving.

We expected Heliokleia back at the midmorning to change for a
meeting requested by the Greek citizens of Alexandria Eschate. They
had done most of the work to organize the celebrations in honor of the
king's marriage—they were the ones who had collected enough food
and wine for the feasts, who provided most of the cooks and servers
and cleaners, who decorated the streets and fetched flowers from miles
around. The king had given them produce and money from his own
wealth, but they'd added to it, trying to outdo each other in welcoming their new Yavana queen. Now that the festivities were over they
lost no time to letting her know why they'd been so welcoming. The
delegation they sent to the queen was ostensibly to give her a gift in
the name of the city, but in fact to present her with a list of their
grievances. It included all the wealthiest landowners of the city, and a
number of prominent tradesmen as well. But when they arrived, in the
middle of the morning, Heliokleia was still not back from the riding
lesson. I started out the back of the palace toward the stables to announce them and bumped into her on the steps: she was flushed and out
of breath from running.

"The delegation is here," I told her.

"*Oi moi!*" she replied, a strong exclamation of dismay. "The time
. . . I told Amage I had to be back . . . I never thought . . .
where are they?"

They'd been shown into the dining room. Heliokleia went directly
there, brushing off her clothes as she went; just outside the door she
paused. "Is my hair straight?" she asked. It had been done into a Saka
braid down the back for the riding, and only a few wisps had come
loose.

"It's straight enough," I said. "But don't you want to change?" As well as the braid, she was wearing trousers and a short riding gown. The clothes were richly made, but nonetheless the trousers had horrified Padmini and Antiochis even more than the fact of the riding lesson, and they had only consoled themselves by choosing a particularly fine purple and gold Greek tunic for the queen to wear when she met the local Greek dignitaries.

"It's more rude to keep them waiting than to go in like this," she said, and taking a deep breath, at once transformed herself from a flushed and flustered girl to a composed and dignified queen. Smiling, she pushed open the door and went in.

The citizens noticed the trousers instantly and you could see they were disturbed by them, worried that she was adopting barbarian customs and might be unsympathetic. But Heliokleia greeted them very graciously, apologized for the clothes, explained about the riding lesson overrunning, asked them their names, seated them, told the servants to bring them sesame cakes and fine wine, and soon they were completely at their ease again. Eukleides, son of Aristagoras, whose family is still the richest in the city, was their spokesman, and he made a long speech welcoming the queen to the Farthest Alexandria before presenting her with the gift, a magnificent cloak woven from purple wool and patterned with silk and gold. Heliokleia thanked them warmly and praised the beauty of the cloak. "Though I have already seen the skill of your craftsmen," she told them, "in a crown my husband gave me which could have been the work of Daedalus himself; it's no wonder that Farthest Alexandria is the marvel of the north, famous among Greeks and barbarians alike." The goldsmith who had made the crown was, as she'd no doubt expected, one of the delegation: he was extremely pleased by the queen's praise. So were the others.

"You are gracious to us, O Queen," said Eukleides, "and yet, what you say is true. The Farthest Alexandria has always been the marvel of the north, the richest and loveliest city beyond the Oxus. But how long will it remain so? It has already shrunk from the glory it had when I was a young man, and soon it may be no better than Maracanda, a barbarian town squatting in ignorance upon a river. We look to you, O Queen, to raise our city up and make it great again."

"I am only a foreigner here," said Heliokleia, frowning slightly. "I don't know what power I have or how to use it, where to tread boldly and where to draw back. I doubt very much, sirs, that an ignorant woman like myself can help you. And yet, if I could help the city, I would take great pride in doing so."

This was encouragement enough for Eukleides. He launched into an account of the difficulties, not just of the city, but of all the Greeks in Ferghana, and Heliokleia listened attentively, occasionally asking a question or calling on one of the others to bear out Eukleides' complaints.

I had grown up with the idea that the Eskati Yavanas were leeches, corrupt bugs sucking the goodness out of the royal administration wherever they could, and unfairly protected by the king who needed their skills to run the system his Yavana predecessors had set up. Whenever someone had had to scramble to meet a new tax, or lost a case in court, or had to pay for a new irrigation channel, he cursed the Yavanas. I was young and not at all interested in politics: not only had I not seen the other side, I hadn't even thought there was another side to see. Eukleides' speech knocked me breathless. The Yavanas, he said, were desperately hard pressed in spite of the king's protection, and the city was struggling for its bare survival. When he had taken Ferghana, Mauakes had continued to use the Greek administration, and often the same Greek administrators, as his predecessors. He had not admitted those administrators, though, to the status of his "kinsmen and friends," his council of advisors, as a Yavana king would have done. The tribal council was always jealous of its rights, and it alone was allowed, officially, to advise the king. In consequence, only the king had any idea what the royal administration was doing. Whenever the king demanded a new tax, or men to build another road, the people blamed the Yavanas who collected the money and enforced the labor—but when the road was opened, or the feast given, they thanked the king. The Yavanas, afraid of the hostility of the Sakas, turned to the king for protection, and in exchange the king demanded total obedience—and money. Eskati, like most Greek cities, had had civic funds—for schools, for buying grain and keeping its price stable, for repairs to the public water and sewage supplies, for providing oil in the gymnasia, for heating the public baths, and for the occasional festival. All these funds had either been completely swallowed by the king, or were liable to be raided when he needed money. The public schools were closed, and citizens too poor to pay for private schools saw their children grow up ignorant; grain varied wildly in price and sometimes became completely unavailable; the city's chief men had had to pay for repairs to the aqueducts and sewage system from their own stretched resources; there hadn't been any oil in the gymnasia for a generation, and the theater had stood empty for three years before the queen arrived. As all the pleasure was crushed out of Eschate, so the people were leaving it—not the true Greeks, who loved it too much and had nowhere else to go, but half-Greeks, now content to pass for Sakas, abandoning it and moving out to remote estates, leaving empty places behind and a heavier burden on those who remained. "Scarcely can I bear the weight of the taxes and the surcharges, the citizens' hopes and the king's expectations," said Eukleides, rounding up in a flow of rhetoric. "What shall my son do, when death has closed my eyes? Will he forget Farthest, forget that he is a Greek—one of those whose spears behind King Alexander swept the world like a thunderbolt, and made the very gods look down in envy? The Jaxartes will be proved to be like the waters of Lethe, the infernal river, whose taste procures oblivion, and this noble city will sink into eternal slumber."

"What can I do?" asked Heliokleia earnestly, when Eukleides' words had ceased ringing and their speaker had sat down.

"Speak to the king for us, O Queen," said Eukleides eagerly. "Explain our situation to him, and beg him to lighten our load!"

Heliokleia nodded. "Indeed, sir, and I will do so. But what do you suggest should be done?"

At this the whole delegation began talking at once, all of them explaining and arguing, alternatively or all together, what each thought should be done to help the city. I could scarcely follow one suggestion, let alone five at once, but Heliokleia listened attentively, occasionally ruling out a suggestion as impractical or reminding the delegates that the kingdom was threatened with war and could not afford to lose revenue, coaxing a heady generality into a specific proposal, until the whole delegation had agreed on a set of concrete and reasonable measures.

"Then I will put these suggestions to the king," said Heliokleia. "And I hope that he finds them, as I do, wise, moderate, and likely to promote peace and wealth in the kingdom. Thank you for your good advice, and thank you also for your gift. Rejoice, O men of Farthest Alexandria."

"Rejoice, O Queen," they replied, and bowed themselves out. I hurried over to show them the way out of the palace. They certainly did rejoice as they left, each of them praising their new patroness to his neighbor—so beautiful! so gracious and courteous! so quick to understand, so intelligent in her comments! so serious and modest in her attentiveness! They had longed for someone to save them, and they happily discussed her every word and gesture, wringing from each glance of her eyes the last delicious drop of hope.

When I'd seen the delegation out the door, I went back to the dining room. Heliokleia was sitting with her face in her hands, taking deep breaths. I thought she was meditating again. It was only much later that I realized she'd been trying not to cry.

The tears were never far away from her then, and they had to be boxed up several times a day. She already knew, wearily, that their true cause was what happened to her in the king's bed—which she hated as much now as she had the first time—but the pain and confusion seemed to spill into everything else she did. Here the city had appealed to her, as queen, for justice and relief it desperately needed. It was a call she'd been waiting for. For years she'd worked to prepare herself for it, dreamed of it, longed for it to come and give her the chance to fulfill her karma. Now it had, and all she wanted was to go away. She felt dirty, humiliated, unsure of herself; anything she tried to do would inevitably become a filthy shambles, despite her noble intentions. She wished she could put it off, even for a few weeks.

It was a pity it had happened immediately after the riding lesson. It had taken all her strength to conquer her fear of horses and struggle onto one. And then Amage's four-year-old daughter, who shared the lesson, hopped up onto her mare's wide back and crawled about it like a little monkey. Heliokleia had been bitterly ashamed of herself; her own efforts, in contrast, were like the floppings of a jointed terra-cotta doll. Amage's child had laughed at her, and Amage had scolded the girl, but gently, laughing herself. Then the lesson had gone on for hours: up on the horse, grip with your knees, no dear put your heels down, no, no, keep your back straight, grip with your knees, your *knees,* not your heels—as the horse lurched forward and she nearly fell off—no, no, you mustn't hold on to the saddle, you need your hands on the reins, no, no, no, no. Heliokleia had not allowed so much time for it all. Grimly astraddle the stout gelding used for training, trying not to hold on to the saddle, she had suddenly noticed, with horror, that the sun stood at the hour she'd allotted for the meeting with the delegation of citizens. She'd slithered off the horse and excused herself to Amage in a rush, then, trying not to cry at the prospect of being late, imagining the delegation standing insulted in the courtyard, she'd run up the hill from the palace stables, wincing with the pain of newly strained muscles, to arrive panting at the back door of the palace where I met her. She came aching, exhausted and humiliated, and, thinking it over, everything she'd done seemed wrong. Had she offered the men too little or too much? Did they think she was discourteous, to hurry them out like that when they were finished? She'd only been worried that the servants would want to prepare the dining room for a meal.

When I came back in, Heliokleia at once lowered her hands and crushed her feelings behind the mask of calm. "Thank you, Tomyris," she said formally.

At the same minute, Inisme appeared in the other door to the dining room, the one that led back to the palace living quarters. "The king wishes to speak with you," she told Heliokleia, folding her hands and looking at the queen expressionlessly. "If the citizens have gone, he said you were to attend him in his study."

"Oh," said Heliokleia. I suppose it was only because her mask hadn't quite settled firm yet that I caught the momentary flicker of dread at Inisme's message. I didn't guess that it was by now her usual feeling at having to attend the king privately. When Mauakes had seen her in the trousers that morning, he'd laughed and said that he'd have to take them off her. She was not as ignorant as she had been, she could imagine that now, and felt sick. "Thank you," she told Inisme, dry-mouthed, "I'll go at once."

The king's study is a small room—at the back of the second court-yard, next to his bedroom and well away from the more public front part of the palace. Mauakes kept tally sticks there, and maps, and emblems of the noble families he ruled, all in an old chest of carved wood under the window; on a shelf opposite it were a row of large cups covered in gilded leather. There were no books or tablets, as

Mauakes couldn't read; he had a Yavana secretary to write his letters
for him, but this man lived in the servants' quarters and came only
when he was summoned. Heliokleia had barely glimpsed the room
before, and she knocked on the door very hesitantly.

"Yes," came the king's voice from inside, and the queen steeled
herself and went in.

Mauakes was sitting in the single chair beside the counting table,
his wide face at its most moonlike and unreadable—but to the queen's
relief, he was not alone. Itaz was standing stiffly by the window. His
face was all too easy to read: he was furious. Heliokleia found the
king's son more hostile and, with his fierce dark stares, more disturbing,
at every meeting—but in the circumstances she was very pleased to see
him.

"There you are," said the king, smiling at her blandly. "And have
the citizens gone away pleased?"

Heliokleia hesitated. She had hoped to have more time to work
out how to put her request on the city's behalf. She understood that she
wasn't trusted, and knew that she must behave in everything as though
she were on trial. "They were very warm in their expressions of loyalty," she temporized, "and seemed very happy indeed to have given
me the beautiful gift they had chosen."

"Oh? And what's that?"

"A purple cloak, sir, a most beautiful thing."

"Where is it, then?" asked Mauakes, smiling with amusement now.
"Why aren't you wearing it?"

She'd left it in the dining room, its abandonment betraying only
too clearly her lack of real interest in it. Unregal stupidity! She took
another deep breath, trying to detach herself and stay calm. "You asked
me to come, and I came quickly," she replied, managing to smile back.

He chuckled, but his eyes were shrewd, judging. "So you did. But
tell me, what did the citizens want? They did have requests to make,
didn't they, my dear?"

She looked down at the floor for a moment, gathering her
thoughts. If she couldn't put it off, she must do her best for the city
now—though clearly it was not a good time. "Sir," she said, looking
up again and meeting the suspicious eyes, "they did indeed have requests, a great number of them, which they begged me to bring to

your attention. And I judged it would be advantageous to you, sir, to hear what they had to say—at some time when you have leisure to listen to them. The city is in a sorry condition, stripped of half its people, impoverished, growing bitter and sour under its burdens, and I thought that any means to restore it to its old wealth and dignity, without loss to yourself, must be a thing you would gladly hear."

Mauakes snorted. "I thought they'd complain to you at the first chance they got. What's the current price for their loyalty?"

"No price at all; their loyalty we have already. You are their protector, and they've turned to you as suppliants, begging for help. No, I . . . shall I speak now, sir?"

"Yes," said Mauakes, with a glance at Itaz, who still stood stiff and silent, scowling, "tell me what they wanted."

Heliokleia carefully set out the proposals decided upon by the delegation, phrasing them as tactfully as she could, and trying to show that adopting them would increase the king's power and dignity without losing him any income—arguments that she knew from her brother's court carried more weight than mere justice. The most important of these proposals were that the chief ministers of tax and finance should have seats on the tribal council and be accepted as the king's advisors; that the city council of Eskati should elect its own magistrates, and not have Sakas picked by the king imposed on it; and that the city council should control its own finances, and be allowed to raise extra money for the king by voting taxes, on trade or roads or waterworks, which could be shared with the Sakas of the region. Mauakes listened seriously.

"Not as hotheaded as I'd feared," he said thoughtfully when the queen had finished. "And I suppose something will have to be done to help the city; it's been declining for years. And I suppose the time to do something is now, to make sure that they keep turning to you—and not to your brother. Hmm. Yes." Then he laughed. "So you propose that I give the Yavanas more power, while my son . . . Itaz! Tell me again what you and your friends want!"

Itaz was silent, his cheeks flushed.

"Are you ashamed to repeat your proposals in front of the queen?" asked Mauakes in a mocking voice. His eyes were not mocking, though; they had the penetrating darkness that Itaz recognized only too well.

"No," said Itaz angrily, "why should I be ashamed? If I were suggesting anything shameful I wouldn't have come here today and told you what we wanted; I would have let the council speak for itself this afternoon. We want you to appoint Sakas to oversee the collection of taxes and the administration of justice—council lords to advise you, and others, subordinate to them, to supervise the Yavanas who do the actual work. And we ask you to allow the councillors to give you a hundred men as a royal guard for the queen."

Heliokleia looked at him in confusion. "What is the point of employing a thousand Sakas to watch a thousand Yavanas work?" she asked. "How would they be paid for?"

"A good question," said Mauakes. "How *would* they be paid for, Itaz?"

"The council lords wouldn't need to be paid," replied Itaz. "The rest . . . I don't know. Perhaps from the taxes, or perhaps by their overlords, or perhaps a mixture of both. That would be for the council to decide."

"Ah. And how would they supervise the Yavanas, seeing that you're unlikely to find a thousand Sakas who can read and do arithmetic?"

"They could talk to the people in the regions and see if anyone has a complaint against the Yavana tax collectors; if anyone does, they can refer it to you."

"There's already a way for them to complain about the tax collectors, Itaz my dear. The courts will assess the complaint and, if need be, refer it to me. So why hire a thousand more men who'll only get in the way?"

"The courts are run by the friends of those same Yavana tax gatherers!" snapped Itaz. "And when one of them oppresses the people, the others all hush it up, so that not one case in ten reaches your ears."

"If it can be hushed up, it wasn't important to begin with," said Mauakes blandly.

"Sir, your son's proposal is a response to the same complaint the citizens of Eschate made to me this morning," put in Heliokleia suddenly and unexpectedly. "Whenever the Sakas see an official collecting

money, they suspect he's embezzling it, because they don't know where
the money comes from or where it goes. And if a region has a poor
harvest, the tax collector knows nothing about it until he actually
arrives with the list of what's due. He still has to raise the whole
amount, and his work becomes oppressive. The tribal council could
have advised him, and spread the burden—but he and it have nothing
to say to one another. It is desirable, sir, to bind together the Yavana
administrators and the Saka lords, and allow them to work together, in
your service."

Mauakes snorted. "Very reasonable, very sensible. But do you
think that I could say that, when the council tells me to appoint these
new Saka ministers? 'No, I won't give you any more power, but I'll
make up for it by sharing your honors among your rivals?' This proposal of my son's has nothing to do with the council's concern at
Yavana oppression: it is all the result of fear—fear that the Yavana
administrators will be loyal to you, and slip off the halter we Sakas
have put on them."

Heliokleia bit her lip.

"It isn't just fear," protested Itaz. "I wouldn't mind seeing Yavanas
on the council: if they were accountable to it, and told it honestly
when they had troubles collecting taxes, I'd welcome them. But how
can anyone know if they're telling the truth, unless we have independent supervisors? And yes, people are worried that the Yavanas will
prove disloyal. They've been treacherous again and again in the past,
even without a queen of their own."

"And that is why you want a guard for me?" asked Heliokleia.
"To oversee me, and make sure I don't . . . slip off the halter . . .
as well? Not a royal guard, but a prison guard?"

"Queen, we have fought wars against your people since King
Alexander's days," Itaz returned. "One of my brothers lost his life
fighting against your father. Can you blame us if we don't instantly
trust you to be our ruler?"

"But she isn't," said Mauakes very quietly. "*I* am your ruler."

"You are," returned Itaz instantly, and he knelt and touched his
forehead to the floor, then remained on his knees, looking directly at
his father. "And I pray to all the gods that you may long remain so!"

"If I am your ruler, why are you making these insolent demands!"

Mauakes replied, suddenly shouting with anger. He slammed a hand down on the arm of the chair. "Telling me that the council wants this and the council wants that, which the council will propose whatever I say! You picked this issue because you knew the councillors would back you on it, didn't you? And you've stirred them up against me; you want to dictate to me through them, don't you?"

Heliokleia flinched.

"No," said Itaz, humbly and quietly. "No, Father. Neither I nor the council are against you. You are our king, and we will obey you as loyally as ever before."

"You've been plotting this behind my back; you have no right to talk to me about loyalty!" shouted the king.

"My loyalty is fixed as ever, and if you order me to stay away from the council meeting, I will!" said Itaz. "But you've made an alliance with our enemies, and taken a foreign queen who might threaten us, if some accident should happen to you—which the gods forbid! You can't be surprised if some of us want to take precautions, even if they're needless ones. If a child's afraid of the dark, you make his bed in the firelight, until he learns that the night won't harm him; you don't shut him in a cupboard to get him used to it! We're doing nothing secretly: we're coming to you, openly in the council, and asking you to allow us some light—and when we've seen that all's well, and there's no harm in alliance or queen, we'll be content to let our precautions drop. But if we have no way to reassure ourselves, how can we stop being afraid?"

Mauakes looked doubtfully at his son's open, earnest face. Slowly, his hands relaxed. He sighed, then rubbed his nose. "Well," he said thoughtfully. "Perhaps." He looked at his wife in a calculating way. Heliokleia was looking at him in silence. She was without vanity, but she knew what she was, a queen descended from many kings, and her chief object of study over some years now had been how to rule. She was perfectly well aware that her husband meant to appease the council by demeaning her own position, which was already restricted on every side.

"Sir," she said levelly, "that you are king here is so evident that it would be ridiculous to question it. I cannot see what Lord Itaz and his friends are afraid of. What am I but one woman? I have no army here, no horde of servants loyal to me. Captain Demetrios and his men left this morning for Bactra; the elephants are in your stables, their drivers subject to your orders, not mine. I have no wealth and no power except what you choose to give me, and what you give I must exercise for you, or relinquish altogether. If I have spoken on behalf of my fellow Greeks, I did so in the conviction that to promote their wealth and dignity would be to promote your own—and I have no way of demanding what I asked. Should you choose to refuse their requests, I can only bow and accept your will, and tell the citizens to do the same. But sir, when you gave me the horses of the royal breed, you said that a queen must have land and money of her own. So she must, to reward those who serve her, or answer those who petition her: otherwise she would be held in contempt by all the people, and her husband would be sneered at for his meanness. And a queen who was guarded like a prisoner—and not even by her husband's men, but by soldiers appointed by his nobles—who was allowed to see only such people as her guards thought suitable—she would be despised."

"There is nothing dishonorable to a queen in having a guard," burst in Itaz. "Every king in the world has one!"

"Under his command," said Heliokleia. "The one you propose for me would not be under mine."

Mauakes leaned back, looking at her thoughtfully. "Indeed, my dear, you are a queen, and you know what's due you," he said tolerantly. "I see no reason to provide you with a guard picked by my council. But a guard of some kind you ought to have anyway, a guard of honor. You may yourself pick a hundred men, who will be at your disposal, and under your command. The army and the levies must be trained soon anyway, if they're to be any use beside the elephants. Perhaps we will have competitions among them, and you may choose your guards from among the victors."

Heliokleia bowed her head, unhappily. The army was entirely Saka, and how could she pick unknowns and know where their loyalties lay? They would certainly spy on her; some of them might turn away people who wished to see her, putting a wall between herself and the Greeks. But at least she would have nominal command. And perhaps the guards would simply stay in their quarters apart from a few ceremonial occasions, and be no trouble to her?

"And perhaps I can tell the council as much," the king went on, looking at Itaz darkly. "As I can tell them that, if they want another tier of administrators, they can pay for it themselves, provided they pay all their regular taxes as well—*and* the additional ones I'm going to demand for defenses against the Tochari. I think you'll see that their enthusiasm for administrating will melt away completely. But since you two both agree on it, I will put Yavanas on the council. As for the other proposals, on either side—well, Itaz, since you and the queen have agreed on one matter, perhaps you should discuss the rest, and see what else you can agree on. If the Yavanas and their worst opponents both support a measure, I have no objection to adopting it."

Itaz and Heliokleia stared at each other, appalled. The king gave a malicious chuckle and heaved himself to his feet. "Have some wine before your lunch," he suggested, in his usual bland forgiving manner.

There was a flagon of wine on the shelf beside the cups, and the king lifted it down. Heliokleia was standing by the shelf; numbly, she began to lift one of the cups, still staring at Itaz, who was watching her with a flushed face and angry dark eyes.

"Not that one," said Mauakes, taking the cup from her. "It wouldn't be appropriate, not for you." He looked at it, smiling to himself, and turned it in his hands before putting it back on the shelf.

"Why?" asked Heliokleia, glancing at it as the king took down another of the cups.

"It belonged to a relative of yours," answered Mauakes. He took down two more cups and poured the wine, then handed one to his queen.

She looked into it a moment: it was gilded inside, and the gold glinted orange through the dark red wine that sat heavily in a shallow pool in the bottom. The gilding was scratched, though, just beneath the rim, and the stuff of the cup beneath stood out white as bone. She remembered suddenly something she had heard about the Sakas and went pale, calculating the shape of the cup's bowl inside its holder of gilded leather. She put it down hurriedly, and looked back at the cup on the shelf. "That's the . . . skull . . . of a relative of mine?" she asked in a whisper.

"Of Nikias, the younger son of Antimachos the God," said Mauakes, with satisfaction. "Your great-uncle. He was in charge of the

garrison at Eskati when we took it. An old enmity, forgotten now—
but you shouldn't drink from it."

"And this one?" she asked, staring at the cup she'd put down.

"Oh, he was a Saka," said Mauakes, and took a swallow from his
own cup. "A prominent traitor. No need to worry about him."

Heliokleia wiped her hands down her trousers, still staring at the
skull cup. "I'm sorry," she said. "It's . . . I . . . that is, killing is
against my philosophy. We consider it best not to eat the flesh even of
animals, and to drink from the skull of a man . . . I ought not do it."

"Would you rather drink from the skull of a woman?" asked the
king, and, when his wife looked up in horror, laughed. "I never had a
woman enemy important enough to merit keeping as a trophy. Very
well, don't drink, if your religion won't permit it." He took another
gulp of his own wine.

Itaz looked down at his own cup, frowning, suddenly wondering
if he ought to drink from it either. The Mazdayists believe that the
touch of the dead pollutes, but he'd never associated dead bodies with
skulls kept as trophies. The custom is very common among the peoples
of the steppes: the Sakas, Issedones, Tochari and Huns all follow it. The
Greeks find it savage and horrifying—but then, they burn the bodies
of their dead, which the other peoples find equally appalling. Itaz had
never worried over his father's trophies before; he'd been proud when
he looked at them, thinking of all the men who had opposed the king
and been crushed. But now something of the queen's horror touched
him and made him uneasy. Perhaps it was savage and arrogant, to drink
wine from the skulls of the dead; perhaps, as a good Mazdayist, he
ought not do so. But he couldn't refuse, not now. Heliokleia was a
foreigner, her refusal based on a meaningless religious prohibition, but
a new and sudden refusal from Itaz would be an insult. Reluctantly, he
took another sip of wine. His mouth full of the sweet red wine, the
cup cold against his lips, he had a bewildering moment of awareness of
himself as two people: one a Saka prince, comfortable in what he did,
and the other—what?—watching from outside. The sensation was so
strong that he almost looked over his shoulder, trying to meet his own
accusing eyes.

"Now," said Mauakes, draining his cup, "lunch is delayed already,
but I think, my dear, you should change from those riding clothes first.

Come with me, and I'll help you take them off." He caught Heliokleia's hand and pulled her briskly out of the study toward the bedroom. He was already looking at the door when he did and never noticed, as Itaz did, her momentary jerk backward in shocked revulsion.

Itaz put the cup down unfinished and stood still a minute, leaning against the wall, miserable, hot, and confused. The proposals he'd made on the council's behalf would go largely unfulfilled; his father, though partially reassured, was again suspicious of him; and his own feelings were an absolute chaos of shame, resentment, pity and desire. Through the wall he heard the king and queen go into the bedroom: the door closing, a thump, the creak of the bed, and then a grunt from his father. Itaz jumped and left the study at a run, terrified of hearing more.

The tribal council met that afternoon on the plain outside the city. The Yavanas of Bactria invariably disregard our council in their dealings with us, assuming, in their usual arrogant way, that any organization they don't possess themselves can't be worth having. That's a mistake. Our council is of great antiquity, and if the kings have reduced its powers, still they must rely on its goodwill if they're to govern at all. They say that the first council members were the heads of the seventy households that made up the tribe upon whose horses the Sun descended, and there are seventy councillors still, each one holding his own estates, his own walled town or fortress, and each leading his own armed men. (I say "his" for convenience—but in fact some councillors are always women. I've said that we Sakas allow women more freedom than the Yavanas do, and a widow habitually takes her husband's place as councillor, while a daughter inherits from a lord who leaves no sons.)

The seventy, then, rode out from the city and from their camps about it to the sacred meeting place. On the east side of the Lesser Lake northeast of the city is a mound which has always been used as landmark, the tomb of a hero who died in the days before King Alexander, and the meeting place is beside it, a double ring of wooden benches with an ancient stone altar in the middle. It's a very plain and primitive altar, a mere heap of stones with a crude bowl on the top, quite unlike the magnificent temple in Eskati, but it's the most revered shrine in all Ferghana. They say that this altar is the same one that was raised by our ancestors when the Sun descended to them, and nearby on an outcrop of rock you can see the twin black-scorched wheel ruts left by the Sun's chariot. That spot is so holy that no one but the chief priests and priestesses is allowed to approach it; the people leave their offerings beside the fence which encloses it. But every day, at the sun's rising, one priest or priestess enters the enclosure and pours a libation on the scorched wheel marks, to show the Sun that we keep the memory of his visit to us ever fresh. The fire on the ancient altar nearby is kept perpetually burning.

The councillors and the king arrived when the sun, seen from the lake, stood above the mound. Each came with ten or a dozen attendants, unarmed and unarmored, as the custom is, dressed in their finest —the tunics or gowns patterned with brilliant dyes and stitched with gold, the harness of the tall horses glittering in the late afternoon sun, their manes and tails fluttering with ribbons. When they arrived beside the sacred enclosure the councillors dismounted, the attendants took the horses aside, and the lords and ladies went up to the foot of the mound and sat down upon the benches. The king arrived after most of the others and took his place on the front bench of the eastern side, in the full rays of the sun; Itaz, who had ridden with him from the city, nervously sat down beside his father. Mauakes had said nothing on the ride out, and wore his blandest expression now, but Itaz could sense the anger behind the mask and knew that the suspicious fury was resting, not asleep.

Kanit, officiating as chief priest, stood up, walked into the center, and turned to the west, where the sun stood halfway down the hard blue arc of the sky. The sacred fire was burning high in the hollow of the altar, and Kanit tossed some horse hair onto it, lifted his arms so that his gold-spangled yellow cloak tossed in the breeze, and prayed loudly for the god to regard their deliberations with favor. The council was met.

In the old days the council judged all disputes between its members, and it used to sit for weeks at a time, arguing over boundaries or dowries, murders or the ownership of disputed horses. But Mauakes had allocated such matters to the courts, where they were assessed by his Yavana administrators and determined by his own judgments. He allowed the occasional boundary dispute or blood feud to the council, when he thought its agreement was necessary to make a judgment stick, but otherwise he occupied it only with discussions of how many men its members could raise for a war, or who needed a new irrigation channel most urgently. Two or three days were usually enough to complete a quarter- or even half-year's business, since the king guided the councillors through the reduced work at a brisk trot. He waited now impatiently while the oldest councillor, a talkative old widow, rose, took the speaker's place in the center with her hand on the altar, and moved that the council vote him its congratulations on his marriage.

Mauakes was in a bad mood. He knew that what his son had told him was true: if the council was afraid, it made sense to allow it to reassure itself that there were no Yavana plots afoot. But it should have trusted him, he felt. He had devised his own methods for keeping a firm grip on his new queen, and they were effective and, just as important, unobtrusive. Nothing he had done would offend the Bactrians: his domestic arrangements in the palace were indisputably his own concern, and the new alliance could sit lightly on both partners. But now the council was asking to set up its own guard on the queen, and proposing new restrictions on his Yavana subjects: the Bactrians could hardly fail to take note of that, and King Heliokles would be bound to protest. It would stand between the partners of the alliance just when there was the greatest need for unity. This, though, was not something the council would take any notice of. Clumsy, interfering, unreliable fools, Mauakes thought, watching the faces around him. The only thing they see clearly is what's in front of their noses: their own power and privileges. Any hint of a threat to those and they'll all turn traitor, even if it means ruin for the country.

Opposition of any kind made him angry—angry and, though he never admitted it, frightened. He had struggled for power all his life, and every man he'd defeated and killed made him more afraid. One day he would not discover a plot in time, and with every victory he grew less certain of his own power. He scowled grimly even when the council unanimously agreed with its oldest member, and voted him its congratulations.

Tasius rose next and walked slowly to the center. He and Itaz had arranged between them that the king's son would break the news of the council's impending proposals to his father, and that Tasius would formally present them to the council—though most of the councillors were already aware of what would be proposed; my father told me afterward that there had been rumors about it all day. Tasius placed his hand on the altar and looked at the king with an ingratiating smile. "Lords of the council," he said loudly and clearly, "while we congratulate our king on his wedding, and praise him for his wisdom in converting our deadly enemies into our friends and brothers, let us not forget how great that achievement is, remembering how dangerous those enemies were and how much assistance they have always received from the Yavanas who live in our midst. We are confident, Lord King, that you will continue to govern those of that nation that live among us with the same wisdom you have used in making this foreign alliance, and will keep us in security for many years to come. It is clear to all how greatly the Yavanas rejoiced when they saw they had a queen of their own race. Most, no doubt, rejoice innocently—but we know the Yavanas. We know that some of them will grow arrogant—or should I say, some will grow more arrogant than ever?—and trusting in their queen to protect them, begin to pillage and oppress the Sakas whom they ought to serve humbly in your name. We of the council know that your mind is much occupied with preparations against the invasion we all fear, and that perhaps you have little time to restrain the pride of your administrators, and so we offer to undertake the supervision of them ourselves, if you consent. I move that, if the king is willing, six lords of this council should receive the control of the offices of finance, of the census, of the control of the waters, of the royal roads, of the army, and of mines; and that they should hold rank superior to that of the Yavanas who presently occupy these offices, and should choose men from among their own followers to supervise those the Yavanas send out. Further, Lord King, we notice that your queen has no royal guard, as a lady of such high rank ought to have, and we therefore beg you to grant us the honor of providing her with one: let each lord of the council provide her with a man for her defense, and let the great lords add more warriors, so that in all her guard numbers a hundred horsemen. We are eager, Lord King, to join with you in preparations against the invader, and to take from your shoulders the burden of such small tasks as might fittingly be allocated to your loyal council. Let those of the lords who agree to make these offers, rise."

A double handful of lords, including Itaz, leapt to their feet at once; then more joined them, and more, until almost the entire assembly was on its feet. Tasius bowed and went back to his bench. There was nothing more he needed to say: the council had made its hatred and distrust of the Yavanas, and its dissatisfaction with the king's own arrangements, plain to everyone.

Mauakes rose as soon as his son-in-law's hand was off the altar and strode to take his place. "I thank my loyal council for its humble and generous offers," he said, his eyes glinting as they swept the assembly. "I agree with you, my lords and ladies, that a lady as distinguished as my queen ought to have a royal guard. But I had already chosen another way to provide one. The army must be raised and drilled this summer, and the horses must have time to become accustomed to the elephants. All of you come here with your own warriors after sheep shearing, and join with me and my standing army in training. While we drill we will hold competitions, and my wife can choose her guard from among the victors. In this way we will institute between us a new royal guard, a force of picked men subordinate in honor only to my own: I myself will pay their wages, and they may have the privilege of riding the royal and half-royal horses. I think that this way of choosing a guard for Queen Heliokleia will better satisfy both her honor and your loyalty. Do you agree, my lords and ladies?"

There was a confused stir along the benches. Mauakes stood straight and still beside the fire, turning his hard, cool stare on one councillor after another; and one after another, they rose submissively. Saka nobles are not submissive by nature—but I've said that the king had immense authority, acquired over many years, and it was not worth opposing him over the differences between his plan and their own. Besides, as my father said later, a new royal guard inferior only to the king's was a golden opportunity for honor and advancement, and, my father said, he had two sons who might be eligible for it.

Mauakes nodded, his hand still on the altar, and the assembly sat.

"But as regards my councillors' offer to supervise my administrators," the king continued smoothly, "I fear that, threatened as we are by invasion, I cannot find the funds to pay any such supervisors. Shall we reconsider this proposal in a few years, my lords and ladies, when we are clear of the threat of the Tochari? Any man who wishes to serve as a supervisor unpaid, I will of course accept gladly, and I will direct my ministers to allot him appropriate duties.

"However, I understand that you are afraid of Yavana arrogance, and—for whatever reason—my own authority over my . . . ministers . . . does not satisfy you. I have therefore decided to admit my six chief Yavana administrators to this council, those who hold the ranks my daughter's husband has mentioned. I will require them to give full accounts of their doings to you, my lords, and you will then have the opportunity to object and reform what they propose. Is this acceptable, my lords and ladies?"

There was a moment of silence, then a confused buzz of voices discussing the proposal in disbelief: Yavanas to sit on the council? Mauakes waited for a few minutes, then asked again, "Is it acceptable that my loyal administrators should also be accountable to you, my lords and ladies?"

There was a stir, and then Azes, who was one of Tasius' firmest supporters, a very powerful man, strode down to the center. He was the father of Itaz' friend Azilises. He slapped his hand down onto the altar beside the king's, and Mauakes politely lifted his own hand from the stone, yielding the right to speak, though he remained standing beside the altar. "Lord King," said Azes, bellowing at the man beside him so that the whole assembly could hear, "it is acceptable that the ministers should report to the council . . ."

"Good," put in Mauakes quickly.

". . . but not that they should have a place as councillors! Lord King, this assembly is ancient, sacred to our Lord the Sun and to all the gods. All here are of noble blood, owners of land and horses. How can you propose to admit a clutch of Yavanas, foreigners to our god and to our land, secretaries and menials?"

He was going to go on, but Mauakes had set his own hand down on the stone, and Azes yielded. "My Yavana ministers are all of noble blood—among their own people—and they, too, own lands and

horses," the king said mildly. "Moreover, they have happily worshipped our Lord the Sun for many years: he is, after all, Lord of the
world, and does not shine on Ferghana alone. I do not understand your
objection, Lord Azes. Please explain it to me."

Azes stood gaping for a moment. "They're Yavanas," he said at
last. "This is a Saka assembly."

"And?"

"And . . . and the Yavanas are our enemies . . ."

"No longer. We have a firm peace treaty, Lord Azes; they are our
allies. It would increase the power of this assembly, and ease the work
of the administrators, if the ministers could take part in your deliberations." Azes tried to intervene, but this time the king did not withdraw
his hand, but continued, now addressing the council as a whole. "We
are faced with a war, my lords and ladies. Last summer the Tochari
came to our very boundaries, boasting that they would drive off our
royal horses, the sign of the Sun's favor to us, and steal that favor for
themselves. You know what it cost us then to turn them back. My son
Goar is dead—and many other sons as well, many husbands, cousins,
friends; in all this assembly, I think, there cannot be one councillor
with no one to mourn. And this very summer, probably, our enemies
will return, in numbers like the flies that swarm above the river. This
time, too, their hatred will be more bitter, for we have injured them;
this time, we have to fear the loss of more than horses—though the
Sun knows that would be loss enough. This time, if they enter the
valley, they will burn and kill where they can, and anyone who falls
into their hands they will take away as a slave. I hope that, by our
courage and by the ingenuity of our allies, we can make them regret
that ever they heard of us. But how can we win—how can we think of
entering such a serious struggle—when we are engaged in a squabble
with our allies and our neighbors, over precedence? Over who has
which title? It is time, my lords and ladies, for all of us to forget that
some who dwell in this valley descend from the Massagetai, and others
from the followers of King Alexander: we all inhabit one land,
Ferghana, and we suffer or prosper together. Let those who agree with
this proposal, and wish to make my ministers accountable to this assembly, now rise."

Itaz rose; after a moment the others began to stand as well. The buzz of discussion rose again; more stood. "I decided for it," my father told me, "though I didn't much like it. But the king has never been wrong in the past, and if he thought this offered us a better hope of victory—well, we should try it."

It was close, though. When the buzz of talk died down and everyone had made his choice, it was not at first clear whether the proposal had passed or not, and Kanit and the priests had to count. There were thirty-eight in favor, a majority of only three—but enough. The king's proposal had been passed. Mauakes nodded, still with his hand on the altar, directed Kanit to summon the six Yavanas to the next council meeting in the council's name, and at once began on his next proposal —the demand for additional taxes to meet the cost of defense. Baffled and cheated, Azes remained for a little while at the altar, then, shaking his head, slunk back to his seat. The other councillors murmured at first, but quickly began to pay attention when they realized they were due to lose money, and the rest of the meeting was the usual brisk procession of business guided through by the king.

When it was too dark to count the votes, Kanit rose, bowed to the king, and covered the altar with earth, preserving the embers of the sacred fire: the meeting would continue at sunrise next day. Even before the glow of the coals had faded, the councillors began talking furiously among themselves; Mauakes was instantly surrounded by anxious men and women inquiring about the new tax, or offering excuses for being late to the army drills. Itaz watched them and his father for a moment in silence, then started toward his horse, striding quickly over the benches and across the thick grass, black in the dusk. The west was still red, the stars were white over the mound, but the moon had not yet risen.

Tasius joined Itaz before he reached his horse, falling in beside him and matching his quick steps toward the picket lines. "You should never have told him in advance!" hissed Tasius angrily. "I should never have agreed to let you tell him! It was fatal. He had time to work out his own proposals, giving just enough to satisfy the council and nowhere near enough for us. If our proposals had come as a surprise, he might've been forced to agree."

"If I hadn't warned him, he would have rejected the idea outright," replied Itaz, though without complete conviction. "When I told him what we wanted, he accused me of 'stirring up the council against him.' He was furious, Tasius. If we'd surprised him, he would have decided we were both guilty of treason. He's still suspicious, even as it is."

"But he wouldn't have been able to suggest this other idea, this notion that the Yavanas should be councillors! He couldn't have sprung it on us, and carried it by surprise."

"He would have proposed that anyway," said Itaz unhappily. "The Yavanas from the city suggested it to the queen this morning, and she suggested it to my father."

"And he accepted it? Just like that?"

"She . . . she put it very cunningly, said that the city was appealing to him for help. And she said it was an answer to the same problem that our proposal addressed."

They had reached the horses. Itaz greeted the guardsmen shortly and went over to his stallion, which was grazing, its bridle loose about its head, the bit giving soft musical clinks as the animal tore at the thick grass. Its black coat was almost invisible in the darkness. He patted its shoulder, reassured by the familiar hardness of bone and muscle. He was in such a condition of confusion and misery that it was relief to occupy himself with the simple operation of adjusting the saddle blanket and tightening the girths, giving his attention only to the comfort of the animal.

"It's an outrage!" declared Tasius angrily, still hovering beside his ally. "To give those clever bastards a place on our council, as though they had any rights in the land! Why on earth did you jump up so quickly to vote for it?"

Itaz turned and looked at his brother-in-law in surprise. Tasius' face was merely a pale oval in the dusk, shadowed by hair, the mouth and eyes dark holes in the white shape. "I don't see anything wrong with having the Yavana administrators report to the council, if we can't have administrators of our own," he said.

"It's a way to make sure we never get any administrators of our own!" snapped Tasius. "And it's worse than that: he's giving his servants equal honor with us, with independent noblemen! And he's making *us* responsible for all their oppression. Now if one of our people suffers, he won't just blame the Yavanas, he'll come to us and say, 'Why didn't you stop it?' "

"Well?" asked Itaz. "Isn't that what we want? A chance to stop it?"

"Don't be so simple! We still won't have any chance to do anything about it. We'll only know what the Yavanas choose to tell us, and we'll have no more power than before. And even what we used to have, the glory of being councillors—that's going to be cheapened, with greasy-fingered Yavanas coming to sit down on the benches among us."

"How does it hurt us to sit by them?" said Itaz. "Nobody's going to think a Yavana minister is the equal of a man whose ancestor met the Sun face to face. And if they report to us, we'll have a chance to make adjustments to what they ask."

Tasius let out his breath in a hiss. "You don't understand, do you? But you're *his* son; you're in the shadow of the royal glory anyway, and the glory of the council is just something to be brushed away."

"I think I do understand," said Itaz tightly. "You'd prefer it that the Yavanas got all the blame for any hardship that comes from collecting taxes, and you only got credit for rescuing the odd case afterward. People would be much less grateful if you merely prevented the hardship in the first place—particularly when you had to agree that some taxes are necessary." He adjusted the saddle girths, then loosened the chinstrap of the horse's bridle and slipped the bit back into its mouth.

"Let's not quarrel," said Tasius, after an uncomfortable silence. "I suppose it could've been worse. There will be a guard on the queen, after all, and some of our people will be on it. And some of our men will be free to supervise the Yavanas, if they do it at their own expense. Perhaps we could work at giving them an official position."

Itaz grunted, tightening the chinstrap again. He was ashamed now of his outburst; after all, Tasius was an ally and a brother. And he was guiltily aware that he might, indeed, have harmed their case that morning. Certainly he had not presented it well. He couldn't help wincing now as he remembered how gracefully and humbly the queen had made her rival submission on the city's behalf. It now seemed obvious that his bluntness was bound to alarm and annoy his father. Yet he'd been trying, trying desperately, to make Mauakes see that the opposition was still loyal—trying, in some obscure way, not to hurt him.

"The queen had some other suggestions, too," he told Tasius, try-ing to make amends for his hostility. "The city's delegation gave her a long list, and she relayed it all very cleverly, phrasing all their demands as humble requests, flattering him. They're suppliants, she kept telling him, begging you to save them."

"Ah," said Tasius, slowly, staring into the dark. "I was afraid of that. He may be merciful to beggars; he won't give lords what they ask by right. Yes. That was clever of her. And will the king grant the other requests, too?"

"I don't know. He didn't say. But he seemed inclined to—and he said he'd grant anything that she and I could agree on."

"What?"

Itaz shrugged, one arm across his horse's withers ready to mount. "He said that anything the Yavanas and their worst opponents agreed on, he would have to grant."

Tasius let out his breath in a long hiss. "He was angry, wasn't he? What else did the queen want?"

Itaz paused, dropping his arm, trying to remember it all. "She wanted to let the city choose its own magistrates," he said at last. "And she wanted the Yavanas to tax the Sakas they dealt with, instead of paying money to the king from their own funds. She said the citizens needed the money for all their Yavana entertainments."

"We're not agreeing to that!" said Tasius fiercely. "Perhaps we can use what he said to you to block it. And we must work at getting some official rank and position for our observers. Maybe if . . ." He launched into a long discussion of what sort of position and rights the observers might be granted.

Itaz leaned back against the horse and tried to listen. The stallion again began to graze, mouthing the bit as it chewed, and he found himself wishing desperately that he and the animal could change places; that he could be aware of nothing but the taste of the grass, the pleasant cool of the evening after the day's heat. There is a simplicity to animals that all of us long for, sometimes: to live wholly in the present, aware of nothing but the world of the senses. Our own worlds are so compli-cated that we ourselves don't understand them. After a little while Itaz found that Tasius' voice had become a senseless drone, and only the chomping and soft snorts of the horse made sense. He felt very tired, and he wanted badly to mount the horse, go home, and sleep.

Tasius fell suddenly silent. Itaz straightened and saw that the king was standing a few feet away, the solid, squat shape of his body unmistakable even in the dark. He had finished with the councillors and come to fetch his horse, which was tethered beside his son's, and here were his son and his son-in-law, whispering together. Tasius made a slight nervous movement, as though he wanted to run away.

"Greetings," said Itaz, before the king could speak. "We were talking about what the administrators' observers would do."

Mauakes grunted and turned aside, collecting his mount's reins—a groom had prepared the beast as soon as the meeting ended. The same groom immediately appeared at the king's side and offered him a leg-up; Mauakes heaved himself into the saddle and drew up the reins. "Continue your talk, then," he told Itaz and Tasius in his blandest tone. "You don't need to stop for me. Or if you do, I'm returning to the city, and you can continue when I've gone."

Itaz sprang into his own saddle. "May I ride back to the city with you?" he asked the king.

"You want to tell me what the observers should do, too?" asked Mauakes, still with the deceptive mildness.

"No," said Itaz, "but we're going the same way, and there's no sense riding separately, as though we were enemies."

Mauakes stared at him for a long moment. Masked look, suspicious glare, surprise: the darkness made it impossible to tell. "You may ride with me," he said at last, abruptly. "Tasius, my son, are you coming back to the city tonight as well?"

"Of course," said Tasius eagerly. "I'll just fetch my horse."

"Catch us up," ordered Mauakes, and turned his beast toward the city. "So," he went on, as Itaz drew his own horse in beside him, "what do you and Tasius think these 'observers' should do?"

Itaz sighed. "We don't even know who'll they'll be yet, or if anyone will be willing to do the job, seeing they have to undertake it at their own expense. Tasius wants them to have some official rank, with the authority to relay complaints directly to the council."

"Does he? And what do you want?"

"I suppose that makes sense, particularly if the chief administrators are councillors."

Mauakes snorted, and rode on for a moment in silence. Behind them a half-moon was rising, covering the sky eastward with a wash of pale gray light. "Tell me," said the king at last, "whose idea was this? Yours or Tasius'?"

"Tasius suggested it to me," Itaz replied at once, openly. "I don't know whether it was his originally, or whether one of his friends had suggested it to him. Father, you know perfectly well that most of the councillors distrust the Yavanas, and always have."

"Of course," said Mauakes in a whisper. "The council wants to rule. They don't dare hate me for ruling instead, so they hate the Yavanas. King Antimachos was lucky: he could send the whole pack of them into exile and rule the peasants directly, and it undoubtedly made things much simpler for him. I have to balance Saka nobles and Yavana kingship, and if I fail, both will fall down together with a crash. But if the noble lords and ladies were honest, Itaz, they would admit that the Yavanas are less of a threat now than at any time since before you were born. Bactria won't help them anymore, and all their hopes center on the queen. And the queen can give them only what I permit—and she understands that perfectly. She is in my hands entirely. So now the councillors prepare to hate her, too. Them I understand. Why do you hate her so much?"

Itaz closed his eyes, trying to stifle the surge of agony, glad of the darkness that hid his too-honest face. Hate her? Yes, he hated her—the coolly devious foreigner, set to get her way by flattery and sweet phrases; the blasphemer, the descendant of a murderous dynasty. But there was also that horrifying sense he had in her presence that he understood her, far better than his father did; he admired her, pitied her, was so desperately in love that his father's claim to her made him set his teeth in rage. She had split him in two. He did not trust or believe the self that loved—but still, it hurt him, and made him wish, not just that the woman were back in Bactria, but that she were dead, safe in the earth and unable to torment him anymore. "You know I don't like the Yavanas," he told his father. "I still wish we'd strengthened our alliance with Parthia instead."

"But I told you why an alliance with Bactria would be better!"

said Mauakes, angrily now. "Can't you see reason when it stares you in the face? And if you can't, won't you believe that I can? I've ruled this kingdom for a generation, and I've never failed its people, never, but still they question my judgment—even my own family. You keep protesting your loyalty to me. Why won't you accept my decision, and submit?"

"Father!" said Itaz, again glimpsing the pain behind the suspicions. "I have submitted; we all have. You are king of the Sakas, the lord of Ferghana, the only man who defeated the invincible Demetrios, and I'm glad to obey you. But there's a war coming, and if—may the gods avert it!—something happened to you, we don't trust our own authority over the Yavanas to match yours."

Mauakes stopped his horse and caught the bridle of his son's mount. "Swear it to me," he said urgently. "Swear that you're loyal."

"I swear it by Ahura Mazda, by the Sun, and by all the beneficent immortals," said Itaz solemnly. "You are my king, and I will never betray you." He took his father's hand and bowed his head to kiss it.

Mauakes sighed, his fingers tightening on his son's. Then he reached over and patted Itaz' arm. "Well. Well, perhaps I'm too suspicious. Itaz, my dear, kingship is a bitter thing."

"I've never wanted it," said Itaz honestly.

"No," said Mauakes, sounding much happier. "Well." He spurred his horse to a trot, and when Tasius joined them, talked with him easily about the council meeting and showed a gracious interest in the proposals for observers.

CHAPTER

VI

The amount of time the king had allotted his councillors to tend to their lands before arriving for the drills was very short, a mere twenty days. My father didn't even bother to leave the city, merely sent my brother Havani back to the estates, instructing him to ride quickly and borrow fresh horses on the way, and return with all our men who were able to fight. Many other councillors did the same. The same men who'd come down to Eskati for the wedding remained camped by the lakeside as the heat of the summer grew, and more slowly trickled in to join them. The city was cramped, the citizens short-tempered; on the plain outside the walls the Saka tents collected a horde of flies and vermin, and a network of cracked-earth paths sprang up through the yellowing grass and dying thistles. There was no news of the Tochari. Mauakes had sent men out into the lands of the Sakaraukai and Dahai, to listen for any reports of raids, but the spies had nothing to report. It seemed that the enemy might not invade this year after all. Some of the councillors grumbled—why wait expen-

sively with all their men, when the fields needed tending and there was
no enemy in sight?—but Mauakes was relieved, knowing that any
additional time for preparation was priceless.

The king set to work at once, without waiting for the tribal army
to arrive. As soon as the council meetings were over, he began drilling
the three hundred men of his guard and the two thousand of his
standing army. Every morning he rode out from the city to the practice field just south of it, with some hundred of his standing troops and
one or two of the elephants, and all day the men would ride about the
great beasts, trotting or galloping, straining to keep their horses quiet
when the animals trumpeted. He tested the artillery as well. King
Heliokles had sent four of the larger machines, the kind they call
"thirty-pounders" from the weight of the rocks they can hurl. These
were nearly twenty feet long and too big to be used in the field, since
they have to be taken to pieces to be moved. They were assembled in
the gate towers and left there, one to each gate. But the rest of the
machines King Heliokles had sent were the kind called "scorpions,"
which are about six feet long and can shoot arrows or fire canisters, but
not rocks: these can be split into two pieces, base and stock, and moved
about or set up in the field. Since the Sakas claimed that the use of war
machines was unmanly, and refused to touch them, Mauakes recruited
some Eskati Yavanas to study their use with the engineer from Bactra,
and these Yavana catapult teams drilled with the army. That was something new: in the past the king had forbidden the Yavanas of Ferghana
to carry so much as a spear, but now he gave them charge of the most
powerful of all weapons, the scorpions and the fire bolts. The Sakas
murmured about it, particularly the fire. There is a lake to the south of
Bactria which produces a stuff called naphtha that burns hotter than
oil; they load an earthenware canister of this—or of oil, if no naphtha's
available—onto a catapult, stick a burning rag in the end, and hurl it,
two or three hundred yards, into the enemy, where it explodes and
clothes everyone around it with a clinging fire. It is a dreadful weapon
—and, of course, especially useful against horses, which are terrified of
fire. The Bactrian Yavanas had used it against us in earlier wars, and the
king's men hated it; now King Heliokles had sent a supply of naphtha,
and the citizens of Eskati were being taught how to use it. The tribal
troops loathed the new catapult teams, and considered the whole busi-

ness a mistake. But the king's men, though just as suspicious, were well disciplined and trusted their commander's judgment. At the king's command they practiced defending the catapults against attack, and arranging the catapult wagons in the line of march, and so on and on, until the Yavanas were fully part of the Saka army.

Mauakes also tried to accustom his men and horses to fire. Not that he had the trainee catapult teams shoot at his own men, of course: they had a range of their own and some straw targets to practice on. He didn't waste any of the precious naphtha in the drills, either; there was only enough of that for two hundred canisters, which were all destined for the Tochari. Instead, he built a row of bonfires, twenty paces apart, and ordered his cavalry to charge targets beyond these. They attacked them again and again, until the horses no longer shied and refused to approach the fires—and then he lit more fires, and more, till the horses had to gallop through a narrow corridor of flame. This many of the men and horses had done before, to prepare for Yavana wars, but they struggled to do it again, and perfectly.

While the king drilled the army, the new queen dutifully studied the administration of her kingdom—and lost even the faint shadow of trust with which the king had regarded her before.

It wasn't that she did anything that was actually wrong; from her point of view, she was simply being conscientious. She wrote polite notes to all the king's chief administrators, saying that she wished to understand her husband's duties and her own, and begging them to explain their work to her at some convenient time. When each of them appointed a time, she went along to his office, escorted by Padmini or Antiochis and two of her Saka attendants as well, and gave the man her thanks for his time and a small gift from her store of Bactrian treasures. Then she would ask him earnest questions about what he did, and listen to the answers with flattering attentiveness, and look at the books with a schoolgirlish gravity. Her questions, though, were anything but schoolgirlish. I think everyone in the palace commented on her intelligence. She learned; she compared what she learned with how they did things in Bactria—and she made suggestions. That was when the trouble really started.

I got a summons from the king one evening round about suppertime, and obediently went to see him in his study. He had a massive accounts ledger, a codex with wooden bindings, open on the table in front of him, and when I came in he slapped it and, without any greeting or explanation, ordered me to read it.

I stumbled over the pages he'd indicated. They held a record of receipts and expenditure of grain: so much received from such-and-such an estate, so much given to the horses of the royal guard, and so on. The king listened as intently as though I were a minstrel at the climax of a hero tale. When I'd read three interminable pages, he asked, "Has anything there been altered?"

I stared at him in surprise, then stared at the book. The ink was all the same color, and the lines were straight. "It doesn't look like it," I said at last.

"Is it all the same . . . how do you call it, the same hand?" he asked.

"Yes," I said, still more surprised.

He grunted and leaned back. "I heard that the queen visited my finance minister today," he said. "And that she suggested some changes to his methods of accounting."

I hadn't been there—it had been Jahika and Armaiti's turn to accompany the queen—but I'd heard her discussing her suggestions with Antiochis, so I agreed. "Yes, that's right. She was saying that you use the grain fund that used to belong to the city for buying surplus grain for your own men; she thinks that if you transferred some other payment into this account you could restore the grain fund, and then the city could use it to stabilize the price of grain again. She said that already grain prices near the city have started to go up, and when all the army is here together, you'll have to do something or the poorer men will starve."

"She said that, did she?" said the king, looking at the ledger with narrowed eyes. "My finance minister was much impressed." He closed the ledger, stared at it a moment longer, then looked up at me and asked, "Has she written any letters yet?"

"No," I said. After a moment I added, "That is, she's written to the managers of the farms you gave her, saying how pleased she is to have them working for her and asking them how the estates are run. But those letters went out through your own steward, so I didn't think I needed to worry about them. And Antiochis and Padmini wrote some letters, to their families in Bactra, but they didn't seem to be about anything but what their children should do in school."

"You saw these letters?"

"Well . . . they read them to each other."

I could see that he didn't think much of me as a spy. His jaw set and he looked back at the ledger. "She's seen all my ministers now, hasn't she?" he asked softly, and when I agreed, he said, even more softly, "Then she doesn't need to see them again."

"What?"

"She has no business making suggestions to my servants behind my back. I do not want her interfering with my administration again."

"But . . . but it wasn't behind your back, my lord. She told your finance minister to speak to you about it as soon as he had a chance. I thought it was a good idea, sir. It's true the price of grain has gone up: everybody's been complaining at the cost of bread. If she understands Yavana accounting, how does it hurt for her to make useful suggestions about it?"

The king gave me a look of unmistakable contempt. "Stupid girl!" he snapped impatiently. "She and the ministers understand it; we do not. Think for a minute: don't you see what that means? Even if she intends nothing but good, it will scare the councillors witless, and the gods know they're jumpy enough already. And if she has treachery in mind, she could tear the kingdom in half. And, no thanks to you, I still know nothing of her real intentions. She must stay away from the government. No, I'm not leaving you to tell her: you may give her my compliments, and tell her that I will discuss the matter with her this evening. But tell your fellows that I do not want her going into the administrative offices again, and if she does, I am to be informed of it at once."

And that was how it was: that evening he told the queen that she was not to speak to his ministers without his permission. She, once again, accepted it—*in view of the disturbance caused by the threat of invasion*—and quietly left it at that. Padmini and Antiochis were rigid with anger about it. I overheard them discussing it that night—I was anxious and homesick again, and couldn't sleep. "She has twenty talents of silver in the royal treasury!" wailed Antiochis. "Can't she even talk to the treasurer? Does she have to ask royal permission to know what's being done with her own money?" "Of course," replied Padmini, sourly. "He doesn't want a Greek queen, let alone a Saka: he wants a Parthian to sit in a harem and spin. He refused to give her her own staff; he refuses her access to his; he shuts her off from her own household every night, and he chooses all her servants. Oh, my dear, she should have been silly as a chicken: he'd have trusted her then."

But they said it among themselves. They didn't want to make things worse by setting queen against king, and when Heliokleia was present they pretended to accept the king's decision. I only understood afterward how much Heliokleia herself was bewildered and hurt by the king's orders. She knew that she was not trusted; she even accepted that it was natural for the Sakas to suspect her. She knew how deep the enmity between our nations went. But she'd accepted as her great object in life the task of making peace. Now it seemed that she'd interfered wrongly, and made unwelcome suggestions that undermined her husband's authority. But how could she show her goodwill except by looking for opportunities to help? She was even more confused when the king did follow the suggestion, and restored the grain fund to the city of Eskati: if he agreed with the suggestion, why was she so wrong to make it? She wrestled with the problem for weeks, and finally, in exhausted exasperation, decided to leave it.

But the king couldn't leave it. He had known, in theory, that his new wife would be able to read the records and accounts of his Yavana secretary and his ministers, which he couldn't read himself—but he hadn't expected that she'd actually bother to do so. Now he searched the city until he heard of a slave, a Sogdian man who'd been captured as a boy by the Bactrians and taught to read and write Greek, then sold to a family in Eskati: this fellow absolutely detested the Yavanas. Mauakes bought him and had him go over all the official files, in case the queen, or a minister favoring the queen, tried to alter them. Even when the files proved entirely untampered with and the ministers regarded him with horrified astonishment, he remained uneasy. But by then his relations with his new wife were beginning to make him uncomfortable anyway.

She did not warm to him. When he took her to bed she volunteered nothing, not a touch or a kiss on the cheek; if he asked her to do something she obeyed at once, but otherwise she lay under his hands like a woman drunken or drugged. As the weeks wore on he lost his first confidence that this would change as she got used to him; he grew impatient, and worse. We in her household knew about it—living as we did, crammed into four rooms, we were all forced into a kind of horrible intimacy with each other: colds and coughs, sleepless nights or stomach upsets, backaches or menstrual pains, we all, slave and free, knew every unwanted detail of each other's bodies, and our knowledge extended to the queen. We noticed it first about the time the tribal army had finally assembled: she came upstairs one morning with her tunic torn, bruises on her thighs, and a red bite on her breast. She sat down to her usual meditation without saying a word about it, but every evening afterward when she went downstairs her face was whiter and quieter than the evening before, and usually she came back with another mark on her. I was revolted and bewildered by it—I was a virgin then, eighteen years old. This was no part of what I'd thought marriage was about, and it frightened me. And I couldn't talk about it: everyone treated the queen's bruises as though they were some unfortunate deformity that only a vulgar peasant would comment on. Padmini and Antiochis were disgusted, but said nothing about it, except to insist that particularly deep bites were bandaged with myrrh to disinfect them. Only the old slave Parendi, who'd lived all her life in the palace and remembered the old queen, said anything to me about it.

"She's not good for him," she muttered to me one morning when she was cleaning up the bath after the queen had gone down to breakfast. "Look at that!"—a scrap of wool smeared with blood and myrrh, used on a particularly nasty-looking bite—"He never did that when Queen Vishaptatha was alive. Twenty years they were married, and he never so much as slapped her. This is against his own nature."

"Why?" I asked in a whisper, and Parendi grabbed my sleeve with her horny red hand and peered up into my face.

"It's because he doesn't matter to her more than a dog," she told me, gabbling the words out almost greedily, her own opinions that nobody usually troubled to ask for. "You look at her when she goes downstairs, she's like a statue. A man doesn't want an image of Anahita to sleep with. He can't stand indifference, no man could: he wants love, but if a woman hates him, at least he matters to her. But this one . . . it's all that meditating. She's indifferent. It doesn't touch her. She doesn't care about anybody. He tries to love her and it doesn't matter to her, so he hurts her, because at least that way she pays attention to him. It's not right. He's a good man, a good king, and he'll hate himself for it, and hate her too. It's a bad business, and it will end in evil, you'll see."

I shook Parendi off, and told her to mind her tongue, because I didn't like what she was saying. But even at the time I thought she was probably right, and as the weeks passed I grew sure of it.

The queen's indifference ate at Mauakes like a sore. He found he wanted her more, not less, and wanted her violently. He had never been a man who derived pleasure from harshness. If he had had men killed, it had always been for what seemed to him good cause. I don't believe he ever struck Heliokleia, even when things between them were at their worst: remembering now I can say with certainty that the marks were all of rough passion, a furious assault on that blind calm resignation. He knew he hurt her, though, and he was ashamed, but couldn't stop himself. The thought of her began to haunt him: in the middle of a meeting with his officers, or when riding out to drill his men, he would imagine her lying naked on his bed, her smooth pale skin blotched red with the marks of his hands, and he would break into a sweat, his flesh going hard and his mouth dry; he would struggle to contain himself and attend to what was happening about him, afraid that people would notice, and think that he was growing old, that the sharp wits that had kept him alive and king were blunted. He could not help feeling angry with his wife, though he admitted freely that she behaved in all ways correctly, and his anger led him naturally to a pervasive vague suspicion of her and everything she did. He was relieved when it was finally time to choose a guard for her.

Heliokleia suffered torments from the king's use of her, of course —but she was a strong woman, and far too proud to beg him to be gentler, and she only struggled all the harder to detach herself. She had no notion that she was stoking the flames that burned her, or even that Mauakes' roughness was in any way unusual. She did not complain, even to Antiochis and Padmini, and she certainly never mentioned her feelings to her Saka attendants or the king. I found out, though. She did, eventually, write a letter, and so of course I had to steal it before it was sealed, and read it, so that I could tell the king what was in it. I almost had no chance to look at it, too, since she was going to seal it immediately after writing—but fortunately the sealing clay had dried out and she had to wet it and wait while it softened, and while she was waiting Inisme distracted her and called her out of the room so that I could read the letter. I can still remember how it went:

Heliokleia to Nagasena her teacher sends greetings. I hope, sir, that this finds you in good health, that your monastery is safe and prosperous, and that your disciples around you are listening to your teaching with delight. I pray daily to the immortal gods that my next life allots me a place like theirs: it would be such great joy to live quietly, taking no thought for the things of the body, but free, serenely at rest, illumined wholly by the marvelous light of the eightfold way. My mind is very dark, here in the north, and it is difficult to meditate; I find myself constantly distracted by trivial matters, and easily brought close to tears by things of no consequence. Sir, allow me to sit at your feet, in imagination only, and teach me, ignorant and weak as I am, how I can follow the way in my new life. I am so tormented by the carnality of marriage that my own body is loathsome to me. I should, I know, subdue the pain of the flesh as I would subdue its desires, but I can't, and my thoughts are like muddy water and won't be still. I am ashamed to beg your wisdom for something so commonplace and inconsequential, complaining over this one thing when my allotted karma has given me riches, good health and authority, but I find myself like a beast in a pen; I run back and forth blindly, seeing no way out. Please, lend me your knowledge to open the gate! The king my husband treats me courteously, but has no understanding of what I feel. How could he, when I don't understand it myself? And I dare not tell him how repulsive he is to me. I notice a thousand things that I should disregard calmly—but I cannot. He has bad teeth—I hate the smell and the sight of them; his body is thick round the middle, and hairy—I hate the touch; he has not bathed since the wedding—I loathe the smell of him. Because my body belongs to him, I feel unclean; I am disgusted at myself, and don't know which way to turn. It is as though these things, which are small things, add up to a sorcerer's potion, which has transformed me from what I am into something brutal and defiled. I no longer know myself.

I fear I am like the woman in the parable, asking, as a cure for her child's ill, black mustard seed from a house where none have died. There is no such house, and the ill is incurable. Suffering, I know, is the first truth, and it is born of thirst; that is the second. That much of the way I remember, and this: suffering ceases when thirst is abandoned and desire destroyed—but how can I destroy my desire to be away from this man? The noble eightfold way, you will answer. But I hold to the eightfold way already, as far as I can. Only in meditation has it become a struggle for me to keep to the way, and that is a most bitter and terrible struggle, when it ought to be relief. Sir, please, advise me, help me, tell me how to meditate or what god to pray to to escape this misery.

The letter shocked me. I had known that the queen hated sleeping with her husband; for all my inexperience, and her self-control, I could see that much. But she had still seemed so calm, so resigned, so—to use Parendi's word—indifferent. All this talk of coming close to tears over trivialities, of a mind like muddy water, of being penned like a beast, full of self-loathing and disgust—I hadn't guessed any of that. I am not self-controlled: if I lose my temper, everyone knows about it. The kind of discipline that could disguise misery like that was a mystery to me. And I don't think I would have suffered so intensely at it in the first place. I wouldn't have liked to marry a man older than my father, but I think I would have accepted it; I wouldn't have felt such a horrible sense of violation. I stared at the letter for a long time and, half-unwilling, read it several times before I slipped it back onto the queen's writing table.

I had to tell the king about it, of course. She sealed it and sent Padmini to deliver it to a merchant who was bound for Sakala in India; the king would know that, and would expect me to report to him. So I told one of his body slaves that I wanted to talk to him, and when he got back from the drill field that evening, Mauakes sent for me.

"She's written a letter to her brother?" he asked eagerly, when I appeared in his study.

"Not to her brother, sir," I replied. "To somebody called Nagasena, in Sakala. She called him her teacher. I think he's a Buddhist monk."

"Oh," he said, disappointed enough for it to show. He didn't expect any revelations from a letter to a monk. After a moment he asked, "What did she say?"

I shuffled my feet. I was horribly embarrassed—at reading the letter, at telling him about it, and at its contents. I simply couldn't repeat to the king what she had said about him; I was ashamed even to know it. Perhaps things would have been better if he had understood what the trouble was, and perhaps I am in some sense responsible for what happened because he didn't understand—but no mortal can see every consequence of her action. "She wanted to know what she should meditate on, and what gods she should pray to," I said at last.

"Oh?" said the king, giving me the penetrating look. "But that isn't all she said, is it?"

I swallowed. "N-no. That is, it was why she wrote. She . . . she said she was very unhappy here."

There was a silence. "Why?"

"She . . ." I stumbled, unhappily, not daring to look at the king. "Sir, I think she just misses the way of life she had before."

"She objects, perhaps, to the restraints put on her here?" asked Mauakes sweetly. "She wishes for more authority? Come, Tomyris, you said I could rely upon you. What exactly did she say?"

"Sir, it wasn't like that!" I protested. "She didn't talk about authority at all. Most of the letter was just religious talk, about how happy monks are, and what the Buddhists teach about suffering. She just said she wasn't happy and was having trouble meditating, and finally asked him to advise her how to meditate. Truthfully, sir, that was all."

"Indeed? So why are you so . . . nervous?"

"I don't like reading her letters, sir, especially when they're . . . personal. It makes me uncomfortable. There was no harm in the letter, though, sir, I swear it."

He looked at me a long time with narrowed eyes. "I see," he said at last. "You may go." I started to go, but when I opened the door, he said, "I hope you are indeed my loyal subject, Tomyris."

I paused and looked back, but he had turned his back on me and was putting out the lamp, so I closed the door behind me and went on to the women's quarters, hating myself and cursing the day I ever came to Eskati.

By this time the councillors had assembled with their men, and the king had begun drilling them. All the two thousand troops of the standing army now had some acquaintance with elephants and some tolerance of fire—though, of course, none of the horses were really happy with either—and the king had enlisted them to help with the training of the rest. He drilled the tribal army hard for another two weeks, and then brought his wife from the city to witness the first of the competitions.

It was past the middle of the summer by then, and hot, as it always is in the valley, particularly in the west end of it where the land is lower. The contests were to begin early, before the full heat of the day, so we all went down the hill to the palace stables in the gray predawn: the queen and the two Bactrian and four Saka ladies. Mauakes had already gone, off to arrange the army. A half-moon was setting and the dew was heavy on the weeds beside the path; the city huddled asleep beside the river. In the stable yard the horses were already saddled, a two-horse chariot was prepared for Antiochis and Padmini, and an escort of a half-dozen men from the royal guard were waiting for us.

The all-seeing Sun knows how I'd been looking forward to that minute. We had chosen the horses for this expedition the day before: royal horses. I'd gone down to the stables with the queen and looked over the ten Sun-descended animals kept ready for her, and when one had been found for her I was allowed to pick one for myself. I chose a mare, a dark gray dappled with brown. She had a lovely deep chest and clean legs, strong round hooves, and she walked like a tigress. I called her Terek, after the river near my home, a dappled stony river, strong and swift as the horse. I'd barely been allowed on her back the day before, and I was aching to make her gallop; when I came down to the stable yard in the dim morning, it was like New Year's morning to find her standing there snorting and shivering. I gave her a sesame cake and she nuzzled my hand with a nose soft as silk.

The queen was also to ride one of her royal horses for the first time. Amage had allowed her to abandon the stout old gelding she'd been learning on and helped her choose a suitable mount. It was another mare, a beautifully trained, feather-mouthed, dapple gray with a gait as soft as snow falling; she was called Shadow. Heliokleia stroked her neck, and the proud head bent and nuzzled her shoulder, looking for the cake she'd brought. Heliokleia fed it to her, crooning the right noises, then mounted, scrambling to get into the saddle, but no longer needing to have the horse kneel for her. She'd had lessons every day for over a month now, and was accustomed to the size of the horses; her muscles were growing used to them as well, and she could look the part of a Saka queen in the saddle now, though anyone who spoke to her about horses soon would realize she was no Saka bred. She'd learned quickly, though. Some heaven-sent instinct seemed to guide her body even when her mind was unaware. Even Amage had remarked how it was wonderful, wonderful; she'd never have believed it, after seeing the queen during that first lesson.

Antiochis and Padmini sighed and snorted and got into their chariot. They were intelligent enough to see that Saka queens were expected to be able to ride; nonetheless, they could not shake their first conviction that there was something scandalous about a woman putting on trousers and sitting atop a horse, even if the trousers were elegantly woven and the horse of the royal breed.

We set out for the drilling field at a sharp trot. Terek's trot was high and jolting, as though she couldn't bear putting her hooves on the ground; I loved every minute of it. Padmini and Antiochis were obviously far less happy. They sat opposite one another on the chariot's benches, pulling their draperies over their heads to prevent the wind from tangling their hair, occasionally rising a little from their seats to look at their mistress riding ahead, then sitting down again, shaking their heads sadly. The queen, however, was just making the surprising discovery that she enjoyed riding. She sat very straight, her cheeks flushed with pleasure, and Shadow stepped as lightly as the wind.

When the queen arrived at the drilling field, the sky behind the mountains was the color of fire, and the birds were singing loudly in the bushes that flanked the aqueduct. The army cheered her. She was wearing a gown and trousers in the Saka style, woven from light cotton because of the summer heat, white patterned with purple and spangled with gold. Her hair was in the usual Saka braid, though she wore a wide-brimmed Greek hat on top of it, to protect her fair skin from the sun, and she had on most of the jewels the king had given her: she looked regal and beautiful and not Greek at all, and the men were pleased. Mauakes, riding over to greet her, relaxed a little from the tension that was now usual when they were together, grinned at her, and nodded to his men.

The king escorted us to a raised platform erected beside the aqueduct, shielded from the sun by an awning of gold-worked cotton; the elephants were picketed beside it. Here Mauakes dismounted and helped his wife down, then helped her up onto the platform and seated her on a couch set on its edge before going back to his horse. Her attendants were escorted up by some of the officers and seated behind her, while our horses were led off to be unsaddled and picketed in the shade. We four Sakas sat cross-legged on the cushions, making ourselves comfortable for what we knew would be a long day. Padmini and Antiochis settled stiffly, looking about with resigned disapproval at the bare platform, the elephants, the horses, and the flies. They were not liking Ferghana, which they found very barbarous.

When the queen had taken her place, the king rode out before the ranks of the army and gave the signal for the first of the contests to begin.

Sakas are addicted to games and contests on horseback; I've watched a good many such events in my time and, I've no doubt, will watch many more. They can take the form of races, of tilting and shooting competitions, or of polo—I've mentioned that before; it's a kind of game. On special occasions it's played with up to a hundred horsemen to a side, but usually done with fewer, and those few need some skill. Mauakes had decided to hold the different kinds of contests on different days, and to allow the queen to choose thirty-three men for her guard on each day. These first contests were tilting and shooting. Tilting is done with the lance, and thus is chiefly the sport of the heavy cavalry, the nobles who can afford armor; shooting is the task of the light cavalry, though the noblemen often join in.

The first group of competitors lined up before the queen's stand, about twenty of them, all wearing helmets and scale armor that had been polished till it glittered; each held a long spear in his hand, and many had decorated the spear shaft with flags. Their strong horses, half- or quarter-royal, were covered with armored blankets, and the riders spurred them, jostling each other, making the horses dance. They all seemed slightly built, and studying the faces under the gleaming helmets, Heliokleia saw that these warriors were boys, none of them much more than fifteen. She glanced around, gave me a considering look for a moment, then obviously decided against calling on one of her attendants for advice when there were army officers who might take offense at it, and glanced round again. One of the officers of the royal guard, an elderly man called Palak, was standing beside the platform. She beckoned him over; he came readily.

"Is there anything you wish me to explain, O Queen?" he asked.

"If you are free to, sir, I would be grateful," replied Heliokleia. "Is this contest only for boys?"

He nodded. "All the less expert warriors will compete this morning—boys of noble family, tenant farmers who train only once a year, poor shepherds who can barely afford a horse, and so on. The tilting won't be much good, but some of the farmers and shepherds are superb archers. These boys will tilt, of course; they're all noble."

The sun shot its first blinding ray over the edges of the mountains, one of the officials shouted, and the group of boys spurred their horses to a gallop and headed down the field. Some hundred yards away was a line of fires; beyond these stood a line of posts holding bronze-covered shields. Yelling madly, the boys charged the fires. Two horses shied from the flames at the last moment, and one of the riders fell off. The others galloped between the fires, and rode on to attack the posts.

"Do they have to hit the shields?" asked Heliokleia.

"That—or fetch down the ring. You see the rings? There, one on each post. They're arm rings, tied on with strings, and if you get your lance through one, the string snaps and you carry it off. The best thing to do is hit the shield on the way out, circle round, and take the ring on the way back; that wins most points. Difficult to do at a gallop, though, and it's probably safer just to hit the shield twice; I'll be surprised if any of these . . . here! Looked like that one managed it."

The young warriors had all struck the shields, though one must have angled his spear wrong, as the impact had tossed him from his horse. The rest had spun round and were riding back, striking the shield or stabbing toward the ring as they did so; one did, indeed, have something gleaming caught in the banner that was tied to his lance. He galloped back toward the fires, standing up in the saddle and waving the long spear triumphantly.

Just as the boys passed the fires, one of the elephants lumbered suddenly onto the course, trumpeting. The oncoming horses shied and bucked, and the young victor, together with one or two others, lost his seat and fell. He was on his feet in a moment, grabbed his horse before it could run off, and leapt back into the saddle. The others had only just managed to recover from the shock of the elephant, and the victor, by galloping hard, succeeded in catching them up. Palak chuckled. "Well done," he said, "but he shouldn't have been showing off before he was home. He should have realized that the king would bring the elephants out. It's the whole point of the training, after all."

Heliokleia had brought one of her chests of silver coins to reward the victors—good Bactrian tetradrachms, not local imitations. The boy rode up to the stand, flushed and bright-eyed with triumph. "Rajula, son of Azes!" announced one of the officials.

Heliokleia stood and smiled at him. "Well done, Rajula, son of Azes!" she said, holding out the coin to him. "It showed true courage not to give up even when you'd fallen. Take this as a keepsake, to remind you of this victory, and may it be the first of many."

It was beautifully done. Rajula's father Azes was one of the bitterest opponents of the whole Yavana alliance, but Rajula seemed to forget that on the spot. He beamed at her, bowed in the saddle, took the coin and kissed it, then turned his horse and rode out of the way. The next group of competitors, archers on shaggy ponies, was already assembling; out on the field a bale of straw had been dragged before the posts to act as a target.

Heliokleia watched, occasionally applauding, as group after group competed. Old Palak stayed near her, leaning against the platform and explaining things, obviously pleased to have found an attractive young queen ready to listen to his gossip and opinions. He was a good man to have chosen; he knew most of the nobles and some of the archers as well, and told her histories of the competing families going back for generations. She listened, trying to take it all in. She awarded silver coins to all the victors, and tried to find kind words for them as well. She would choose the guardsmen in the evening, and she watched the faces of the men she handed coins to, trying to guess which might be friendly to her. Eager boys' faces; scarred leathery old men's faces; open, admiring eyes and sullen, suspicious ones; dirty shaggy beards and dandified polished ones; gleaming armor and leather jerkins patched with a few scraps of bronze; deep-chested half-royal horses and quick light ponies; lances fluttering flags and scratched horn bows hung over the saddle: all the endless variety of the Saka army, one after another, and no guessing, really, what was in their minds when they bowed their heads to thank her for their bits of silver stamped with her brother's image. She sat very straight and smiled at them all. The sun crawled higher in the bleached sky, and the air above the grasslands shimmered with heat.

After a morning that seemed endless, there was a break, and men and horses went to rest through the midday heat. The elephants went back to the shade of the aqueduct; the men tethered their horses in the bushes and lay down in the shadows. On the drilling fields the bonfires burned down to embers and gray ash. Mauakes rode back to the pavilion and dismounted. "You can have lunch with me and my officers," he told his wife as he helped her down from the platform, and she bowed her head in assent. She was very hot, and her trousers clung round her waist and thighs, soaked with sweat; her back ached from sitting still.

It was a working lunch, not very different from the kind the officers would eat on campaign, taken in a large tent behind the pavilion. The queen ate the tepid mutton and rice in silence, listening while the men discussed the morning's performances and the kind of training used by the lords of the council. It was hot and close inside the tent, hard to concentrate. The officers went on and on about so-and-so's hunting parties and what's-his-name's economies in armor. After an hour, Antiochis and Padmini gave up trying to discuss anything else, even in whispers between themselves, and went outside to sit down in the fresh air; after a while, we joined them. But Heliokleia remained by the table, listening, saying nothing, trying to connect what she heard with the victors' names she'd been given that morning. It was hard to remember even the names of the officers she dined with; they all looked alike, in their coats of scale armor and their helmets. Only

Itaz, who had a nominal rank in the royal guard and was in the party, stood out. He watched her incessantly: every time she looked round, she found his fierce black eyes fixed on her. After a while her head began to ache.

When the sun was halfway down the sky, the bonfires were built up again and obstacles were dragged onto the courses: walls made of straw shocks, hedges of whip-thin saplings, and huts of wicker. These contests were to be for the more expert: for the king's army and the picked men of the councillors. Heliokleia took her place on the platform again and watched yet another group of men lining up to ride at the targets. She set her teeth, straightened her back, and struggled to pay attention. I managed to slip forward and tell her that my brother Havani was one of the competitors, and pointed him out to her. Havani's a good rider, though not much of an archer, and since he was competing so early in the afternoon while the most skilled were competing later, I had hopes that he might be among the victors.

It was at once clear that everything had become much more dangerous. A horse, jumping the straw shocks, fell heavily, rolling over its rider; another, shying from an elephant, tossed a man into a fire. He rolled out, flames lining the edges of his armor, shouting and beating at his clothing. Havani, however, stayed on, didn't take the ring but did hit the shield, and rode back in front of the others. I clapped madly when he came to collect his prize, and he grinned at me before bowing deeply to the queen.

"Havani, son of Thrita," said the herald; and Heliokleia, smiling, handed Havani his coin and said, "Well done, Havani! It would seem that your sister is not alone in your family in her courage and her skill with horses."

Havani looked startled, and kissed the coin when she handed it to him. Then he turned, rode to the side, and the next contest began.

A noble was thrown when his horse shied at an elephant, and broke his arm. A horse tripped over a log, broke its leg, and had to be killed. An archer missed the gap in the hedge of saplings at full gallop; he shot at the target regardless, but when he came to collect a prize, later, you saw the bloody slashes the wood had left on his hands and face. The queen smiled at him, but he stared back soberly, dark eyes unblinking beneath the weals. Old Palak was gone now, helping some of his own relations prepare for the contests, and there was no one for her to question.

It was dusk before it was the turn of the final competitors, the three groups from the royal guard, and Heliokleia felt limp with exhaustion and longed for the day to end. One more coin gone; another party of guardsmen forming at the line—with a shock she noticed Itaz' straight, alert form on his tall black stallion, lining up among them. But of course she should have remembered that he was a member of the guard, and he'd be bound to take part with the others, just to show good fellowship. This contest was one of the most difficult. The men had to jump the straw shocks, weave about the huts and between the fires, go through the gap in the hedge, then strike the shield, shoot as often as they could into a straw archery target, take the ring, and repeat the obstacle course on the way back. Heliokleia found herself watching the black horse, not sure whether she wanted its rider to come first, or last.

Itaz made no attempt to push his horse to the front as the group started, but rode leaning low across the stallion's shoulders, both hands on the reins, holding the horse as lightly as if it were a small bird. The black leapt the wall easily, despite its blanket of armor, and began to speed up as it wove between the huts. Itaz checked it as it neared the fires, took it between the flames at a flowing canter, its shape showing like coal against the hot glow. As the horse found the gap in the hedge, it speeded up again, and Itaz pulled out the spear from its holder by his knee and leveled it as he galloped up to the post. He struck the shield with a flourish, shoved the spear back, rose with his bow at his shoulder, and began shooting; impossible to say, in the dusk, with what accuracy or even how often. The dark horse showed vividly a moment as it turned, the firelight catching in its armor, covering it with flame, then vanished into shadow. An elephant lumbered suddenly out from behind the huts and trumpeted; Itaz steadied his horse without a glance, stowing his bow in its case and snatching up the long lance again. He spurred his horse, crouching sideways, lance at an angle—then he was past the post again, slipping the ring from his spear onto his arm. The black stallion galloped faster, overtook another warrior between the hedge and the fires, leapt an ember that fell into its path, passed the huts, jumped the wall, and galloped home ahead of all the others.

Heliokleia let out her breath, and was only then aware that she'd been holding it.

The king's servants were already counting the differently marked arrows in the target; in a moment it was Itaz who came forward to receive the prize. They had lit torches by the platform by then; again the red light painted the young man's armor so that he was clothed in fire. He was carrying his helmet under his arm, and the eyes he raised to her had the same fierce black glare as before; the torchlight gleamed on them and on the sweat that wet his cheeks and forehead. Heliokleia sat straight and stiff, her head aching, feeling strangely short of breath. She almost offered to lend Itaz her own cotton scarf to wipe his face with. Her hand tingled as she offered him the usual victor's coin. "It was very beautifully done," she told him softly.

He looked at her in surprise, then reached up to take the coin, saying nothing. His fingers brushed hers. Then he tossed the coin in the air and caught it again, looking away from her at last. He turned his horse and rode back to his friends. The next contest, the last, was already beginning.

Heliokleia scarcely saw it—but, of course, it was dark by then. She handed out the day's final coin and sat numbly, waiting.

Mauakes again trotted up and dismounted, and this time jumped onto the platform and sat down beside her. He made a signal to the officers; there was a stir of men and horses, and then all the day's victors, some eighty in all, trotted up out of the darkness into the torchlight. The king stood.

"Free men of Ferghana," he shouted to them and to the others listening in the darkness beyond, "you all know that today's victors may be rewarded with more than a silver medallion, for from your number the queen will choose her guard. It is a great honor to be chosen as protector to my wife, a lady descended from so many kings; and those she chooses will have rank second only to my own guard, and pay and equipment equal to it. But it may be that some of you are unwilling to serve the queen; let any such withdraw now." No one moved, and the king nodded with satisfaction. Heliokleia noticed that Itaz and the others from the royal guard were still in their places. They had no reason to want to change the king's service for her own. Mauakes must have ordered them not to withdraw, to strengthen the appearance of solid loyalty and devotion and reconcile the army to her presence. She was not surprised; the king lost no chance to make the Yavana alliance more acceptable to his people.

Mauakes continued, "Thirty-three men will be chosen tonight, and one to command them, and thirty-three more after each of the two other days of contests we will hold—but those chosen tonight will be the first, and theirs will be the first honor. Ride past, and the queen will give another coin to those she chooses."

They began to ride past, slowly, each pausing, watching her with questioning eyes. Heliokleia stared back with a splitting head and a dry mouth. After the first five had ridden by, she started, then stood, moving to the edge of the platform. "Keep going," she whispered, and louder, "Ride by once, first, and come back, good sirs: you are all so skilled that I have to see everyone together before I can decide."

They heard, and the slow pace speeded up. They hurried by now, one after another, into the torchlight and out again. Itaz was the second from the end, scowling slightly, only joining the line to show comradeship with the others. The line had circled about; there was a gap— and then the slow procession began again. Heliokleia signaled the first, the boy Rajula who'd distinguished himself at tilting, and when he stopped she handed him a coin. His face lit up; he touched the coin to his forehead and spurred his horse suddenly to a gallop past all his fellows, holding the silver shining above his head. Heliokleia turned back to the others.

She chose, half at random, half from guesses and fragments overheard: there the boy, here a bowlegged archer, tenant to a poor holding in the east; here a bulky, armored freeman with a blunt honest face; there a wary young lancer from the king's army. She chose Havani, with a faint smile and a sideways glance at me. She chose the man who'd ridden through the hedge. She chose and chose again, counting them out in her mind, counting out the coins in her hand, twenty-nine, thirty, thirty-one . . . there were no coins left, and the line was almost at an end. She signaled as the second-to-last rode by; he had been watching her, as he always was, and he stopped so suddenly that his stallion reared up, snorting, astonished.

"You can command them," Heliokleia told Itaz, in her low clear voice.

The stir around her was like a herd of grazing horses suddenly scenting something and standing heads up, sniffing the wind. Without turning, Heliokleia was aware of the king getting to his feet behind her, his eyes now fixed on her as well.

"What do you mean?" demanded Itaz furiously. Even the red of the torches couldn't cover the flush of rage.

"You wished, sir, to be sure of my . . . safety," replied Heliokleia. "You were the one who suggested I have a guard. I would like you to command them."

There was a heavy silence. Itaz stared at her, appalled.

"Lord Itaz," she said after a minute, "I wish all the people of Ferghana to know that I am not ambitious. If it's you who commands my guard, they will be certain that I have no chance to be. I beg you, sir, to accept the command."

She heard Mauakes snort behind her. Itaz looked down at his hands suddenly, almost as though he were afraid.

"The queen offers you a considerable honor, Itaz my dear," said Mauakes drily, coming forward. "Command of a body of picked men. Don't you mean to take it?"

Itaz opened his mouth, closed it, looked at his father. Reluctantly, he looked back at Heliokleia. Then he bowed his head. "You do me honor, O Queen," he muttered. "I accept the charge."

⊐⊒⊐⊒⊐

Havani found a chance to slide up beside me in the dark while I was bridling my horse to start back to the city. He grabbed me, and I yelled. He laughed.

"I was just testing whether you're the same Tomyris I used to know," he said. "You looked so ladylike up there on the platform I scarcely knew you. But you still yell like a goatherd."

I snorted, then hugged him. I was very glad to see him, but the thin hard presence of him made me realize how much I missed all my family. "Congratulations," I said, "guardsman!"

He gave a snort of pleasure. "By the all-seeing Sun!" he told me. "That's something, isn't it? And for a queen like that! She's a queen to adore, your queen is. We're lucky!"

I didn't say anything. After a moment, Padmini called: the others were already setting out. I hugged my brother again, jumped on my mare, and followed them. I thought about what Havani had said most of the way back, though. A queen to adore? I didn't adore her, and it made me angry, somehow, that Havani did: I felt he'd been deceived. For my part, I realized, thinking it over on that hot dark ride back, I neither trusted her nor liked her.

Looking back on it now, I can see that most of the things I disliked her for weren't her fault at all. Inisme was pretty and neat and had perfect manners, and led the others in looking down at me because I was none of those things; Padmini and Antiochis disapproved of me; I was forced to sit about all day when I wanted to be riding; I had become a spy: none of those things were Heliokleia's fault, and yet it was toward her that I felt resentment because of them. It's true she was nearly as neat as Inisme, always tidy and rarely with a hair out of place —but that was the doing of Padmini and Antiochis. She never obviously sneered at me, though I knew, somehow, that she found me amusing, in that superior Antimachid way. But it certainly wasn't her fault that I had to spy on her. And certainly, she seemed kind. She'd spoken to all of us, her new attendants, asked us about our families and our wants, and tried to fit our different tastes comfortably into the household. She remembered what we'd told her, too—she'd known, for example, that I was the best attendant to consult about horses, and the most likely to be informed about tilting contests. She was gentle and forbearing with the slaves, too. In the first few days she was in the valley, she'd called them together and told them that if they could give her the chance of showing them kindness, she'd be grateful to them, for her philosophy considered that merciful deeds benefit the doer even more than the recipient. And when one of the slaves, Parendi's sister Asha, took up her offer, and timidly asked permission to take a week off to visit a sick grandchild, the queen not only gave her leave, but handed her some money to pay for a doctor as well.

Yes, I told myself, watching her white-cottoned back going slowly ahead of me through the close dark, yes, she speaks kindly, and she's never done anything unkind or improper—but I don't trust her.

It was as though she was always wearing a mask, like an actor in a play; she was always saying and doing things, not because she wanted to, but because they were appropriate to her chosen role. "She doesn't care about anybody," Parendi had said. But already I knew that it was more complicated than that: there was a face behind the mask, one which I had glimpsed but never seen. Pain, and a longing for freedom I knew about from reading her letter, but what else could hide behind that flawless calm? Anger? Hatred? Ambition? I was sure that her compliant silence about the restrictions the king had placed on her wasn't really submission, but pride. If he wasn't going to give, she wasn't going to beg: a philosopher and a king's daughter doesn't ask anything from anyone. I could sense something in her like thunder in the air on a hot still day, and the passion seemed worse, and more dangerous, just because it was hidden. Also, she was brilliant and tremendously strong, and she frightened me. She alarmed the king, too—I suppose for the same reasons. He was himself a master of deception and smooth-faced self-concealment, and he recognized a mask for what it was. Perhaps he was right to distrust her and spy on her. But, I realized, I didn't trust him either, and I liked him no more than I liked her.

I sighed to myself and wished again that I were safely home.

Mauakes rode beside Heliokleia on the way back through the dark fields to the city. As they entered the gates he began laughing. "Very cunning," he told her affectionately, "and very clever. No one will be able to question his opposition to you: you've hobbled the whole pack of your enemies in one move, my dear. But are you sure you can manage him?"

The queen shook her head. "He'll do his best to be fair and honorable, won't he?"

"I suppose he will. He adores honor. Very clever indeed—and by the Sun, you astonished him! He looked like a startled sheep. When did you decide to do that?"

She shook her head again. "I hadn't even realized he'd be there, until I saw his horse with the contestants from the guard. I . . . I . . . ." She was not sure what she meant to say, was not sure why she'd chosen Itaz. She'd realized the political advantages to such a decision, but only after she'd made it. She wished she wasn't so tired, and that her head would stop aching.

But Mauakes was only half listening; he laughed again, to himself. "Like a startled sheep," he said again. "Baaa."

When they reached the palace he lifted her down from her mare and, without waiting for Antiochis and Padmini and the carriage, pulled her off to his bedroom. Heliokleia went with him numbly, saying nothing. She had expected this.

Mauakes was cheerful and delighted. The men had performed better than he'd hoped, and his queen had been everything anyone could ask for: he was aware, with great satisfaction, that most of the army had been charmed out of its instinctive opposition to his marriage—for the moment, anyway. And Itaz, he felt, had been paid back properly for his interference. She was clever, his wife; she was graceful and lovely; all the men in the army had admired her—and she was his. He led her into the bedroom happily and lit the lamp, then turned to embrace her—and found her standing stone-still, her face as remote and unchanging as the sky. He knew that look now, and he'd grown to hate it. The delight turned in an instant into a furious sense of disappointment. It was not right, it was not fair, that she should be like this with him, her rightful lord. He grabbed her shoulders and shook her. "What is the matter with you?" he asked her.

This she hadn't expected, and she stared at him in astonishment. "What do you mean?" she asked.

"What is the matter? You look like a priestess in a trance, trying to prepare herself to prophesy. Is there some Buddhist ban on pleasure?"

She bit her lip, still staring. She had been trying to detach herself from what was about to happen; it was unbearable otherwise. She had always assumed from his passion that he didn't notice. "I'm sorry," she said feebly.

"Sorry!" he snorted. "What good does it do to say that? What's wrong, why do you hate me so much? You're my wife, you should love me!"

"I'm sorry," she replied again, looking away. She was trembling, horrified at the enormity of his demand. It was too much, it was wrong even to ask it; he had no right. "I can't help it," she said.

"I'm not good enough for you, am I?" he shouted, flying into one of his sudden rages. "A pure-blooded Antimachid like you! You arrogant Yavana vixen, you simply can't bear to yield yourself to a barbarian, isn't that it?"

"No! It's nothing to do with that! I simply . . . simply . . ." She tried to shut her mind to the image that had begun to torment her when she thought of her husband, the nightmare picture of being violated by a beast. She simply couldn't stand the touch or the smell of him—but she couldn't say that to him, and she stopped. "I simply don't like the carnal act, sir."

He shook her again. "But you ought to! If you love me, you ought to!"

But she didn't love him. All at once, she felt a sick wave of guilt. He was right—a wife ought to love her husband. She had failed. But how could she love *him?* "Sir," she said sharply, the whole tangle of pain between them becoming perfectly clear to her, "I have tried to do as you wish, all along; I have obeyed you as a wife should. More than that you can't ask. Leave love to the gods: I can't give what I don't have."

He frowned. "What do you mean? You don't like me, you prefer someone else?"

"No one else," she said—and even as she finished saying it, she thought of Itaz, and how her hand had tingled when his fingers brushed hers, and again she felt short of breath. Someone else. Appalled at it, disbelieving, she pushed the thought of him from her mind, but her vision was lost again, and she was plunged in confusion. "There must be something wrong with me," she told Mauakes wretchedly, nearly in tears.

He reached out and put his arms round her, gently at first, to comfort her—but when she flinched involuntarily, jerking her arms protectively across her breasts, the gentleness turned into a grab. It was harder than ever to make herself yield; she was slow, forcing down each cramped tense limb by conscious effort, and her husband was impatient, angry, reluctant to wait, tearing her clothes off and dragging her to the bed. She thought of animals, scrabbling at the earth, and turned her head away. The lamp's shadows crouched blackly in the corners of the room, as though it were a cave, or a tomb, and she were buried in it alive. She closed her eyes, struggling to show no resistance as Mauakes thrust himself into her as though he meant to stab her to death. Then it was over, at last it was over—for the present. Mauakes rolled over heavily, and looked at her bleakly. She stared at him a moment dispassionately: the thin arms; the heavy body with its stiff gray hairs poking from the skin like a scalded side of pork; the stomach sagging above the thick gray thatch over the groin; the loose red genitals, half-buried, animal-like, in the fur. She lay still, bruises aching, torn, sore, and sick, trying again to force the nightmare image from her mind. How could he convince even himself that she should enjoy it?

Heliokleia gathered herself up and picked up the gown. "My women will be waiting for me upstairs," she told the king in an unsteady voice. "I would like to bathe, after such a hot day, so if you'll excuse me, sir . . ."

Mauakes grunted and closed his eyes. Heliokleia slipped the gown over her head and went upstairs, clutching the trousers and jewels in a bundle before her.

We'd been waiting upstairs. Antiochis and Padmini had insisted that the queen would wish to bathe, and the slaves had been sent for the water. The tub was growing cold when the footsteps stumbled up the stairs to the door, but steam still rose from the hot water jug beside it, twisting snakelike in the light of the single lamp, casting a faint, dreamlike shadow over the floor. Heliokleia shoved the door open, stumbled over to the couch, dropped the bundle of clothes, and sat down, shivering.

Padmini pulled gently at the gown, drew it off again, then stood still a moment, looking at Heliokleia's shoulder, her dark face perfectly expressionless. The shoulder was covered with blood, not just a wisp or smear but a dripping mess, dark and shiny in the lamplight. Heliokleia glanced down at it, touched it, then fingered its source, a torn ear. "My earring caught in my gown," she explained. She unfastened the earring and looked at it, bent catch, blood caking in the scrollwork and under the inlaid rubies.

"Oh, my dear!" exclaimed Antiochis, taking the earring away.

Padmini shook her head and spread the gown out on the bed, examined the matching tear in the gold-spangled neck. She looked back at Heliokleia, who slouched wearily on the bed, naked, her slim body marked with bruises and bites. At last the deformity couldn't be ignored. "He's very rough," Padmini said in a toneless voice.

Heliokleia had grown up dreading that voice, which had always been used only for the heaviest condemnations, when scolding was far too mild; now it brought a sudden sense of release. So Mauakes was rough, very rough, more than Padmini felt proper in any man, let alone a king? She was not entirely to blame? "It's my fault, it seems," she said with just a hint of the anger she felt. "I don't love him, and it makes him angry."

"Love!" exclaimed Padmini. "He didn't marry you like a romantic fool, for love; he has no right to expect it."

"Your mother never loved your father in the least," put in Antiochis, "but he always treated her decently and honorably. If he wanted love he found himself a woman whose business that was, and he kept her quietly and well away from the palace: that's how a gentleman should behave."

I simply stared at that. That's not how Saka gentlemen behave. A Saka husband who kept a mistress would be an oath breaker, foresworn before the all-seeing Sun. His wife would be well within her rights to divorce him, take back her dowry, and marry someone else. But the Yavanas see things differently.

"You don't . . . fight him, do you?" asked Padmini hesitantly.

"Of course not. I do what I'm bound to."

"No man has a right to expect more. What a barbarous country!"

"I'm sure it happens everywhere," said Heliokleia wearily, and stooped toward the steaming water. When she had washed she would have to return to the king's bed for the night, and to give in to anger and revulsion would simply exhaust her to no purpose.

CHAPTER

VII

Heliokleia went to bed drained and defeated, but woke angry. Even before she was awake the anger was there, a hard knot in her throat and chest, pushing her out of confused dreams into wakefulness long before the morning. Still half-asleep she tossed in her bed, already repeating to herself the scene of the previous evening, this time not with any sense of her own failure, but with furious indignation at the outrageousness of her husband's demand. When the anger was nearing hatred she came fully awake and tried to check herself.

It was dark, and everything had the deep stillness of the night's end. The room was hot; the single cotton top sheet was tangled about her legs, and the bottom sheet damp with sweat. Mauakes lay in a hot heavy lump beside her, his breath whistling a little through his teeth. She was thirsty and her bruises ached, but she lay quite still, watching as the gray light grew imperceptibly in the bedroom. Carefully, coolly, she turned her position over in her mind. She had done her best to be a good queen of the Sakas, and the king had no just complaint against her in anything. But her efforts had been greeted only with suspicion. She recounted to herself the bitter evidence of how little she was trusted: the separation from her own household; the lack of her own staff; the ban on speaking to the king's men; the Sakaraukai slave and the king's investigation of his own files; request after request on the city's behalf refused; the appointment of a guard. It seemed to be getting worse, not better. And the most painful thing of all, the misery of sleeping with the king—it now seemed it wasn't enough just to do it, she was supposed to like it as well. At this her cool assessment grew hot again, catching in her throat. Love and pleasure were no part of a queen's business, she told herself indignantly, and it wasn't wise for an aging king to introduce any consideration of them. If she gave any value to love, she would . . .

Here she and her anger together tumbled over a precipice, a sheer crag that had just appeared at the edge of the barren plateau of her life. If she gave any value to love, she told herself unguardedly, she would look for it with Itaz.

For a moment she regarded herself and her feelings as she had in the hot misery of the night before, with disbelief. Then, deliberately, she thought of Itaz—the fierce dark eyes and the long, keen face lighting with enthusiasm; the strong hands that were so sensitive on the reins of a horse; the white flash of his teeth when he smiled; the tall, sharp shape of him, the quick stride, the hot honest passion and the amazing gentleness and humility with his father. It was as though, at the thought of him, a part of her she had not known existed, a part long crushed down and trampled like a weed underfoot, began to open, petal on petal, its rich purple flower, fragrant incense lying on the barren stone. For a moment she did not know who she was. The room, the gray light, her own soul, became in an instant unfamiliar and strange, lit up suddenly from within. Then she came to herself and remembered that the man was her husband's son, and her enemy.

She sat up, appalled at herself. This was sheer wickedness. If she was in love with her own stepson, she was guilty of a wrong great enough to make everything her husband had done mild in comparison. She must destroy this desire at once—and destroy her anger at her husband, which verged so near a ruinous hatred. Whatever Mauakes did, it didn't affect her own duty to behave correctly. She hadn't expected happiness, and she had come to make peace between her people and the king's: if that was difficult, surely there was all the more merit in what she endured to bring it about? That, surely, was a cause for pleasure, even if a bittersweet one. Besides, she reminded herself, she had not been long in the valley—not even two full months. Both king and people might come to trust her better, given time. She crossed her legs, folded her hands, closed her eyes, and struggled to detach herself from sense and empty her mind of all trivial thoughts.

For weeks she had found meditation a painful struggle, but this time the trance came with astonishing ease, as though she had come out of rough country onto a paved road. In a moment she became unaware of her bruises, the torn ear, the heat, the brightening morning; she didn't hear the first birds begin to sing sleepily in the palace gardens, or the sounds of the first risers preparing the day's work. There was only an utter stillness—and then a sense of joy welling up within her, like a lotus rising slowly through calm, dark water. She did not think anymore of desire or of anger, but sat perfectly still, gradually releasing the joy into a profound watchfulness. The lotus opened, its petals unfolding like a rainbow, and in its heart shone a brilliance like the sun. She was not aware that she breathed; she had forgotten her body and the rhythm of her heart. Her mind was still, a mirror like calm water, releasing everything but the image of Heaven.

How long it lasted—a minute, a year—she couldn't say, but then, suddenly, the mirroring waters were shaken, and the image dimmed and was lost; almost in the same instant she became aware of her body, of a hand on her arm and a voice speaking, saying a name. She took a deep breath, still numb; recognized the voice as Padmini's and the name as her own. She opened her eyes and looked into her lady's tight, anxious face.

"Child, it's late," said Padmini. "The king was up hours ago and he's asking for you; you must get up and get dressed quickly."

She tried to move and found that her legs were asleep. It was full day in the room and beginning to grow hot; she was still naked, still bruised, still married. She put her hands to her face and burst into tears.

When she went downstairs a little later she had regained her air of calm self-possession. Arriving at the dining room she found the king sitting at the table with his Greek secretary, going over a list; a couple

of the officers from the army were arguing at another table, and half a
dozen council lords were having an earnest discussion by the door.
Mauakes looked up impatiently when she came in.

"There you are, properly awake again," he said. "My dear, the
Tochari have come. I want you to leave the city today."

"What?" she asked stupidly.

Mauakes gave her a straight, shrewd stare. "The Tochari have begun their invasion. One of my men brought the news at dawn. He says
that, when he first had word of them four days ago, they were among
the northern Sakaraukai a day's ride north of Maracanda, and making
directly for Ferghana. The Sakaraukai and the Sogdians are still gathering their armies, and haven't been able to make any resistance. It isn't
clear how many of the enemy there are, but they should be here in a
couple of days. We plan to meet them just north of here, at the fords of
the Jaxartes, but we may have to fall back on the city, and if we do I'd
prefer it if you were safely somewhere else."

Heliokleia drew a deep breath, trying to calm herself, telling herself that she had known, they had all known, that the invasion was
coming: it should not be so stunning that it had finally arrived. But it
was stunning, nonetheless. It had been expected so long that she had
almost forgotten it. In three days the city could be under siege! And
how could she run off, abandoning her city and her husband in time of
danger?

"Sir," she said quickly and quietly, "please let me stay. If I go, the
citizens will say that, since you send your wife out of the city, you
expect it to fall; they'll lose confidence in you and in their own defenses. And I'm sure I could be of use if I stayed. I could rally the
citizens behind you, and I could help organize the city's defenses. I
. . . I know I'm young and clumsy, but I think I could act bravely.
And if the city falls, I'm unlikely to be safe anywhere else."

He shook his head. "I would prefer you to leave Eskati altogether.
You have a fortified farm in the foothills of the southern mountains:
you can go there."

"Sir," she began again—then stopped, taking in the penetrating
stare and the bland smile. She realized that he wanted to send her away,
not because he was afraid for her safety, but because he didn't trust her.
He thought that, if the city were besieged, she and the citizens might

make terms with the Tochari and open the gates to them. She stared at him, her face hot with indignation, the anger swelling again in her throat. She had given him no cause! she told herself; he condemned her out of blind suspicion. "Sir," she said, still quietly, "I'm not afraid to stay. If I stayed, you could be confident of my complete loyalty and obedience."

He merely shook his head again. "As I am of your love?" he asked drily. "My dear, you must go. I will give you an escort to your farm in the mountains; go tell your servants to pack. You can leave at noon."

She stared at him a minute longer, choking back the shouted, futile demands. Then she bowed her head. "As you wish, sir," she said quietly, and left the room.

The queen had probably been the last person in the palace to hear the news. The rest of us had been wakened with it. When she came back to her room, I was sitting by the window, looking down into the courtyard below and worrying about my father and brothers. I wished, not for the first time, that I could ride out and fight the enemy like a man: a thousand times better that than sitting in the city and waiting for news. (Of course, we'd all assumed that we *would* wait in the city.) The others were fidgeting, each in her own way: Inisme rebraided her already neatly braided hair; Jahika and Armaiti whispered in a corner; Antiochis, who was musical, began to tune her kithara; Padmini sat down to her weaving. The slaves were luckier: they had work to do. Then the queen came in, as composed as ever, and announced, "The king wishes me to leave the city at noon; we will have an escort to a farm I own in the mountains. We must pack."

We all stared at her open-mouthed; even Padmini gaped. After a moment, Heliokleia added, "But there is no reason for all of us to go; the city isn't expected to be in any danger. I will take only two attendants, and the rest of you can remain here."

Padmini's mouth closed with a snap. "You will not leave me and Antiochis," she declared grimly. "We will not be left, child. And you must take at least two of the Sakas . . . to reassure your husband."

It was the closest Padmini had ever come to saying that she knew the rest of us were spies. Heliokleia looked at her a moment; the Indian stared bleakly back at her. The queen inclined her head. "Very well, if you wish to come . . . it's a hot season for a journey, though. Inisme . . . and Tomyris, will you come as well?"

I wondered why the queen asked me, instead of Armaiti. Inisme was her ladies' favorite, but Heliokleia must have noticed how much they disliked me. Nonetheless, I was glad to go. If I couldn't ride out to war, I'd still feel happier riding *somewhere*, and a farm in the mountains was a good place to be—and if it came to that, a good place to die. I had none of the queen's loyalty to the city: Eskati wasn't my home, and I didn't even like the place. I jumped up and started packing at once, before the queen could change her mind.

Heliokleia half hoped, half feared, that her escort would be the first third of her guard, with Itaz to command it—but the king, it seemed, did not want to spare his best warriors at this crisis. When we descended to the palace courtyard at noon we found our horses, the chariot, and a cart flanked by a mere twenty men: all of them old; eight of them missing a foot; five of them missing a hand; one missing half his face; and one with an appalling cough. Old Palak seemed to be their commander. Heliokleia looked at them in silence while the white-bearded captain saluted. She was smiling—the Antimachid smile at the world's absurdity. The cougher hacked loudly in the silence, then spat. Beside me, Antiochis and Padmini bristled.

"Greetings, O Queen," said Palak. "King Mauakes has allowed me to take charge of your escort. Your luggage is already stowed in the carriage, and the king has ordered us to go quickly: may I help you in?"

"Thank you, Palak," said Heliokleia. "I'm pleased to have your company on the journey. But I'd rather ride than sit in the chariot—is my mare saddled?"

The mare was saddled, and Palak smiled approvingly when she mounted it. Some of the old men whispered among themselves and slapped each other's hands, and I realized they'd been making bets as to whether she'd travel like a Saka or a Greek. Antiochis and Padmini climbed resignedly into the chariot, and Inisme joined them. I vaulted onto Terek. That completed the party, and we rode out of the stable-yard, the wheels clunking on the rain gutters, into the road that led round the citadel and into the marketplace.

There was a crowd in the market square, gathered as Greeks always gather in times of crisis, to talk about what has happened and argue over what may come of it. They fell silent as we rolled out into the square, one knot of discussion after another stopping, turning, staring. It wasn't until then that I realized what they would think when they saw us leaving. (I learned about the scene in the dining room after we got back.) As we rode past the temple of the Sun and slowed our horses for the crowd, we saw the fear come into all the faces around us. The same question was sweeping through a thousand minds: if the king is sending his wife out of the city, does that mean he expects it to fall?

Heliokleia drew rein in the middle of the square. "Palak," she said, "stop the men. I must speak to the citizens."

"The king said to hurry, O Queen," Palak told her reprovingly. "Come along."

She turned her mare without replying and cantered back to the temple. Palak swore and cantered after her, calling anxiously that we had orders to hurry. Not sure what I was doing, I followed him. Heliokleia ignored us, dismounted, and climbed up onto the terrace. I caught Shadow's bridle before she could bolt: she was a well-trained animal, but the tense crowd had made her nervous.

Heliokleia stood in front of the altar and looked over the market square. Palak had stopped before the terrace, dithering and nervous, and the rest of our party was stranded in the middle of the square, Antiochis and Padmini arguing with the old men of the escort—but the people were hurrying across eagerly to gather round, and pouring out of the houses to listen. Heliokleia raised her arms. "People of Farthest!" she called in the pure, musical Greek of her dynasty. "Do not be alarmed!"

Palak stopped his anxious glances about, obviously concluding that she couldn't be dragged off like a runaway slave.

"You have heard by now that the Tochari are approaching, and that our army will meet them in a few days," continued Heliokleia. "The king my husband is confident that they will never succeed in crossing the Jaxartes, but as a precaution, he wishes you to prepare for a siege. He is not in the least afraid that we will lose; if we don't get the victory at the Jaxartes, we are certain to obtain it here in Farthest. And I wish with all my heart that I could remain here, and join with you in that victory. But my husband has decided otherwise." She stopped, staring down at the upturned faces around her, the hungry eyes, then with a sudden lift of the head, she went recklessly on. "I am new to this land, and the king fears that my loyalty and love will not endure the stress of war," she declared, raising her voice to carry to the edges of the crowd. "I know the honesty of my own heart, and I am faithful to the honor of my house, which was committed to this alliance—but how can my husband be as sure of me as I am of myself? My house was his greatest enemy until this spring, and I have been queen here for only a few brief weeks. Because of this, he has asked me to stay at one of my farms while the war lasts. This is bitter to me, people of Farthest. I swear by all the gods, I would rather die honorably than run away. But my duty is obedience. How else can any of us convince our king of our loyalty? So I must go. But I leave you behind, to testify in my place to the courage and honor of the Greeks, and to show to the Tochari and to all the people of Ferghana, that with your wisdom added to the strength of the Sakas, we are invincible. May Anahita preserve you and Good Fortune guide you! I will return to celebrate your victory."

The citizens of Eskati cheered. Heliokleia jumped down from the terrace, her head up with pride and anger; grinning, I brought Shadow over to her. Though I didn't realize it for some time, I had just left the king's service and entered hers. She was magnificent. All her strength and brilliance were in the open for once: she was angry—angry for the honor of her house. When she said she would rather die than run away, I had no doubt at all that she was speaking straight from the heart. That was something I did understand, and by the Sun, I loved her for it.

As we trotted back across the square, the citizens went on cheering, clapping, stamping their feet and shouting aloud. She had done more than simply calm their fear: she had given them some of her pride and a determination to prove themselves the equals of the Sakas. They poured after us down the street as though she were already leading a victory parade, singing and cheering for her until she was out the gate.

When the city was safely behind us, Palak tilted back his helmet and wiped his forehead. "By the Sun!" he remarked. "What did you say to them?"

He didn't speak Greek and hadn't understood a word she'd said. "I told them that my departure didn't mean that the king thought that the city would fall," Heliokleia told him, calmly handing him a half-truth, "and I added some words to give them courage."

"Ah," said Palak, satisfied. "Well, it sounded as though it worked. King Mauakes had told me to leave the city directly, and to hurry, but if you've managed to put some fiber into the Yavanas, the delay will be well worthwhile. We must hurry now, though." He touched his horse to a trot.

Heliokleia followed silently. Much later she told me that she was wondering how Mauakes would view what she'd done. Had it been honesty or anger that made her shout out to the citizens a thing which the king himself hadn't admitted? And had she been right or wrong?

It was senseless to worry, now, with an invasion at hand. If the war were lost, no one would care; and if the Tochari were turned back, small irritations would be forgotten. The king might even be dead when she returned to the city. Dead as the omens had promised.

At this thought she felt a shock of hope, and, instantly, of shame. Did she really hate her husband so much that she wanted him dead?

No, answered something inside herself. No, she only wanted not to be married to him. She bowed her head, trying to discipline her mind. The heat was baking, and the mare's neck was already shiny with sweat. She took a deep breath and closed her eyes, swaying to the mare's motion. I saw the mask settle over her again, and remembered my distrust.

It took four days of hard riding to reach the farm in the southern mountains. I ached after the first day—for two months I'd scarcely ridden, and muscles forget and grow soft. Heliokleia had never ridden any distance before, and must have felt much worse—but she continued on the mare. "Why don't you join us in the chariot?" demanded Padmini in exasperation on the second evening, and the queen replied, "The escort has been betting I'll do that. They think Yavanas are soft."

For the first three days we rode through the close heat of the valley summer. Women were starting to harvest the alfalfa on the upper fields, stooping to the cut of their sickles; they called out to us as we passed, asking for news of the army. Heliokleia left it to the escort to answer and rode with her eyes fixed in front of her, ashamed to be running away, but if anyone asked if the Tochari were going to win, she would declare firmly, "I am as certain of my husband's victory as I am sure our Lord the Sun will rise tomorrow," and the people would cheer.

I couldn't help it; I started to like her again. No, she wasn't soft, and she wasn't going to let the old men win money betting she would be. She rode on, straight as a spear, and never faltered. One thing I could trust her to do, I realized: whatever she did, she'd do it like a queen. Queen Heliokleia of the Ferghanans, I told myself, trying the sound of it. Perhaps she was a queen worth serving, after all.

On the fourth day we left the South Road, the track that goes along the Mountains of the Sun. We turned directly south and began climbing, up a steep, stony track into the foothills. Soon the air grew cooler; small streams chuckled across the rocks, flanked by rhododendrons, balsam poplars, and twisted pines, and flooded summer pastures were green with lush grass; the sky was full of eagles. I was used to the riding again, and I sat up in the saddle, drinking it all in, at home in my own kind of country. All day we climbed, and the road grew smaller and stonier, the signs of settlement less frequent. The mountains towered before us, ice and stone, frowning down on our straggling group of old men and young women. The sun slipped down the sky, sending its orange rays sharp and horizontal between the tall peaks. Finally at evening, Heliokleia straightened a back aching from the unaccustomed riding, and saw a fortress, a wall of stone and a single gate, squatting on a crag below a sheer peak. "What's that?" she asked Palak, who'd been riding beside her, uncharacteristically silent with weariness.

"Ah!" he exclaimed happily. "That's it! That's your farm, Eagle Crag." And he ordered one of the old men to gallop ahead and warn the servants of her arrival.

It looked, she thought, like a prison, and she rode on toward it slowly. "Why is it so high in the mountains?" she asked. "There doesn't seem to be anything else near it."

"Well, of course not! All the land round about is yours, and it wouldn't support someone else's beasts as well. It's summer pasturage, O Queen; when the snows come they drive the horses down to the Eagle's Brook, just beyond where we turned off the main road, in the valley. But there's not much pasturage there in this season, so many of the farm workers come here with the animals each spring."

She'd heard this before, but not understood it. She stared at the grim walls again as the track turned to take us up the side of the crag. "Why is it built like that?" she asked. "You don't need walls like that to pen horses."

"It's old," replied Palak. "It was built before there were kings in the valley. Clans used to raid each other—and they say that before people came here, griffins used to roost in the cliffs, guarding their gold, as they do in the north. It's a strong place, O Queen. That's why your husband sent you here. Here we might hold out against even the Tochari—for a while at least."

Heliokleia nodded, but could not shake off the sense of the fortress's menace.

It was dark by the time we reached our destination; the gate under the single tower was standing open, and the queen rode through, followed by the chariot, the cart, and the escort—and then the gate swung shut with a dull thud. Heliokleia jumped and glanced back, then looked around. We were in a stone-paved courtyard, surrounded by a number of squat buildings of wood and stone; the yard was full of people, some of whom held torches that cast a red, unsteady light over their waiting forms and gleamed crimson on their eyes. The moon, nearly full, shone cold and gray on the rooftops, and the mountains loomed breathless and enormous out of the darkness.

After a moment, the people poured up to us. One of them detached herself: a tall, solid woman of middle age with lank gray hair. "Welcome, O Queen," she said to Heliokleia, "I'm Tabiti, wife of Galat the Steward. Let me apologize for the state of the farm, my lady. We would have prepared it for you, if we'd known you were coming. And my husband would have been proud to greet you himself, but he's with the army, and I'm the only one left to take charge of things. We've been shorthanded, with the men gone, and the house has suffered for it. But what we can do to make our lady welcome, we'll do gladly."

Heliokleia glanced about again. The people in the yard were, indeed, all women, children, and old men. Wives and mothers, fathers and young sons and daughters, whose men had gone down to Eskati to train and might by now be dead. Already the crucial battle would be over. And she could give them no news, other than what the old messenger must have delivered already, that the Tochari had arrived. "It's all right," she said stupidly. "I know I've come unexpectedly." She felt suddenly quite dizzy with exhaustion. The long journey, on top of the strain of the weeks before it, had left her aching and disoriented. It seemed to her that the mountains were like a tiger, crouching behind the farm, ready to spring, and she glanced at the moonlit peaks to be sure they hadn't moved.

Tabiti made another speech, which the queen was too tired to understand. She answered it randomly, with another apology for arriving unexpectedly, and slid off her horse. "Please," she said, "my horse is tired and should be stabled—and I'm tired, and need to sleep." Crude and stupid, she thought, but she didn't know how to put it more elegantly, and she was desperate to get out of the prison yard and lie down.

After some muttering, some women took our horses and Tabiti led us into the main farm building. There was a kitchen with an open hearth, bunches of herbs and dried meats hung about the eaves, and looms stood by baskets of carded wool. Tabiti showed the queen up a ladder and into a loft; she spread a blanket upon a pile of straw heaped into a long wooden box; other boxes stood nearby, partially screened by curtains of coarse brown wool. Padmini, who'd scrambled up the ladder after her mistress while Antiochis stayed below, stared at the bed in disbelief. "Do you call that a bed for a queen?" she demanded.

"If we'd known she was coming," said Tabiti unhappily, "we would have brought a bed from the city, and fitted up one of the sheds to be a proper bedchamber. But it would take days to prepare properly."

"Well—make a proper mattress, at least! Surely you can do that, even here in this howling wilderness!"

"Padmini," said Heliokleia.

"This is perfectly comfortable!" Tabiti retorted testily. "I've slept in such a bed all my life, and slept well, too."

"I've no doubt of it! But my lady is a queen, not a dirty peasant used to sleeping in a manger! You can't expect—"

"Padmini!" said Heliokleia, more loudly, and the Indian woman stopped and looked at her in surprise. "I will sleep in the bed. It's clean, and I've no doubt I'll sleep well; I'm very tired. But Tabiti . . . my ladies are gentlewomen, and tired from journeying. Please try to make them at home. I need to sleep now."

She lay down on the blanket at once, without even taking off her horse-scented gown and trousers. She didn't see Padmini's stare of surprised concern. The world seemed to spin about her as she closed her eyes, as though she were flying, and she was asleep even before Padmini and the steward's wife found her another blanket as a cover.

The rest of us were found beds without too much difficulty—there was plenty of space. Not only were all the men of the farm away with the army, but many of the married women were down in the valley, helping to get in the harvest. Padmini and Antiochis sniffed at the stained sleeping mats Tabiti offered them, but were tired enough to make no more fuss, and I curled up in my box bed and listened to the mountain breeze whispering in the wooden walls, and the sound of cattle shifting in the stables next door, in perfect contentment until I fell asleep.

I woke up next morning at milking time, rolled over and went back to sleep, and woke up again at dawn. Padmini was already up, stiff and fastidious and wondering aloud where the servants were; the queen was still fast asleep.

"There you are," said Padmini, when I sat up and rubbed my eyes. "Hurry and get dressed, girl: I want you to translate for me. Our lady will want to bathe when she wakes up, and I want everything to be ready for her. Antiochis, dear! Inisme! Wake up!"

It took us some time to arrange a bath. First, all the farmwomen were working, and we had to rouse Tabiti from the cow sheds to get help. Then there wasn't a bathtub, and then there was only the one main room of the farm to stand the washing tub in, and then there wasn't enough wood to heat the water. Tabiti saw no point in wasting good firewood on the Yavana passion for hot water, and I had to point out soothingly that the used bathwater would be perfect for laundry or cleaning tack. Padmini scolded and issued peremptory orders, which I translated diplomatically, leaving out the comments on the general level of cleanliness at Eagle Crag and Tabiti's shortcomings in particular. It was perfectly clear, to me anyway, that they were very short-handed, and it was only to be expected that the housework would be neglected in favor of the farm work. The new mistress must have been the last person the women of Eagle Crag wanted to see that summer. But the water was, indeed, hot when the queen descended crumpled and smiling from the loft.

When Heliokleia first woke, she felt light-headed and improbably happy. Straw was poking through the blanket into her side, and she could hear birds fluttering on the roof above her head. She rolled onto her back and looked up: the sunlight slanted through the cracks in the wooden loft, and the dust motes danced in the criss-crossing beams, glittering and spinning, then vanishing into the soft gold shade. She lay and watched them for a long time. How delicious to lie still in the morning, alone, with no one beside her! The sense of menace and imprisonment she had felt the night before seemed remote, part of a long nightmare from which she had now at last awoken. For as long as she was here, she thought suddenly, she would be free. The escort of old men were unlikely to interfere with her, and the servants were her servants and bound to obey her. She could do exactly what she wanted. She had never been able to do that before, and who could say if she'd ever have the chance again? She had time now—a few days anyway—to do . . . what? Lie in bed and watch the dust dancing, wander in those green mountain meadows, picking flowers, with her hair in tangles and her clothes in a mess?

There was a sound of feet on the ladder and Padmini appeared, climbing carefully in her long skirts, her mouth set firmly in disapproval. Heliokleia found herself smiling, and sat up.

"You're awake, then!" said Padmini, unexpectedly smiling back. "I was quite worried about you last night, child; you looked ill. By Anahita you're a mess, though; your hair's full of straw. Really, they ought to have at least one mattress in this abandoned place!"

Heliokleia laughed. "I slept very well," she said, and stood up, stooping under the low roof. She looked down at her crumpled riding clothes and smiled again. "Can I have a bath?"

"They don't have a tub, of course, the filthy creatures," said

Padmini. "But I've found a large basin for you, and set up some curtains to screen it off from those silly old men. I knew you'd want to wash, and we've got the water hot."

When she'd finished washing, Antiochis appeared, with a Greek tunic she'd just unpacked. Heliokleia shook her head. "Trousers, please," she ordered. "I want to ride about the farm today."

"Child!" exclaimed Antiochis in horror. "Haven't you had enough riding? Why should you wear such ugly things when you don't need to?"

"But I want to," said Heliokleia. "Just fetch them, Antiochis dear. The saffron ones, if they're clean." Antiochis went off, shaking her head in dismay, to find the Saka gowns and trousers. Heliokleia dressed and, to Padmini's irritation, asked for her hair to be fastened in the Sakan braid.

The farm looked different in the light of morning; the wood and stone buildings seemed to grow comfortably out of the earth, and the mountain peaks behind them were a blaze of light. The old men of the escort sat about in the paved stableyard, talking with the busy farmwomen, carving wood or mending harness or just sleeping in the sun. Some children tussled with a dog in a straw-covered corner, and doves cooed from the rooftop. The stables were empty.

"We put the horses out to pasture, my lady," said Tabiti, who took charge of showing her new mistress around. "The ones you came on, too, after a good feed and a rubdown. They need a proper rest after the journey."

Heliokleia nodded. "But I'd like to ride around the farm," she said. "Is my mare too tired to take me?"

"I should think so, my lady. But all the horses here are yours. I'll have one of the girls run up to the near paddock and fetch you another one. Most of the royal horses are up in the high pasture, though, my lady; I think . . . no, all the royal horses are off, I'm very sorry, my lady; we wouldn't dream of riding them, so we put them far from the house. There's a fine half-royal gelding, though, my own horse, which is in the near paddock; you'd be welcome to use him, and you could ride up to the high pasture and choose one of the royal beasts for yourself. Or we could fetch one for you. It takes two hours, more or less, to get there."

A leisurely two-hour ride up the mountainside, away from her attendants, was an enticing prospect. "I'll ride up there myself," Heliokleia said at once.

Tabiti nodded, though she seemed a bit surprised. "I could show you the pasture, my lady . . . or would my daughter do?"

Heliokleia accepted the daughter, a slim thirteen-year-old named Adake, and Tabiti nodded with evident relief. Heliokleia understood that she found her mistress, foreign and unexpected, a bit alarming, and smiled at her with a touch of extra warmth to reassure her.

The queen had a brief argument with her ladies and the escort over who else should accompany her on this expedition. Palak offered his company, though without enthusiasm, as the quick journey had left his old bones aching. Antiochis and Padmini urged her to accept, pointing out the suitability of an armed escort to a queen. But Heliokleia firmly refused. "I don't need an escort to ride about my own property, do I?" she asked. "I'll just go with Tabiti's daughter."

"You must take someone else!" said Antiochis plaintively. "It's improper for a lady to go riding about on horseback with just a peasant girl for company. Oh, Padmini and I should've learned riding, too!"

"We should not!" snapped Padmini, scandalized. "But take the maids. They can ride."

"Very well—I'll take Tomyris," said Heliokleia.

The ladies looked as though they weren't quite sure whether this wasn't worse than taking no one. Again I wondered why she'd picked me. To have my advice on choosing a fresh horse, I supposed. I was surprised at her decision to do more riding, too: it wasn't what I'd expected, either of the calm and flawless queen or of the passionate unknown behind the mask. Still, I liked the idea of a ride up to the high pasture. I suggested, though, that we take a picnic, since it was already midmorning.

In a little while, the three of us—the girl Adake, the queen, and I —set off with bulging saddlebags, riding out of the gate at a brisk trot in the clear mountain sunlight. Tabiti watched us go with scarcely disguised relief and turned back to her work. Heliokleia rose in the saddle and looked all around: the high peaks, the green meadows, the view of field and stream and rocky mountainside dropping down and down along the faint dun track into the blue haze of the valley below.

An eagle soared close by, wheeling about the sun, and she craned her neck to watch it, smiling.

She remembered that day till the end of her life. We rode east along the mountainside, then turned south where a little stream had cut a gorge in the peak, and followed a goat track winding from bank to bank up into the mountains. Creeping thyme, pale-leafed sage, and wild jasmine perfumed the air; birds sang among the dark rhododendrons and the trembling poplars. Trout darted under stones in the blue-green rock pools; the blue sheep and mountain ibex leapt away from us up the crags. Once we glimpsed a snow leopard, cream and gold, slinking off across the rocks of a distant hill. "Sometimes there are tigers," said Tabiti's daughter, "but the men kill them to protect the horses. Last year my daddy shot one, and we dried the skin and kept it for a rug."

"Aren't you frightened to ride about when there are tigers?" asked Heliokleia.

"Oh, no!" said the girl disdainfully. "Tigers don't hurt people. They always run away. If someone says a tiger hurt him, it wasn't a real tiger; it was a demon in disguise. And demons never come to these mountains, because they belong to our Lord the Sun."

"They can't all be sacred mountains," I protested. "The Sun only lives in a part of them. There's a corner of them that's a fragment of Hell." My own family's estates were by the Mountains of Heaven, and I didn't care for the exaggerated claims of the southerners.

"That's the Terek Pass," said Adake authoritatively. "That's different. That's in the Mountains of Heaven."

"It's between the Mountains of the Sun and the Mountains of Heaven," I corrected her. "I'm from the Terek Valley; I ought to know."

Adake shot me a look that mixed awe and pity. "I wouldn't like to live in that valley," she said bluntly.

"There's nothing wrong with the valley," I said shortly, "just the pass. We don't even get tigers, demon or otherwise."

"But the pass is haunted?" asked Heliokleia, innocently curious. Adake and I both stared at her.

"No one can cross that pass," said Adake, after a moment. "No one has ever been there and returned alive."

"Ah," said the queen in a noncommittal tone. "I've heard of a number of passes that are said to be haunted. But usually they're only haunted occasionally." She smiled, the mocking Antimachid smile.

I felt a stab of my old dislike. Superior Yavana philosopher, who thought she knew more about the gods than anyone else, and was amused by our barbarian simplicity! She was smiling at something she knew nothing about.

"The Terek Pass is different," I snapped. "It's been closed since your ancestor's days, and for his sin."

"Indeed?" asked the queen, still with the condescending curiosity. "What sin did my ancestor commit? Which ancestor, by the way— Antimachos?"

"No," I replied, "King Alexander." We rode on for a minute in silence. Ordinarily, people from the Terek Valley don't talk about the pass, and we only tell the story in whispers. I remembered my dream— the stillness of the dry river—and I shivered. I understood suddenly that the terror I had felt then had been because I was in a place forbidden to me; too loud, too clumsy, too alive for that wall of sky and bare stone. I understood it because I felt the same sense of trespass now.

But it was a clear, bright day without a shadow on it, and we were a long way from the Terek: after a moment I went on and told the story.

"They say that in the old days the pass was open," I told the queen. "In the days before there were kings. It leads between the Mountains of Heaven and the Mountains of the Sun, out from the valley into the east; they say that beyond it the land is dry, a great desert flanked by the mountain water courses; and beyond the desert is a waste of salt; and beyond that is the country of the Silk People, a land rich and fortunate beyond measure, the most blessed of all lands upon the earth. In the old days, some Sakas went through the pass and settled in the lands on the desert's edge by the mountain rivers, which were suitable for irrigation, but they did not cross the salt waste. Then King Alexander came, pursuing his enemies the Persians across the Oxus as far as the Jaxartes. He subdued our ancestors and founded Eskati upon the river, and he sent scouts out into the valley of Ferghana beyond.

"When the scouts reported that Ferghana was a rich and fertile country, possessed of fine lands and horses and the favor of our Lord the Sun, Alexander determined to add it to his empire, and leaving his generals at Eskati, he rode with some of his army right down the valley. The councillors were afraid of him, and they thought that, anyway, he wouldn't stay long, so they came and made submission to him, bringing him gifts of tiger skins and gold and swearing allegiance. And he rode on down the valley without a spear raised against him, until he came to the Terek River. Then he looked up at the mountains and asked the local nobles what lay beyond.

" 'There is a pass through into the land of Khotan, where our cousins live,' they told him. 'And beyond that?' he asked. And they told him what I told you, what they believed, but added, 'The gods willed that there should be a boundary between this world and the world eastward, and they have made that road impassable; the Silk Road is not for mortals, but for the deathless ones.' 'But I will travel it,' said Alexander, who was always ambitious to exceed every limit set upon mortality, and arrogantly transgressed every boundary he faced. He sent out fresh scouts to investigate the way east. They never returned. After ten days he sent out more; of these, only one came back, three days later, staring mad and raving of poison and burning; he died the next day, without regaining his right mind.

"That night, King Alexander dreamed, and in his dream a woman appeared to him, dressed in black and crowned with fire, and told him that the gods had released into the pass a creature from the Underworld to punish him for his presumption, and that death would seize all those who tried to cross. When he woke, Alexander decided to give up his attempt to go east by that road. Without it to lure him on, he lost all interest in Ferghana. He built an altar to the goddess Nemesis, whom he believed was the woman of his vision, and returned to Eskati, and from there turned south toward India. But from that day to this, no one who has gone up to the Terek Pass has returned alive, and we regard the slopes of the mountain with dread. They're quiet—too quiet. The thing is there still; we know." I rode on a little farther, then added, "I once met a goatherd from East Terek, who went up almost to the pass one autumn after a strayed goat: he said he'd heard a sound that froze his blood, and he turned back, leaving the goat, which he never saw again. He wouldn't say what the sound was; only that it was like nothing earthly."

We rode on up the stream, through the scent of pine and balsam and the shadows of the leaves. "The sound your goatherd heard might have been an avalanche," said Heliokleia.

"People in the Terek Valley know what an avalanche sounds like," I replied.

"But if they're alone in the mountains? Near a place they regard with dread anyway? Ready to be terrified at the least sound?" I looked at her. The sound of an avalanche near the pass would have been reassuring—but it was pointless to say that to Heliokleia. She'd only invent some other explanation. I looked away, angry.

"I'd heard that there was a pass from Ferghana into the East," the queen said after a moment. "There are other passes, through the mountains from Bactria, but they're very mountainous and wild. Sometimes, though, you get white copper from the eastern lands, which they say comes from the Silk Country; and certainly the silk trade goes through India. This world and that aren't separated *so* inflexibly, whatever may be in the Terek Pass. It's a pity the pass is . . . closed: the silk trade is a great source of prosperity to the Indians."

There was no point in arguing. I knew what we in the Terek Valley all knew: that the pass to the east was touched by something unearthly and terrible. We had lived with it all our lives; we had all felt it, brooding there, sometimes, in the white silence of winter, watching the light fade on the distant peak. Whether it was the mysterious Nemesis who'd closed the pass, or as many said, Anahita; whether it had come because of King Alexander, or whether it was some ancient hatred left over from the earth's beginning—it was there. But the queen wouldn't believe me, and the more I said, the more superstitious and barbarous she'd think me. If I'd merely said the pass was unhealthy or infested with tigers she'd have taken my word for it, but about this she thought she knew better than me. So we rode on in silence.

Just after noon we came out from the gorge into an upland meadow. A lake as blue as a butterfly's wing shimmered in the sunshine under a pine-covered peak, and grazing on the thick grass were the horses, mares and foals, dappled and golden bay, knee-deep in the rye grass and purple vetch. Heliokleia drew rein and sat watching for a long moment. A foal red as a fox cub cavorted across the meadow, flicking its little tail and kicking its heels, then darted abruptly to its mother's side. The queen laughed.

"We call that one Frolic," said Adake. "Her mother's Honeycomb. My cousin Banai should be somewhere watching them; she's staying with the herd for the summer . . . here she is! Banai, look, this is the Yavana queen! She's come to stay here while the men fight the Tochari —the Tochari have come, and they're fighting now!"

Banai was a shy young woman about my age, mounted on a massive gelding. She bowed nervously to her royal visitor, murmured an unanswerable question about the war, then sat in paralyzed silence, leaving Adake to point out the individual horses. Heliokleia listened happily, asking no questions, wanting nothing more than the sweetness of the radiant air.

"Let's have lunch," I suggested when all the horses had been named.

We went down to the lakeshore, hobbled the horses, and ate the picnic on an outcrop of flat sun-warmed stone that jutted out into the lake, taking off our boots to trail hot feet in the icy blue-green water. There was fresh bread and new cheese, fresh grapes, still a bit green and sour, honied sesame cakes, and flasks of a pale white wine. An osprey plunged into the water a few yards away, quite unafraid, and flew off again, shaking bright gobbets of water from his feathers, clutching a fish in his claws.

"Which horse do you like best?" I asked.

"What do you mean?" asked Heliokleia.

"Have you decided which horse you want? That was why we came up here, wasn't it?"

"Oh. Of course—that is, not really. I just wanted to come up, and see." She turned to Adake and asked, "Would your mother mind if I used her horse for a few more days?"

"Oh no!" said the girl, as surprised as I was, but recovering quickly. "She'd be pleased; she's been so busy about the farm she hasn't had time to ride it herself, and it needs exercise."

"Then let's leave these horses. All the older mares have foals, and I wouldn't know how to ride the younger animals. Besides, they look so happy here it would be a pity to drag them away."

Adake grunted happily and leaned back against the warm stone of the lakeside, eating a grape. Banai pulled at her arm and drew her off to one side, and began a whispered discussion of small events at the farm.

Heliokleia crossed her legs and trailed her fingers in the lake. I looked at her, sitting there golden and smiling in the sunshine, and I laughed. "I didn't think you were this sort of person at all," I said before I could think better of it.

"What sort?"

"Oh—the sort to ride up just for the ride. I thought you were more like Padmini."

At that, Heliokleia laughed, meeting my eyes openly. Perhaps she'd always done that, but I felt as though it were the first time we'd looked at each other as equals, as two young noblewomen, and not as maid and mistress. "Like Padmini!" she said. "By Apollo, no! I'm the bane of Padmini's life. I'm everything a queen shouldn't be."

If I'd been surprised before, now I was dumbfounded. "What do you mean?" I asked after a pause to recover myself.

She shrugged, looking away. After a moment she began to smile again. "When I was small, I used to be given silver bracelets, little thin ones that jingled together. I used to lose them—they just slipped off my hands when I wasn't paying attention, and I usually wasn't paying attention. I don't know how many I lost in all, but once I lost three in five days. And I dropped things, and I got ink on my fingers at the wrong times, and my hair was always in tangles. Padmini used to say I'd drive her mad. I still won't wear what she thinks I should, and I do things like . . . go riding . . . but she's given up scolding me now; it doesn't do any good." Another mocking smile, but this time I realized that the mockery was directed at herself, and wondered if that had always been the case. "She scolds you instead."

"Well, not exactly scolds . . ." I began, then stopped myself and asked, "Look, why did you choose me to come up here?"

"Who should I have chosen? Inisme? It wouldn't have been much fun with her; she wouldn't have seen the point of it at all. She'd be sitting there with her knees up and her gown pulled straight over her ankles, worrying about the ants." She uncrossed her legs, sat up, and jerked her own gown straight with an imitation of Inisme so primly accurate I couldn't help grinning.

And there were ants, of course. I brushed a few of them aside, frowning again.

"I shouldn't have said that about Inisme," Heliokleia said after a moment. "It wasn't easy for Padmini and Antiochis to come here. They miss their families—Antiochis' youngest girl is only eight, and I know she worries about her, though she won't say so. And Padmini . . . she had to work very hard to find acceptance at my father's court. In Sakala the Indian nobility and the Greeks work side by side, but in Bactra the Greeks look down on the natives, and Padmini suffered for it. She was terrified that in Eskati it would be the same thing again. Inisme helps them. She understands how they like things done and she's willing to defer to them. Being treated with respect makes them feel that their journey was worthwhile. Really I'm very glad to have Inisme."

"But why did you bring me?" I asked.

She sighed. "Because I like you."

"But . . . why?" I asked, bewildered, guiltily remembering her letter.

"Why not?" she replied. After a moment she added, "You don't belong in a palace. People inhabit such different worlds . . . Probably I don't know what I'm talking about, but sometimes I wish I were"— she smiled at me, as though it were already an old joke between us—"a big bold country girl who shoots tigers and speaks her mind."

I thought of growing up in a family where your mother was dead and your brothers murdered your father and each other. Perhaps the only way you could manage in a world like that was learn to look calm and practice detachment. Perhaps the really remarkable thing wasn't the calm, but the fact that underneath it she still wanted to ride up a mountain just to sit in the sun. "You could have waited a day," I said. "To come up here, I mean. You could have rested first."

"We won't have much time here," she replied soberly, with just a hint of passion. "Whatever happens."

We looked at each other for another minute. My suspicions had been wrong, wrong, wrong. There were no black secrets behind the mask—only feelings as commonplace and straightforward as my own.

Sitting there in the sun, liking the woman I served, I felt big with happiness. With all the enthusiasm and ignorance of the young, I burst out, "You may be what a Bactrian queen shouldn't be, but you're exactly the right queen for me. You know, I hate that palace, I was planning to ask my father's permission to leave. But I won't now. You don't like it any more than I do, do you? You just go along with it. And so things are bound to get better, once Padmini and Antiochis go back to Bactra."

Heliokleia stopped smiling and shook her head. It wasn't until afterward that I realized she dreaded the prospect of the ladies' departure. They were her only link with the past; they had worried over her and scolded her in her earliest memories. When they went, something large and solid, something she had braced herself against all her life, dropped from her world and left her staggering. And she was more experienced than me, and knew that their departure wouldn't help her situation. "When they go," she said sadly, "I think you'll see that it makes no difference."

"Oh, I didn't mean things will get better *because* they go. But you're bound to get more authority, as people get used to you and see that you're the kind of queen we want, aren't you? Padmini's sort of queen wouldn't even have learned to ride. Who knows? You may even reconcile the Eskati Yavanas to Saka ways. *I* understand Greek; I know what you said to them before we left. I think the king was wrong to send you off."

"You shouldn't say that," replied Heliokleia dutifully, some more of her pleasure vanishing at the mere thought of the king. "Anyhow, now that I am here, I like it."

At that moment, Banai and Adake exclaimed and began to point into the water. I abandoned all unhappy thoughts of politics and jumped up to see what they were looking at.

There was a trout as long as my forearm sheltering by the rock. "I've seen him here before," Banai told me. "But I've never had a net with me."

"I once caught a trout in a scarf," I said. "My brothers drove it toward me and I just scooped it up. If we caught it now, you could have it for supper."

We took off our trousers, kilted up our skirts, and waded into the

lake, trying to catch it; the queen stood on the rock, shifting from one
side to another to follow the turns of the fish and pointing it out to the
rest of us. Banai and Adake drove the trout toward me, and I clutched
my scarf, which was a fine gauze one, almost as good as a net, waiting.
But at the last moment the fish darted off sideways; I lunged for it and
fell headlong into the water, and the trout disappeared to some quieter
lurking place. The water was cold as ice, and I came up spluttering and
blowing to the sound of the other three laughing. I laughed too, and
climbed out, dripping and goose-pimpled, and lay down on the flat
rock in the sun to dry. It was now the full heat of the day, and the air
over the rock shimmered like an oven. I was still tired from the
journey, and fell asleep while I was still damp.

Heliokleia lay on her back staring through slitted eyes at the hard
blue of the sky, listening to the lake lapping at the stone and the wind
in the grasses. An eagle wandered over the meadow, balancing on air,
feathered hands gripping the wind. After a long while she sat up again.
Adake and Banai were asleep as well. The horses had moved nearer,
chomping the grass noisily, round and sleek with contentment. Heliokleia stood and wandered into the meadow, barefoot, her toes curling about the cool uneven roots of the grass. A butterfly landed on a
flower of vetch and she stooped to study it. Its wings were dusty blue,
marked with orange and gold; it fanned them as it crawled about the
flower. She put out her hand and the insect crawled onto it, and she
straightened, the butterfly's delicate legs hooked to her finger, its pow-
dered wings opening and closing as evenly as breath. She was flooded
suddenly with an immense joy. She wanted to pray, or perhaps meditate, but that was wrong: she wanted nothing, nothing at all; what she
had already was Heaven. She raised her hand and the butterfly fluttered
from it, drifting across the field under the warm sun, lost among the
flowers. She sighed, turning back to the lake, and saw one of the horses
standing very close to her, watching her mildly.

It was a stallion, and she supposed he must be the king of this small
herd. He was unquestionably of the royal breed, and finer and more
splendid than any horse she'd seen before, slim-legged, deep-chested,
with a powerful arched neck. He was white, the glittering, almost-blue
white of new snow, but his eyes were dark and warm. She held out her
hand to him and he came over, moving so lightly he scarcely seemed to

bend the grass. "Rejoice," she said to him in Greek; and he bowed his proud neck and sniffed at her hand. She stroked his head. "I think there's a sesame cake left, if that's what you're hoping for."

He snorted and nuzzled her palm, so she went back to the picnic rock and fetched the sesame cake from the saddlebag. The stallion sniffed it, then condescended to eat it; when the cake was gone he nuzzled her shoulder, and she stroked the smooth straight back. It made her hand tingle. "You're beautiful," she told him, and he bowed his head in gracious assent. "Are you broken to the saddle? If I were better at riding, it's you I'd want. But I think maybe nobody rides you; you're a horse for the gods, aren't you? Well, if they ever come to me and say they want a horse for a sacrifice, I won't give you to them; you're too lovely. There was a mare . . ." The horse nuzzled her shoulder again, and she leaned against him, one arm across the warm, shining back. "There was a mare they killed for my wedding," she whispered in his ear, relieved somehow to be explaining this even to a horse. "And she tried to flee the knife. Who could blame her? What was the point of her dying, why should the Sun be pleased by a dead horse? Surely he'd prefer it alive, running upon the earth where he can see it, than as smoke in the air and some charred bones buried in a pit? We took a terrible and beautiful creature, descended, they say, from the immortals; we destroyed it, and gave the god a carcass: that's our worship. Ah well, I suppose we mortals need to do something to show the gods how we honor them; and no doubt the gods take our gifts in the spirit they were offered. But it's a bad omen, for a victim to struggle, and if you believe omens at all, why twist it and say it applies to a war? If killing the horse means anything more than a mare's death, what it means was meant for the marriage. And somehow or other, I think the omen was a true one. The marriage is a bad marriage, and there's death in it, for someone. I felt it then, and I've felt it growing around me, and I can't get out. Perhaps it will just be my death. That's probably the best way out—better than nothing happening, than just going on. Only sometimes . . . now . . . I feel that there's something here I haven't seen yet, something wonderful I ought to grasp, now, here, while it's so close—only I can't, I don't know how, I don't even understand what it is I'm looking for. But it's so near, and I have so little time!"

She found that her voice had risen, that she was clutching the horse's mane, shaking with the intensity of a longing that had sprung, like the joy, from nowhere. The horse nodded his head as though he had understood—then suddenly turned, leaving her staggering, and galloped off across the meadow. He ran with a lovely flowing gait, skimming the grass as lightly as a swallow, and vanished among the trees at the far side of the field. Heliokleia watched until he was gone, then sat down and rested her head on her knees, blinking at the inexplicable tears. The sun was warm on the back of her neck; a beetle, green and shiny, burrowed in a crack in the rock. After a moment she wriggled her bare toes as the happiness of the morning crept back over her.

In a little while Banai woke and began counting the horses. This woke Adake and me, and we yawned, stretched, put on our boots, saddled the hobbled horses, and got ready to go back to the farm. Banai was rounding up the mares as we left. Heliokleia looked back at them, trying to hold the memory of the animals, grazing peacefully in the high meadows, perfect and joyful and untouched by the misery of the human world. "Where's the stallion?" she asked Adake after a moment.

"We don't keep stallions here, not at this season," the girl replied. "Just mares. The stallions are down in the forest pasture, with the common horses."

"But there was a stallion, a very beautiful white one. He was here earlier. Did he stray from a different pasture?"

Adake stared at her. "A white stallion?"

"Yes. Of the royal breed."

"You must be mistaken. We don't have any white horses here, mares or stallions. It must have been Cloudburst; he's a light gray gelding, and he strays sometimes."

"No, he was white, and a stallion. He came right up to me and ate a sesame cake out of my hand. You were asleep."

Adake stared, then looked away, muttering something. I stared, too. I was frightened. A white stallion, a very beautiful stallion of the royal breed, descended from the horses of Heaven. There were no white royal horses at Eagle Crag: I knew the breed well enough to know that. White is a color especially sacred to the Sun, so all the

white horses of the royal breed are kept near Eskati, on the high
priest's lands, and are never ridden but only used for sacrifices. But if
the horse had eaten from her hand I didn't see how even Heliokleia
could have been mistaken about him. I remembered again the carved
stone on my father's lands, the name of Antimachos masked by the
offerings of flowers. Would Antimachos' descendant see a thing that
might be forbidden to others?

"What's the matter?" asked Heliokleia.

"Nothing," said Adake, sullen with fear and awe. "But we don't
keep stallions here."

There seemed no point in continuing the discussion; it would only
shake the day's fragile happiness. Heliokleia turned the gelding back
down the gorge and we rode home in a silence broken only by the
clopping of the horses' hooves and the calling of the birds returning to
their roosts. When the farm appeared on its crag before them, Heliokleia found herself praying that no one would come to summon her
back to the city, not for a long, long time.

CHAPTER

VIII

We were not at Eagle Crag for long, though perhaps we had a bit more time there than Heliokleia had expected. It was nine or ten days before we even heard the result of the king's encounter with the Tochari. In that we were still better off than most people in the valley, who knew nothing about the whole war, until it was over. For my mother, and for the rest of my own people down the east end of Ferghana, it was a summer of work; they worked dawn to dusk, and whenever the moon was bright as well, trying to get the harvest in without the help of any of the men. "Everyone was saying that the king should have called the drills earlier," my mother told me afterward. "But no, he was too busy with his Yavana alliance, they said. So he calls them as soon as his wedding's over, when it's convenient for *him,* without a thought of the harvest! If he couldn't call them before sheep shearing, he should have waited till the harvest was in. That's what they all said—and what would have become of us, I wonder, if he'd done it?"

Of course, the Tochari had picked the harvest season for their invasion deliberately. They were true nomads in those days, neither planting nor harvesting, living off their sheep and cattle and wandering from place to place for the grazing. They had nothing to lose by attacking at harvest time—but they knew that we were different. They sheared their own sheep, gathered their horsemen, and rode south, scarcely pausing on their way, expecting to find us unprepared. Three tribes of the enemy, this time, more than fifty thousand mounted archers: they darkened the plains like smoke. But Mauakes had, in his own private deliberations to which he admitted no advisor, expected nothing else—and we were ready for them.

The king set out from Eskati on the same day as his wife. The Mountains of Heaven come down toward the Jaxartes in a ridge and the river turns northward beyond it; a tributary of the Jaxartes joins the main stream from the tip of the ridge, closing off the entrance to the valley altogether. The king planned to meet the enemy at a point below the tributary where the Jaxartes is fordable—at least in the summer—reckoning that they would come that way, rather than the more southerly route, which besides being the long way round is over steeper ground. He set off, then, on the same day we did, but took the road that goes up the north bank of the river. It was shortly after noon when he rode out, followed by the lancers and archers, the elephants and the artillery, some twenty thousand men in all. The citizens of Eskati cheered him loudly as he rode from the palace, clapping and stamping their feet. Mauakes only scowled. He had been told of his wife's speech to the populace, and was very angry about it.

"They've never cheered for you like that before," one of the king's officers said to his lord when the city gates were closed behind them.

Mauakes grunted. "It seems my wife told them that they must prove her loyalty for her, since I doubt it and won't give her the chance to prove it herself."

"Well, it seems to have been the right thing to say. I'm glad; I wouldn't like to have the city hostile to us, just at the minute."

Mauakes grunted again. "Yes," he agreed at last, and shut his mouth with a snap.

Itaz, riding just behind, could hear the unspoken addition: "But she had no business telling them something I never told her." He sighed and looked down at his horse's neck, thinking that he should be pleased that his father now seemed as suspicious of the queen as he was of everyone else. But he was not pleased, and he puzzled over it a moment, poking cautiously at his own feelings, like a man poking a stick at a snake to be sure it's dead. Was he grieved at this? Now, with a war about to begin, he still had space to grieve because his father distrusted a woman he himself both loathed and desired? Sheer senseless stupidity! But there it was, he was sorry for the woman—and sorry for his father, too. Mauakes had again outwitted or overmastered everyone: the Tochari, the councillors, and his own family—and he was alone, horribly alone. He rode at the head of a great army, dressed in the gilded armor and crowned helmet of a king who has received the Sun's glory—but he might as well be riding out on his own. Each follower might be an enemy, and there was no one to be relied on.

Had it always been that way? Sifting through memory, Itaz decided no—Mauakes had trusted his first wife; had trusted here and there cousins who were now dead; had even trusted his eldest son for a little while. But year by year the suspicions had grown and the trust had shriveled, and for a long time now, probably, there had been no one whom the king admitted to his secret mind. Itaz remembered his years in Parthia, already becoming dreamlike and remote. If he'd come home years earlier—if he'd been recalled before his brother's death— could he have won his father's trust? Perhaps—and perhaps not. The king might, in a rush of tenderness, have admitted the new queen to his confidence—if she'd been younger, less clever, less cold and unloving —or simply more honest. But he would never rely on the sort of woman she was, a brilliant and beautiful mystery with a heart like a locked box. Though from what Itaz could gather, there had been nothing to object to in her speech to the citizens of Eskati which so annoyed the king.

Itaz looked back at his father. The king sat stiffly on the bay stallion in its gilded armor, scowling thunderously. His officers talked among themselves in whispers, if they talked at all. Under the helmet Mauakes' face was tight and pale, and his eyes flicked quickly over the road ahead. He was not angry, Itaz understood suddenly; the nervous officers thought that, but in reality the king was afraid. It is fearful enough to ride out to meet the enemy when you go joined in the fellowship of your friends; it must be a blind horror to set out alone. On impulse, the young man drove his horse forward to ride beside his father. "How did you know the Tochari would be coming now?" he asked.

Mauakes gave him a sharp, irritated glance. "It's what I would do, if I were a Tochari leader," he said shortly.

Itaz smiled at him. "You never said that to the council."

The king snorted, but with somewhat less anger, encouraged, as his son had hoped he might be, by the memory of his own cleverness. "Of course not. If I tell the councillors what I think will happen, if it happens as I say, they believe it was their own idea, and if it doesn't happen, they remember how I was mistaken. And I could have been wrong."

"You were right all along, though, weren't you?" Itaz said quietly. "And I was wrong. A Parthian alliance wouldn't have helped at all. The Parthians wouldn't have come at harvest time, not with no enemy in sight. And the enemy have given us no time to summon anyone now. I was thinking like a child when I opposed you; we all were. I'm very glad we had a king in Ferghana to plan wisely for us."

The king looked at him in surprise, suspicion, and, finally, a touched, nervous pleasure. "You're young," he commented, smiling with an odd shyness. "You'll learn."

"Let me stay beside you in the battle," Itaz asked him earnestly. "Let me see myself that no harm comes to you."

That brought another look of suspicion, which, in turn, relented slowly. "I thought of sending you off with the queen," Mauakes grunted.

"When I heard you were sending her away, I was afraid you might do that. I was glad you didn't."

"Hmm. If I'd sent my son as well as my wife away, the Yavanas would've been convinced there was no hope. Besides, we need all our heavy cavalry. No, Itaz, you ride with the guardsmen. I expect you to show all the army the courage of our house. But for my part . . ." The king suddenly gave a harsh laugh. "I'll fight this battle riding on an elephant. Show everyone what I think of my alliance."

Itaz stared at his father in surprise, then looked back at the elephants lumbering just behind the royal guard, their great heads showing plain and terrible above the glittering helmets and tossing flags. Our kings are expected to lead their armies, and have always done so on one of the horses of the Sun. This battle, Itaz realized, would be different from any we'd fought before. But he had an unpleasant feeling that his father chose to ride an elephant not to emphasize the alliance, but because it would be safer. He swallowed. "I will do my best to be a credit to our house," he managed to say. Mauakes snorted, and was content.

They reached the ford of the Jaxartes about the middle of the afternoon on the second day after leaving Eskati. The land slopes down steeply on the eastern bank, but the river where it bends has a wide, gravelly bed, dotted with trees and scrub. The west bank rises again into rolling, dry, scrub-covered hills, and the road, which is little more than a dirt track this side of the ford, on the other side stops altogether. If you take the south road from Ferghana it's different: that road goes to Maracanda, to Tarmita and Bactra, settled lands, and it's a good road, partly paved, and set here and there with markers, shrines to the gods, memorials. The north road goes only to the steppes, the nomads' country, a land without cities and pathless as the sky, where a thousand tribes have lived, fought and died and left no mark.

The king was just sending out his scouts to look for the Tochari when there were shouts, and the vanguard pointed excitedly at the Tochari scouts splashing off at full gallop across the river. Mauakes paused, watching as the horsemen galloped up the hill on the far side of the Jaxartes, then continued giving orders to his own scouts as though nothing had happened. The whole army, though, began shifting and whispering, like a flock of birds settling to roost: the battle was almost upon them, and the king had been proved right again.

The king's scouts returned in less than an hour and reported that the main body of the enemy were not far away, traveling in a great mass toward the ford with their wagons in the middle of a cloud of horsemen. By then the king had already arranged his artillery on the slope facing the river, and he ordered his men to water the horses at once, tether them, and make camp, but to keep themselves and their mounts ready to fight at any moment. He himself sat down beside the elephant he had chosen and began ordering the companies both for the camp and for the line of battle. Itaz stood and watched him for a moment, then set to work arranging the affairs of his own men. He had thirty guardsmen and a troop of the standing army: not a large command, for a king's son, but still one that required his attention.

The Tochari arrived at about the time of day the ploughman turns his oxen homeward. One moment the hills beyond the river were empty slopes of bleached grasses, bending in the wind—and the next a line of horsemen showed black along the top, then spilled down toward the river, darkening all the hillside. Mauakes stood, staring at them intently, one hand half-raised, prepared to give the signal to his men to mount. But the cloud of horses stopped halfway down the hill, spreading itself out; the wagons rolled onto the hilltop and circled about. The Tochari too were making camp. It was too late in the day to fight a battle, and they wanted to rest before they attacked. The king sat down again, waiting.

Even before the wagons had stopped moving, the enemy sent a party down to the river to parley. Twelve men rode from the camp down the hill, carrying a bronze bowl altar slung between two horses. The smoke from the sacred fire trailed sullen and gray behind them. At the riverside the riders thrust their spears into the ground, hung up their bowcases, set down the altar, and waited. Mauakes left the elephant and went to his horse, signaling Itaz, Kanit, and some of his officers to follow him.

"What do they want to talk about?" Itaz whispered to his father as they started down the slope. "They can't think we've come here to surrender!"

Mauakes snorted. "They never expected us to be ready for them. They thought they could take what they wanted from us without a battle. Now they want to see if they can get at least some goods without fighting, if we're willing to buy them off."

"Then why are we talking to them? If we attacked now, before they've had time to rest and water their horses . . ."

His father looked at him in forgiving amusement. "We won't attack. We want them to attack us. No, no, let's hear what they have to say for themselves—they may back off altogether this time, though I doubt it."

They continued down the slope to the river in silence; they could hear the rush and gurgle of the water over the stones as they approached. The Tochari on the other side were perfectly still, only a horse occasionally tossing its head or swishing its tail against the flies. The Tochari horses were unarmored, except for breastplates attached by straps to the saddles, but their harness was adorned with gold, and tassels hung from their bridles. The armor of the men was clumsily made, though it was stitched not just with plates of steel and horn, but with bronze and gold as well; one man had plaques of jade decorating his shoulders. Three of the men wore helmets decorated with griffin heads of gold—the lords of the three tribes who had come to attack us. The lowering sun burned at their backs, casting an orange light over the dry hillsides, the stony banks and trembling poplars, and the sleekly rushing water. Mauakes thrust his spear into the gravel by the riverside and rode into the stream, and his followers did the same. As the last spear crunched into the gravel, the Tochari too rode out into the river. On a shoal of sand and gravel in midstream, the two parties met.

Mauakes spoke first. "Greetings, O lords of the Tochari," he said with his blandest smile, "what brings you here to Ferghana?"

The Tochari all speak a language very similar to ours, though one tribe, the Kushans, also speak a different language of their own. They understood the king without difficulty, and looked at each other questioningly, uncertain which of them should speak first. Itaz, sitting motionless on his horse behind his father, the water curling about the black stallion's legs, studied them carefully, trying to guess how they would fight. Looking at the handkerchief-sized tassels that hung from the reins and bridles of the horses, he realized with a shock that they were human scalps, trophies taken from the dead. He remembered his brother Goar, killed by the Tochari the year before, and he set his teeth and clutched the reins hard to make himself sit still.

"We have come to avenge the wrong you did to our brothers last year," said the one with the jade shoulder plaques—he, we learned later, was Kajula, the lord of the Kushan tribe, a very bold, cunning, and violent man. His son Huviska, who now rules the Kushans, is another of the same stamp, and their tribe is beginning to attain preeminence over the others.

"Wrong?" asked Mauakes, still smiling. "Some bandits, renegades, no doubt, and criminals cast out by your people, attacked us last year with a view to some common horse stealing; we punished them, as indeed such creatures ought to be punished. But we have committed no wrong against any people of the steppes, and we wish only to go about our own business in peace."

"You slaughtered thousands of my people!" shouted one of the other Tochari leaders, the lord of the Pasii, the tribe we had met before, his face contorting with rage. "We will avenge it! We will take your famous horses, and whatever else we want, your wives to be our whores and your children to be our slaves!"

"Oh, so you are more bandits!" exclaimed Mauakes, with pretended surprise. "Indeed! Well, you are welcome to come and take what you want—if you're strong enough. But I think you'll find that you manage no better than before. I drink my wine from the skull of your brother, bandit lord, and I shall toast my victory from yours."

Kajula put up a hand to restrain his colleague, who had his dagger half out of its sheath. "We need not fight," he said, matching Mauakes' mild tone. "Our people have lost land, horses, cattle to the violence of the Huns, and as we cannot go without, we must take what we need from others. But still, we need not fight. Look, lords of Ferghana: see the army that faces you on the hill behind us? Twice your number and more again, and all of them skilled and brave. But give us some horses of your royal breed—say, a hundred for each of our tribes—and a few thousand of your other horses, and with them some gifts, and we will go away and leave you to go about your business in peace."

"The royal horses are the sacred gift of the Sun to us and to the king's glory!" exclaimed Kanit hotly. "It is sacrilege to demand them from us."

Mauakes made a soothing gesture and gave the Tochari lords his forgiving look. "We are most willing to give you gifts," he said sweetly, then as they stared in surprise and the beginnings of contempt, went on in the same soft, mild voice, "but they'll be gifts of our own choosing, and I think you'll get no pleasure in receiving them. You're welcome to cross the river, lords of the Tochari. Come, come tonight, come tomorrow, come whenever you wish. You can see that we are ready. Why should we worry over numbers, when you are a ragged troop of bandits, scraps left by the Huns, and we are free men and warriors? Your brothers found that—we piled up their bodies and burned them like vermin, as we shall do to you in your turn. A tiger isn't afraid to face a pack of stinking jackals; nor are we afraid of you —dogs." He turned his horse abruptly and rode back across the river, his attendants following. Itaz looked back and saw the Tochari arguing among themselves, the Pasian lord with his dagger now drawn apparently eager to ride after the Sakas and begin fighting on the spot. He was relieved when he was able to pull his spear from the gravel and hold it securely in his hand.

"They may attack this evening after all," said Kanit to Mauakes, in a worried voice.

"They won't," said Mauakes. "They're not such fools. They've had a day's hard riding and they haven't even watered their horses yet."

"Why did you insult them?" asked Itaz quietly. He knew his father well enough now to be sure that there was a reason.

Mauakes grinned at him, baring the bad teeth. His face had gone pale again, but he seemed pleased with himself. "I wanted to be absolutely certain they attack us promptly. I don't want to keep the army waiting in the hot sun for a day or two. We can't attack, since we can't afford to lose the advantage of defense; we have to wait for the Tochari. But they've come farther than us, and come fast, and they and their horses could use a rest. They won't want it now." He snorted.

Mauakes' followers looked at each other. "Our lord the Sun favored us," said Kanit piously, "when he chose Mauakes as our king." Itaz only looked at his father and grinned with pride.

The two armies spent the night facing each other across the river, bristling with sentries. Both were up before the dawn and watered the horses at the river, silently observing an undeclared truce. Itaz washed his face and hands in the quick water, then stood staring across the shallow stream while the stallion drank, to where the horses of the Tochari drank with bowed heads, wrapped in the pale banners of the dawn mists. After a moment he turned back to the east, where the sky over the mountains held the first saffron smear of dawn, and raised his hands in prayer, commending himself to the keeping of the Wise Lord, Ahura Mazda, the Lord of Infinite Light, who holds those who follow him securely, whether they live or die in him.

When the sun came up, white with the summer heat in a sky as delicate and pink as rose petals, both armies had breakfasted and were drawing themselves into the line of battle. Mauakes, who had addressed his troops the evening before, watched impatiently as the three tribes arranged themselves over the whole of the opposite slope. The king's standing army was already prepared for battle. They stood beside their horses: first the royal guard, with the king and the elephants, then the two thousand others, waiting for his order. All around the lords of the council were falling into place, addressing their own men: the hillside was bright with flags and armor, full of the sound of horses and metal, and the thrumming of bows being tested. The Tochari too were mounted and ready, but their lords began to ride up and down before their own men, encouraging them to the fight; the horses began to prance, the flags tossed, the armor flashed in the light, and the men plucked at their bows to make them sing. Mauakes snorted with impatience, then, at last, turned to the chief of the Yavana engineers, who was waiting beside him. "Begin shooting," he ordered. "Just the arrows, first: use the fire only when the enemy have begun their charge, and have reached the river."

"But they haven't attacked yet," protested Kanit as the Yavana nodded and went off to give the order.

Mauakes shrugged. "We'll only interrupt the speeches."

The Tochari were well out of bow shot, and had thought themselves quite safe. They must have seen the catapults among the army, but none of them had understood the range of the machines, though some had met them in their attacks on the Yavana cities of the Oxus the year before. They went on with the speeches, not even glancing at the machines as they were cranked up, swung into line, and loaded; the Yavanas sighted carefully along the stocks and there was a sharp, stuttering crack! of iron-sheathed catapult arms striking iron heel plates, sixteen almost in one moment. The first volley hit the Tochari like a frost at planting time, devastating because unexpected. Kajula's horse was shot dead under him, and a handful of men in the vanguard were killed; the actual damage was not great, as most of the men working the machines were only half trained, but its effect was stunning. The engineers cranked up the scorpions and fired again. The Tochari milled about in complete confusion, their shouts coming faint and bewildered across the river; they surged forward—then wavered, looking about for orders, for directions everyone was too astonished to give. The catapults fired a third time. My father, who fought in that battle, said it seemed as though we were eagles watching death from the skies, untouched by it; it was nothing like war, he said, nothing like anything anyone had tasted before. For hours, it seemed, the Tochari stood on the hill opposite and the catapults fired on them. Then, at last, the enemy began to swarm down the slope toward the ford. When they were nearing the bank, the Yavanas hurled into them the canisters of fire.

The imagination of the Yavanas holds horrors, to invent such weapons. Burning alive! The first ranks of the charge dissolved into screams, horses rearing, men howling with anguish, alight like torches, hurling themselves down the slope into the water or rolling in the dust: the following ranks trampled them, or twisted about on themselves as their horses bolted from the flames. The catapults adjusted their aim and fired again, hurling more fire, or bolts that struck with a force to pierce armor of steel. And all the while we stood still, not firing an arrow or lifting a single spear. Mauakes watched impassively as the moon, and would not give the signal to attack.

The Tochari might have retreated and regrouped, if it hadn't been for the fire. The naphtha had set the dry grass alight, and the flames were already racing backward through the army of screaming horses toward the camp and the wagons. The cool green water of the river seemed to promise safety. The horses charged on toward it through the catapult volleys and the fire, galloping into the stream, manes or tails trailing flames, stumbling on the rocks; some tried to cross above or below the ford and were swept off their feet by the current. But more pressed down, and the riverbed was wide enough to allow the men to regain control of their mounts, gather themselves up again, and hurl themselves with shrieks and curses onward toward us. When the first-comers reached the near bank, the king finally gave the signal to attack, and the council levies cantered down to meet the enemy, the archers already firing their arrows. The king climbed onto his elephant.

No one in the middle of a battle knows what's happening. When you are fighting for your life, it's hard to think of anything more than the next blow; my father says the most he can ever do is shout to his own men to turn and gallop round to attack again. Battles against the nomad peoples, all the battles he'd seen before, that is, have a lot of galloping, charging an enemy who melts away and reforms again.

Archers gallop toward each other and away, shooting as long as they have arrows; the armored lancers charge, turn, and charge again. It ends when the horses are tired, and may move off and begin again somewhere else next day; usually the casualties aren't too heavy. But this battle was different. My father and brothers rode down with their friends and tenants, and to begin with, it was the usual whirl of men and horses, archers galloping past each other, arrows hissing, the pull of the bow and the shock of the lance—but then the trumpeting of the elephants began and the horses went mad.

The king had arranged everything with the greatest care. The council levies took the first shock of the enemy charge, holding them back for a moment, boxing them in on the riverbank; then the king's army descended on them with the elephants and the sheer weight of the royal guard and threw them terrified back into the river, where they were penned. The trees on the farther bank were still burning, and the horses shied from the fire and the elephants both. The Tochari made a few futile attempts to break back through our ranks, but the horses were rearing and screaming, trampling men under their feet, packed together too closely for the men to shoot. When they spread out they staggered in the deeper water, falling and drowning, or abandoning weapons and swimming for the shore; and all the while our archers rode relays along the bank and fired into them and the lancers made charge after charge into the struggling mass of men and horses in the ford. It was a slaughter, not a battle. They dammed the river with dead and the water was red: miles downstream the Sakaraukai saw the Jaxartes flowing with blood and wondered at the omen.

It was over well before noon. Kajula and the Kushans soon galloped north through the shallows of the river, fleeing the horror, and the rest followed them. Mauakes sent the army after them, on our side of the river, shooting at them across the stream. The Tochari didn't even try the usual maneuver of wheeling back: they galloped till they were clear of the fire, then headed up the bank and away, leaving their wagons to burn and their dead to lie unburied. It was not the first battle we fought with the Tochari, nor was it the last, but it was the greatest. More than eighteen thousand of their number died in the space of two hours—and our own losses amounted to only three hundred. So great was the glory of our king, Mauakes of Ferghana.

Itaz had led his own men in the charges when the enemy were trapped in the ford, and followed them northward on the near side of the river until they galloped off. When it was over and the Tochari had disappeared into the hills on the far side of the Jaxartes, he rode slowly back along the stream. A few bodies lay in shallow water, at first, and there were a few wounded men struggling alone up the hill out of bow shot; the poplars and scrub still smoldered, but the hills were blackened and dead. The fire was still burning, though, out of sight beyond the hilltops, and a curtain of thick black smoke hung motionless in the hot still air. As he drew nearer to the ford, the water was threaded with red, and when he rounded the bend of the river he saw the dam of corpses choking the stream. He stopped his horse a moment, then continued on, staring at the twisted bodies of men and horses, heaped together in the water where they'd died. He followed the pile to the place where the stream entered it, high and muddy, and there he stopped again and covered his face with his hands, shaking, with the taste of tears in his throat. There was no pride and no glory in that massacre for anyone but the king. And in fact, though everyone in the valley is proud of that great victory, I have never met any Saka who can tell of his own part in it with anything but shame. Only the Yavanas who had charge of the artillery are proud. They will tell you how many times their catapult fired in a minute, or how the string snapped and how they fought to replace it, recounting the struggle as though it were a heroic single combat against a valiant man. War is a science for the Yavanas; they write books about it. But they aren't warriors.

Itaz' friend Azilises touched him on the shoulder, and Itaz lowered his hands, struggled to calm himself, then ordered his troop up to see the king and learn what to do next.

Mauakes was standing beside his elephant halfway up the slope, where he'd been that morning, cheerfully shouting congratulations and orders at officers and men, taking an occasional gulp from a sack of wine Kanit had given him. Everyone around him was beginning to laugh, joke, slap each other on the back: the Tochari were defeated! Itaz dismounted and pushed his way through the crowd. Mauakes saw him and beamed, then rushed forward and embraced him, slapping him on the back; he stood a full head shorter than his son, and his hands clanked and jingled on the hot heavy scale armor. The king leaned back on his heels, smiling up into his son's face. "Well, we've done it, eh?" he exclaimed happily. "And you were a credit to our house, Itaz, my dear: there's no better commendation of your courage than that."

Itaz didn't know what to say. Courage? He still felt sick with shame and disgust at the slaughter. It was growing very hot, and he was drenched with sweat under the heavy armor, and he longed, passionately, to be somewhere else—somewhere high among the snows of the mountains, cool and bright and silent, with no one else around. After a moment he realized he should have congratulated his father on the victory; Mauakes loved praise, and deserved it. But already it was too late; already the king was letting go, turning to someone else, shouting another order. And the words of congratulation seemed limp and feeble in his mouth. When the king turned back, Itaz said only, "Let me really show my courage, Father. Let me follow the Tochari."

Mauakes laughed. "I've already got scouts out after them to see where they go, and make sure they keep going there, but why engage them in another battle? We've got more to lose by it than they do. No, no, let them go. But if you want something more to do, take the guardsmen, all of them, and round up any enemy stragglers you can find, them and their horses. We can sell them as slaves, eh? They wanted to make slaves of our wives and children, but they'll end up on the block themselves, ha!"

Most of those round the king laughed excitedly; Itaz bowed and went off to collect the rest of the guardsmen.

It was just after noon, and the air was baking. Everywhere men were sitting down in whatever shade they could find, pulling off helmets and armor, unsaddling sweating horses. They looked warily at the stream, which had to be cleared before they could drink. Itaz and the royal guard picked their way cautiously through, round, and over the corpses and spread out along the far bank, looking for the stragglers. They found many of these downstream, men who had lost their horses and weapons in the river, injured men and broken-legged horses lying groaning by the water's edge. They killed those who were badly hurt, and roped the rest, with bound hands, behind their horses. There were too many for the royal guard to deal with alone, and they had to send back for men from the army to join them.

Men were still clearing the ford when Itaz returned with the prisoners late in the afternoon. Most of the bodies were already piled in a
heap on the blackened earth on the west side of the Jaxartes. Kanit and
some other priests watched as the bodies were stripped. Armor, bows
of horn and daggers of iron; gold arm rings, brooches set with lapis
lazuli and jade; bridles and harness decorated with griffins and eagles in
gold; woolen clothes dyed bright colors and leather ones stitched with
gold: all the things the Tochari had worn proudly, and lost, like the
battle and the world of the living, were piled in heaps to be divided
among the victors. The river pulled impatiently at the remaining
corpses, twisting the burned, hacked trampled limbs in its clearing
blue-green stream.

Itaz led the prisoners to his father, who had left the elephant and
was sitting before his tent counting out tallies of his troops and of the
dead, trying to determine the division of the spoils. He stopped,
though, when Itaz arrived, and watched with satisfaction as the long
line of captives was paraded past him. There were nearly eight hundred
men and some five hundred stray horses.

"Excellent," said the king, smiling genially at his son. "We can sell
them back to their own people at a gold tetradrachm a head—if they'll
stop running long enough, and if they think these dogs are worth it. If
not, we'll sell them to the Bactrians. But not that one." He leaned
forward, his eyes gleaming, and gestured for the procession of prisoners
to stop, then rose and came over to inspect one man. It was the lord of
the Pasian Tochari who'd been so eager to fight, who had drawn his
dagger at the parley. Itaz had noticed him as well, but said nothing
about him, silently hoping that Mauakes wouldn't. The man had fallen
on the bank when his horse was killed under him, hitting his head and
breaking an arm; the fire had swept over him without doing much
more than giving him a few burns on face and hands, but he was dazed
and in pain, scarcely knowing where he was; he looked back at our
king blankly. "The gods must have brought you here," Mauakes said
to him, grinning. "I said I would toast my victory in your skull, and
the Sun, in his justice, has put you in my hands. And so I will fulfill
my promise. Itaz, cut his head off."

Itaz winced. He was never a man to kill a prisoner willingly, and
he had had too much of killing already that day. "He doesn't even

understand you, Father," he protested quietly. "He hit his head. Please, leave him. Let him go back to his tribe and remember this day for the rest of his life."

"I said I would drink from his skull," said Mauakes, raising his voice slightly. "And the gods saw how he urged his people on to attack us, and have punished him. Do as I said, Itaz!"

Itaz drew his short sword, then hesitated again, looking at the prisoner, who still stared blankly in front of him, swaying on his feet. Probably this was the man who had instigated the whole invasion, and he'd clearly been eager to fight: nonetheless, Itaz found his whole being revolting against killing a man captive, stunned, and in pain. "But if you send him back," he said, "he'll be a living witness to your power to all his people. If we kill him, he'll just be another death for his brothers to avenge."

Mauakes looked at Itaz, the satisfaction ebbing from his face. He had thought that his son was finally won over to loyalty; he had felt closer to him than ever before—and now Itaz was contradicting him in front of the whole royal guard, with the sun not yet set on his magnificent victory! Still he was on trial; still no one would trust him. It hurt. "Why are you disobeying me, Itaz?" he asked in the mild voice, only the edge of the explosive anger showing.

"I don't like killing helpless prisoners," Itaz answered at once, meeting his father's eyes honestly. "Please, don't ask me to do it."

The prisoner finally seemed to understand what was happening, and began to look about himself in horror. "Kill him," said Mauakes, quietly and savagely, not looking at the prisoner now, but at his son. "Kill him as I told you to."

Itaz drew a deep, unsteady breath. No one in the army would see the killing as shameful, though they might have applauded a decision to spare the man. Itaz himself could see the rightness of the death—with a part of himself. But another part of himself was sickened by it, sickened by all the deaths that day but most by this. It watched in silence as the prisoner gave a bewildered wail of dismay and tried to stagger off, and Azilises caught his arm, kicked his legs out from under him, and tossed him on the ground before Itaz. The enemy lord caught his broken arm, screamed in pain, then began to whimper in confused anguish. The sound seemed to burn into every nerve; Itaz set his teeth against it, suddenly wanting nothing more than to get the awful business over with, stop the noise and the pain and the misery together. He knelt down on the prisoner's shoulders and, holding the sword with both hands, struck with all his strength: the neck broke with a loud clear snap and the sobbing ended. In the silence, Itaz hacked through the rest of the neck, then stood, picked the head up by the hair, and handed it to his father.

"That's better," said Mauakes, and went back to his chair. He sat down and dropped the head beside his feet without looking at it. "Tie the rest of them up and keep them in the middle of the camp: we'll send a messenger to their friends and see if anyone wants to ransom them."

Too disgusted with himself to speak, Itaz bowed to his father and obeyed in silence.

CHAPTER

IX

The army remained at the ford of the Jaxartes for some days, negotiating ransoms and burying the dead. The night after the battle the Tochari camped on the blackened plain some twelve miles from the ford and two miles from the river. It was a miserable encampment, without water or grazing—or shelter, since they'd lost all their tents and provisions in the burned wagons. Mauakes' messenger, sent to parley with them that night, found the enemy hungry and subdued, huddled beside their horses in circles across the plain. They agreed to ransom their captive fellows, and sent a gold arm ring for each man—they had no coins of any kind—on the day after the battle. As soon as the prisoners joined them they rode off northward as hastily as they could—they'd lost all their spare horses as well, and we kept the beasts we'd captured, so many of them had to ride pillion. But they were willing to suffer that indignity to get away. The Sakaraukai confederacy had begun assembling its men when the Tochari first appeared, and the Tochari were in no mood for another battle with a fresh enemy.

The Sakas did not burn the bodies of the enemy dead, as Mauakes had suggested: after the fire, there was nothing to burn them with. Instead they dug pits in the hillside, tossed in the bodies, a hundred at a time, and covered them with stones. For our own dead they built a cairn, which you can see at the ford to this day, and the horses of those who had fallen were sacrificed to the Sun and buried with them. All in all, the army did not return to Eskati until ten days after they'd left it, though the news had been rushed to the city at once.

The citizens had prepared a welcome for their king when he finally returned. He was showered with flowers the moment he passed the gate, and the streets were again decked with banners. All the way to the palace he was greeted with songs and shouts of triumph, and in the marketplace the chief men of the city presented him with the gift of a gold crown, a thing they'd never done before of their own free will. The Sakas were all astonished, but in no time they had joined the Yavanas in the singing and shouting; the royal guardsmen leapt off their horses and danced in the marketplace with the citizen girls. Eukleides, who'd led the delegation to the queen, also presented the city's gift to the king, and being a Yavana he made a speech then as well. He praised the king, praised the victory—and reminded everyone that what had been achieved had been achieved only through Yavana ingenuity, since without the catapults, the elephants, and the king's Bactrian alliance we would have suffered either crushing losses or defeat. All the Yavanas cheered even more loudly at this, but the Sakas didn't contradict it.

Mauakes only smiled blandly in response and thanked the city for the crown. But when he had reentered the palace and tossed the gold down on the dining table he snorted and said, "Well, I suppose the queen didn't do any harm with her speech." Then he looked up at Itaz, who had followed him silently from the marketplace, and said, "You'd better go and fetch her home. She's at Eagle Crag."

Mauakes had said little to his son since Itaz' insubordination over the prisoner, and Itaz had said nothing to his father. He felt very tired, shamed, and depressed; he dreamed at night of butchering men packed into pens like cattle, and sometimes of killing the white mare at his father's wedding. He found the company even of his friends oppressive, and ached to be alone, to have time to think and pray. "Why me?" he asked now, scowling at the thought of Heliokleia. The only advantage of his misery had been that it seemed to have killed desire.

"You're the captain of her guard, remember? Take your new guardsmen with you, and escort her here quickly: we'll wait till she's back before we hold the victory celebrations. The people will like that. Go on, you can set out now. There's an hour or two of daylight left, and if you hurry you can cover some distance before nightfall."

Itaz stood motionless a moment, then sighed, bowed, and went to obey.

The thirty-four men of the queen's guard, mounted on their chargers, made better time to Eagle Crag than the queen had with her escort of old men. They arrived at the farm early in the afternoon of the third full day after leaving Eskati. The news of the victory at the ford of the Jaxartes had arrived long before, and they were welcomed enthusiastically, but the queen was not there.

"She went up into the mountains this morning, with her lady Tomyris and my daughter Adake," the steward's wife told Itaz. "She'll be back at nightfall, though, and you can leave tomorrow morning."

"My father wanted her to come back quickly," Itaz replied. "He's waiting for her to arrive before he holds the victory celebrations. I'd prefer to start back this afternoon, if we can. Where has she gone? If her ladies can start packing, I'll ride up and fetch her."

After some discussion, Itaz was provided with a boy to guide him, and he set out into the mountains while the rest of the guardsmen helped the escort arrange the chariot for the queen's attendants.

As they set out, Itaz noticed a stone altar beside the gate. Adake had told her mother about the white stallion. If that in itself hadn't been enough to impress the farmworkers, the queen had innocently confirmed all their wondering suspicions by seeing the horse again. Since she gathered from people's awkward silence that the stallion really wasn't hers, she had tried to make the herdswomen capture it to return to its owner: this altar was the only result of that order. Itaz saw that it had been newly decorated with flowers, and fragrant pine smoke was rising from its hollow. "Is that for the victory?" he asked his guide.

The boy, a shy ten-year-old, shook his head. "No, we put that up after the queen arrived, because . . . It's for the god Antimachos."

Itaz looked at it again, sharply this time, remembering the delicate, amused face smiling from the coins, mocking its own declared divinity. So, Heliokleia was encouraging her ancestor's worship? He snorted like his father and rode on in silence.

The boy was Adake's little brother, and he explained that his sister had planned to visit an eagle's eyrie, since the queen had expressed an interest in seeing the nests of the great birds. Itaz nodded and urged his horse forward impatiently, eager to collect the queen and be gone. But the eyrie turned out to be farther away than he'd expected. They rode for nearly two hours, galloping over the high pastures, scrambling over rough tracks up a succession of steep slopes, past the occasional flock of sheep, winding along gullies toward walls of seemingly impassable stone. At last they came to a grove of pines and dark rhododendrons by a mountain stream, and the boy pointed toward a steep crag in the distance. "There are half a dozen eagles nesting there this year," he said: and sure enough, two of them were flapping with heavy wings toward the crag even as he spoke. Itaz nodded impatiently, exasperated. They could never return from there in time to start for Eskati that night; he might just as well have waited with the others for the queen to return in her own time. But having come so far, he was bound to continue.

He was just starting his horse into a trot when he heard, through the noise of the rushing water and the hush of the wind in the pine trees, the sound of women laughing. They stopped. "That's probably them," said the boy. "They must have seen the eagles already and stopped for a drink on the way back. There's a pool that way." He pointed into the thick undergrowth in the direction of the sound.

Itaz nodded and turned his horse in the direction of the sound, then, faced with a wall of dark leaves, he dismounted and led his beast along the bank of the stream.

Bending his head under the low branches of pine, he came suddenly upon a small clearing, where pink heather and wild thyme flowered about the edges of a rocky pool tinted gold with pine needles. Flowing from the pool the stream plunged in a little waterfall down the farther slope, its babble concealing the noise of his approach. Three horses were tethered to the trees beside the pool, and three women were laughing in the sun on the far side. One crouched on the rock, calling encouragement to the others, who stood thigh-deep in the wa-

ter, staring eagerly into it, holding between them a gauze scarf. One of
the women in the water was Heliokleia. Her dark gold hair was loose
in tangles over her shoulders, and her white cotton gown was wet,
clinging to her breasts, kilted clumsily about her waist; her white legs
shone through the water. She was laughing, and she looked scarcely
older than the peasant girl beside her. Itaz stood rock-still, not daring
to breathe. It was not desire that he felt, not then. It was wonder and
astonishment, as though he'd suddenly found a door out of a prison
into the sun, as though the bloodstained waters of the Jaxartes were in
memory transformed to light.

"He's gone that way," shouted the woman on the rocks. (That was
me, though Itaz didn't notice that at the time, having eyes for no one
but the queen.) "No, over there! There! You've got him! Oh, look,
look!"

The two fisherwomen lunged, pulling the scarf between them, and
drew it up quickly: a large trout flapped in its folds. "Got him!"
crowed the peasant girl. "Quick, quick, give me the other end of the
net!"

But the queen was laughing too much to comply, and the fish
flopped itself out of the scarf and back into the water. The girl
groaned; the queen sat down on a rock, laughing even harder, brushing
her hair out of her eyes—and then she saw Itaz.

The laughter vanished at once. Heliokleia leapt to her feet, her
cheeks going red and the blue-green eyes staring into Itaz' own, wide
with alarm. Itaz opened his mouth but could say nothing. He felt his
own face going hot. He couldn't move; he felt like a man in a dream.
The moment seemed to last forever.

"Greetings, Adake!" called Itaz' guide, pushing past him. "The
king's son has come to escort the queen home."

Heliokleia abruptly looked away. She jumped out of the water,
hurriedly pulling down her skirts and looking about for her trousers.
"Please, sir," she said, without looking at Itaz, "I need to dress. Go
back to the path, and I'll join you."

Itaz swallowed, nodded, and turned his horse. Glancing back he
saw the queen pulling her trousers off the branch of a tree, and the
image of her standing, reaching up, seemed to burn itself into his eyes
like the sun, so that even when he turned away he found it stamped

behind everything else he saw. And as soon as she was behind him the desire that had been suspended before struck him violently. He led his horse back to the path and waited, setting his teeth and trying to think of something else, but the image of the queen standing reaching up still dazzled him. He couldn't banish it: his eyes ran again and again down the line of her body from the upraised arm over the curve of breast and thigh to the slim legs, all revealed with appalling clarity by the clinging gown. He tried to think of other women; tried, in desperation, to recall one of the images of the battle that had tortured him all week— and found it all lost, confused, sunk in a hot fog of longing. He closed his eyes, blinking at tears, and leaned his head against his horse. The stallion nuzzled its master's shoulder, comfortingly solid, and he tried wretchedly to pray.

The queen dragged the trousers on hurriedly, pulled off the wet dress and wrung it out, then pulled it back on, crumpled. She was still flushed with an embarrassment that, even then, seemed to me excessive for merely being caught fishing by the king's son—though I knew he didn't like her, and put it down to that. We emerged onto the main path in a few minutes, dressed—though Heliokleia's hair had been fastened so hastily that it left loose wisps about her face. She was leading Shadow, but stopped before she reached Itaz and mounted while Adake and I were still stooped under the rhododendrons. Itaz jumped hurriedly onto his stallion and started down the path in front of her, afraid to look back.

They rode in complete silence for about an hour, Itaz first, then the queen. Itaz was miserably aware that in respect to his father's wife he ought to allow her to ride in front—but he didn't want to ride where he had to look at her, and he pressed his horse, eager to get back to the safety of the escort. Meanwhile, Itaz' guide, who'd been hurried up before, now rode next to his sister and made up for his earlier rushed silence by talking to her and to me nonstop, and the three of us gradually fell behind the silent pair in front. Soon the two of them were disappearing around the bends in the path ahead, and each time they reappeared they were farther away.

At the top of one of the slopes, where the path snaked down through a tangle of sage and mountain laurel to a pasture, Itaz glanced back. Heliokleia was not far behind him, riding stiffly with her head turned away from him: the rest of us were nowhere in sight. Reluctantly, Itaz paused. The queen stopped beside and just behind him, but neither of them looked at the other. They sat for a moment in tense silence, looking down, over the pasture, over the foothills, into the heat shimmer of the valley far below. Then Heliokleia said, suddenly, softly, "Look!"

A horse was cantering across the pasture at the foot of the slope, a white horse running as lightly as a cloud. Itaz caught his breath, watching it: the white of its coat shone like snow crystals against the green grass, and the gait was like water flowing. It crossed the pasture to a wooded stream at the far end, paused, glanced back directly at them—then vanished among the trees. Itaz let out his breath in a sigh. "Is that one of your horses?" he asked the queen, momentarily forgetting his misery in his wonder at the perfect beauty of the sight.

"I don't know," replied Heliokleia. "Everyone here says I don't have any white stallions, that there aren't any at Eagle Crag. But I've seen him a number of times now. Once he ate a sesame cake out of my hand: he's not wild, and he's obviously staying here, even if he has strayed from another herd."

Itaz looked at her a moment in puzzlement. Of course he knew the lineage of the royal horses, and he remembered that it was true. But even at a distance the horse had been unmistakably of the royal breed, and a stallion of the royal breed is not an animal that can be lost casually without anyone noticing. "He must have strayed somehow," he said. "We ought to bring him back to the city with us and return him."

Heliokleia shook her head. "I tried to get someone to do that shortly after I arrived. But no one wanted to look for him. They said that if anyone had lost such a horse, he'd come looking for it. The second time I saw him I ordered the herdswomen to search for him, but they came back and said they couldn't find him. They didn't look very long, though. I suppose they think he's not royal, just one of the common horses, and I'm too inexperienced to know the difference—and nobody else ever seems to be around when I've seen him. They probably think I'm inventing him to make extra work for them—at any rate, they don't want to talk about him at all and don't seem to like it when I mention him. I haven't pushed the matter hard, I . . .

haven't wanted to disturb things. Now you've seen him as well, I—what is it?"

Itaz was staring at her in shocked disbelief. Without replying, he started his horse down the slope, urging it at a reckless speed along the steep path. Reaching the pasture he galloped in the direction the white stallion had taken, down to the stream. But the mysterious horse was nowhere to be seen. Itaz dismounted and walked along the bank: there were no tracks, either leading up to the water or going away from it. But the ground was stony. He stopped, standing perfectly still and listening. The stream ran quick and clear, whispering to itself, and the poplars shivered, green and silver, casting long shadows in the level afternoon sun. Horse hooves thudded in the meadow behind him and he spun round—but it was only Heliokleia riding up. She stopped by the stream and sat for a moment looking at him, motionless in the shifting black and gold of the sunlight through the leaves. "Do you know who he belongs to?" she asked him at last.

Itaz shivered. "Yes. Perhaps." He tossed the reins over his mount's neck and vaulted back into the saddle.

"Who, then? If he's not mine, I ought to return him."

"Don't try and pretend you don't understand!" Itaz shouted furiously. She had cost him fear, misery, tears and sleepless nights; it was unbearable, unbelievable, that she could have caused such pain in innocence, and it was a relief to turn on her with hatred, finding her out in what had to be a lie. "You probably arranged it somehow: you brought the horse in yourself! Just like you had them set up that altar!"

"What altar?" she demanded sharply, her face not moving but her eyes brightening with anger. "I have no idea what you're talking about. Please explain."

"The altar to Antimachos at the farm! You had them garland it, didn't you?"

He saw at once that she hadn't, that she hadn't even known there was such an altar. In fact, she'd been out riding every day since our arrival, hadn't been consulted about the altar, and had never asked about it. "I thought that was to the Sun, to ensure a victory," she said after a moment of bewilderment. "But if it is to Antimachos, it's nothing more than a courtesy. And I don't see what it has to do with returning a strayed horse."

Itaz let out his breath with a hiss. "A white horse, a stallion, a horse so beautiful it stops the heart, a horse that runs so lightly it leaves no tracks—that shouldn't be there, that no one else has seen? You don't understand? You're not stupid, Queen, whatever else you are."

The expression on her face didn't change, and her voice remained low and even, but he could see the anger in the set of her shoulders, the grip of her hands on the reins, the stiffened back. "You've seen him," she replied. "And I don't understand—whatever else I am, sir. What do you mean to say? I would like to know, sir, what you believe I'm guilty of—other than being of the wrong nation and family."

Her eyes met his with a directness to match his own. Again he felt the bewildering shock of understanding for her, and knew that she wasn't merely angry, but hurt, and afraid. She was alone in an alien world, distrusted by everyone for no fault of her own, and faced with a sudden accusation she couldn't understand. He looked away. Everything was confusion again: he didn't even have the satisfaction of hating her. "Maybe you wouldn't think of it," he admitted helplessly. "You're a foreigner. You're a Buddhist. Do you even believe in the gods?" He looked back, met the angry, injured eyes and went on, "But you must be able to guess what people here think you've seen."

She stared at him, frowning. "Do you mean that they think the horse is . . . is one of the horses of the Sun? That's why they won't talk about it?"

He nodded.

She shook her head. "But that's absurd." After a moment the look of amusement came over her face. "I fed him a sesame cake."

Itaz turned his mount wearily back toward the path. "So?"

"What would an immortal want with sesame cakes?"

"What do the gods want with sacrifices?"

"I don't believe the gods do want sacrifices," she replied unexpectedly. "A god who needed mere mortals to support him wouldn't be divine or worth worshipping. God, if he is truly god, lacks nothing, but is perfect, sufficient in himself. Why should we think we can give anything to a god who created the things we destroy in his honor?"

Itaz stopped his horse again, looking at her: she looked back, challengingly. "Do you believe the gods don't care about us?" he demanded. "That it's nothing to them whether we honor them or not?"

She shrugged. "I don't know. I suppose we ought to honor the gods. If we don't, we may try to take their place. But it's blasphemous to say the gods need honor, or anything else, from creatures like us."

"Blasphemous? Isn't it worse to say they don't care? And as for trying to take the place of God, your great-grandfather did just that!"

"That was poetry," she said, though a bit shamefacedly. "Kings are like gods. They rule the worlds we inhabit, and make the laws we live by; it can be easier for people to understand what a king is if they think of the gods. Antimachos was the first king of Ferghana, and he had to explain that to his people in a way they could understand. I don't suppose the real gods minded, any more than a king minds the boy kings of children's games."

"You talk as though everything in this world had no more value than that!" exclaimed Itaz.

"Well, does it?"

"Of course! The world's no toy, and it matters what we do in it, to us and to God! The earth is a battlefield, not a . . ." He stopped himself. It was senseless to get into a religious argument with her; he might say things impossible either to live with afterward or retract.

But, "Go on," said the queen, still watching him. "Tell me what it is you believe. We'll have to work together now; I might as well know."

Itaz took a deep breath. He started his horse back toward the path again and rode staring straight ahead, trying to master the confusion of his soul. He felt strangely frightened of trying to explain his beliefs to Heliokleia, to show the demon of lust the secrets of his defense against it. It was like stripping off armor on a battlefield, and standing naked to the spears. And yet he wanted to make her understand. "At the beginning of existence," he said at last, "there were two spirits. Some say they were the two sons of Zurvan, the Lord of Infinite Time and Space. And the Holy One, whom we call the Wise Lord, Ahura Mazda, saw that the universe was empty, without limits and without form, and from himself he made the world, out of the love of what is, so that the universe should be full of delight. But when the other spirit saw what his brother had done, he was filled with jealousy, and from jealousy created evil, which fell on his brother's world like a disease, invading and wounding it, creating grief and suffering where before there was only joy. And the Holy One said to the one who is evil, 'Neither our thoughts, nor our wills, nor our choices, nor our words, nor our deeds, nor yet our souls agree.' And since that hour the two have been locked in a battle for possession of the created universe, Ahura Mazda to restore it to joy, and Angra Mainyu to ruin it forever. All things on earth belong to one side or the other, and humanity, which has allegiance to both, must ultimately choose between them. The world is both good and evil, both a house of joy and a miserable prison; the choices we make here are part of a struggle fought in heaven, and when we worship Ahura Mazda—and I believe we can worship him as the Sun, which is his shadow—we choose joy, and delight God, who loves us like a father."

Heliokleia rode in silence for a long time; glancing sideways he caught her profile, the eyes lowered in thought, her lower lip caught between her teeth. "It is not as ridiculous as I had thought," she said at last. "But I could never believe it."

"Why not? Because you believe all the world is evil? Or because you believe the gods aren't interested in mortals at all?"

"I don't believe the world is evil—only that it's futile, and full of suffering. Evil, good—evil to whom, and good for what? A man who was about to hang himself from a tree found a treasure hidden among its roots: he left the rope and took the treasure home, rejoicing. But the man who had left the treasure, returning and not finding it, took the rope and hanged himself. The good of one was the other's evil."

"No! You're playing the usual Yavana tricks with words. Good was life, for either of them; evil was needing money so badly they wanted to die. In a good world there would be no money, and nobody would ever die for lack of it."

"Even so . . . is it meaningful to talk about good and evil, in the world? My philosophy loves goodness. We who follow it are required to struggle for equity and charity, and to avoid every kind of wrong-doing—but is the *world* good and evil? If a man steps on a snake, and it bites him, is the snake evil? Oh, I know, you say all snakes are evil—but suppose the man were a robber, about to murder an innocent traveler? Or say the man tripped over a rock, and fell, and hit his head, and died: is the rock evil? That same rock might be used to build a temple to worship the gods: is it still evil? Only choice knows virtue and vice, justice and wrongdoing. If there is such a thing as natural evil, it is bound up so closely to good that you could not have one without the other."

"That's more Yavana word games," said Itaz impatiently. "Everyone knows what evil is. Starvation is evil; pestilence, disaster and cruelty are evil; all the suffering and death of the innocent are evil."

"And war?"

"Yes!" Itaz said fiercely, remembering again the horror at the ford. "Yes, war is evil. A necessary evil, sometimes, to overcome a greater evil, but an evil for all that."

"If you can only fight evil by evil, how do you expect to win? Isn't it better to renounce evil, even if you have to renounce some good as well?"

"You cannot renounce good! How can anyone back away from what's good, pure, and joyous, just to escape the risk of suffering? It would be like a coward running away from a battle!"

"More like finding release, like a slave that's been tortured and rewarded in turns, without reason, by a capricious master."

"There's more to the world than that!" Itaz cried, looking at her directly. "There must have been a time when you were happy, when you felt that you stood with one hand touching Heaven. Think of that, and then say if you think the world is futile, and good meaningless."

Heliokleia flushed. "There was a moment . . . but most of the times I've felt joy it's been in meditation, in the quest for release. If you had looked for release yourself, seen the beauty of it, you wouldn't talk this way about it."

"Beauty in that? In release from life—into what?"

"I don't know. Nirvana. Your Infinite Time and Space, perhaps."

"It sounds like death, to me. It's not . . . when I came up to that pool, when you were fishing, in the sunlight, laughing—how can you say that death, or infinity, or nirvana, would be better than that? There was nothing so lovely in all the world. Even looking at you made my blood sing for joy."

She stopped, staring at him doubtfully. The setting sun painted her cheeks with gold and gilded the crease lines in the crumpled gown. Slowly as in a dream he reached out and touched her hand. "Heliokleia," he whispered. It was the first time he had said her name.

The hand moved from under his, rose and rested against her cheek; she stared at him for a long moment, in doubt, in bewilderment, in longing. Then she shook her head and touched the horse to a trot. "I don't understand what you mean," she shouted back over her shoulder, in a tone that meant she didn't want to understand.

Itaz stayed where he was for a moment, furious with himself and elated. He had been right to fear a discussion of religion; it had made him forget himself and forget the danger the queen presented. At the same time, his blood began to sing again. The hand he had touched had rested treasured against her cheek: she felt something too. Not for his father. For him.

He spurred his horse and caught up with her. "We ought to hurry," he told her. "The others must have overtaken us while we were down at the stream, and we'll have to ride hard to catch them up again."

Heliokleia was glad that the summons back to Eskati had come too late for her to depart that day: she wanted time to give up her happiness gently. That night she lay awake on the straw bed for a long time, looking at the moonlight that slid through the eaves above her, trying to remember everything she had loved at Eagle Crag—the dance of the dust; the butterfly; the horses grazing; the fish in the pool; the white horse running. She didn't think of the horse as I would have, with awe at a sign of the god's favor, but remembered it simply for its beauty and freedom. Perhaps I was unfair to the Yavanas earlier: most of them aren't impious—merely skeptical and careful. But whatever the reason, they don't believe in miracles easily. You can't find books of rules about miracles, and investigations of them don't explain much, so the Yavanas treat them like hornets, and keep their distance from them.

But if the memory of the horse didn't remind her of the gods, it did remind her of Itaz, and the calm, melancholy recounting of memories became something much hotter and more confused. She realized, first, that she hadn't asked him about the battle or about his father's health. Of course, they'd had news of both when the Tochari were defeated—but still, she should have asked. She twisted in her bed: how callous she was! How despicable!

Then, despite fierce efforts to forget or dismiss the memory, she thought again of how he had spoken to her, passionately defending the loveliness of the world and treating her as an example of it; how he had touched her hand and whispered her name; his eyes, warm and alive, fixed on her. The starved girl inside the queen, who longed simply and straightforwardly for happiness, for kindness, for love, glowed again. She told herself the passion was girlish, weak, contemptible, but it remained truer and sweeter than anything that had touched her before—and she was torn in two. All her certainty about herself and what she did, her confidence in her cold philosophy, suddenly vanished. Like a landscape in a mist, the familiar world became unknown, and she wandered in it, groping for landmarks. She twisted about again, and again put the hand to her cheek, her heart beating in her throat. She had struggled before to discipline her mind; she hadn't thought of Itaz since the Tochari first appeared, and she'd believed that she'd succeeded. She saw now how desperately she had failed, and she was terrified.

> "Dione's daughter, Love," says the Yavana poet,
> "Why should you be insatiate of evil?
>   Devising always loves that stray, deceits
>   and charms that crash the strongest house in blood?
>   If you were kind, you'd be in every way
>   by nature sweetest of the gods to men."

Everyone has known desire, of course, and often we use the word *love* to cover that—but true love that comes suddenly is a terrible divinity, not a game we play for pleasure. All the things we thought we were, all that we believed in, everything we expected for ourselves —it can all be stripped away, leaving us strangers to ourselves, empty and helpless. I remember standing one morning, much, much later, in my father's house, and my father saying that he would speak to the family of a certain young man whose name I had confided to him the previous evening: I remember I seemed to myself like a jug in the kiln, both empty and burning, and with no more power over myself than a

pot in the potter's hands. I was terrified. And yet that was a calm and
orderly business: two families arranging the marriage of their children,
with smiles and compliments and a businesslike discussion of the
dowry. To be helplessly caught in a love that can go nowhere without
calamity and evil—what anguish and terror that must be!

Heliokleia stopped pressing her hand to her cheek and bit it instead, bit it till she tasted blood, as though she could break off the link
between herself and her stepson by punishing the place where he had
touched her. Then she rolled over onto her stomach and linked her
arms behind her head, trying to detach herself. She thought of her
brother's kingdom, of the Tochari, of the importance of the alliance;
she thought of the citizens of Eskati, their reliance on her, the speech
she had made to them. She thought of her husband, waiting for her in
the city. That was a mistake. The humiliation and shame she had felt at
his lovemaking before, when her body was closed and asleep, seemed a
thousand times more horrible now. And she must return to it. There
was no escape; she must live with it for the rest of her life. She began
to weep helplessly and quietly into the straw, shaking with dread, with
the rebellion of the flesh against what the will demanded.

After a long time, she heard a stirring in the bed next to her, and
then Padmini's voice said, "Child?"

Heliokleia sat up, trying to cram the sobs back into her mouth
with clenched hands. "I don't want to go back, Padmini," she whispered helplessly. "I don't want to; I hate him."

I was sleeping just along the loft from them, and I woke up,
hearing the Greek whispers. I lay very still. I felt it was something I
shouldn't hear, and never admitted afterward I had heard, but I lay
there listening intently and unwillingly in the darkness.

"Hush," said Padmini gently, and put her arms about her mistress.

"But I hate him!" said Heliokleia, still in a desperate whisper,
pressing her head against Padmini's shoulder like a young child. "I
can't, I can't go back to it."

"Hush! What are you saying? You don't mean to stay here?"

"How could I? What reason could I give? No, I know, I know, I
must go. Oh, by Anahita, I wish I were dead!"

"Hush! You're tired and you're talking wildly. He is a king, and,
for a barbarian, a great king. In most ways he's behaved quite properly

toward you—he's given you lands and attendants, treated you publicly with respect, and he hasn't expected you to share his house with a horde of mistresses. Many queens endure far worse, even among the Greeks. I'm sure you have too much sense to indulge yourself with tears and passionate talk for long. You have a position to uphold."

Heliokleia nodded, but she was still shaking with revulsion; Padmini could feel the shudders, deep and irregular, trembling against her own side. She stroked the tangled hair. "There's another matter," she whispered. "I meant to discuss it with you later, after we'd returned to Farthest, but I might as well tell you now. It's been clear, to me and Antiochis at least, that in some ways your husband treats you in a fashion that is not suited to your rank. That is something we must deal with. You are the daughter of Eukratides, the niece of Menander, the descendant of Alexander the Great. You have a right to respect, in private as well as in public, and if you feel such a horror of your husband that you wish you were dead, he ought to be told flatly to treat you better. If you consent, I will go to him with you when we return, and I will explain to him what is due to a princess descended from so many kings."

"Padmini!" whispered Heliokleia, pulling away from her attendant, shocked. "He . . . he hates to be contradicted. Even his son . . . the very least he'd do would be send you back to Bactra in disgrace!"

"That's the very most he could do," Padmini corrected her. "I'm not *his* servant. And if he does that, what harm does it do to me? The disgrace would be his, as soon as I told your brother why I was sent off. Child, I've been considering this since we left the city, and I think it would be best."

Heliokleia peered at her doubtfully through the darkness. She was astonished. Despite Padmini's sharp matter-of-fact tone, it is no small thing for a lady-in-waiting to lecture a king on his duty to his wife. Padmini was offering to risk her position, and possibly even her life. The queen was at once deeply ashamed of her own passivity—and deeply touched. "What about Antiochis?" she asked.

They both glanced to where Antiochis lay, in a bed the other side of her mistress, sound asleep and snoring softly. Padmini sniffed. "We talked the matter over, while you were off on all this riding, and we're both agreed that something must be done—though you know Antiochis; she lacks forcefulness, she's afraid to speak her mind. But she agrees with me, and has said that she'll stand by me if I do the talking. It's most improper for a king to use his queen like a concubine, keeping her to warm his bed all night and every night, overriding her command of her own household, refusing her access to his, directing her to come here and go there as he pleases, expecting her to adopt at once the scandalous customs of his own people, then sending her off on long journeys with an escort of disreputable cripples to live in squalor on the other side of his kingdom, because of stupid, ugly, and groundless suspicions. We came with you from Bactra to see you honorably established; it's our responsibility to ensure that no one treats you with disrespect."

"Oh, Padmini . . ." Heliokleia stared at her for a long minute, then bowed her head in shame. "I am a coward," she said. "I should either have borne it quietly or defended myself."

"Don't be a fool," snapped Padmini. "No well-brought-up virgin could be expected to deal with this kind of problem. And you, child, have always been too unworldly for your own good, too set on this monastic self-denial. That is why you need attendants of rank and experience. Trust us. Of course, the king may behave more properly anyway, now that the savages have been defeated; men are often impossible during a war. We'll wait for a while once we're back in the city, and see. But if matters are no better, Antiochis and I will take them in hand. Now, darling, lie down and go to sleep. We have another of these miserable journeys tomorrow."

Heliokleia lay down, and heard the rustle of the straw as Padmini did the same. The queen lay on her back again, staring upward; the moon had set now, and the loft was dark. She couldn't sleep. She had little confidence that Padmini would be able to achieve anything, but she was touched, and deeply comforted, by her loyalty. She thought again of her husband, with resigned misery now, then again remembered Itaz. She sat up. Padmini was asleep now, and everything was profoundly still. Heliokleia crossed her legs and struggled again for the abandonment of thirst and the destruction of desire. When I fell back into sleep she was still sitting there, motionless and intent in meditation.

She can't have slept more than an hour that night, and was worn and quiet with exhaustion when we set out for the city, early next morning. She did not speak to Itaz at all. He seemed perfectly happy with that, and spent all his time urging the party to go faster.

This time the journey took three and a half days, though a messenger sent ahead on the third day announced our impending arrival to the king the night before we reached the city. The queen spent most of the journey riding beside her ladies' chariot, beside me, or talking to old Palak. Only when we were in sight of the city did she take a place at the front of the party, next to Itaz—and then each sat staring straight ahead, carefully avoiding the sight of the other.

As we rode toward the east gate, however, we saw that the king had decided to make our arrival part of the celebrations of his victory. The gate stood open, hung with banners, and the walls were lined with people who cheered loudly as we approached. Itaz hunched his shoulders unhappily. "Merciful Anahita!" he muttered. "Another parade! I wish he'd at least let us rest first."

Heliokleia relaxed sufficiently to glance over to him and take in the look of tense misery that showed, transparent as all his feelings, on his face. "I thought you were eager to celebrate this victory," she said. "You seemed in such a hurry."

"I wanted the journey to be quick," he told her. "But as for celebrations . . . well, it wasn't a joyful victory, not for me."

She frowned. "I was told that it was a great victory, and a very cheap one, in lives lost."

"Oh, it was. Yes." His eyes finally stopped sliding off her, as though she were made of glass, and fixed on her face. "But it was . . . different, not like the kind of battle we're used to. There wasn't any real fighting. You didn't need strength, hardly needed skill, and could manage without courage; there was no glory. The enemy . . . we killed thousands of them. For them it was not cheap."

She was bewildered. The Yavanas have athletic games to show off strength and skill: war for them is a serious business, to be won at all costs, not a sport; they hope for success, not glory. I said before that they're not real warriors. But I suppose that for them, the penalty of loss has always been death or enslavement. For all the time we've been a settled people, our warriors still remember the ways of the steppes:

lose a war there, and you go somewhere else. "If the enemy losses were high, doesn't that make it more worth celebrating?" Heliokleia asked Itaz. "Surely they'll be less likely to come back now."

"I suppose so," he muttered, hunching his shoulders again—but she could see that both the question and the answer were nothing to do with what troubled him about the battle, and the fact that she asked such a question had put her outside some boundary between honor and contempt. She stared at him, still confused, and with a shade of anger. Itaz looked back, then went on, suddenly, "My father wanted me to execute a prisoner afterward. For me, the whole battle was like that. There was no doubt that the man had been eager to attack us, but he was injured and helpless, and I pitied him, I didn't want to kill him. It's good that I'm not king: I would have tried to meet the Tochari in fair fight, and we would have lost."

Mercy was a thing she understood much better than glory. "Did you execute the prisoner?" asked Heliokleia after a silence.

"Yes. In the end. But I was reluctant. My father's angry with me about it."

"He's angry with you? Why? Surely, if you did as he said . . . ."

"I should have obeyed him with delight!" Itaz said vehemently, suddenly angry, detesting her and the part of himself that agreed with what she said. "He'd sworn that he'd drink to his victory from the man's skull; he'd given the Tochari a defeat they'll remember for a lifetime; he was proved right in everything he'd done; the gods themselves brought the man there as a prisoner—and when he asked me to chop the fellow's head off, I dragged my feet and made excuses. He's right to be angry! I was wrong; I should have been glad to do anything he asked me to."

Heliokleia looked away and was silent for a few minutes. They rode up to the gate, and a choir of citizen girls and boys on the ramparts began to sing an ode, welcoming the queen to the victorious city. The queen raised her hand and waved acknowledgment rather absently. "It seems to me," she told Itaz, when they were inside the wall, speaking so softly that he had to strain to hear her over the shouts and the singing, "that he's entitled to obedience, but delight is something no one can demand by right."

Itaz shook his head angrily. "What's the use of doing anything by form, if the heart's not in it? Nobody likes obedience without love."

She winced. Mauakes certainly, bitterly, disliked obedience without love. "Do you love him?"

"Yes, of course!" said Itaz angrily. He remembered again the scene over the prisoner, and this time saw, as he hadn't at the time, the pain beneath the rage in his father's eyes. He felt a stab of rueful affection, bewildering pity and protectiveness toward a man who had always been victorious and powerful. "He's my father," he added defensively.

"Does one love someone just because he's a father? I scarcely knew my father. I always tried to be dutiful and obedient to his wishes, but if I'd said I loved him, it would have been a lie. Should I say that I shouldn't have been dutiful, because I didn't love?"

"This is more of your Yavana cleverness," Itaz said angrily. "More tricks with words. I don't know why I mentioned the matter to you in the first place. No Yavana ever put their whole heart into honor."

Heliokleia tilted her head back and looked at him disdainfully, not admitting to herself that she was hurt. "I spoke as I did because it seemed to me you had more cause to be angry than he did. You obeyed; he was angry only because you wanted to be merciful. I am a Yavana and a Buddhist, of course, ignorant how to do good, but we believe that it is meritorious to be merciful, and that killing is evil even when it's necessary . . . but maybe your faith views things differently." She snapped her head away and waved at the shouting crowds. Itaz could think of nothing more to say, and rode with her into the marketplace in silent anger and resentment.

The king was standing before the temple of Zeus Helios, dressed in his gilded armor, with all the priests and priestesses of the Sun flanking the altar behind him. The royal guardsman had formed an aisle through the dense crowd, and the queen's party crossed the square slowly, the guardsmen falling in behind them and leaving a seamless carpet of faces behind. They stopped before the terrace. Heliokleia was painfully aware of all the eyes upon her. She was wearing only the white cotton riding clothes, dusty from the journey, with a wide-brimmed hat and no jewels. Mauakes on the terrace blazed with gold. She wished he'd sent a message, telling her what he had planned so that she could prepare for it.

Itaz jumped off his stallion and offered his hand to help her down from her mare. Heliokleia ignored the hand and slipped off by herself; I dismounted and held her horse and my own. The queen took a deep breath, her head turned away from Itaz and Mauakes both, trying, as always, for detachment—then climbed resolutely up onto the terrace and bowed to the king. Mauakes caught her hands and kissed them, and the people cheered. She looked up into his face: it was unchanged. Rounded, clipped gray beard, bad teeth, thick neck disappearing into the gilded scale armor; unreadable brown eyes. He smiled at her blandly and kissed her again, on the mouth this time. The people cheered even more loudly at that.

"Welcome home, O Queen," said Mauakes loudly so that everyone could hear him. "You have indeed returned to celebrate my victory, as you promised." He gestured to Kanit, and the priest came over, carrying the purple cloak and the gold crown, the city's gifts. Mauakes set the cloak about her shoulders; she took off her hat and he placed the crown on her head. She saw herself a moment in the cheers of the people: a disheveled traveler transformed by their ruler back into a queen. No words were needed: he had showed the citizens again that what she was, was his gift, and done it in a way they liked. With the part of her mind that had studied power, she admired it. But the woolen cloak was suffocatingly hot, and the crown slipped forward uncomfortably over the Saka braid. "Perhaps you'd care to address the people again?" Mauakes asked, leading her to the edge of the terrace.

She could not tell whether this was a barbed reproof for what she'd said the last time she'd addressed the people, or whether it was an honest invitation. Either way, it would probably offend him if she refused. "If you wish me to, my lord," she said hesitantly. He smiled and stood back, inviting her words with a wave of his hand.

She stared out at the carpet of faces before her. The marketplace was packed, and people hung out of the windows of all the surrounding buildings, and stood crouched on the pedestals of the statues. Much of the army and all the citizens were there, jammed sweating together in the hot sun, watching her—happily, because this was victory, release from fear and hope for the future. "People of the Farthest Alexandria," she began, in Greek—then paused. She felt suddenly faint and ill. She straightened her back, set her shoulders, and went on, "I promised to return to celebrate your victory, and, by the gods' will, I have!" There was a cheer. "Let us first praise the immortal gods, who have granted us safety from our enemies; and after them, let us praise the king, our benefactor, whose wisdom has averted calamity. For it was because of his foresight that the enemy did not find us unprepared, and have suffered such a defeat that they will think well before they ever ride out against Ferghana again. So must we all agree, Sakas and Greeks together—but because I am a Greek, I will say more: I will praise the king for his wisdom in choosing to ally himself and his nation with us!" Another rousing cheer, mixed with laughter. "Yes, and I thank the king, too, for giving us the chance to prove ourselves to him. For you have truly proved yourselves now, citizens of Farthest: proved yourselves as brave and loyal as those who are the king's subjects by birth, restoring the honor of the Greeks to the level of their merit, and I rejoice with you greatly." There was a perfect thunder of cheers at this, with a rhythmic clapping of hands and stamping of feet, and it was some minutes before the queen could continue. When the people had finally quietened enough for her to make herself heard, she went on, in Sakan, "And you, Sakas of Ferghana, I rejoice also with you, and praise your boldness and loyal strength, that barred the river with dead and threw your enemies back into the wilderness. The minstrels will sing of your courage to your grandchildren's children, and you can be glad! Saka and Yavana are joined now in joy, joined in peace by this victory. And I pray to the gods that our rejoicing may last, and good fortune bless our kingdom for generations to come. Praise the gods, O people of Ferghana!"

They praised the gods, cheering, stamping, and raising the victory shout with the Saka yell and the Greek paean together. Mauakes smiled and took his wife's arm. "Why is it," he asked, murmuring the question into her ear, "that all you Yavanas are so clever with words? But you study speaking, don't you. More than you study war. Well done, well done."

The king had arranged a sacrifice of horses to the Sun to follow the welcome to his wife, and Heliokleia stood stiffly in the hot cloak, watching while Kanit and the other priests and priestesses killed one white colt and one white filly of the royal breed, and a dozen of the Tochari horses captured in battle. After this there was, as usual, a feast

—in the market square for the people, and in the palace courtyard for the nobles. I was able to get back on Terek and lead Shadow off to the royal stables, and rest and change before going down to the feast. Heliokleia went up the steps with her husband directly to the palace courtyard, where she took her now-usual place beside her husband and sat through the festivities, smiling grimly. At the height of the feast the king's servants brought in the king's newest drinking cup, now cased in embossed leather and lined with gold, and he toasted his victory, as he'd promised, from the skull of his enemy. He gulped the wine from it greedily, and licked the drops from his beard with a thick wet tongue. Heliokleia remembered Itaz and his reluctance to kill an injured prisoner, and felt so sick she could scarcely swallow the forced sip of her own wine from the simple glass goblet.

By the end of the day her head ached savagely and she felt very ill. She managed to excuse herself at the end of the feast, when the men began the heavy drinking, and went upstairs to her own room. She dropped the cloak onto the floor and collapsed across the couch in the dusty riding gear. The crown dropped onto the floor, falling with a soft clunk to the tiles.

The queen lay motionless for a long time. The lamp was lit, but none of the attendants were present: Padmini and Antiochis, exhausted by the journey, had gone up some time before and were already asleep in the adjoining room, and Inisme and I were in our own room washing. We heard the queen come in, but it had been agreed that Armaiti and Jahika could look after her. Heliokleia wanted to sleep; but felt too ill, hot, and dirty; she wanted to bathe, but felt too exhausted to move. After a while, Armaiti did appear and asked her if she wanted anything.

Heliokleia pulled herself onto her elbows and asked for a basin of warm water. That was the expected answer, of course; the slaves had been heating it in the kitchens, and they at once fetched it in. Heliokleia sat up and greeted them wearily, then stood for Armaiti to help her off with the stained and crumpled white cotton shift and trousers. When the bath was ready, Heliokleia washed herself slowly. The water was deliciously cool, scented with spikenard; it seemed to rinse away the sticky sickness that had clung to her from the moment she entered the city, delicately peeling off the feast's spilt wine, the blood of the dead horses, her husband's touch. Clean at last, she stood naked by the bed, combing her hair, feeling the coolness of the night air against her skin. The headache, still present, was fading into a shadow crouched upon her shoulders. She had been indulgent and selfish, she thought, looking at the elegance and space around her, the slaves clearing up the bath water, the clean sheets. Most women endured far more misery than she did, and bore it quietly. So must she.

There was another knock on the door, and Jahika came in. "My lady," she said with just a shade of apology, "the king is going to bed now, and asks you to come to him."

Heliokleia's resolution vanished in a flood of revulsion. She was only just clean—how could she plunge back into the filth at once? She dropped the comb, then picked it up again. Not tonight, she thought, with a rising sense of panic. She was too tired. Wasn't that reason enough? It had been a long journey; surely even Mauakes would understand that? "T-tell the king," she stammered, "that I'm not well, and very tired from my journey, and beg him to excuse me."

Jahika accepted that without comment, bowed, and went out. In a minute, however, she was back. "The king commands you to come, my lady," she said—smiling, as though the king's insistence were charming. She was a hot-blooded creature.

A Saka wife might still have refused such a command; women here regard it as their choice, whether to sleep with a man or not. But all Greek husbands, and not just kings, have the right to their wives' bodies whenever they wish, and it didn't occur to Heliokleia to disobey. She bowed her head, then looked about for something to wear going down the stairs. Armaiti handed her the purple cloak, which had been picked up and hung across the clothes chest. Appropriate. The queen pulled it over her head and, holding it fastened with a bent arm, went slowly down to her husband's bedroom.

CHAPTER

X

Mauakes was sitting naked on the bed, half-drunk and irritated. "Why did you refuse to come?" he demanded as soon as his wife came in.

"I didn't refuse, sir," she replied quietly, closing the door behind her. "I begged you to excuse me, since I was tired and feeling unwell. You commanded, and here I am."

He snorted, squinting at her. "You're unwell? What kind of excuse is that? You seemed fine all day."

"Sir, I could hardly excuse myself from your victory celebrations for a headache. I had to pretend to enjoy myself, for the sake of your guests."

"Then you can pretend to enjoy yourself for my sake. Come here."

She came, stiffly. He began to jerk the cloak off—then, to her surprise, he stopped. Very gently, he brushed her damp hair off her cheek with the edge of a bent finger. "I'm sorry," he told her softly. "I didn't mean to quarrel with you again, not tonight. The war's over, for now, and I wanted to make peace with you as well. But I had something I wanted to say to you, you wouldn't come, and I've had too much to drink. Here, let's try again. Things haven't been happy between us. Perhaps I should have been gentler with you, and been aware that maybe you weren't as sure of yourself as you seemed. Perhaps I put too many checks on you. And perhaps you should have been more honest with me. Let's forget it all, everything that's happened before. I'm willing to start over. Are you?"

It must have cost him agonies to make such a speech, particularly after the queen's first refusal to come to him. He had planned his offer in the strength and confidence of victory: a new beginning, old mistakes corrected, the Yavana woman transformed from an aloof and superior rival into an affectionate and willing partner. The confidence had not lasted long. When she came into his room, cloaked in purple with the distant masklike face, unfailingly correct and subtly reproachful, all the old doubts entangled him again. But he longed for a marriage of gentleness and affection, like his first marriage, and he tried to set the doubts aside, spoke as he had intended, and now he looked at her with oddly open, childlike eyes, his hand cupping the side of her face.

She looked back doubtfully. A part of her guessed, with astonishment, that this might be the nearest thing to an apology he had ever uttered. But most of her was still curled up in dread of what came next, recoiling from his smell of wine, dirt, and blood, from the thick hands and hairy beast's body. Her mind was slow with fatigue; it took long moments to realize what the moment meant, to think of something to say in answer, a way to agree. It was already too late when she thought of it. The silence had lengthened between them without a word into coldness. The king still didn't take it as refusal; instead, he leaned forward, clumsily pulling the cloak aside, and kissed her breast. It was meant as a gesture of tenderness and intimacy, a promise of the new start, but she shuddered at it, violently and involuntarily. He looked up, the open eyes darkening with hurt, still like a child, but now a child who's been struck when he looked for comfort. "By our Lord the Sun," he whispered, "I can win the greatest victory my people have ever had, then rub my face in the dirt to please you—and you're still too proud to let me touch you."

"No!" she stammered. "No, it's not that, it's just that I'm so tired. I can't think straight."

But the damage was done. "There's no pleasing you, is there?" the king said bitterly. "I could offer you my heart on a platter and you'd spit on it. It's not good enough, not for you! Great-granddaughter of a god, aren't you, and too fine to be dirtied by barbarian hands! My parents were noble, I won the kingship by my own efforts, and I'm the only man in the kingdom who knew how to conquer the Invincible Demetrius or defeat the Tochari. What's wrong with me, eh?"

Something in her snapped. "Don't blame it on our ancestors," she said icily. "The fault's your own. You are older than my father would be if he were alive, you are ugly, and you stink. Do you expect me to faint with rapture when you touch me? You can't really believe that I should enjoy sleeping with you; you don't even try not to hurt me, let alone please me."

He jumped to his feet and stood staring at her. He glanced suddenly down at his own body, then looked at her again with the hurt child's eyes, as though he had only just understood that he was not the splendid young man he might once have been. Then he became angry. "I was wrong, then, was I?" he began, raising his voice in the choked roar common to such quarrels in every land and every condition of life. "You're not the cool lady I took you for, but a commonplace bitch yearning after some hot young—"

"I came to you a virgin," Heliokleia interrupted, her voice snapping and imperious. "And you and the gods both know I've been chaste since. I don't need pleasure and I don't need love. I'm perfectly content to honor you, to be faithful to you, to obey you; I swore my marriage oath in earnest, and I mean to keep it. What more can you reasonably expect? You didn't marry me for love."

He stared at her for a long time in silence, his hairy gray barrel chest heaving in the dim lamplight. Heliokleia sat rigid on the bed, her hands joined between her knees, the purple cloak hot and itching over her shoulders, meeting the stare with a calm mask fixed proudly on her face. Behind it, she was horrified, already regretting her loss of control. What had she said? The face that looked into hers was first shocked, then angry, and then, finally, perfectly moonlike and unreadable.

"No," said Mauakes at last, "I didn't marry you for love." He

moved a step nearer to her, and she had to tilt her head back to keep
her eyes on his. "I married you for your brother's elephants and artillery, and those have been very useful." He took another small step
nearer. "And, I admit, I had hopes that you could swing the Yavanas of
the city behind me—and you've done so, very nicely. So I have no
reason to complain, have I? It was my mistake to believe that we ought
to love each other anyway, if we could, that it would make things
pleasanter for both of us. Clearly, you'd prefer to leave the arrangements businesslike. Have you loved anyone? Ever?"

She blinked at him in silence for a minute. The headache was back,
worse than ever. Still she couldn't think, not clearly, not quick enough.
His question had been acid, almost rhetorical, but she found herself
considering it with her full attention, honestly and seriously. Had she
ever loved anyone? She looked back across her life through a chaos of
years and faces, and it was empty, barren and dry. There were people
she liked, people she was bound to, but no one whose death or absence
would break away a part of herself: no love. And no hatred either. The
shape of Itaz loomed in the foreground, fringed with light, but she saw
with a bitter clarity that it was because she felt she might love him, not
because she did. She felt a terrible regret and shame at her cold emptiness, but an equal conviction that she couldn't honorably end it. "No,"
she replied at last, quietly. "When I was small I had a nurse whom I
loved. But I don't think I've loved anyone else. Ever. I am content . . ." She paused, fighting off something inside her that screamed
that she was choosing a living death. "I am content to leave things that
way."

"So. Perhaps you'd prefer it if I found myself a mistress and left
you alone? That's what the Yavanas do in such circumstances, isn't it?"

"Yes," she said, her voice roughening with hope, "I would prefer
that. There'd be no worry then, either, that I would threaten the
succession with children."

"You perverted bitch! You want to make me an adulterer!"
Mauakes shouted, with the terrifying transformation from bland rea-
sonableness to fury. He dropped to one knee on the bed, grabbed her
shoulders, and shook her violently. "Do you think we Sakas tolerate
the kind of depravity your people prefer? You whore, how dare you
make such a suggestion to me?"

"It was your suggestion!" she protested, gasping. "I only agreed to it!"

"Don't contradict me!" he roared, and threw her back onto the bed.

There was a blinding pain in her head, as though the swollen headache had burst her skull open like an overripe fruit. Everything went red and spun around her, and she felt as though she were falling into a pit. There was a jolt, and a beast was tearing at her. She tried to scream, but her voice was gone, tried to move, but her hands had been changed to stone and she couldn't lift them. There was another splitting stab of pain in her head, and she was falling again. With astonishment, she realized she was dying, wished it wouldn't take so long, prayed desperately to the gods for release. Then there was another jolt, she drew a deep breath, and realized she wasn't dying, after all. There was horrible pain, though. She hadn't realized a headache could be so painful.

Then there was a blur of light around her and a hand on her face, and a voice, distorted and unintelligible, saying something. She felt sick and tried to roll over onto her side to vomit, but when she lifted her head, there was another sudden pain that sent her spinning back into the pit. Then there was someone holding her shoulder; she was on her side and retching violently. Everything stank, everything was confused and distorted and terrifying. She closed her eyes and tried to focus her mind on the prayers of her faith. "The jewel is in the lotus," she whispered, and someone said, "What?"

She didn't answer. There was a coolness at the back of her head now, and if she lay very still the pain was small and everything around her was less blurred and sickening.

"She'll recover in a few days, if the gods are kind and there's no splintering of the bone," said a voice on one side of her, in Greek. "But she should not be disturbed. It's best if she stays where she is for some time."

"Of course," said another voice on the other side of her, speaking the same language but with a heavy accent; it took her a moment to recognize it as her husband's. He had never spoken to her in her own language. "She'll be all right now, though? She's not moving . . ."

"She shouldn't move. She has a bad concussion. Probably she'll go to sleep soon. With your consent, O King, I'll stay here and watch her for you, to be sure she comes to no harm."

Heliokleia opened her eyes. Everything was still blurred and dizzy, and she closed them again. "Did I hit my head?" she asked, in her own language. Her voice was only a tiny whisper, like the pattering of a mouse's foot in the dark.

"What's that?" asked the first voice eagerly.

"Did I hit my head?" she asked again, more loudly.

"You fell and hit your head on the bed frame," said Mauakes, in Sakan. "I've brought in your countryman Apollodoros, a doctor, to attend you. Lie still, my dear; he says you'll be all right." He patted her hand.

"Oh," she said. It was a relief to understand what had happened, to know that the pain had a natural cause, and had not leapt at her blindly out the chaos of the world and her own empty suffering. She relaxed her mind's struggle for attentive detachment at last, and slept.

Upstairs, we were awakened by the sound of the king's servants running to fetch the doctor. Jahika, who was wakeful anyway, went down to see what the fuss was about, and came running back up looking terrified, just as Padmini came out of her own bedroom with a lamp. "The queen's hurt," she blurted out. "They're sending for a doctor."

"Merciful Anahita!" exclaimed Antiochis, coming half-dressed to the door and somehow understanding the Sakan words perfectly. "He's killed her!"

Nobody commented afterward on the fact that none of us contradicted this. It seemed horribly possible to all of us that he'd killed her. Padmini snapped at the others to stay where they were—"They won't need a gaggle of servants about"—then took me to translate, and went downstairs to find out the truth.

The doctor still hadn't arrived then. Heliokleia was lying unconscious on the king's bed with the cover drawn up to her chin. Her face was very pale in the lamplight, there was blood all over the sheets, and her hair was wet and red. The king was dressed, sitting anxiously by the door, and looked wretched. When we came in, he got up and came over. "Your lady fell and hit her head against the bedstead," he said, in Greek since he knew Padmini spoke little Sakan. We looked at the bedstead, and saw the blood on it, and a scrap of skin and hair twisted in the gilding. "A doctor has been sent for. Please go back to bed."

"Is she alive?" asked Padmini, apparently quite calm.

"Yes."

Padmini nodded, then went over to Heliokleia and touched her forehead. "I would prefer to stay here in case she wakes," she said softly. "I will be quiet, and sure not to disturb her. She is her mother's only child, and has been my chief duty since she was born." She looked up at the king questioningly.

"Stay, then," he said, "but be quiet."

Padmini nodded and settled silently on the floor beside the bed, dismissing me back upstairs with a wave of the hand.

After the doctor had arrived and made his diagnosis, she came back upstairs and told us calmly that the queen was not in any danger, and had in fact already woken and asked what happened. Then she sat down on the queen's couch. After a moment she put her arms about herself as though she were cold, and, after another moment, her sharp calm face crumpled and she began to cry. Antiochis sat down beside her, hugged her, and cried as well. Inisme fetched them both a pitcher of water.

"She should never have come here!" Padmini exclaimed passionately when she could speak again. "King Demetrios' granddaughter, thrown against a bed and raped by the same barbarian lout that murdered her great-uncle! How could Heliokles have agreed to it? Savages, wild, unprincipled savages, animals!"

"Not animals," said Antiochis quietly. "Darling, the maids are listening; don't say things you don't really mean."

Padmini burst into tears again, and Antiochis held her and comforted her. Inisme, after a moment, beckoned the rest of us back to our own room to bed.

"She was saying horrible things about the king," said Armaiti, shocked.

"She was very distressed," said Inisme reprovingly. "Of course she was. When the marriage was arranged, they put her whole life's work into it without thinking of her in the least, but if it all goes wrong, everything she's done is ruined. It's very hard for her, very hard for both of them; even to come here was hard. They had their own households in Bactra, and husbands and children, and here they're strangers. They're married ladies of quality and rank, and they're treated just like us, expected to share a room and live like unmarried girls. And now the queen is injured. Naturally Padmini's very distressed. We couldn't possibly repeat anything she said at a moment like this—could we." She stared challengingly at Armaiti and at me.

I stared at Inisme. I'd assumed from the first that she'd been trying to curry favor with Padmini and Antiochis; when Heliokleia had spoken about her with gratitude, I'd thought I understood better than she did. But I'd been wrong. Inisme liked the two ladies-in-waiting. She was of the same breed, and she understood them far too well to feel anything for them but sympathy.

"I wouldn't tell anyone what she said," I said. Armaiti echoed me, and Inisme, contented, put out the lamp.

When she'd had her cry, Padmini went back downstairs to sit by the queen's bed, opposite the doctor; when she came back next morning to get some sleep, Antiochis took her place. The queen slept until the afternoon.

Heliokleia woke to the sound of someone playing the kithara, picking it softly in little ripples of music that slid and turned around themselves. She lay still, staring straight in front of herself with open eyes. She was still in the king's room, she saw, lying on one side on his bed. The dim light no longer blurred and twisted around her. After a while the music stopped and Antiochis appeared before her, holding the instrument with one hand. "Are you awake?" asked the lady eagerly.

"Yes," Heliokleia answered. Her head still hurt and she thought she might be sick if she moved, so she remained motionless.

Antiochis stroked her forehead. "Do you want anything, my dear? Should I call the doctor? He's sleeping just in the next room."

"What happened?" asked the queen, not replying—then, after a moment, "Oh yes, they said I hit my head."

"Indeed, darling. The king got you the best doctor in the city— he's a Greek, of course, and trained in Bactra; he seems to be quite knowledgeable. He says you have a concussion, but he expects you'll recover soon—though you must rest, darling, and try not to move."

"What time is it?"

"About three hours before sunset. You've been asleep since the middle of last night. Doctor Apollodoros was worried at first, but about noon today he said he was satisfied that you were just resting in a normal sleep, and he went off to rest himself. Padmini and I have been taking turns to sit with you. We've been very worried."

Heliokleia made no reply for a while, but lay there, thinking. "Antiochis," she said at last, "can I go up to my own room tonight?"

"The doctor said you weren't to move," Antiochis said. "Your husband has given you his bed until you're recovered; he had the servants bring in another bed for himself, so he wouldn't disturb you."

So, he'd be coming back to the room in a few hours? She tried to sit up, then felt sick at the blinding pain and lay still again. "I'd rather be in my own room," she said. "Please, Antiochis. Have someone carry me up there."

"The doctor was quite firm, darling." Antiochis looked at her anxiously, then, leaning forward and lowering her voice, "What happened? When you hit your head, I mean. Padmini thinks . . . well, never mind. How did it happen?"

Heliokleia thought for a moment. "It was an accident," she said at last. "We were quarreling. He threw me on the bed, and I must have hit my head on the frame."

"You were quarreling?" Antiochis repeated unhappily.

"Yes. I said some things I shouldn't have. I . . . I don't want to see him. Not yet. Please, I'd rather be upstairs."

A door opened, and Mauakes came in; she recognized the heavy step even before she saw him, and bit her lip. She was too exhausted and ill to restrain the tears, and she blinked up at her husband through them as his face appeared over Antiochis' shoulder. It was as round and unreadable as ever.

"I'm sorry," she said miserably before he could speak. "I said some things I shouldn't have, some shameful things."

But this seemed to embarrass him. "Don't think of it," he told her hurriedly, and patted her shoulder. She flinched at the touch, and he pulled the hand away—then put it back, gently.

"Please, sir," she said, "I'm in your way. Let me go upstairs to my own room until I'm well again."

"The doctor says you're not to be moved," he replied. "Just lie still and rest." He stood a moment looking at her, then added, "I'm glad to see you're awake again. I'll go now, so as not to disturb you." He patted her shoulder again, kissed her on the mouth, and left.

Heliokleia rubbed the kiss off her mouth with a shaking hand. "I wish you'd let me go upstairs," she said. "I'd be much happier there."

Antiochis was looking at her anxiously. "He threw you so you hit your head? What had you said to him?"

The fumbling hand rubbed at the tears, then dropped. "Things I shouldn't have. What's the point in talking about it? There's nothing to be done. It was an accident." And in fact, she told no one the details of the ugly scene until long afterward, when they no longer mattered.

Antiochis did not reply, but her soft, plump face set angrily. She looked at her mistress for a moment longer, then picked up the kithara and turned her head away, watching her fingering on its strings, playing rapidly a song without words.

Heliokleia lay back in the bed, her eyes closed, listening in silence until Antiochis stopped and set the instrument down, thinking that her mistress was asleep again. But the queen opened her eyes. "Antiochis," she said dreamily, "do you remember my old nurse?"

"What, that woman Datis? Yes, I remember her. Why, darling?"

"I was just thinking of her. I remember her sitting by me once when I was ill, singing something . . . I don't remember the words. They were in Bactrian, though, weren't they?"

"Most likely," said Antiochis disdainfully. "She was a Bactrian, and spoke Greek like a peasant."

"I loved her."

"You did. I remember that," Antiochis answered, smiling now. "Mai-mai, you called her. 'I want Mai-mai,' you'd say when one of us tried to comb your hair for you. Nobody but Mai-mai was allowed to touch it. I remember you toddling after her—Herakles! you can't have been more than two!—tugging at her skirts and beaming at her till she picked you up. It always annoyed us, since we never liked her."

"I remember that. I never understood why."

"Well, she was just a silly peasant girl. She'd got herself pregnant by some young man, then lost the baby. She wasn't a suitable person to nurse a queen at all, really, but she was the first wet nurse your father could find after your lady mother died. She was a big slovenly creature; if she'd lived she would have married some stout guardsman and had as many children as a prize sow. She used to indulge you and fuss over you in the most mawkish way, and she used to contradict us when we tried to correct her. Sometimes she used to talk to you in her own language, which wasn't allowed—though I think it probably helped you when you took up barbarian tongues later on. Ai, looking back I suppose she was a very good nurse. She certainly loved you, and you were such a happy child then; you'd smile if anyone so much as looked at you. I'd almost forgotten it. But when she took ill and died, merciful Anahita! Padmini and I were at our wits' end. You cried and whined and wouldn't do this, and screamed if we asked you to do that, and you were off your food for months. Every time a door opened you'd run to see if it was her, and burst into tears again when you saw that it wasn't."

"I remember that, too."

"Do you? You were still very small, certainly not more than five."

"I do remember it, though. I don't think I've ever really loved anyone since then. Not even you and Padmini. I'm sorry. It must be bitter, spending your lives and loyalty for such barren land as me. I wish I were different. Virtue is cold and arid, and obedience without delight pleases no one. Probably even the gods hate them."

"Child! You can't measure love by the devotion a child has for its nurse! Why, if that were the standard, none of us would ever love anyone again. It's a phase. You would have outgrown it, you know."

"No," said Heliokleia thoughtfully. "No, it would have changed, but I wouldn't have outgrown it. She could have been here with me now."

Antiochis gave a ladylike snort. "Be that as it may, you've been quite loving enough to please any reasonable person: no court lady ever had a kinder or more considerate queen. Oh, it annoys us, dear, when you haven't had enough respect for your position, but we've counted ourselves lucky, too. Why, they say Menander's queen Agathokleia is a proper tyrant, and as for your brother's wife! Well, you know about that. No, darling, don't worry about us. And . . . don't worry about anything your husband may have said on the subject either. Probably he's come to his senses now."

Heliokleia gave a small, unconvinced smile and said nothing. After a moment, Antiochis picked up the kithara again, privately resolving once more to speak to Padmini, and after that, to the king.

The following morning, Padmini and Antiochis met the king as he was leaving his room and asked if they might speak with him. He was slightly taken aback, but waved them toward his study.

"Not there," said Padmini firmly. "I don't wish to upset the queen, should she overhear us."

He hesitated, then ushered them to the guestroom the other side of the study. It had just been vacated by one of the king's officers, who had returned to his own estates now that the victory celebrations were over; it was dirty, the bedspread was over the floor, and the rugs were askew. Padmini sniffed. The king sat down on the couch and looked at the two ladies in anxious inquiry. "Do you have some reason to be afraid for the queen's health?" he asked them, politely speaking in Greek.

The two looked at each other. "Yes," said Padmini. "May we speak plainly, O King?"

"By all means."

"Sir," said Padmini formally, "we two came from India with Queen Laodike, Queen Heliokleia's mother, and we have been your queen's attendants since her infancy. Our whole lives have been dedicated to the house of Antimachos, and we wish you first to understand that what we say, we say only from love and loyalty, not malice. We accompanied our lady to your kingdom, to see that she was established in the honor and dignity proper to her rank. We thought that, in a year, she would have a proper household and new lady attendants, young women suited to a young queen, as well as stewards, servants, perhaps even a child. We thought that we could return confidently to Bactra and devote all our attention to our own families, secure in the knowledge that our mistress was happy and our duties all discharged. But the gods have allotted otherwise, and for some time now we have been viewing our lady's situation here with concern. At this latest . . . accident . . . we feel that we cannot keep silent any longer, but as we value our duty to the royal house of Antimachos, and to King Heliokles, we must protest to you at your treatment of her. The daughter of Eukratides and niece of Menander is not a captured harlot, to be thrown against a bedstead and raped."

Mauakes stared at them, his face completely expressionless, but his nostrils flared and narrowed quickly as he breathed. "I do not understand you, ladies," he said quietly. "Please explain yourselves."

"Sir," said Padmini sharply, glaring at him bleakly, "you understand me perfectly well. You say it was an accident, she says it was an accident—and no doubt you never meant her to hit her head. But you must have thrown her hard, to hurt her so badly—and when you allowed me in to attend her, I saw how her blood was smeared all over the sheets: you'd kept on at her for a while, even though she was injured and unconscious. And she has fresh bruises. You used her barbarously—most disastrously this time, but this time wasn't the first time. She hasn't complained, but she can't hide the marks, not from us. All she's told us is that you're angry because she doesn't welcome you with love. Love, sir, isn't a proper concern of queens."

"Ladies," said Mauakes coldly, "it's not your place to lecture me on how to treat my wife. But I believe you are speaking from loyalty to her, if speaking wildly, and I will pardon you."

"Indeed, sir?" said Padmini, even more coldly. "I am glad to hear it; I haven't finished yet. A queen ought to have command of her own household, with supreme authority over her own people and attendants. You have given her a pack of girls loyal principally to you, all Sakas without a Greek among them, and . . . I have observed, sir, that you summon them from time to time to report upon their mistress. You have weakened her authority further by keeping her in your bed every night, so that she goes to her own rooms as scarcely more than a visitor. You have not given her her own steward or any household officials, but all her estates must be managed through your people, and you have forbidden her to speak to them; for all her wishes she is reduced to begging from you. This is, of course, the custom of many savages—but I had heard that the Sakas did otherwise; that Saka queens could, if anything, expect more power than Greeks, not less. Queen Heliokleia is a lady admirably fitted to play a part in government, but you've made her little more than your plaything and a channel for the petitions of your Greek subjects. And still you distrust her; you buy slaves to tell you what she writes; you give her a guard only to spy on her. And worst of all, when war threatened, you packed her off, with an escort of useless cripples, out of the safety of the city and into a dreadful squalid wilderness without any of the comforts that any civilized person, let alone a queen, ought to expect by right. But the gods know she's done nothing to deserve such treatment, indeed, she's done more to submit to you than you had any right to expect. She has adopted the language and customs of your people to a degree that will seem scandalous to her own when it's reported in Bactra. She's even accepted that miserable brat as your heir, in place of any children of her own line. Sir, it is intolerable. I call on all the gods to witness that I, Padmini, say this not from any ambition or desire to harm, but from regard to the rights of my lady's house, which I have served since my girlhood. May the gods grant that it is for the best."

The king squinted at her for a long minute. "And have you," he asked at last, "said all this to the queen?"

"Indeed not," said Antiochis, answering for her earnestly. "We've always been careful to call her attention to the honors you've shown her, and we've kept quiet about the rest. We didn't want to make trouble between you. We only came here today, O King, because . . . because we felt you had exceeded the limits of decency."

Mauakes grunted, still squinting at them. "But on the other matter? You have, I think, told the queen that I ought to get myself a mistress."

"I may have said something of the sort," Padmini said coolly, "but she hardly needed me to say it, with the examples of her father and brother before her eyes."

"We Sakas do not approve of adultery," Mauakes said bitingly. "We differ from the Greeks in that respect."

"But it isn't adultery," replied Antiochis in bewilderment. "Not for a husband. Just for a wife."

"It is for us," said Mauakes. "Ladies, you are the servants of the king of the Bactrians, as you've pointed out. You do not understand our customs or our language here in Ferghana, and have no business advising me how I should or should not arrange matters in my own kingdom. It seems, moreover, that you have tried to corrupt the morals of my queen by your foul advice. If you were my subjects"—the calm slipping, but not quite lost—"I would have you both flogged. As it is, you must go, both of you, back to your own people at once. I will not be lectured by servants. Go pack!"

Padmini glared at him venomously and gave a curt little nod,

Antiochis wrung her hands. "But Heliokleia's ill!" she cried in distress, "She wasn't to be disturbed; how can you send us away now?"

Mauakes ground his teeth and hunched his shoulders with the effort of restraining himself. "You should have thought of that before you decided to insult me!" he told them. "But very well. Despite what you've said, my queen's happiness is very dear to me; I do not want her distressed while she's ill. You may stay until she is recovered. You will tell her nothing of this conversation, and make no effort to disturb her with accounts of it or pleas to be allowed to remain: if I find either of you doing so, I'll have you whipped, despite your allegiances. When the queen is well enough to climb the stairs to her own room, you must go. Now, stay out of my sight!"

Padmini and Antiochis bowed with frigid correctness and stalked out. They went directly upstairs and told us—that is, the four maids, after sending the slaves out—about the conversation and its outcome. We were stunned. I was amazed that the king had taken it so quietly; I had never heard of him enduring such a lecture from anyone in his whole life. Inisme kept shaking her head, and afterward deplored the lack of judgment shown by the two. "They simply don't understand anything about the Sakas!" she complained in dismay, and it was quite true. But Padmini also relayed the instructions that no mention of the argument or their departure was to be made to the queen until she was better. "A very sensible precaution," said Padmini. "I pray to all the gods that it's true what he said, and that our lady's happiness is indeed dear to him; more than that I cannot do—except entrust her and her honor to you." She looked at each of us, then reached out and caught Inisme's hands. "I know you have some care for these things," she said earnestly, and quite suddenly, switching from Greek to a clumsy mixture of marketplace Bactrian and Sakan, "Be faithful to my lady. She is a very kind and honorable queen."

Inisme kissed the hands that had taken hers. "She will come to no dishonor here," she promised, and Padmini smiled weakly.

The king, meanwhile, went down to the stables, took his horse and his armor, and went to slaughter targets on the practice field for an hour, until the horse was lathered and he felt calm again. When he returned to the palace he went first to see his wife.

Padmini and Antiochis were back in the king's room by this time.

Heliokleia was sitting propped up in the bed, listening while Antiochis read to her; nearby, Padmini sat spinning. The two ladies jumped up when the king entered and backed off quickly. Mauakes ignored them and went directly to his wife. She was very pale, huge-eyed, her loose hair dark in the dim light of the sick room; she looked lost in the magnificent bed, fragile and frightened. He kissed her forehead tenderly and patted her hand. "I'm glad to see you sitting up again," he told her.

He hadn't meant to hurt her. He hadn't realized at first that he had hurt her. She had lain very still on the bed after he threw her onto it, but she always lay still, locked into her detachment. He had, as Padmini had said, "kept on at her"—until the awful, unforgotten moment when her head had lolled brokenly away from him, and he saw that her hair was a mass of blood. For a terrible instant he knew he was embracing the dead, and he been shaken to the roots with the horror of it. It had been some minutes before he could bring himself to touch her again even to see if she was still alive. The beat of her pulse under his finger had been like the river to him, giving life to the dry land. He had wanted only to master her, cancel the sting of her words and her rejection; the thought that she might die drove him to unexpected tears. When he saw that she would live he'd been happy to forgive her anything.

He had made a mistake, he'd decided. When she first came, he'd been fooled by her confidence, and had taken possession of her casually, as though she were a well-trained riding horse. Now he realized that she was young, innocent, and high-strung, an unbroken high-bred mare: naturally she'd been hurt and frightened, and had tried to throw him. He would be gentler now, he would be kind, he would undo all the effects of his roughness and impatience. Eventually she would stop flinching and shying away when he touched her; she would calm, understand he loved her and wanted her and meant her no harm; she would yield to him and love him. Most of the problems, he told himself now, had been caused by her attendants. She herself was honorable and compliant; she had adapted to his ways, they hadn't. It was them, it was her brother's court, that had taught her that love was not a proper concern for queens. He would send the women home, and soon she would settle to his view of things, and be guided entirely by him.

He never asked himself why he so desperately wanted her to love him, when love had been no part of his plans for the marriage. He didn't understand why her rejection had stung. At the time he seemed to me arbitrary and unreasonable. Only when I looked back on it long afterward did it become clear to me, as I think it never was to him, that he was haunted, more even than the rest of us, by the mocking ghost of Antimachos the God, from whom he had stolen his kingdom. It didn't matter that Antimachos had died when Mauakes was a boy, that Mauakes had defeated Antimachos' heir Demetrios. He had ruled always with that shadow at his shoulder, that comparison half-made in the minds of his people. An unfair comparison. Antimachos had put down no rebellions—but with all the Saka nobility in exile, who was there to lead one? Antimachos had doubled the arable land in the valley, and enriched its people—but he had all the wealth and ingenuity of the Bactrian Greeks at his fingertips, and Mauakes had only a land at war. Yavanas are too clever, skilled at too many things. No Saka king, even Mauakes, could ever match the technical ingenuity of a Greek, and when a claim to something beyond mortality is added, how could a Saka nobleman compete? How can a man conquer a god? Mauakes hadn't tried: he had left the cult of his predecessor alone, and rarely even spoke of it. And not just from policy, I think: what he felt for that bright shadow was more than mere rivalry. He too was Antimachos' heir, and he loved the smiling ghost as much as he hated it. To him Heliokleia was an image of Antimachos—brilliant, beautiful, and remotely disdainful of himself and his people. From the moment he had seen her, he had ached for her to love him, to reconcile the ghost and make it rest. If she'd been different—if she'd been ugly, or silly, or even had a different smile—she wouldn't have had such a power to disturb, and he wouldn't have been so desperate to win her over. And he didn't realize that he was painfully in love with the mere shadow she cast on his mind, and didn't really know or understand her at all.

CHAPTER

XI

The queen was recovered enough to walk upstairs on the sixth day after the accident, and we broke the news about Padmini and Antiochis' dismissal then. She said nothing, merely looked at them in horror, then embraced them. They didn't ask her to plead for them to the king, and she didn't offer to do so. She felt, I'm sure, that if they continued in Mauakes' palace their lives would be intolerable. But she wrote them letters thanking them for their loyal and devoted service, and she showered them with gifts.

The king duly made arrangements for the two to be escorted back to Bactra. He had wished to send an embassy to the neighboring capital anyway, to give his ally King Heliokles an accurate account of the battle and to ask for more naphtha. He now felt some anxiety about what the two ladies would say to the king of Bactria, and decided to send a gift of some of the captured Tochari horses and weapons as well, along with a letter dismissing the women's claims as ignorant feminine hysteria coupled with homesickness. He dictated the letter to his

Yavana secretary a dozen times before he was satisfied with it, then
entrusted it, the embassy, and the escort, to his son.

Itaz had never been to Bactria, and was reluctant to go. He protested that he had no experience of embassies, that his Greek was
clumsy, that he ought anyway to be organizing the queen's guard in
Eskati, not running back and forth across the Oxus. But Mauakes was
insistent. "The captain of the queen's guard should escort the queen's
ladies home," he told his son mildly. "It's the most appropriate thing.
And Heliokles will treat you with respect in front of his people, where
he might disregard another man. You can uphold the dignity of
Ferghana, can't you, my dear?"

Itaz hunched his shoulders, miserably aware that his father wanted
him out of the way. He guessed that the king was planning some
oblique move against the councillors who had opposed him. However,
he was bound to obey, and so, one hot clear morning in late summer,
he set out from Eskati with twenty guardsmen (including my brother
Havani), two supply wagons, the ladies in their chariot, and two dozen
horses loaded with captured daggers and gold.

The two-week journey was an uncomfortable one. The ladies
treated him with stiff, disapproving politeness, and the guardsmen's
talk bored him. He had found it increasingly difficult to talk to his
friends; the easy fellowship he'd enjoyed before somehow slipped from
him, and the sense of loneliness was worse, as it always is, in close
company. He was relieved when they finally arrived at Bactra.

Bactra is a wonder. I went there myself in the end, ten years ago,
and it's the most splendid city I've ever seen. It's laid out four-gated,
like Eskati, but the two roads that meet in its marketplace are no
ordinary thoroughfares. One is the road from Ferghana, which also
comes from the steppe lands rich in furs and gold, and goes through
Bactra into the highlands and across the spice-filled deserts of Gedrosia;
the other is the great road which runs from India and the eastern lands
of silk as far west as rumor can guess, to Seleukeia-upon-the-Tigris, to
Antioch and the Middle Sea: they are the two greatest trade roads of all
the world. The streets of Bactra are decorated with statues and colon-
nades, stone carved with all the ingenuity of the Yavanas, so that the
way seems crowded with gods and kings—and it is crowded, in fact,
with the horsemen and elephants of the royal guards, with the carriages

and camel trains of the merchants; with the mass of people on foot, dressed in the styles of all the tribes from here to India. In the marketplace you can buy furs and gold from the north, cotton and pepper from India, pearls from Taprobane, incense from the Gedrosia, purple, fine woolens and glass from Syria and Egypt—yes, and silk from the farthest east, as well! In the middle of the marketplace is the temple of Anahita, one of the wonders of the east, suspended on its columns like the magical floating palaces of a children's tale; inside is a statue of the goddess three times the height of a man, made entirely from gold and clothed in a cloak of beaver fur. Just south of the temple is the citadel, and the palace of the kings. It makes the palace of Eskati look like a shepherd's hut, for Bactria is the jewel of Asia, and its wealth is the stuff of legends.

Itaz had announced himself and his purpose to the governor of Alexandria Oxiana when he crossed the Oxus, and received an additional escort for the journey through Bactria proper. He and his party were allowed into the city at once, and escorted by the guards from the gate to the citadel. He rode slowly, gaping. I gaped the first time I saw the city—by the Sun, I did. I hadn't realized that mortals could build anything so magnificent, or that so many people could be brought into one place without being summoned there by a war. Eskati is the only city in Ferghana, and it's tiny beside Bactra. Of course, I came prepared to admire. Itaz hadn't forgotten his hatred of the Bactrians, his contempt for the Eukratid dynasty, the death of his second brother in a Yavana war. He came angry and reluctant, wanting to prefer the Parthians—and still he gaped at the Yavana capital. Its variety and beauty disarmed and confused him.

King Heliokles the Just, thirty, ugly, and affable, came out to meet the son of his ally and brother-in-law in the marketplace. He held the bridle of Itaz' horse while he dismounted, then formally embraced him, calling him "kinsman." Itaz muttered an inarticulate reply, acutely uncomfortable. Part of himself still insisted that kinship to Heliokles was a disgrace; another part remembered Heliokles' sister, and accepted the courtesy readily. For lack of anything better to do, he handed the king his father's letter, and the king smiled and thanked him.

Though it was evening, much of the populace had gathered in the marketplace to watch the embassy's reception, and King Heliokles, like a true Yavana king, prolonged it for them. He made some show of receiving the captured horses and armor, and at once dedicated some of the spears and bows to the goddess Anahita, hanging them up in her temple. That's a Yavana custom after a victory: they thank the gods for it, but they publicize it as well by displaying the trophies. The king kept the gold, however, and had it put in his own treasury.

Antiochis and Padmini disappeared even before the dedication among a horde of servants and attendants, and after the ceremony Itaz' guardsmen were taken to the luxurious barracks reserved for the escorts of visiting princes and given a banquet, which Havani afterward described to me in great and wondering detail. Itaz himself was ushered into the palace. The servants showed him to a bedroom the size of his father's dining hall, offered him a bath—which, to their surprise, he accepted—cut his hair, made him a gift of a new cloak, and escorted him to have dinner with the king.

The palace, for all its splendor, didn't disconcert him. The Parthian Surens, with whom he was fostered, have a splendid palace of their own—though they're not city dwellers. But the prospect of dinner with King Heliokles was more disturbing. He no longer knew where his loyalties lay: the queen's accident, which all Eskati had been whispering about from the moment it happened, had plunged him into such a confusion of conflicting passions and loyalties that he tried not to think about it at all. Now he was Heliokles' guest, emissary of Ferghana to a land he still regarded with hostility, bound to justify his father's conduct toward Heliokles' sister. He had no skills as a diplomat, and his Greek was coarse and clumsy, picked up from the traders and administrators of Eskati. Heliokles spoke the tongue like a orator, and spoke no other. Itaz wished, passionately, that his father had found some other ambassador.

But the king, again, was all smiles and courtesy. He seated Itaz on his own couch—the Yavanas always sit, or rather recline, two or three to a couch, and they usually have three couches at a dinner party, ranged along the sides of three tables set together in a sickle shape. They make a great fuss over who sits where; the top, host's couch is the most honorable. Heliokles had invited some of his officers and ministers to share the dinner, but he paid particular attention to Itaz, seeing that he was served with food, pouring the wine for him, and thanking him for his trouble in coming as ambassador from "my most valued ally, King Mauakes." The ministers, however, smiled behind their hands. Itaz had only ever reclined to eat in the brothel, and he knocked his cup off the table with the folds of the cumbersome new cloak, which he hadn't draped properly—Yavana cloaks are very large, and the gods know what they do when they drape them. I won't wear one; I can never get the folds to stay in place. Itaz set his teeth and ignored the smiles.

Mauakes' letter was sitting, still unopened, under a gold basin of rose water. Itaz glanced at it and felt as though he were sitting with a plate balanced on the edge of the table, about to fall off any minute; he waited unhappily for the king to read the letter and lose his good nature. But Heliokles was in no hurry; he asked instead for an account of the battle against the Tochari, then discussed and admired it with his officers. Itaz struggled awkwardly through the meal, feeling more and more angry and uncomfortable. The Yavana ministers smiled at the mistakes in his Greek; he spilled his wine; he trailed the edge of the cloak in the sauce; he dropped his bread; he felt in all ways a clumsy savage, and he despised himself and the Yavanas both.

At last the main part of the meal was over and the king ordered the servants to pour out more wine, and begged his guests to allow him to read his ally's letter, "So that we can discuss anything that needs discussing." Itaz clenched his fists under the table and waited. Heliokles read it out to the company, gradually slowing as he did so and raising his eyebrows, then gave Itaz a quizzical look. Itaz looked at the floor. It was a mistake, he saw, to have given the letter to the king directly; he should have kept it and handed it to him privately. But he'd wanted to get rid of it, and he hadn't realized that Heliokles would suppose it was official business.

"Your father seems concerned that I not listen to what my sister's attendants have to say about her," said Heliokles. "What *do* they have to say about her, Lord Itaz?"

Itaz scowled unhappily into his drink. He knew roughly what they had to say. Everyone in Mauakes' palace knew, though how they knew was impossible to say. Palaces are like that. "She had an accident a little before we left," he told Heliokles. "Her women think it was my father's fault. And they think he wasn't giving her enough authority.

They . . . they don't understand that he can't simply give her the rights most queens of our people enjoy. The lords of the council won't accept it, not until they know her." He remembered his own opposition to her and went red, wishing again that his father had sent someone else.

"Ah." Heliokles folded the letter and put it in his purse, then offered his guest some prunes stuffed with pepper. He took one himself and chewed it reflectively.

"It was an accident," Itaz said defensively. "In fact, my father values your sister greatly."

"Umm," said Heliokles, and swallowed. "So he says, in his letter. What happened to her?"

"She fell and hit her head against the bedstead. She was already recovered when I left Eskati."

"I see."

"The whole kingdom admires your sister," Itaz went on, aware that he was babbling but unable to stop himself. "Much more than we'd expected beforehand." One of the ministers smirked, and he went on hotly, "We never expected her to speak our language or show such understanding of our ways. We thought—I thought—that a Yavana queen would sneer at us, the way so many of your people do." The king cast an amused glance at his friends; they smiled back condescendingly. "Your sister's not like that. When she rides out. . . ."

"Rides? You mean, on a horse? My little sister?" The king stared. The smirking minister laughed out loud.

"Of course—when she rides out among the people, or to view the army, the Sakas forget she's foreign, and admire her as much as the Yavanas do."

"On a *horse!* To view the *army!*" said King Heliokles. *"Ma ton Apollon!"* He shook his head and took another sip of wine. "And your people approve of this? Your father approves of it?"

Itaz stared at him in confusion. Most of the Yavana women in Ferghana had already adopted some of the customs of their Saka neighbors; he hadn't until then understood how different things were in the royal court of Bactria, and how drastically the queen had abandoned the ways of her own people. "Of course," he told Heliokles. "A queen of the Sakas must be able to ride. How . . . how else could she be a queen? She can't sit in a cart, like a farmer going to market."

Heliokles shook his head again. "Merciful Anahita! Still, I suppose it's creditable that she adapts herself to your ways. Though, between us, I wish I'd kept her back and married her elsewhere." He took another sip of wine thoughtfully and added, "I never noticed her much when she was small, but when I sent her off I thought it was a pity to lose her. She's pretty, isn't she?"

"She is as lovely as the sun in Heaven," said Itaz, honest and unguarded, and found himself adding, "And she is honorable, brilliant, and brave. She is a jewel that would shine anywhere." Then he bit his tongue.

Heliokles looked surprised, then smiled, dismissing the words as the extravagance of an illiterate barbarian. "She's pretty, and clever," he conceded, "and very seriously given to virtue. You're right, she'd make a fine wife for any man—and for any other man she'd produce heirs who would unite his power and mine. With all respect to your father, whose friendship I value as half my kingdom, an ordinary treaty of alliance would have served. I was . . . overpersuaded"—with an ironic glance at the smirker—"to confirm the treaty with my sister's hand." There was an awkward silence. After a moment, the king went on, "If her children are not to be her heirs, that may cause trouble between my successor and your father's. I make no claims, of course; it was understood when we made the treaty that your father wished his firstborn's firstborn to succeed him—still, it would preserve peace into the next generation if your father's successor and mine were cousins. You might tell your father to consider that. I make no claims to direct him, of course."

Itaz stared at him uncomprehendingly. Heliokles looked back inquiringly, completely unconcerned about his sister's well-being; it was as though her only purpose was to produce half-Yavana heirs to rule Ferghana. Itaz remembered the queen saying farewell to her lady attendants—thin and pale, still unwell, embracing them and watching them go with resigned grief. She was worth more than this. "I heard," he said, suddenly rash with anger, "that your ministers advised you to agree to the marriage alliance because they were afraid your sister would tell you about some of their own misdoings."

There was a sudden absolute silence. The ministers stopped smiling. Heliokles blinked at Itaz. "Indeed?" he asked at last. "Where did you hear that?"

"From . . . from a relative, a nobleman who'd visited Bactra about the time of the wedding. He said that, because your sister speaks the language of your subjects, she'd learned things your ministers were anxious to prevent you from finding out."

"Indeed?" asked Heliokles again. "Was this common talk, in Bactra? What sort of things?"

"I don't know. I know nothing about Bactrian affairs, King Heliokles. I'd simply heard this reported as the reason your sister was able to marry my father without his disinheriting my brother's son. But having met your sister, and seen her intelligence and her ability, it seems very likely to me."

Heliokles' eyelids drooped and he looked from Itaz to his ministers. After a long minute he smiled. "Of course, I probably know my little sister less well than you do," he said. "I have always been so busy with affairs of state; I leave matters in the palace to my ministers, in whom I have complete confidence. But I doubt that rumors your relative heard among the shopkeepers in the marketplace have any substance. I do remember that my sister was an odd child, though. I'm sorry to hear what you say of her, that she's taken to riding out among the men of the army—in those dreadful trousers, too? Herakles! There is such a thing as adopting too many of the customs of one's barbarian subjects. It must be useful to speak their language, however. Perhaps I should learn Bactrian myself. What do you think, Archedemos?" he inquired in a tone of polite inquiry to the smirker.

"I see no point in studying barbarian languages," replied Archedemos. "It seems to me to be beneath the dignity of a king descended from the conqueror of the world. We are the masters, and those who wish to deal with us should learn our tongue. Would you like your court to be like King Menander's, where half the men they call royal kinsmen can barely speak Greek, and Alexander's descendants mingle their blood with Indian barbarians, and bow to native monks and holy men? And the Indians at least have their own nobility, while the Bactrians are all slaves by nature. But of course, if you think it would be advantageous, O King . . ."

"It sounds as though it could be very advantageous," replied Heliokles, smiling. "One hears such interesting gossip."

Archedemos looked away and began to talk about an interesting piece of Yavana gossip he'd heard, changing the subject. Nothing more was said about Heliokleia, and Itaz, pleading fatigue from his journey, left the dinner and went to bed as soon as he decently could, then prowled about the huge bedroom, silently cursing King Heliokles. He hadn't realized that he'd been hoping the king would intervene and extract for the queen some freedom from his father, or perhaps even insist on a divorce. Now he was left, not merely disappointed, but angry with Heliokles, and ashamed of himself for wanting something disgraceful to his father and his nation. Eventually he lay down on the bed and tried desperately to pray.

Itaz and his party spent four days in Bactra, resting the horses a little before the return journey to Ferghana. They were escorted about the city and given gifts of money and fine clothing. The young men of the escort spent all the money in the markets and brothels, and sold their spare clothes and jewelry to spend more. Havani came back laden with presents. He gave me an onyx signet ring engraved with a leaping horse, which I have still; it was brought from the west, and the lines of carving are as tiny and as perfect as the wings of some jewel-like little beetle. Itaz, however, didn't join the others. On the second day of the visit, during a tour of the city, he found a Mazdayist fire temple, and he felt a desperate need to pray.

Bactra was a Mazdayist city before it was a Yavana one; some say that the prophet Zarathushtra was born there. There's a very fine and large temple outside the city walls which was built before the days of King Alexander. Itaz visited it and made an offering, but found it too public and too full of Greeks for private worship. But while he was being shown about the city, he noticed a small shrine on a alleyway off the North Road, built very much in the Yavana style, with a rectangular central building surrounded by a columned porch. Itaz wouldn't have known what it was, but the guide the king had given him indicated it and said, "That's a temple to Zeus-Mazda. It was built by a Parthian trader; it's quite new."

The old temple outside the city was also dedicated to "Zeus-Mazda"; it was immediately obvious that the Yavanas identified the

Wise Lord with their own chief god. Itaz stared at the building curiously. "May I go in?" he asked.

"Not unless you're a fire worshipper, a Mazdayist," said the guide. "They don't like it if people from other faiths go too near the fire altar."

"But I am a Mazdayist," replied Itaz, and started eagerly toward the temple.

There was a Yavana sacrificial altar on the temple's porch, and beyond it a door leading into the temple proper. Itaz tried it; it was unlocked. His guide sat down resignedly on the temple steps as he went in.

The interior of the building was dark, lit only by a few window slots high up near the ceiling. The altar to the sacred fire was at the far end, shrouded by curtains; looming above it through the gloom was a Yavana statue of Zeus, crowned with the sun disk and gripping a thunderbolt. There was a smell of incense, charcoal, leather, and soap. A small shriveled man in the white robes of a priest was busily washing the polished marble of the floor. In a large temple that would have been beneath his dignity, but Itaz guessed that a small chapel like this would lack temple slaves, and the priest and his family would care for congregation and building both. The priest sat back on his heels when Itaz entered blinking in a cloud of daylight. "What do you want?" he called, in Bactrian.

"I wish to worship the god," Itaz replied, in Sakan, which he had found was easily understood. "I am a follower of the good religion visiting from the North."

"Ah! Then you are welcome!" The priest pulled out a leather mat and arranged it in the middle of the room, where the floor was already dry. " 'May the bright heaven, the all-blissful paradise, come toward you twelve hundred steps for every step,' " he said, quoting from the Mazdayist service—then went back to washing the floor.

Itaz sat down on the mat and tried to pray for guidance. Bactria left him more in need of that than ever. All his old certainties had abandoned him: he found he didn't even hate the Yavanas now, and couldn't say what was right and what was wrong. He felt entangled in a net of contradictions; he couldn't even be honest with himself, as he didn't know anymore what his self was. He begged Ahura Mazda, the

Lord of Light and of Truth, to illumine his darkness and confusion, and to protect him from the power of the Lie. But it seemed as though the god had turned his face away, and his pleas went unheard.

After a long, silent struggle he heard a rustling near him, and opened his eyes to see the old priest standing over him. The floor was clean. "You seem troubled, my son," the old man said gently. "Do you want prayers or counsel?"

Itaz nodded wearily. The old man squatted down on the prayer mat beside him. "Happy is the body which labors for its own soul," he said. "What troubles you?"

Itaz was silent for a long time, then said heavily, "I am being tormented by an evil demon of lust," and already this seemed a kind of betrayal of his feelings, to put so simply something so much deeper now than lust, and so ringed with doubt.

"Ah," said the priest tolerantly. "That is an affliction common among young men; strive against it, my son, and avoid whores, who are a trap set for you by the Lie. But be comforted by the thought that others suffer in the same way."

Itaz shook his head impatiently. "You don't understand. The woman . . . the woman is married."

"Oh." The priest pulled at his thin white beard. "Oh, I see, that is much worse; you are right to pray to the god for help. Is she a believer?"

"No, she's . . . an unbeliever. But she's honest; she doesn't encourage me. I try to put her out of my mind but I can't."

The priest was silent a moment. "You are a nobleman?" he asked at last. "Of the Sakaraukai?"

"I am a Saka of Ferghana."

"Ah!" said the priest, in a changed voice, his old face sharpening. "So you are; I saw you at Anahita's temple and I recognize you now: you are the son of the king Mauakes. Forgive me. I didn't know you were a Mazdayist." That pleased him; Itaz resignedly saw that he would boast of it to rival sects. He set his teeth, wishing he'd kept his troubles to himself. But the priest was nodding now. "Ah, I see now why you are so troubled. It is very much worse for the son of a king to be tormented by lust for the wife of one of his father's subjects than it is for a private citizen. You dare not even speak of it in your homeland, at your own temple, in case the husband should learn of it and take offense. No, no, have no fear, it is safe here. I will tell no one." He frowned. "You have prayed against this trouble and it hasn't got better?"

"I've prayed, I've offered sacrifice, and it's only grown worse every time I see her," Itaz said wretchedly. "I'd avoid the woman if I could, but I can't."

The old man made a sympathetic noise, frowning. "It must indeed be the work of some demon, then. We must have a ceremony of purification to drive it away."

"Yes!" said Itaz, catching a glimpse of hope. "I'd be glad of that. When could we hold it? I must leave the city again the day after tomorrow."

"Ehh . . . Midnight tonight? It is an auspicious day tomorrow, the Thanksgiving for the Creation of Earth. If we hold the ceremony at night, you will have the benefit of the thanksgiving in the new morning."

"Excellent!" said Itaz, smiling at the old man.

The priest beamed back at him and patted his hand. "I will prepare it for tonight, then, and my grandson and I can conduct it; my son will take the morning service for the people. But"—with embarrassment— "I must ask you to give some money to the temple. We have many poor, here in the city, and then there are visitors, and sometimes they have been robbed on the roads—whenever there is a war the bandits gather like vultures, and we have men come in in rags, with all their goods lost, begging only for food to give them strength enough to get home . . ." He trailed off shamefacedly. Itaz noticed that the white robe was patched, and felt a stab of liking for the old man. "And then there is the haoma," the priest finished, snorting ruefully at himself. "The cost goes up and up." Haoma is a mountain plant, used by the Mazdayists in their ceremonies. A decoction of its root is said to bring visions; the Mazdayist laypeople usually take only one sip of it from a common cup, but for special services the priests sometimes get very drunk on it and say they see all the secrets of Heaven and Hell.

Itaz took his purse and tipped all its contents, which included the gifts of King Heliokles, out onto the mat before the old priest. "Take what you need, and give the rest to the poor," he said, and the priest beamed, caught his hands, and thanked him warmly.

Itaz told the guide, and later the servants of King Heliokles, that he wished to return to the temple for a special service that night, and they shook their heads in tolerant amusement. He left the palace after supper, refusing the offered attendants, and went directly to the temple. The door was still unlocked, as he'd hoped. Inside the only light now came from the sacred fire, a faint orange glow just visible through the curtains. He sat down on the floor in the dark and prayed, impatiently now, hoping that in a few hours all his doubts and anguish would be cleared away.

The old priest came in an hour or so before midnight, carrying a lantern and accompanied by a boy. He greeted Itaz quietly, bowed to the fire, and he and the boy lit the lamps that hung on silver chains down the length of the building. Then the priest put on the cotton mask and the gloves, which they wear to stop their breath from contaminating the holy fire, and drew back the curtains round the fire on the altar. He added sticks of sandalwood and sage and the flames burned up brilliantly, giving a clear light and a sweet clean smell; the priest turned from it to Itaz and said, "Blessed are the pious who come to this offering!"

Itaz stood and whispered the sentence of the service, "I arrive in the world, I accept affliction, I am contented with death."

The service was a long one. The boy sang, the priest prayed and recited the long hymns and invocations, the fire burned. Sometime after midnight Itaz went up to the altar and the priest marked his palms with the consecrated water, then scattered more water about with the bundle of consecrated twigs of tamarisk and pomegranite. He lifted the mortar with the haoma root in it. "Come hither with a weapon for the pure, to protect the body, O golden Haoma," he intoned solemnly. "Against the spirits of lust, endowed with magic art, causing desire, whose spirit goes forward like a cloud driven by the wind; bring hither a weapon for the pure, to protect the body." With trembling hands, the old man crushed the haoma, blended it in milk, and poured it into a golden cup. He took one sip, then handed the precious drink to Itaz. "Drink all of it," he whispered. Itaz obeyed, and the priest prayed again, holding out his hands over the holy fire and begging the god to

destroy the demon that tormented his worshipper, and to purify his
mind, as fire purifies the earth. When the prayer was finished, he led
Itaz to an alcove to one side of the fire altar, where there was a soft
rug. "Now sleep," he told him. "Wake in the morning to give thanks
for the creation of Earth, new and purified with a clean heart."

Itaz nodded; he felt very dizzy and was glad to lie down. When his
eyes shut, though, the room seemed to spin about him so madly that he
opened them again. It must have taken longer than it seemed, because
the priest was nowhere to be seen, and all but one of the lamps had
been put out. That one hung just before the alcove, and its flame rose
high, burning still and orange-gold. It made him think of Heliokleia—
and the memory struck him with a stab of pure longing, making his
flesh stand up and bringing tears to his eyes. He sat up and began to sob
in loss and despair. The god had changed nothing. He was still in love.

After a while he began to feel cold, and he pulled the rug up about
his shoulders and sat huddled in the alcove, waiting for morning to
come. But the temple seemed to grow steadily darker and colder; the
stone creaked as though something heavy had settled on it, as though it
were being buried a long way beneath the earth. The lamp still burned,
but it seemed as though its rays were being smothered by the thick
darkness, and it grew dimmer and dimmer. When it was only a faint
blur he could bear the crushing weight of darkness no longer, and he
stood, stamped his cold feet, and stepped nearer to it. The wick was
almost burned out, and the flame guttered in the oil. He saw by its
faint light that the floor was covered with snow. He did not think this
odd, at the time, but merely looked for something to trim the lamp
with. There were no tongs nearby, so he drew his dagger and pulled up
the wick with this; the flame leapt up again, casting a circle of gold
light. At the edge of that circle he saw his father, staring at him with
accusing eyes. He knew, the moment he met that bitter glare, that the
king knew everything, all the secret longing he had never confessed—
knew it and despised it and was wounded by it to the heart.

"Father!" he said aloud, paralyzed with guilt.

Mauakes stepped nearer, drawing his sword. Itaz found his own
knife settling in his palm, ready to be used. He looked at it in horrified
disgust. What kind of man murders his father out of lust for his

father's wife? Wildly, he hurled the knife away into the darkness. "Father!" he said again. "I don't *want* to do it!"

In answer, Mauakes raised the sword. Then there was a sudden horrifying noise from the blackness, and his father whirled about, his mouth falling open in a soundless shout as an immense shapelessness hurled itself at him out of the night. There was a confusion of teeth and eyes, curved horns and yellowed claws and rags of hair, snake coils, a smell of blood; the nameless thing flung itself about the king and began to crush him. Mauakes struck it with the sword, but the iron snapped uselessly in his hand. He screamed once, a bellow choked into a shriek, and then his face had vanished into the horror, and the arm that held the sword was torn off and hurled aside to fall bleeding at Itaz' feet. Itaz screamed, clutched helplessly at his empty belt, then ran toward the deadly tangle, slipped in the snow and fell. Something hot went over him and he screamed again, climbed to his knees, staring wildly around himself.

His father, the horror, and the snow were all gone. He was kneeling by the foot of the fire altar, and the old priest was crouching beside him, holding his shoulder and saying, "Son, son, be calm. You're safe here, all is well."

Itaz stared for a moment longer, breathing in hot gasps. He felt in his belt. The dagger was there again. He leaned back on his heels and put his hands to his eyes, trembling.

"You have seen a vision," said the priest. "What was it?"

"My father . . ." said Itaz. "There was . . . there was a thing . . . it tore him to pieces . . . oh merciful Anahita!" He was choking on tears.

"Come and sit down," the priest said soothingly. He led him back to the alcove. When Itaz saw it, he stopped dead and shook his head.

"No!" he said. "I'm not going back there!"

The priest hesitated, then led him in the other direction, out of the temple, and across the street to a small house. The stars were fading, and the sky was gray; the street was hot with the Bactrian summer. Itaz shivered, a little of the chill beginning to leave him. The old priest took him into the house and sat him down in the kitchen. The room was full of loaves of plaited bread, shiny with glaze and smelling of cassia, and of pots of earth and clay shapes of men and animals, ready for the morning service of thanksgiving. The priest fetched him a cup of water. "What did you see?" he asked again, when Itaz had drunk it.

"My father . . . there was a thing, a monstrous kind of . . . a thing like nothing on earth. It attacked him and tore him to pieces. I couldn't help. His arm fell at my feet, there was blood . . ." He looked at his boots. There was no blood on them.

"Hush," said the priest. He was silent for a moment, then smiled and patted Itaz' arm. "It must have been the demon that was tormenting you. You saw what it wished to do—tear up your father's kingdom by seducing you into an act of wickedness with the wife of one of his subjects. But you've been too strong for it. What you saw is something that can't happen now."

"Can't it?" asked Itaz doubtfully.

"We have made certain of that!" said the old man. "The ceremony has driven it off. You have seen its true shape, and won't be deceived by it again."

"But I still love . . ."

"No, no," said the priest confidently. "You'll find that that will pass now. Rest awhile, then come with me and join in the thanksgiving for the creation of earth."

Itaz didn't believe him. But he was too tired to argue, and anyway, he liked the old man. He rested, then went back across the road with the old priest and his family to watch the priest's son conduct the thanksgiving service for a congregation of local shopkeepers and Parthian traders. But he had no confidence in the old man's interpretation of the vision, and had never felt less thankful in all his life.

CHAPTER

XII

The morning before he left he sought out Padmini and Anti-ochis, thinking that the queen would want to know how they were.

Both the ladies had married officers in King Heliokles' guard, and had apartments in the palace. Itaz was directed to Padmini's room, and found both of them there, weaving. Padmini's daughter, a slim dark sixteen-year-old, sat beside her mother, and Antiochis' youngest, a plump girl of eight, was spinning laboriously, her tongue between her teeth. When Itaz was admitted to the room, both girls were promptly sent out, as too young and modest to be exposed to the gaze of an unknown young barbarian. Again he realized how much the queen had left her past behind when she married a Saka.

"Ladies," said Itaz politely, "I came to ask whether you had any message to send to Queen Heliokleia."

"Thank you, Lord Itaz," said Padmini, as usual speaking for both of them. "Send her our love and loyalty, and tell her that we are well."

261

There was an awkward pause. "Your families are well?" he asked.

"They are. They, of course, are pleased that we're back."

"Tell her my eldest has enlisted in the royal guards, in his father's troop," put in Antiochis. "And Padmini's Nikolaos won first prize in the school competition for speech making. My little Gorgo won the girl's contest on the lyre for her age."

"I'll try to remember. You . . . you have some position in the court, still?"

Padmini sniffed. "The king neither blames nor commends us for what we've done. So we keep our rank as the "king's friends" but have no duties. We are at liberty to devote ourselves to our own homes; thank the gods we have plenty to occupy us!"

"He doesn't believe what you told him?"

Padmini looked at him with narrowed eyes. "He believes us, but pretends not to. Your father has no very great reputation for kindness, here where people have endured his raiding parties. The king knew when he agreed to the marriage that his sister might be made to suffer. Do you understand that? He wanted the Tochari weakened and kept away from his people; he values his alliance too much to shake it with protests to your precious father. If our lady had written to complain, he might have been forced to take note of it, but she hasn't, and won't. She accepted the risk of unhappiness as much as her brother did; she won't yield or run away now. But *we* were free to protest, and we did. We thought King Heliokles should know the kind of reception a Greek princess can expect among the Sakas."

Itaz looked away, ashamed.

Antiochis said suddenly, "Why did you tell the king that our lady was going to inform him of some crimes committed by his ministers?"

"It was what I'd heard," said Itaz. "Wasn't it true?"

"She'd heard things," said Padmini, "but she wouldn't have said anything without evidence. It is true that the ministers were alarmed— especially Archedemos. You've stirred up a wasp's nest there. The king is investigating the matter now and the whole palace has been turned upside down."

"Has it?" asked Itaz in surprise. "He didn't seem . . . that is, I thought he dismissed what I said as a rumor."

"Oh no," said Padmini. "Do you think he's stupid? He's a very able king, and not one to favor corruption. He's regretted not making a better bargain in the marriage and he'd wondered why Archedemos pressed so hard for it. But he never hears what anyone says in Bactrian. He wishes—now!—that he'd thought harder before he married off his sister. He should never have agreed to the marriage"—vehemently—"never."

"Your father doesn't deserve her," Antiochis put in. "I always hoped she'd marry her cousin, Menander's son Straton. Well, I pray to the gods that it turns out for the best."

Itaz nodded, looking sick.

Both women stared at him in surprise. "What is it to you?" demanded Padmini. "You're the one who disliked her most, who tried to stir up the council against her."

"I . . . I've changed my mind," replied Itaz. The two women stared at him again with curious, suspicious eyes, and he suddenly wanted desperately to get away from them, go . . . not home, but out, alone somewhere. "I must go," he told them. "My men are ready to return to Eskati now. Rejoice! I'll tell your news to the queen."

"Rejoice!" they replied, puzzled, and he fled.

Heliokles rode with him to the gates, then gave him two letters, one for Mauakes and one for Heliokleia. "A private query, eh?" he said, handing Itaz the letter for the queen. "Concerning some friends of hers here in Bactra. Give it to her, not to your father's secretary. A pleasant journey, kinsman. Rejoice!"

Rejoice, rejoice, they said, but Itaz rode out of Bactra even more confused and wretched than when he'd ridden into it. He pushed the pace, hurrying the escort home, though he dreaded the arrival. The men grumbled: it was hot; there was no reason to hurry; the horses were tired. Itaz replied curtly: they had been gone too long. The effort of hard riding was comforting: watching the road, judging the horses' limits, urging the men on, took all his attention, and he had no time to wallow in the black confusion. They reached the Oxus in a day, Maracanda in three, and turned east on the high road toward Eskati.

Water is scarce along the ridge at the end of the summer. The plentiful streams of the spring thaw are mostly dry, by then, and the winter rains are still ahead. Itaz was forced to spare the tired horses, and halt earlier in the day wherever there was a trickle of water dampening a streambed. The guardsmen set up camps, hunted for game, and sat about the campfires eating the fresh meat and talking over the wonders of Bactra or singing songs and telling the old stories of heroes, monsters, and wars. Itaz sat with them silently. Every time they stopped, his misery seemed worse. It seemed to grow by itself, no longer confined by the situation that had caused it, but spreading out like a tree, entangling everything he did in its deep roots and thorny branches. He no longer worried simply whether it was right to love his father or the queen; he found himself questioning all the rules he lived by—the way of life of his own people, the sanctity of oaths, the value of love, the goodness of the gods and their wisdom in creating the world. He was angry; angry with the laughing young guardsmen, with the dusty road and the dry streams, with the Bactrians, with the people of Ferghana, with his father, the queen, and himself. The anger choked him, welling up suddenly over little things—a broken halter or a stone in his stallion's hoof; he sat with the others about the evening fires tasting the rage at the back of his throat and not trusting himself to speak.

At dusk on the third day out from Maracanda, his horse slipped its halter and bolted up the latest streambed, and he swore aloud, consigning it to Angra Mainyu. He almost wanted to shoot the animal and have done with it. But even if it hadn't been a cherished servant, it was a stallion of the royal breed, and had to be recovered. He picked up the halter and a handful of grain to tempt it back to him and stamped off up the stream after it. The others laughed at him, none of them offering to help. They were tired of his hurry and his tempers, and he couldn't blame them. Probably, he thought, he'd be better off dead— and the complete seriousness with which he thought it shocked him momentarily calm again.

The black stallion had stopped just round the bend of the stream and was browsing on the willows. Itaz approached it slowly, whistling and clicking his tongue, but it laid its ears back and began to walk on up the stream, snatching mouthfuls of leaves as it went. He swore again, under his breath, and went after it. It would be too tired, he thought, to go far.

But that evening a demon had got into the horse, as sometimes happens. It walked on up the stream, not hurrying, but never letting him get near, shying and laying its ears back when he got too close. It

ignored his calls, his whistles and his curses, scorned his offered handfuls of grain or leaves. Itaz lost his temper and shouted; the horse shied
and bared its teeth and stayed farther away than ever. It grew dark, and
the gully was steep. Itaz could scarcely see the horse, but he heard it,
crunching leaves or scrambling up the bank beyond him. He remembered that this was good country for tigers or snow leopards; it wasn't
safe to leave the horse in the hope that it would find its own way back
onto the road home. Wearily, he struggled on. He stumbled and turned
his foot on a stone; he stood, shaking with anger, and stared at the
horse, then only a few paces away. It snorted and started upstream
again. Itaz gave a shout of exhaustion and exasperation, and the animal
broke into a trot, vanishing into the darkness. Itaz leaned against a
willow and rubbed his ankle. He found that he was trembling with
weariness, and had no idea how far he was from the camp. Around him
the trees whispered to each other in the vast empty stillness of the
mountain; there was that sense, suddenly, which everyone who's been
alone in the wilderness knows, that the world is other than it seems,
and is watching, hostile. Itaz closed his eyes, put his hand on his dagger,
whispered a prayer to calm himself, then struggled doggedly on after
the horse.

He had not gone a dozen paces when he smelled wood smoke. He
paused, then pressed on more hopefully. The slopes were used as summer pasturage by Sogdians and Sakas both, and there was nothing odd
in finding a herdsman here; perhaps the fellow could help him catch
the horse.

The streambed opened out into a meadow, gray and uneven in the
darkness, and there was the fire, burning low on the gravel where the
stream was dry. A man sat before it cross-legged, no more than a black
shape in the red light, staring into the embers. Behind him were two
horses: a white, tethered; and Itaz' black, cropping the dry grass. Itaz
climbed out of the stream bed and stood panting before the fire. The
man glanced up, then stood. "Your horse?" he asked in Sakan.

"Yes," said Itaz, looking at the animal with loathing.

The other chuckled. "Led you a chase, has he? Let me catch him
for you."

Itaz grunted and sat down by the fire. His ankle ached and his

temper was in shreds; a fresh, calm man had far more chance of catching the horse than he did. He watched to see how long it took him.

No time at all. The other simply walked toward the black horse
slowly, hand outheld, caught its nose, and led it over to its master.
"Here you are," he said.

Itaz gave a whistle of admiration and climbed to his feet. He
slipped the halter over the animal's head and fastened it securely, then
patted the stallion and stroked its neck, trying to reassure it and himself, after the angry chase, that he meant it no harm. The horse nuzzled
his shoulder and looked for the grain he had offered it before; Itaz took
the handful out of his purse and let the animal eat. "Thank you," he
told his unexpected helper.

"Think nothing of it," replied the other. "You're camped down by
the road? He has led you a chase, hasn't he? That's a steep climb, in the
dark, and the footing's treacherous."

Itaz grunted, still stroking the horse. His anger seemed to have
burned itself out, leaving only an immense tiredness.

"Worse footing going down," said the herdsman. "If I were you
I'd wait for moonrise before I tried it. You're welcome to share my
fire."

"Thank you," said Itaz. The other gave him a length of rope, and
together they went to tether the black horse beside the white. The
white, though only a pale shape in the darkness, was still obviously a
hand higher than the black, and Itaz paused, staring at it in puzzlement.
He glanced around the meadow: in the black night it was hard to say,
but there seemed to be no animals resting in dips and hillocks. He
looked at his companion, who was tying the horse to a bush. "I
thought you were a herdsman," he said.

"Oh no." The other went back to the fire and sat down. "I'm
traveling on business. The pasturage is better off the road." He put
some more wood on.

Itaz stood over him, staring. The fire, burning up, caught the
other's red and purple cloak, the glint of a gold brooch, and a pair of
sharp, amused eyes in a shaven face under a flat hat. A wealthy Yavana.
He sat down. "What business?" he asked, feeling a sudden, instinctive
liking for the other. "If you're going to Eskati, you could join us."

"I'm coming from Eskati," replied the other. "I had to see a man."
He smiled. "Where are you coming from, good sir?"

"Bactra."

"A fine city. Had you been there before? Ah, what a pleasure to be
young, and see Bactra for the first time!"

"Not much pleasure to me," said Itaz sourly. "I . . . was busy."

"What a pity." The Yavana sat in silence for a moment, watching
Itaz with shrewd, sympathetic eyes, then said, "If I can say as much
without giving offense, I'd say that you seem troubled. Was it such a
sad business, whatever took you to Bactra?"

"Yes." Itaz sat in silence a minute, staring into the fire, remembering again the queen's white face as she said goodbye to her ladies. He
hunched his shoulders and looked up, found the traveler still watching
him with silent sympathy. He had a sudden urge to confide in this man,
briefly and namelessly encountered on a dark mountainside, who
would never connect a lone man met chasing a strayed horse one night
with the son of the king of Ferghana in daylight. "I had to take a
message to the kin of my father's wife," he said.

"She's unwell?"

"She's unwell, the marriage is unhappy, her kin don't mind."

"And you do."

"Yes. I used to hate the Bactrian Yavanas. But she's . . . I don't
know where I stand anymore. On anything. I've tried to hate her, but I
can't. I try not to hate my father, but I do."

The Yavana said nothing, watching Itaz with gentle absorption,
ready to listen or change the subject, as he wished.

"Oh, not hate," Itaz admitted. "That word's too strong, far too
strong. But he's wrong. He was wrong to marry her, but if he had to
marry her, he should have treated her gently, trusted her, tried to
understand her. He's like a peasant with some cunning Yavana machine,
twisting it about to make it work, and breaking it more with every
turn. He doesn't know what he's doing, but I can see it even when I try
not to. She's . . . merciful Anahita! . . . she's—well, there's no
sense talking about it." He fell silent again.

"I take it she's your father's second wife," said the Yavana drily.
"And nearer your age than his. He married her for money or connec-
tions, and you're in love with her."

Itaz looked up sharply, biting his lip and regretting his honesty. But the other just looked amused—amused and touched. "Never fear," he said gently. "I'm in no position to tell, even if I wanted to, which I don't. It must be painful enough to be in your situation; I've no wish to make it worse. But it isn't exactly unheard of, you know. One can't help falling in love, and these things happen whether we want them to or not."

"Oh, by all the gods, I am in love with her," Itaz said, passionately now. The words, out loud, were an immense relief; there never was a nature less suited to concealment than his. "I've never felt like this before about any woman. When it started, I wanted her, worse than I've ever wanted any woman, but now it's even worse than that, though I didn't think it could be. I don't know what to do. I've prayed to the gods to help me, but they haven't, and now I scarcely know where I am. I have to go back there. I have to see her every day—and she . . . she feels a little the same about me, I'm sure of it. A little bit at least. I don't know what to do."

"You prayed to the gods?" asked the Yavana, frowning, after a moment. "Involving gods is a dangerous business: divinities don't always do what we expect them to. I found that out through some rash claims of my own once. Which gods did you pray to?"

"Ahura Mazda. And Anahita. I am a follower of the good religion. That makes it worse: I know what's right; I know this is evil—but I still can't escape from it. I thought at first that this desire was caused by some demon, but I've prayed, I've sacrificed, in Bactra I went to a temple and undertook a full purification ceremony, but the only vision I received was a nightmare so terrifying I don't like to remember it. The god won't help me and the trouble's worse than ever. I swear I've done nothing to deserve this, nothing!"

"Why is it evil?" asked the Yavana unexpectedly.

Itaz stared at him a moment in disbelief. "She's my father's wife!"

"But not your mother. Saka custom would allow you to marry her if your father were dead."

Itaz felt hot and sick. "To preserve his line, yes, it's allowed! But he's not dead; I don't want him dead! I'm not so wicked as to want him dead!"

"It hasn't even crossed your mind?" asked the other, gently ironic.

Itaz caught his breath and stared into the fire. The hot sickness relaxed its clutch on him, then vanished as utterly as his earlier anger. He looked again at the black morass he'd been struggling in, and saw, quite clearly, the greatest horror, the root of his anger and hatred, the beast that had torn his father to pieces, had been this.

"But I don't want him dead," Itaz protested, quietly and in bewilderment, more to himself than to the other.

And to his surprise and relief, the words were true. It was as though he'd suffered a painful injury a long time before, but had refused to examine the wound or treat it, for fear of what he'd see; and finally, forced to it, discovered not a twisted mass of gangrene but a clean, common slash, sore perhaps, but easily cured and nothing to be afraid of. "I don't want him dead," he repeated in wonder, looking up again. "That is, there is an evil in me that wishes it, yes, but *I* don't. I love him and my own honor too much. I couldn't live with myself if I won happiness only through his ruin; I'd end up hating the woman and myself. I hate the thought so much I wouldn't allow it to cross my mind. Even in the vision I threw my dagger away, rather than use it on my father."

"It might have been easier for you if you'd let it cross your mind and shot it down," said the Yavana drily. "But never mind. Apart from that, is it evil to love this woman? I mean, is she an evil woman? You were speaking of her with some admiration."

Itaz thought for a long moment. The old loathing and distrust wavered like dust clouds before a strong wind. He saw that for a long time now he had been using them to screen himself, trying not to see her as she was. But it was too late to tell himself any more lies. "Yes," he said at last, and the doubt vanished on the word. Again he felt weak with relief, as though half the branches of the tangle tree of contradictions had been lopped off at one stroke. "I do admire her. She's very brave. She's noble and strong and self-sacrificing. She also takes herself very seriously, insists on seeing everything with the eyes of the mind and not the body, and doesn't know when to laugh—but she could learn, so easily."

"Then my objection stands. There's nothing inherently evil in you loving this woman; the evil is secondary, in the circumstance of her being married to your father. I know, I know, spare you from Yavana philosophers! But it seemed to me that you were very angry with the gods for failing to help you. Things look different from Heaven than they do on earth. Look, what's that?" The Yavana pointed at the trickle of water in the gravel of the stream bed, which glowed golden red with reflected firelight.

"That?" asked Itaz in confusion. He reached over and touched it lightly. "Just water, of course."

"Just water. But what is that? It is vapor in the air, it is snow, it is rain, it is great rivers and caverns of ice. It gives life to the earth and wears mountains into dust. It forms seas deeper than the mountains are tall, and in the wide waters live things no man on earth has names for. Without it we are all of us dust. You Sakas water your cattle by it, and grow rice and wheat; we Greeks can run it through channels and draw it from deep wells; siphon it and pump it and use it to turn wheels to grind stone like grain. But do either of us understand it?"

Itaz stared at his wet fingers. "What does this have to do with the gods?" he asked after a moment. "Are you trying to say that they won't hear or understand our prayers?"

The Yavana smiled. "Not in the least. But why should you expect them to respond as a human being would? We humans live in a world our own minds have made. We say 'water'—or 'hydor' if we're Greek —and we dig our irrigation ditches and think we know the truth about things. But the gods don't live in that world at all. Our rules and our beliefs and our names for things change from place to place and from time to time, but if a god is a god, he lives with what is true always and everywhere. Water for him is the thing above or beneath all our names and uses, the thing itself. And love is at least as deep as deep water, and certainly just as hard to grasp. It isn't bounded by those channels we cut called "marriage" or "desire," though no doubt it flows in them happily enough if we don't ask it to go uphill. But our human laws aren't any part of its nature, and it can slip through them as easily as that stream slips through stones. And if the gods are concerned with it at all, they're concerned with the thing itself, not human rules about it. So if you go praying to them to deliver you from it, they're likely to be a bit disconcerted. If there's anything certain about mortals, it's that they want love; they can't live without it; never have enough of it; are always begging the gods for it. When you invoke a god to get rid of it and say "Go away, evil demon!" it won't work. It's not evil, and the god may have struck you with it in the first place. All the evil is ours: our corruption of marriage, our greed, weakness, lust, and self-deceit."

Itaz gaped at him for a moment. He had followed the argument; he had even agreed with it—but the conclusion was a contradiction of his faith. "In the good religion we worship a good god, not a law-breaker!" he said hotly. "Anahita is nothing like your Yavana whore, Aphrodite!"

"Yes, but," said the Yavana, "whose laws are you breaking?"

"The sacred laws of marriage, which are sworn by our Lord the Sun, who is the image of the Wise Lord."

The other sighed. "But what do they include? When your ancestors roamed the steppes, they allowed married men and women to sleep with anyone they pleased. A man simply hung up his quiver outside a woman's wagon and enjoyed himself without misgivings. Your cousins the Massagetai live that way to this day. Well, you've changed your customs, now that you're a settled people, but your ancestors swore marriage oaths by the Sun as much as you do. How do you think the Sun remembers what rules you're using now?"

"This is nothing but Yavana trickery," said Itaz angrily. "I shouldn't have spoken."

The man stared at him for a moment, then gave a smile of amusement, so open and affectionate that Itaz found his resentment melting. "I'm not saying this out of mere sophistry," said the Yavana.

"Then what do you mean by it?"

"Which is the greater evil, marriage without love, or love without marriage? Don't you think that that's a question that shouldn't have to be asked? It's human perversity that forces a choice: if the world were good, as the gods surely meant it to be, the two would be the same. Don't blame the gods because your own people misuse marriage laws. And don't beg them to kill your natural feeling for this woman, as though it were a centipede, because your circumstances don't permit you to marry her."

Itaz frowned. He remembered his answer to Heliokleia's story of the two men and the treasure: that the contradiction was an illusion, since the real evil was in the world's need for money. He shook

himself. "Adultery is evil!" he declared fiercely. "It's perjury and theft
and betrayal all in one, and in this case it would be incest as well.
Whatever rules other people live by, these are the ones we've accepted,
and they're better than the customs of the steppes. Everyone knows
that, and no ordinarily decent person would deny it. If all these fine
words about the gods and love add up to nothing more than an excuse
for adultery, then, for all their cleverness, they're senseless."

"But you don't want to commit adultery," the Yavana pointed out,
smiling. "And you don't want your father dead. You've said both those
things now. So. You're simply in love. The deed is evil, but is the
thought?"

"Thoughts father deeds!"

"True. But what is your thought? You said it was not just desire.
What is it, then?"

Itaz stared at him, frowning, silent. The fire hissed softly; a horse
shifted beyond them in the darkness, and far off an owl hooted sorrow-
fully.

"Humans define things too quickly," said the Yavana regretfully.
"In the end the body only knows four wants—hunger and thirst, desire
and weariness. And all the thousand impulses and yearnings of our
minds we define with those four words. I remember once I was riding
along a stream and I suddenly saw how one irrigation channel from it
would water as much land as sixty teams could plough. I was on fire
with longing for that channel, for rice paddies and fields of alfalfa full
of grazing horses where there was only baked earth and thistles. That's
what my mind wanted. But I tell you, all my body knew was an agony
of lust. How else could it understand? Desire can be true and false at
the same time. If satisfied lust was all there was to it, we could dip into
a brothel and out again, and be all our lives as content as a baby at the
breast. But most of the time the act of generation is almost irrelevant.
What is it that you want? Why do you want this woman, and not
another?"

Itaz sat in silence for a long time. It was suddenly possible to think,
where before his mind had shied away from one intolerable yearning
after another. He imagined Heliokleia again as he had seen her first,
standing outside the city walls in her saffron robes, smiling up at his
own restless, passionate hostility. The scene looked different now; ev-

erything looked different, but particularly himself—that young man who had looked back at the queen in fear and pride, a prince with a headlong longing for goodness and honor who had just discovered, in the angry refuge of a brothel, that his father and his country had no use for him at all. "All my life I've been in a narrow place," he whispered, more to the night and the fire than to his listener. "When I went off to be fostered I was a stranger among a foreign people, without duties and without rights. I was never taught anything but fighting—riding and shooting and using a lance, and heroic deeds sung by minstrels. I'm an ignorant Saka barbarian, yes." He glanced up quickly at the other, looking for the superior contempt.

There was none. "My own people are far from wise," murmured the Yavana. "Merely clever."

"But there was no one much to fight," Itaz went on. "And it wasn't enough, to sit waiting. So I took up the good religion. And then I came home. Home is another narrow place, an even narrower place. Any step I take outside a boundary is a step into treason or wrongdoing. I won't cross the boundary, but I can't be still. I'm like a weasel in a box, dashing from one end to the other. Where could I go, what could I do with myself? But she was calm. From the beginning, calm as a light in a still place. So I wanted her. To hold her, to be with her. Partly, I suppose, because she is very beautiful, and it makes my blood burn to be near her. And partly because . . . it's as though she were a side of myself I can't otherwise know, where there is space to breathe. She is so different from me . . . different from what I thought I was, but when I'm with her I find I understand her, and I think and feel differently. Not to love her is to lose things . . . knowledge . . . that I haven't yet discovered. It's as though I'd been blind, and have to put out my eyes when they first start to see, because they see things that are forbidden." He looked up and grimaced, angry with the other for asking the question and with himself for answering. "That," he said heavily, "is what I want, and why."

The other chuckled. "Well said! And do you need . . . possession . . . for that? For the knowledge, I mean, not the fire in the blood."

Itaz began to answer, then stopped. "No," he said in wonder.

"Good," said the Yavana. "Unsatisfied desire is painful enough without fighting it and hating your own heart. Fires can be trusted to go out, in time, if they're not fed."

Itaz looked down into the orange embers, still blinking with amazement. Peace. Yes. After all the turmoil and confusion, that was the way to peace—and more than that, to a kind of bittersweet happiness. He could love her, he could learn from her, he could try to help her, he might even teach her to laugh; and if he didn't touch her, all would be well. He might even learn to forget how desperately he wanted her, marry somebody else, and grow peacefully old in her company.

His eyelids drooped with an immense tiredness, as though he'd finished some long struggle and could finally sit down and rest. "You clever Yavanas," he said aloud. "Thank you."

"Think nothing of it," returned the other, smiling. "The moon still isn't up; do you want to sleep here for a bit, and rejoin your friends in the morning?"

"Thank you," Itaz said again, and lay down, rolling his cloak under his head for a pillow.

When he woke it was dawn, and the red light was pouring across the meadow, turning the damp trickle in the heart of the streambed the color of new copper. He rolled over onto his back and looked up at the sky; the moon was still up, but pale now, fading into the blue; the morning star shivered white above the peaks. He sat up.

His black horse was lying asleep by its bush, alone. The fire had gone out, and the white horse and its master were gone. Itaz stood and limped over to the stallion, stiff from the night sleeping on the streambed. He looked about for the Yavana; then, thinking the man might have taken his horse to a better watering place, looked down at the ground for tracks. The ground by the bush was damp, holding a little of the moisture from the bog the meadow would be in spring: his own tracks, and his horse's, were printed plainly in the soft ground: going up, standing; going back. But of the other, man or horse, there was no trace.

Itaz stared at the ground for a long moment, cold with shock. Then he went over it carefully; walked back to the fire and studied the gray ash. He could see the hollows in the gravel where he had sat and slept; but there were no other marks. If it hadn't been for the dead fire, he might have dreamed the whole thing. He glanced at the brightening east and made a gesture to ward off evil, then went hurriedly back to his horse and untied the picket rope.

The horse snorted and climbed to its feet. Itaz looped the rope across its neck and fastened the loose end to the halter to form a makeshift bridle. Holding it, he paused again. Caught in the bush were three long white hairs from a horse's tail, three hairs that seemed to glow of their own in the fresh light. He plucked them free hastily and stared at them, then turned eastward. The sun was just showing over the edge of the mountains, too brilliant to look at, and the birds were singing loudly by the stream. He was filled suddenly with an up-welling of sheer joy. He lifted his hands to the Sun, wanting to sing, and not knowing words or music to match the morning. Why should you expect the gods to respond as a human being would? But they had heard him, and set him free. Finally he said simply, as he had before, "Thank you," shoved the three horse hairs in his purse, mounted, and began the ride back down the gully to the road.

When he reached the camp, he found that the others were packing the supply wagons and anxiously discussing his own whereabouts. He cantered the black into the middle of the camp and reined in, grinning.

"Lord Itaz!" cried the boy Rajula, who was one of the party, "Where have you been? We were afraid you'd been killed by a tiger!"

"Don't be a fool," said Itaz good-naturedly. "The horse led me such a chase that when I caught him I decided to wait until daylight to come back. Is there anything for breakfast?"

When he had given the horse some fodder and eaten some break-fast, and the party was once again on the way back to Eskati, he drew his horse in beside Rajula's. "Rajula," he said, as quietly as he could and still be heard, "I remember you said you got a coin from Bactra you wanted to keep for luck, an old coin of Antimachos the God. May I see it?"

Surprised but compliant, the boy fished the lucky coin out of his otherwise empty purse. It was a silver drachma. Itaz studied it in the clear light of morning: the shaven face, the shrewd, amused eyes under the flat hat, and the delicate, self-mocking smile. He let out his breath slowly, clutched the coin in his fist and looked back at the sun. Then he handed the drachma back to Rajula. "Thank you," he said.

"Why did you want to see it?" asked Rajula.

Itaz was silent a moment—then laughed. "I think I had a vision last night," he said.

"Really?" asked Rajula, awed. He looked at his coin with respect. "Of him? Of Antimachos? What did he say?"

"Never mind. It's cheered me up, anyway. Much needed, you'll say, and rightly, too; I'm sorry. By the Sun, it's going to be another hot day; I'll be glad when we're home."

CHAPTER

XIII

In Eskati, Heliokelia's recovery from her head injury was slow. Though she was able to walk within a week of the accident, she had frequent blinding headaches and spells of dizziness; she felt sick and exhausted and didn't want to eat. The king, worried, ordered us—that is, her Saka attendants—to take turns sitting with her during the day. The king himself was with her at night. She still went downstairs and slept in his bed, but he didn't touch her, and slept on a mat beside the bed so as not to disturb her.

The king was spending a lot of time with his wife. He courted her like a young lover, giving her presents of flowers, jewelry and fine clothing. He consulted her about the Yavanas of the city, and agreed to a few more of her requests on their behalf. He called in minstrels, storytellers and clowns to entertain her; he was all tender concern. And it was perfectly clear—to me, at any rate—that she hated it every bit as much as she'd hated his earlier blunt roughness. She had no interest whatever in the jewelry or clothing, and would sit with a frozen smile through the songs and stories, too polite to tell the singers and tale tellers to be quiet and let her rest. Whenever Mauakes left, she would immediately sit down and meditate, and often she was still meditating when he next appeared, and had to be called back reluctant to the waking world. She rarely left the palace women's quarters—though that was partly due to her new guardsmen. There were always two of them at the stairway to the women's quarters, every day from dawn to dusk, and if she left they asked where she was going and made sure they came along and watched. Since the armed levies had returned to their lands, the king appointed the other sixty-six men of her guard himself, and he appointed them from among his own followers. The new men, who owed nothing to the queen, considered themselves to be under the king's orders, not hers, and behaved more like a prison guard than a guard of honor. She said nothing about it, but I could see she hated it, and was reluctant to go out at all under armed escort.

One hot night, when I roused her from meditation with the king's order to come downstairs, she sat still a moment, staring at the lamp, which burned yellow-white in the thick dry air. Then she reached out and snuffed the wick. She studied the ash on her fingers. "Where does a fire go when it's put out?" she asked dreamily.

I looked at the thin trail of smoke from the wick. Outside the window the stars wavered in the heat haze, white and huge as thistle heads. "Does it go anywhere?" I asked. "It's gone, that's all."

She smiled the usual slight, mocking smile, and, as usual, I wasn't sure whether it was my simplicity or her own subtlety she found ridiculous. "We are all on fire," she said in a whisper, the smile fading. "Everything we see, hear, smell, taste, or touch, and all the conceptions of our minds, are burning us alive. Passion tortures us. Our only hope of escape is to put the fire out, and become as indifferent to pleasure as to pain. Where does it go, a quenched fire?" She looked up at me earnestly, as though I could tell her the answer.

I realized then that the idea wasn't her own, but a part of her philosophy. Not being philosophical myself, I didn't know how to reply, so I simply asked her if she was hot, and if she wanted me to fetch her a drink of water. She shook her head, looking back at the ash on her hand. "Thank you, yes," she said after a moment, in a small, humble voice. "I am thirsty."

I brought the water and she drank it, then stood a moment, staring down into the golden cup. The gold was misted with the cool of the water, and gleamed only dully. I could see she'd had another thought about the fire that burns all things, but this time she didn't share it. Instead, she went to the niche by the door and set the cup down, carefully and precisely, beside the alabaster pitcher of water. "Good night," she said politely. Her face became as mindlessly calm as a statue's, and she went on out. Only after she'd gone did I realize that the question was really about death.

It was at this time that she wrote another letter to Nagasena— though she hadn't yet received any reply to her last letter.

Heliokleia to Nagasena her teacher sends greetings. I hope, sir, that this finds you in good health. For my part, I am unwell, being troubled by a head injury received in a fall; I pray the gods give me the strength to endure it quietly.

Sir, I am ashamed to beg your help along the eightfold way yet again. I find my strength of will and my attentiveness is almost gone, and, though I have every luxury around me, in spirit I am shut into a dark, dry place where I stifle. Oh, sir, even my love of the way, the divine and glorious path to release, seems shriveled up; even that looks arid and cold to me, a water-less steppeland, with no river to bring it life. What use is virtue without joy? It's hateful even to those who get the benefit of it, and no benefit at all to the virtuous. I find myself dreaming of my nurse, of human love, longing to sink into the illusory contentments of the sinful world. Thirst, yes, I know, the thirst that is the root of our suffering. I have not the strength to abandon it. You must know many remedies for such weariness of spirit, sir; please tell me one.

The king my husband has sent away two women who came with me from Bactra. They were ladies of the court, worldly women, but honorable and decent, and they had raised me from my infancy. I so long for them to be here that I find myself thinking of worldly things more often than I ever have in my life before, simply to remind myself of them. I have failed them.

It has been made plain to me that if I meddle in public affairs here, I undermine my husband: I have no opportunity to do anything meritorious, and so I fail again. I find it no easier to submit to my husband than before; I detest his touch, and now he too is grieved because I do not love him: I fail him as well. I cannot will myself to love, and I can scarcely even manage common dutiful kindness anymore. My will is a feeble thing, my mind and imagination are weak as a child's, as though I had fallen back even from the point on the path I had reached before, into the hatreds and longings of those to whom sense is everything. Sir, help me. The world's wheel turns over me; teach me to turn with it, and find release.

The queen wrote this letter in her own apartments in Eskati, then sealed it at once. If she had given it to me, I would have done as she ordered, and given it, unopened, to a Yavana merchant bound for Sakala. I hadn't liked spying even when I didn't like the queen, and I certainly wouldn't have pried off the seal and shoved my nose into her private anguish again. But when the queen finished her letter it was Inisme's turn to sit with her. Inisme offered to take the letter to the merchant at once, and Heliokleia entrusted it to her—and of course Inisme brought it instead to the king.

Mauakes summoned his Sakaraukai slave, who read the letter out. When the man had finished stumbling over the queen's words, the king frowned. "Do you know anything about this Nagasena?" he asked Inisme.

"No, sir," she replied, embarrassed. "She said she was writing to her teacher."

"That much is plain from the letter," snapped Mauakes. He signaled to the slave to read it again. This time the tone of profound unhappiness struck him less; he decided that her grief was all the result of illness. If anything, it was encouraging that she found herself longing for love, afraid of undermining his authority, and reproaching herself for failing him. Whatever she expected of this Nagasena, she clearly didn't expect him to tell her to resist her lawful husband. And he would comfort her, would give her another task that she would come to see as better and richer for her than any kind of authority or any cold philosophy: to be a loving wife and mother. "Well," he said when the slave finished, "I suppose there's no harm in it." He took the letter back, stared at it a moment, then returned it to Inisme. "Give it to the merchant, as she told you."

"Yes, sir. What . . . what should I tell him about the seal?"

"Tell him that I read it, of course. It's my right. Here, give it back and I'll seal it again; I don't want anyone else reading her private thoughts, even if they are religious and harmless."

"What do I tell the queen?" asked Inisme as the king resealed the letter with his own seal.

"Don't tell her anything," replied Mauakes without looking up. "I don't want her worried."

When Inisme arrived back at the queen's rooms, I'd returned from exercising my horse and was rinsing some of the dust off myself. Inisme slunk in nervously, avoiding the queen's eyes.

"You were gone a long time," Heliokleia said quietly. "Did you deliver my letter?"

"Yes . . . I, uh, couldn't find the house at first," said Inisme.

I stared at her, realizing what had happened without need of any more words than that. I felt sick with rage. I'd learned to like Heliokleia up at Eagle Crag, and now she was wilting before my eyes like a tree uprooted and planted in a desert; and still the king wouldn't leave her alone, and still the others spied on her.

Heliokleia looked down at her own folded hands, tasting again the salt, stifling dark of unshed tears. "Did the king ask to see it?" she asked, still quietly, looking back up at Inisme.

Inisme went red, stammered a moment, then said, "No, my lady, I thought it was a private letter!"

"It was," she replied wearily. "Never mind."

She was not surprised. The king had boxed her in so closely that it was not to be expected that he'd leave her private letters alone.

"Do you have another headache?" asked Inisme anxiously. "Should I fetch some leeches, or some chilled wine?"

"No," returned Heliokleia, "I will meditate." She crossed her legs where she sat on the couch and closed her eyes.

Inisme stood looking at the queen until I pushed her out of the room. "You did show it to him!" I accused in the corridor outside.

"Of course I did," returned Inisme. "He ordered us to. You've shown him letters, too."

"No I haven't. I told him what was in the other letter, but I didn't show it to him. And that was before I knew her."

"He gave us all orders to tell him what she does," Inisme retorted, glaring up at me. "He made it clear we were to obey him when he first chose us. If you don't like it, you should go tell him you don't want the job."

"And leave her to treacherous little things like you?" I said in disgust. "There was nothing treasonous or improper in that letter. That's all he wanted to know about, and all he needs to know about. He had no business seeing it; it wasn't to a lover or an enemy."

"You know nothing about it," replied Inisme. "You weren't there when she wrote it, and you don't know what was in it or even who it was addressed to."

"I don't need to have read it to know she's honest. She's been here long enough for any reasonable person to know that. Ten to one it was to that Nagasena fellow in Sakala, her teacher—that, or to Padmini."

"It was to Nagasena," Inisme said, somewhat taken aback. And suddenly she was telling me everything about it—what the letter said, what the king had said, how "I was ashamed to do it, but how does it hurt her for him to know what she really thinks about him? She never tells him anything!"

I didn't want to know. I tried to interrupt, but Inisme just went on. I suppose that she hated the spying as much as I had, and it eased her conscience to talk about it. Or perhaps she was trying to involve me, even against my will.

In the end I yelled "Be quiet!" so loudly that they must have heard it in the kitchens, and Inisme stopped. She glared at me, breathing fast.

"The queen keeps her misery to herself," I said. "You've no business spreading it about the palace. Spy if you must, but leave me out of it. For my part, she's my lady and I'm her loyal servant, and I give you warning I'll have nothing more to do with treachery. You didn't fool her either; she knows you betrayed her."

"He said he didn't want her worried," Inisme said defensively.

"And you think it doesn't worry her to be spied on all the time?" I asked furiously. 'I will meditate'! Merciful Anahita, she does nothing but meditate all day now! And it's all because she can't bear being where she is, locked up like a Parthian in a harem, and spied on. She's got the ability to be a queen in a thousand, but she's not permitted to so much as think out loud! If I were her, I'd send you packing. But she wouldn't be allowed to, would she? He'd intervene. 'No, no,' he'd say, 'she's a loyal servant'—and you'd stay, safe as a flea on a hedgehog. A proper Saka queen could demand better loyalty than that, but because she's a Yavana everyone thinks they can treat her as they please, and all she can do is meditate. But she won't trust any of us now, not even me."

"She doesn't anyway," observed Inisme viciously, and whirled about and stalked back into the room.

Heliokleia trusted none of us, and after long striving in meditation, resented nothing. She had come to Ferghana hoping to be a proper queen, prepared to be dedicated and hardworking, ready to take great pains over the least of her subjects' demands. But it seemed that a queen of that sort—at least, a Yavana queen of that sort—was unwanted, and for all her earnest study, she had none of the ferocity she would have needed to become one anyway. That, too, was karma, and must be borne patiently and with dignity. Ill and exhausted, blocked by her guards and servants from the common people, kept from real author-ity, she withdrew into herself and neglected the world. The headaches grew no better, she lost weight, her hair began to fall out and her gums bled. She was still beautiful—she had the kind of face that would look beautiful even as a corpse—but you could see at a glance that she was very ill. The king watched her anxiously, and was more attentive than ever.

Then Itaz returned from Bactra.

He arrived in the city late one afternoon in early autumn, and went first to the king, delivering King Heliokles' letter, which con-tained appropriate greetings, congratulations, and a promise to send more naphtha "and any other supplies you might need." He left Mauakes discussing this with his officers and his Yavana engineer, and went to see the queen.

Heliokleia was in her room, playing Four Armies. It's an Indian board game: she had a board and set of pieces which had come with her mother from India, and to pass the time she'd taught the four of us

maids to play, though only three of us played at once, since it's a game
for four players. The pieces are called horsemen, footsoldiers, elephants,
and chariots, and every player has one king piece, which the other
players try to capture. Heliokleia was very good at it, and beat the rest
of us easily. I'd liked the sound of the game at first, but after being
beaten a few times I liked it less: I hate losing, even to a victor as
gracious as the queen. She was watching resignedly as I made a fatal
mistake with a horseman when there was a knock, the door opened,
and Itaz came in, dust-stained, smelling of horses, and carrying a bunch
of orange day lilies. His eyes met hers across the room and she felt as
though the ground beneath her had vanished.

Itaz edged cautiously across the room and from arm's length offered her the flowers. "For you, O Queen," he said. "A . . . at your
brother's wish. I'd hoped to find you completely recovered, but it
seems you're still unwell."

Slowly, Heliokleia took the lilies; the flowers were leopard-spot-
ted, orange and brown, and smelled hot and wild. She looked at them
in consternation. She did not believe that her brother, obsessed with his
kingship, would ever have thought to ask Itaz to bring her flowers—
but it was almost as incredible that Itaz would look for them himself.
"I am much recovered, Lord Itaz," she said. "Thank you."

"You don't look it," he replied.

She dropped her eyes, then looked up again. "You had an agreeable
journey?"

"It was hot." After a moment, he continued, "Your brother is in
good health, and your ladies are well, and safely reunited with their
families, O Queen. They've been allowed to keep their rank at the
palace, though without duties. Umm . . . Lady Antiochis said to tell
you her eldest has enlisted in the royal guards, in his father's troop.
And Padmini's son won first prize in some school competition, while
Antiochis' daughter Gorgo won another contest, in music, I think."

"Oh!" She stared at him in surprise. "Thank you. It would be
music. Gorgo was always very musical. Like her mother. So they're
well, they're happy?"

"They were worried about you. Apart from that, they were
happy."

"Oh!" She thought of them, happy in Bactra, surrounded by their families, and looked down to hide the tears that forced themselves into her eyes. It was not that she was jealous of their happiness; the tears were of relief. Despite her own failure, Padmini and Antiochis were well; in fact, they were probably far happier than they would have been if they'd stayed. The weight of guilt dropped so suddenly made her almost light-headed. "Thank you," she said again.

Itaz nodded and sat down beside me on the couch. He pulled King Heliokles' letter from his belt and set it down on the playing board. "Your brother sends this," he said. "He said it was a private query concerning some friends of yours in Bactra, and asked me to give it directly to you."

Heliokleia picked the letter up and saw that the seal was unbroken. She looked at Itaz; he was studying the playing board. She handed Inisme the flowers and told her to put them in some water, then broke the seal and read the letter silently.

I didn't read it; she told me what was in it afterward. King Heliokles wished her health, was sorry to hear that she had suffered an accident and still sorrier to hear that her husband had, by some reports, treated her unkindly: he was confident that a daughter of Eukratides would surmount all obstacles with dignity. He had heard that she had formed suspicions of the conduct of his ministers Archedemos and Demochares; could she say who'd informed her of their misdoings, and what they were alleged to have done? Did she have firm evidence, or was it only guesses and rumors? He regretted—by Apollo!—that he had not spoken to her before agreeing to the marriage; he regretted the whole marriage, which was a bad mistake, but he dared not risk offending Mauakes by intervening now, with the Tochari still posing such a threat to his northern borders. Could she recommend a useful Bactrian speaker to advise him on marketplace rumors in the future?

Heliokleia put the letter down. Her investigations of Archedemos and Demochares, all-absorbing at the time, now seemed remote. Someone else had done that; an earnest young woman who expected to become a reigning queen. Her brother's sudden intense interest in them seemed fantastical. To write to her about the deeds of his ministers in Bactra! She had a sudden vision of him energetically questioning, in his melodious Attic Greek, one of the Bactrian cleaning maids who'd told her about the market rumors, and for the first time in days she found herself smiling. Itaz looked up from the playing board and smiled back; he had a smile that lit his whole face and glowed for a moment in his eyes even when his mouth was serious again.

"Is it funny?" he asked.

"He wants . . ." she began—then stopped. But what did it matter if Itaz knew what he wanted? "There were some of his officials I'd heard rumors about, when I was in Bactra—I used to hear stories most people at the palace missed, because I could speak Bactrian. Somehow or other he's heard about this, and wants all the details. So he sends a letter to *me* about his own ministers in Bactra!"

"That's my fault," said Itaz. "I'm sorry."

"Your fault? How do you know anything about it?"

"I'd heard a rumor that the reason your brother's ministers persuaded him to marry you to my father was because they wanted to get rid of you. I said as much to King Heliokles. He'd been annoyed with the ministers for pushing the marriage anyway; he believed it at once."

She stared at him. "But . . . but . . ." She remembered the smooth, self-satisfied Archedemos, who was supposed to have embezzled and sold alterations to the tax census; and the scrawny, wet-lipped Demochares, whom rumor connected with the smuggling of slave girls, some of them free-born and kidnapped. If it hadn't been for them, and for her investigations, she might still be in Bactra, a virgin, whole, earnest, full of hope? Mauakes might still be just a name—she might even have gone to India, and married a cousin at the court of her uncle Menander. She might be in Sakala now, listening to the sermons of Nagasena and the disputations of the scholars. "But . . ." she said again, and pressed her hands to her face to stop the tears of anger and despair; her life wasted, all her suffering, because Archedemos and Demochares wanted to get rid of her! Itaz jumped up, started toward her, then stopped.

"I'm sorry," he said again. "Did I do wrong?"

"No," she said thickly. "I just never knew there was a reason. I thought the alliance alone was important enough."

"I'm sure it is."

"No. My brother wouldn't have agreed to it, not unless my children were designated the heirs. I didn't think of that at the time, but of course it's perfectly clear now. It's all pointless, all of it, there was never any reason for me to come here at all; it's all for nothing!"

"I'm glad he married you to my father," said Itaz. "If he hadn't, I never would have met you."

She looked up at him, her face streaked with tears. "You've hated me from the moment I arrived," she said, bitterly calm again.

"I did. But I don't now."

She looked at him doubtfully, then gazed down at the letter. She folded it and slipped it in her belt. "You must excuse me," she said, not looking back. "I didn't mean to make a display of womanish emotions." She wiped her face with her sleeve.

"Please . . . I don't . . . that is, you're entitled to them. Womanish emotions, I mean."

She gave him a scathing look. Yavana queens are not entitled to any such thing. "My brother's family is well?" she asked after a silence.

"Yes."

There was another silence, then Itaz indicated my mistakenly placed horseman. "You're going to lose that piece," he told me.

"Can you play?" asked Heliokleia in surprise.

"Yes, I learned in Parthia. We played it a lot there."

"You can take my place," I said, jumping up in a hurry. As I said, I hate losing—and I had a vague, if still very doubtful, hope that a game with Itaz might cheer the queen up.

When Mauakes came in a half hour later he found his son and his wife sitting together over the game board, with Armaiti and Inisme reduced to watching and moving pieces to order. Itaz was frowning furiously down at the pieces; Heliokleia sat with her chin on her hand, her eyes shining and a faint, triumphant smile on her lips, watching him. They seemed to him to be sitting in a place of their own, the air around them different from the common air in the room, brighter, mysterious, still. Mauakes stopped in the doorway. He felt for a moment as though his heart were buried in dust—then he realized that he didn't need to worry, it was only Itaz, who hated the queen. He came on into the room; the queen looked up at his footstep and the faint smile vanished. Itaz glanced round, then stood politely, smiling a warm welcome. He had returned from Bactra, thought Mauakes, almost indecently cheerful. "What are you doing here?" the king asked his son.

"I came to give the queen a letter from her brother," replied Itaz at once. "And to tell her the news of her friends in Bactra. I stayed to play Four Armies. I haven't played it since I left Parthia. I was losing." He grinned.

"You inherited a weak position," said Heliokleia politely.

"I inherited a dangerous opponent," corrected Itaz.

Mauakes looked at the interrupted game. "Perhaps I should learn to play," he said. "Would you teach me, my dear?"

She looked down, her face scarcely moving. "If you wish it, sir."

"I could teach you too," offered Itaz. "It'd be easier with two players who know the rules. Though I'd stake my horse on it you'll be very good; it's a war game, so you'll win it."

Mauakes only grunted. "What was the letter?" he asked. Probably, he thought, that was the reason for the queen's smile.

"It was from my brother, sir, concerning some acquaintances of mine in Bactra."

The king grunted again. "What did he want?"

The queen shrugged. "He wanted to know if they were honest."

"Let me see it."

Heliokleia's hand dropped to the letter in her belt and she stared at the king. A half hour before she might have given him the letter or, at least, told him more of what it contained. Now she found herself irritated. "Sir," she said smoothly, "I'm very sorry. The letter is a confidential one and it would be very improper for me to show it to you. My brother expects to keep secret his deliberations over appointments in his own palace, and I'm sure you will forgive me for preserving a decent silence to you about his affairs, as I would to him if he asked about yours."

He stared back at her, his face shifting to its bland mask. "You are my wife," he said mildly. "Surely you don't rate your loyalty to a brother equal to that owed to me?"

"Sir, indeed not," she returned sweetly. "If you command me to give you the letter, of course I must obey. But I am certain that you value my loyalty too highly, and have too much respect for my modesty and discretion, than to give me such a command, and break the confidentiality owed to the affairs of an allied king by abusing your authority over his sister."

She knew how to do these things. But it was only to be expected that her resistance would stir the king's ready suspicions. Mauakes watched her with narrowed eyes. "I would—if the letter does indeed contain only what you say it does," he remarked softly. "I have only your word for it."

"Sir," she replied without a tremor, "you will undoubtedly see my reply to this letter, and so assure yourself beyond doubt of the truthfulness of my report of it." The voice was quiet and unemotional, but the contempt in it was deep enough to drown you.

Mauakes set his teeth, the muscles of his jaw rippling under the thick gray beard. He started toward her, then stopped. He put his hands behind his back, as though he were afraid his self-enforced gentleness had reached its limit. Then he stood still and reasoned with himself. She had a point, after all; she was not simply being contradictory. An ally's appointments in his own palace were his own business—and if the letter contained anything more than a request for references, he'd learn it from her reply. "Very well," he said more calmly, "keep the letter. Itaz, I have a few more questions to ask you about Bactra." He summoned his son with a jerk of the hand and stamped out of the room. Itaz, looking shocked and bewildered, gave Heliokleia an apologetic nod and followed him.

Heliokleia leaned back on her couch, pulled the letter out of her belt, and held it in both hands. She closed her eyes for a moment, trying to release the sense of triumph, as she would have tried to release hatred or anger. Then she opened her eyes again and glanced over the interrupted game. She brushed the pieces aside with the edge of the letter. "Put it away," she ordered. "There's no sense finishing it now."

As Inisme began to comply, the queen reread the letter. It was not really true, she admitted to herself, that it would have been a fatal breach of confidence if Mauakes had seen it. It contained a few things that Heliokles would be embarrassed to have his ally read, and of course if Archedemos and Demochares were innocent, it would be awkward if they were charged with negotiations with Ferghana again: still, it was nothing that Mauakes couldn't hear for himself from any traveler who'd recently visited Bactra—and she'd explained most of it to Itaz already. Nonetheless, she did not want her husband to see the letter now. The best thing to do would be to destroy it. She glanced around the room; none of the lamps were lit. She got to her feet. "I am going down to the kitchens," she told us.

"No, my lady, you should rest," said Inisme. "Tell me what you want and I'll fetch it."

"I want fire to burn this," replied Heliokleia evenly.

"I . . . I could take it down for you and put it in the oven," Inisme stammered after a pause.

"I think not," said the queen coldly. "I will take it myself."

I grinned. This was a deal better than meditating about it, in my opinion. "I'll come with you," I said. Inisme sniffed, but Armaiti smiled at me.

We went out of the room. The usual two guardsmen were on watch at the foot of the stairs, and they snapped to attention and asked the queen where she was going. Heliokleia looked at them coolly. "I do not require you to come," she said. "You may remain here." And she set out again, leaving them disconcertedly wondering if they ought to obey. Across the courtyard, into the annex that held the kitchens: the cooks watched in astonishment as their queen went to the bakery furnace and dropped the letter, still folded, on the banked-up embers. It crumpled slowly, blackened, then faded to gray ash. Heliokleia took a poker and stirred the embers to be sure, then gave the ashes one last, angry jab and put the poker down. I banked the embers up again and closed the furnace door. We looked at each other; I was still grinning. "Done like a queen," I told her. "He has no business spying on you, my lady. And our own customs say you ought to have much more freedom and authority than you do. You shouldn't just meditate; you should fight back. You ought to get rid of Inisme."

Heliokleia looked at me appraisingly, then started back toward her rooms without saying anything. When we were alone in the corridor, however, she stopped. "Would I be allowed to, if I wanted to do that?" she asked.

I stopped grinning. "I don't know. You ought to be, so you ought to try."

"If I were a Saka queen," Heliokleia said slowly, "you and the other girls would be people I'd brought with me from my father's house: you'd be my friends and servants, and I could hire and dismiss you as I pleased. As it is, the king chose all of you, and I would have to ask him to dismiss you. Would he dismiss a servant for doing nothing more than he told her to? And even if he would, is it just to punish Inisme because she obeyed the king? Her family run one of his estates, don't they? They would be furious with her if she offended him, and accuse her of treachery. And your family are related to Kanit, aren't they?"

I felt my face going hot. I had been vaguely aware that she had known that the king wanted me to spy on her, but this was the only time she'd mentioned it to me—and it was typical of her to do it so carefully and obliquely: "Your family are related to Kanit" rather than "Why should I think I can trust you any more than I can trust Inisme?" I suppose, looking back, the real surprise was how little Uncle Kanit still mattered to me, and how completely my loyalty had shifted —but at the time I didn't even think of that. "Well . . . yes," I stammered, looking at her weary, hopeless, appraising face, "Yes, Kanit's my uncle, and neither he nor my family would like it if I offended the king. But look, my father is a council lord in his own right. We're loyal enough to the king, who's made us strong, but there are limits. My father and mother would agree with me in points of honor, and we all believe a servant should be loyal to her lady. The king . . . if you left things up to the king, there'd be no council, no private lands, no independent nobility at all. I'm not like Inisme, my lady, please believe that. I want to see you strong. I know, it was different at first, I admit . . . he wanted me to report to him about what you did, to spy, and I did, a little bit. But you're not what I thought; you're much more of a Saka than I expected. You could make a queen such as Ferghana's never had before. And I'd be glad to help you. My parents named me after the queen of the Massagetai who defeated the Great King, and that's the kind of queen I want to serve." The words came out in a rush, "Just give me a chance, my lady," I said. "Trust me and *I* won't fail you."

As soon as I finished speaking, I saw that, once again, I'd made a mistake. I'd called her a queen of the Sakas, and summoned up the memory of the famous leader of the Massagetai, but Heliokleia looked back at me with a face purely Antimachid—distant, rueful, self-mocking. It wasn't so much that I'd missed the mark as that I hadn't even been shooting at the right target. She would not fight for her rights. It wasn't for lack of ability, or even of desire, but in some way I couldn't understand the whole question of royal authority wasn't the thing that mattered. She wanted it, she was humiliated by the lack of it—but it didn't shake that reserved and elusive heart. I was perfectly right to say she could be trusted: the central thing for her, the thing the king deprived her of that cut deep, was something else, something I couldn't name. I stared at her in dismay.

"Oh, Tomyris!" Heliokleia shook her head. "I'm not a Massageta queen, or even a Saka one. I am a Greek in blood and an Indian in faith. I am the daughter of Eukratides, who made many wars on your people, and the great-granddaughter of Antimachos, who conquered you and sent your nobility into exile. I'm the last person any Saka in Ferghana would support against the king: every restriction my husband places on me will be too little for most people in the valley. I can't possibly call on the council's backing, you must see that! I have nothing here at all, except what my husband is willing to grant me. Perhaps Inisme should stay and it's you who should find another service."

I didn't know what to think. I just looked in confusion. "You want to dismiss me?" I asked at last. "You'd tell the king what I just said?"

"No," said Heliokleia wearily. "No, of course not. But I'm no Queen Tomyris of the Massegetai, and not likely to become one either. The king doesn't trust me and the people never will. I'm simply the wrong kind of queen, for him, for them—and for you as well. You've never belonged here, and unlike me, there's no reason for you to stay." She touched my shoulder, lowering her voice. "And my dear friend, it could get worse. If I were so unlucky as to bear a son, you'd have to choose between being fellow prisoner, guard—or going back to your home."

"You underestimate yourself, my lady," I said after a shocked silence. "And you underestimate the world; it's not as bleak as you think. There is some hope sometimes; it's not nothing but suffering and more suffering. People would support you. I know the valley better than you; I know what they'll accept. The Yavanas all support you anyway, but some of the Sakas would as well; it's our *custom* to give queens some freedom; it's not *right* for him to read all your letters and make you manage your estates through his officials. There were Sakas who fought for the house of Antimachos when Mauakes came back to the valley, and there are councillors who'd support you. Everyone can see you're not an ordinary arrogant Bactrian Yavana, the kind everyone hates. Look at Lord Itaz. He used to distrust you more than anyone: he tried to talk his father out of the alliance and he drank himself silly the night before the wedding, but now he's changed his mind."

The hand dropped from my shoulder and she looked away. I didn't understand it then, but of course she didn't want to think about Itaz. Hostile he'd been disturbing enough, but friendly . . . against her will, she saw his smile again, the long, sharp face lighting up, the teeth flashing, the warm glow resting a moment in his eyes. She took a deep breath and started walking again. "So he says. He also says I'm a dangerous opponent. Perhaps I'm simply muzzled enough that he's no longer afraid of me. He has a brave and generous nature: he likes to fight when he's equally matched, and be merciful to the defeated. If I had the authority you wish, he'd be much less trusting."

"No, I think he's simply decided you're honest," I said stubbornly, hurrying after her. "He might even be willing to support you if you told the king you wanted officials of your own, and attendants you'd chosen. He didn't open your brother's letter, and he was shocked that the king could even ask it; I could see that. Perhaps . . ."

"Tomyris, that is enough!" said Heliokleia sharply, turning back into queen and mistress on the instant. Then, more gently, she added, "No more of this, not now. I am very tired; I wish to rest."

I wanted to grab the woman and shake her. What's the point of suffering passively when there are things you can do about it? But I remembered how easily she had tired since her head injury, and I followed her the rest of the way back to the room in silence.

I was right about at least one thing, though. Itaz had been shocked by his father's demand to see a private letter from an allied king, and more shocked to discover that any reply would be intercepted. Dragged off to the king's study, he answered his father's questions about Bactria absently, wondering, in his newfound eagerness to help the queen, how he could convince his father that this was wrong— until he realized that Mauakes was asking circles about the central

problem of how King Heliokles had viewed what Padmini and Antiochis had told him. Then he stopped halfway through a stumbling
reply and stared at his father; Mauakes stared irritably back.

"Go on," he commanded.

"Why don't you just ask it outright?" Itaz said, bewildered.

"Ask what?"

"Did the king believe what the queen's ladies told him?"

Mauakes squinted and grunted, then was silent for a long moment.
Itaz realized, with a chill of dread, that the king was was afraid to ask
that question. He'd suspected before that Heliokles might regret having
disposed of his sister so cheaply, and now the Bactrian king had a
pretext to intervene, even to suggest a divorce. And that prospect was
so disturbing that Mauakes was afraid even to consider it—because he
wanted her more than he thought right, and had no intention of letting
her go. No wonder he'd been anxious to see the letter.

"Very well," Mauakes said at last, "did he?"

Itaz looked away. "He seemed to me to accept your account of the
matter and let it drop. The women, though, said he did believe them,
but that he pretended not to, so as not to offend you. Whether or not
that was true I don't know; they may only have been saying it to
console themselves."

Mauakes grunted again, this time with relief. Whatever King Heliokles believed, he was not going to *do* anything.

Itaz stared at his father's feet. His feelings toward the queen had
changed, but clearly his father's had as well. This anxious possessiveness
was something new, something more than the mixture of domineering
satisfaction and distrust with which the king had viewed his wife
before. Now his own mind was thrown back into confusion. Why did
he feel this dread? For the queen's sake, because it might hurt her—or
for himself, because his father loved her and she might learn to love
back?

Itaz took a sharp breath. Feelings were treacherous. Best to forget
them, and go on as he had intended. "He would be very offended if he
knew you were demanding to see his letters to her," he said.

The king laughed contemptuously. "You think so? He probably
expects it. He's no innocent. Not like you. I don't suppose you read
that letter? By the all-seeing Sun! First you demand guards for her and

precautions against her, then, when you have the simplest and most obvious of precautions in your hand, you don't even use it!"

"King Heliokles mentioned the letter to me. He said it was . . . what she said it was. They were all in a stir in Bactra over some ministers suspected of corruption, and there was a story that she knew about it, and they'd pushed the marriage to get rid of her. No, I wasn't worried about that letter at all. And I thought . . . before you married her . . . that she would be a real queen." Itaz slowly picked his way as though along a cliff edge, trying not to topple; he sensed, instinctively, that his father's jealousy, once woken, would never sleep again. "I thought she'd have the usual rights and powers, and would be an opponent to be reckoned with. I didn't understand that you meant to . . . control her this way."

"I meant to keep an eye on her," Mauakes replied. "I admit, I've tightened things up more than I originally intended to. She's more dangerous than I'd expected. You and Tasius saw that too, didn't you? And came up with your own plan to watch her. All unnecessary: I never needed royal guards. There are easier ways to keep a tight rein on a woman. But . . ." He paused and looked at his son assessingly. "But I like her more to, eh?" He was silent for a moment, his face heavy, satisfied and troubled at the same time. Itaz knew he was remembering her body, and felt suddenly a wave of that hot sick anger he thought he'd escaped. He looked down at his hands, clenched together in his lap, and told himself again and again that his father had a right to the queen; it was he himself who had none.

"I like her more than I expected to," he managed to reply at last. "She's honorable and honest. And Bactra . . . wasn't what I expected either. King Heliokles is . . . well, he's a lot like you."

Mauakes stared at his son in offended surprise.

Itaz grinned. "I meant . . . he always goes at things roundabout, and thinks before he says anything, and keeps his followers guessing, but he seemed to have the good of his kingdom at heart. He's a good ruler."

Mauakes gave a pleased chuckle. "There's my son. So, you've come round to my view on everything, have you? The Yavana alliance, the elephants, and even the queen."

Itaz spread his hands in acceptance. "So much so that I don't think

you need to read her letters. I don't believe she'd do anything treacherous . . . and it looked as though it worried her. She looks very ill,
Father." He had been shocked by this, too. "I thought she'd be recovered by now. I . . ." He had to give his father a reason for his sudden
concern for the queen, and the reason was there, an honest one, too, as
far as it went: "I pitied her."

"That was why you stopped to play Four Armies, was it?" The
king was genial now, content that King Heliokles would not interfere.
He looked at his son's open, earnest face with affection. "Head injuries
often leave the sufferers weak and depressed, or so her doctor tells me.
But he's content now that there's no lasting damage, and she'll make a
full recovery, given time. No, I want to keep a close hold on her now,
Itaz. It's true, she's not treacherous—but she has a restive streak in her,
and she doesn't give much away. I never know what's in her mind—
but I want to trust her, I want to be able to trust her. She's not an
ordinary woman. She inherited more from Antimachos than a smile.
She's clever and capable and could be more than just a symbol of an
alliance—if I could be sure she were mine, and loyal! I want to know
everywhere she goes, everyone she sees and what she says to them; I
want to know everything that's in her mind and heart. And when I'm
sure of her, then I can relax my grip. Not before. She's worth taking
trouble over."

"But . . ." Itaz remembered her face, the remote blankness slipping over it when his father came into the room. A "restive streak"?
What did that mean? He had never met a woman less restive, more
self-controlled. He had a sudden horrifying suspicion that the "restive
streak" was the whole of her true nature, which his father had
glimpsed, didn't understand, and didn't want. "But . . . but how can
you expect to know *everything* that's in another's mind and heart?" he
stammered. "You can't; half the time we don't know what's in our
own! You have to take some things on trust. If you're confident she
won't betray you, that has to be enough. You can't expect to hold her
closer than that without hurting her. She's . . . she's not the confid-
ing sort, she's very . . . contained, and when people go poking about
in her private feelings, it hurts her. You've made her very unhappy
already."

Mauakes, caught by surprise in a rare moment of openness, was stung, the more so because he knew instantly that what Itaz said was true and couldn't admit it to himself. He shied from the knowledge that he had made her unhappy and would continue to make her unhappy, and blinked at his son. "Don't you lecture me!" he said furiously. "She isn't unhappy, just depressed because of an injury: her doctor says that's perfectly natural and to be expected. And I'm the one who'll make her better, I'm her husband, I'll make her happy. Do you think I'm too old to do that, eh? You think you could do it better, do you? Or do you hope to come to an agreement with her, trade some power for her against some power for you? Get out! Leave now, and I'll try to forget you said that."

Itaz opened his mouth, then closed it. He stood, bowed to his father, and went to the door. He paused there, glanced back to see Mauakes hunched anxiously at his desk, still blinking, and once more was unexpectedly moved by pity for the old man. "I'm sorry," he said softly. "I didn't mean to offend you, Father."

Mauakes only grunted. Helplessly, Itaz left the room.

He wanted to pray, to recover the peace he had felt that morning. But he remembered that he was commander of the queen's guard, and decided that his duty required him to check it first, so he went to the palace barracks, intending to pray afterward.

He arrived to find the queen's guard having a brawl. The new guardsmen had been given the smallest of the barracks of the king's guards, and the king's guards had been crammed into the other buildings with their comrades. The king's guards were annoyed to be moved; the queen's guards were also annoyed, because the barracks were too small, cramped for the seventy-nine men who'd been left in Eschate, and very cramped now that the twenty who'd gone to Bactra had returned. The men who'd gone to Bactra were claiming that, as the queen herself had chosen them, and done so weeks before the others were selected, they should have the best places; the others responded indignantly that they'd been sleeping there for three weeks now, the king had chosen most of them, and they weren't obliged to move. When Itaz arrived, a few men had gone beyond insults to blows and the rest stood about in a ring, yelling encouragement.

"By our Lord the Sun!" exclaimed Itaz. He grabbed a riding whip from a bystander and waded into the ring, beat the brawlers apart, and shouted at the whole troop to explain themselves. Shamefacedly, they did so. He listened, looked down the length of the barracks, and decreed that the sleeping places were all to be allotted over again. To avoid argument, they should arrange themselves about the room as though it were the valley of Ferghana, those from Eskati at the west end, those from about the Terek river at the east, and so on; and if there were any more quarrels about the matter, the quarrelers wouldn't sleep anywhere, and could spend the night cleaning the latrines.

The men were satisfied—a system like that, which everyone can understand and agree on, is usually satisfactory. But it took some time to determine everyone's new position. By the time everyone's sleeping mat or hammock was in its proper place, it was dark and well past suppertime, and Itaz gave up any hope of worshipping the gods that night. He started wearily back to his rooms in the palace. At the barracks door, however, he met his friend Azilises.

"Welcome back," said Azilises, looking him up and down. "How was Bactra?"

Itaz shrugged. "Hot."

Azilises laughed. "So I've heard! But my little brother said you didn't indulge in the heat at all, and spent all your time at some Mazdayist temple. It's not good for you, you know."

Itaz smiled, not offended; Azilises was only very rarely serious. "Worshipping the gods isn't good for you? It's bad luck even to suggest such a thing. You ought to go offer them something to appease them."

"I was just going to do that," Azilises returned, grinning. "I have a big offering to make to Aphrodite, over at Gyllis' brothel. Want to come along?"

Itaz laughed, but shook his head. "Aphrodite's a Yavana whore. Anahita will do well enough for me."

But at this Azilises stopped smiling and scowled. "What's the matter with you?" he demanded, "You haven't been anywhere but army drills and the palace all summer—that, and schemed with Lord Tasius and my father. Have you grown too proud to go about with your old friends?"

"No!" protested Itaz. "It's just that . . . I've had too much else on my mind."

"Well, drop it for tonight. I told my little brother Rajula that I'd take him to Gyllis', to celebrate him getting picked for the queen's guard, and between the war and him going off to Bactra, tonight's the first chance I've had to take him. Come along with us. That little Philomela has been asking where you are; you haven't been back since the wedding."

Despite his promise, he had not gone back. He balanced in the doorway a moment, absurdly unhappy about a ridiculous promise made to a young whore, aware of his friend's resentment. Azilises' brother Rajula came up behind him, bright-eyed with excitement. "Oh, are you coming along as well?" he asked eagerly. "I wanted to invite you, sir, but I thought you'd be offended."

"I'll come along just for a drink," he said, making a rapid decision. "But I can't stay long; I'm going to have to try to sort your lot out tomorrow, and from the look of you it's going to be a long job."

Rajula laughed shyly, and the three young men set out for the brothel.

Philomela was in the dining room when Itaz entered with his two friends, and her face at once broke into a smile. She started toward him eagerly, then nervously stopped and went back to her place. The brothel was not crowded, as every young man in the valley had already visited Eskati that summer, and wouldn't come again before the New Year's feast—still, there were a handful of men, Saka warriors and Yavana merchants, already reclining in the dining room and watching the show. The madam made a great fuss over Itaz, who put her off by indicating Rajula and telling her that this was the young lord's first visit, transferring the fuss instantly to him. The three were seated on the top couch, given wine, given food; two girls danced while another played the flute and Philomela played the lyre. Rajula watched delightedly. "It's as good as Bactra!" he exclaimed when one of the dancers flung herself over in a backward handstand without dropping her castanets.

"Is it?" asked his brother. "I would have thought the Bactrians would be better at it, being ruled by Yavanas. Of course, we have a Yavana ruler now, too. Perhaps that helps."

"She's not allowed to do very much ruling," said Rajula. "But she wouldn't help brothels if she was."

Azilises laughed and boxed his brother's ear. "He admires our queen," he explained to Itaz. "He thinks any woman that beautiful has to be good. I wish it were true!"

"Well, what's she done that's in any way dishonorable, right since she arrived?" demanded Rajula hotly. "And everyone in Bactra thought it was a mistake they'd let her go. Whenever I said I came from Ferghana, they all said so. They know what she's worth, if we don't. I'm not ashamed to be her guardsman; I'm proud she thought me worthy!"

"Well said!" exclaimed Itaz.

"I thought you didn't like her," said Azilises suspiciously.

"I changed my mind," said Itaz for the second time that day.

"He had a vision on the road," put in Rajula suddenly. "Of King Antimachos the God."

Philomela stopped playing, and the flute player stumbled to a halt after her; there was a sudden heavy silence. I've said that Antimachos is worshipped, still, throughout the valley, and his shadow had hung behind the marriage from the beginning: no one doubted that he might well appear to defend his descendant from her enemy. Everyone stared at Itaz. He looked at the floor, cursing inwardly.

"What?" asked Azilises, staring at Itaz. "Is that true?"

"His horse strayed one night and he went up the mountain after it," supplied Rajula. "When he came back next morning, he told me he'd had a vision of King Antimachos—didn't you, Lord Itaz?"

"And you have to announce it in a brothel!" snarled Itaz, getting to his feet. "What I saw or didn't see is nobody else's business."

"Did you see him though?" asked Philomela from her place at the side, watching Itaz round-eyed with awe. "What did he say?"

"Nothing that concerns you!"

Philomela looked down, blinking, and he felt uncomfortable. He told himself he owed her nothing, but he didn't leave, as he'd meant to.

"I'm sorry," said Rajula humbly. "I shouldn't have said anything. I didn't realize you meant to keep it secret."

Itaz sat down again. The madam hastily topped up his cup with wine, and Philomela began playing again, singing this time in Greek, an old song:

Some say the cavalry, some say the infantry
some say the navy's the fairest thing of all to see
but I say it's that one, whoe'er she be, where'er she be
you long for.

Evidence easily jumps out for all to see:
A woman who in beauty surpassed all mortality
the mightiest of husbands abandoning, set out to sea:
Love stunned her.

Queen Helen came to Troy; no more could she
remember her daughter, her parents, or her family;
wealth she lost most lightly, for love quite easily
had won her.

And just in the same way, it's Anaktoria I wish to see
Her bright face and light step lovelier by far to me
Than all the armored soldiers and all the Lydian chariotry
You long for.

Love, love, love: it's true that no mortal ever had enough of it. Singing of a love that toppled a city in fire and blood, which set ten thousand griefs upon two nations, and left a plain littered with dead, Philomela looked wistfully at the man she had once believed to be in love with her, and he stared deep into the saffron flames of the lamps upon the rack, remembering Heliokleia.

He had intended to have a drink and go, but Gyllis refilled his cup, his companions urged him to stay with them, and he was tired from prayers and journeys and it was hard to leave. Half-drunk, dazed with lamplight and music and the twisting, leaping bodies of the dancers, he found that the men were making their choices, and Gyllis was at his side, whispering, "Do you want Philomela tonight, sir? Or someone else?" And the girl, with Azilises' arm round her waist, was looking pleadingly at him.

"I'll have Philomela," he said; and she was beckoned over, and went with him, flushed and smiling, up the dark stairway to her bedroom.

She closed the door behind them and pressed herself against him, setting his hand on her breast. "So you do like me?" she asked him, whispering it against his neck.

He could not answer. He had not meant to come, and remembered that he ought to go—but his hand liked her; his body liked her. He stood with her a few minutes, caressing her and trying to tear himself away, then found himself sitting on the bed, with Philomela half-naked on his lap.

"Why didn't you come back?" she asked him in between kisses. "You said you would come back soon, but it's been months; I thought you'd never come back at all—at least, not to me."

He pulled away, put a hand against her face to stop the kisses. She went very still, and her eyes looked sadly into his. "Then you don't like me?" she said. "You didn't have to say you did, you know. Nobody else says anything like that."

"I do like you," he said. "But . . . Oh, Anahita! I shouldn't have come back at all. I didn't mean to."

She frowned at him. "Azilises told me that Mazdayists think whoring is evil. He said that was why you hadn't come back."

"Yes," he said, relieved. "That's why."

"Oh." She touched the side of his face lightly. "Why do you think it's evil?"

Itaz opened his mouth; stopped; shook his head. He found his hand straying again, despite his intentions. "It's . . . it's an abuse of creation," he said at last. "Ahura Mazda created men and women to love and to people the earth. Angra Mainyu created whores, to trick men from the path of Rectitude, and waste their seed and their souls in sterile ground."

"The evil god created us?" She got off his lap. "You think I'm evil?"

"No . . . no, not you. But . . . this is; you shouldn't be here. You should marry and have children. That's the good path. Not this."

"I can't!" she protested. "I'm a slave. It's not fair, that you should blame me for something I have to do! I don't want to be a whore! I love children; I got pregnant this summer, but Gyllis gave me a potion. I didn't want to take it, but she made me, she said she'd use the stick and then sell me to an India trader if I didn't drink it, so I had to. And it made me sick, and I lost the baby, and I cried and cried and cried.

And I thought maybe you would buy me and set me free, and I could have your baby, a little tiny baby of my own, and a little house . . ." She was crying again. "And you said you'd come back, but you didn't, and now you say I'm evil . . ."

"Not you! The whole business!"

She sat down on the bed and sobbed. He put his arm around her, and she leaned against him and sobbed harder. "It is," she snuffled. "It is. I hate Gyllis. I hate her, I hate her, I hate her. Oh, I wish I were free!"

"I'll buy you. I'll set you free," he said desperately. "Stop crying, please!"

She stopped, looked up at him sniffling, wiped her nose with the edge of her Indian cotton tunic. "You will?"

"It seems I have to, doesn't it?" he said resignedly. Probably, he told himself, she tried this line on all her lovers. He felt that she'd made a fool of him—then, seeing her eyes shining, he didn't mind.

"Oh!" she kissed him. "Oh, thank you! You promise?"

"I swear it by Ahura Mazda."

"Oh, I thank the immortal gods! And you'll buy me a little house, and come visit, and maybe—"

"No."

"No? What—"

"I shouldn't have come here. It's . . . it's not right. I can't keep you—I'll give you a dowry instead. If I give you six half-royal horses, you can probably marry any farmer you like. You wouldn't mind that, would you?"

Her lip trembled and she wiped her nose again, staring at him in complete bewilderment. "I don't understand," she said plaintively. "If I stop being a whore, why would it be wrong? Has your father told you to get married? Then why . . ." She stopped, the lip trembling more. "You're in love with someone else."

He winced and said nothing. Philomela wiped her nose again and rubbed her eyes. It was one of the rules of her world that men always fell in love with someone else, someone free, and left you. It hurt, but not agonizingly: not like losing the hope of a little house of her own to putter about in, one lover, and her own baby. Nearly all whores are slaves, sold in infancy and prostituted when they're no more than twelve years old, and if they survive long enough to lose their looks, they're usually sold off to a slaver and die in some filthy den in India or Parthia. If no lover bought and freed her, Philomela had nothing to look forward to but sweaty nights, forced abortions, and early death. Freed from the fear of that, of course she was happy. Still, she'd been ready to love Itaz, ready to adore him unstintingly, and she blinked at more tears and wrapped her arms about herself, holding in the grief. "I don't understand you at all," she said. "If you're not in love with me, why are you willing to buy me?"

"I like you," he said without thinking. "Why shouldn't you be happy, if I can make you so?"

She looked back into his face, still blinking, and tentatively touched his hand; when he didn't pull it away, she clasped it in both of hers. "You're so kind to me," she said humbly. "I hope she makes you happy, whoever she is. Is she very beautiful?"

The thought still hurt him. "Yes," he said shortly.

"Why do you say it like that? Is she married already?"

"Leave it be!" he snapped; and at once she left it and bowed her head, desperate not to offend him in case he changed his mind and went away again, and this time really didn't come back. Not knowing what to do, aching with desire and confusion and exhaustion, he kissed her again, and finished the night in her bed, as he'd meant all along not to do.

CHAPTER

XIV

Itaz bargained with the brothel keeper Gyllis the next day and, after some haggling, settled on a price for Philomela. It was a high price, and Gyllis wanted the money in coins, not livestock, so Itaz went to his father and asked him for a certain sum.

"I can give you the gold out of my share of the spoils from the ford," he told Mauakes, "but the damned woman wants money with a king's head on it and won't take anything less."

The king snorted. I've said already that he was not rich in silver. Horses we have, goats, camels, sheep, woolens, even metalwork of gold and bronze—but Yavana silver we have to trade for, and the king must tax for, and he never has all that he'd like. "What do you want it for?" Mauakes asked irritably.

Itaz flushed and shuffled his feet. "A girl," he said in embarrassment. "A whore out of Gyllis' brothel. I want to buy her and set her up on my farm near the city." And even as he said it, he realized that it

305

was the best thing he could have said. If his father had any suspicion of his true feelings for Heliokleia, this, if anything, would lull it.

Mauakes stared at him a moment, then chuckled. "And free her?"

"Well . . . yes."

"Hmm. What's her name?"

"Philomela."

"Young and pretty?"

"Young, pretty—and sweet-natured. She hates being a whore; she'd rather settle down and have babies."

"Ha! You're not to marry her. Get some bastards now, if you like, but give her a dowry to buy herself a husband of her own rank when you drop her. You understand that, I hope. I won't have my son marrying an Eskati whore. When it comes to a wife for you, we need a Parthian or Sakaraukai princess to keep up the old alliances. One of your lord Suren's daughters, if he's willing: he has enough of them."

Itaz swallowed hard. "I don't mean to marry the girl," he said. "This . . . this other business . . . you haven't approached anyone about it, have you? I . . . I would have to get rid of her if you had."

"I meant to send you off to Parthia again in another year or so, to put the proposal to Lord Suren. But there's no hurry." He chuckled again. "Here, I'll tell the treasurer to release the money to you: go and buy your girlfriend."

He was genial again, the previous day's quarrel forgotten, the monstrous suspicion which had stirred then snoring once more, still unacknowledged. Itaz thanked him, went to collect the coins, then took the small clinking sack to the brothel and came away with a tearfully radiant Philomela. He summoned the foreman of a small stud farm he owned, a place just outside the city where he kept a few royal horses, and told him to take the girl there and make her comfortable. So Philomela went off, riding behind the foreman and clinging tightly to his saddle, so radiantly happy that everyone who saw her smiled back. Itaz watched her go, then turned back to the palace and spent the rest of the day reorganizing the queen's guard. When he rode out of the city that evening, his men nudged each other and laughed. He told no one that his only destination was the Mazdayist fire temple.

He spent three days drilling the men, testing them and watching to see how they worked together; then, on the morning of the fourth day, he assigned them to companies, five companies of twenty apiece, balancing archers with lancers, commoners with nobles, choosing those he thought would work well together. Havani, who ought to know, said that he chose very well, and that all the men respected him. "He's easy to work for, even though he demands a lot," he told me. "He's fair, he doesn't have favorites, and he always knows what to do. The king ought to put him in charge of the whole royal army." Each company had its own officer, and he chose for these positions experienced men loyal to the queen. (Havani wasn't chosen—he had the loyalty, but not the experience.) When he had assigned each man to his place, he summoned them all to attention in the barracks square, and made them a speech which they all remembered.

"Free men of the queen's guard," he said in a clear, calm voice. "You know that you have been established for an honorable task, to guard your king's wife. My father has said that, among all the warriors of Ferghana, your rank is second only to the men of his own royal guard; and other than that guard you alone have the right to ride upon the royal horses, descended from the horses of our Lord the Sun: that is a great honor. And I wish you to be certain that the honor of your task is second to none! The lady whom you serve is descended from many kings; she is brave, beautiful, and wise, and Bactria grieves that they ever let her come here. But she has left her own people, and without a backward glance, adopted our ways to become our queen. I've heard some of you calling her 'the Yavana,' and debating among yourselves whether or not you should obey her directions. If my father had intended you to be her keepers, he would have attached you to his own guard, and not set you in a body under her command! She's Ferghana's queen, and you are Ferghanan, all of you, and her subjects; you are to obey her as you would the king himself.

"I know it's been said that I suggested this guard to my father as a check upon the queen, and that's true, I can't deny it. But since I did so, I've been convinced—by my father, by the queen's noble conduct in the war, and by the jealousy of the Bactrians—that the lady we will guard is in every way worthy of our loyal obedience. That duty of obedience I now accept with a whole heart, and as your commander I will require the same of you. If you do not wish to obey Queen

Heliokleia, your best and most honorable course is to leave her service now."

There was a moment of stunned silence; then a rustle as every man looked at his neighbors to see if they were as surprised as he was; then the beginnings of a mutter as they all demanded of each other, "Does he mean it?" Though the first guardsmen, the ones the queen chose at the contests, had taken their position at face value, those the king had appointed had assumed that their chief work was to guard the people from the queen, not the queen from the people, and the others, thinking of who was to command them, had reconsidered: now they all had to think again. The murmuring grew, then suddenly snapped into a question, shouted at Itaz from the thick of troop: "Sir! Is it true that you had a vision of King Antimachos the God, and he commanded you to give up your enmity to the queen?"

Itaz was silent for a long moment, standing very straight and staring at the ranks of his men, the eyes watching him, curiously, anxiously, or impassively. Then he replied, still in the clear calm voice, "Yes."

There was a buzz of talk; Itaz allowed it to continue for some time, then rapped the barracks wall to get their attention and asked if any man wished to leave the queen's service.

No one wished to leave, of course. It is a great honor, as Itaz had said, to be a member of a royal guard, and not something to be given up lightly. Even those who had misgivings kept quiet about them. When his question was answered by silence, Itaz thanked the men, then, commanding them to wait at the barracks, summoned the five officers and took them into the palace to present them to the queen.

Her rooms were being guarded by two of the king's men, since her own were busy. Itaz told one of these to ask the queen if she would receive the officers of her guard. The guardsman was surprised, as he expected the officers of the queen's guard simply to knock and go in, but he did as he was told, and came back in a moment saying that the queen would receive them. They all filed up the stairs and into her room.

Heliokleia was sitting over the gaming board with me, Jahika, and the king. Itaz felt a stab of acute disappointment to find his father there, but set his teeth and reminded himself of the rights of the matter.

The queen looked very white and remote, and the king was particularly moon-faced and inscrutable, but something about his bland gaze and the set of his shoulders told Itaz that he was in a foul temper. Itaz bowed his head, first to his father, and then to the queen, and stood aside to let the others line up by the door.

The king had pressed his wife to teach him Four Armies—in his son's absence—the day after he saw her playing it with Itaz. But it's a complicated game, not easily learned, and Heliokleia played it very well. She beat him each time they played. He hated to lose even more than I did, and when she tried to let him win it was even worse. After a while she gave up making false moves on purpose, and played instead with cool, detached ferocity, ending each game with humiliating speed, trying only to get it over with. But every time Mauakes lost, he insisted on playing again, even though the other players were desperate to stop, and the queen herself was white with headache. I began to hate the sound of his feet coming up the stairs, and I almost wished I could meditate like Heliokleia to calm myself afterward. Itaz' arrival was a great relief. We all hoped that afterward the king would be content to put the game away and let us rest.

Itaz bowed to his father, then to the queen. "Queen Heliokleia," he said, "these are the men I think best suited, in skill and in character, to officer your guards. May I present them to you, and ask if they are acceptable to you?"

Heliokleia nodded once in agreement, stood and moved round the gaming board to receive the men. She was dressed in the Yavana style that morning, in a white cotton tunic and a purple cloak—a cotton one she'd brought from Bactria, not the woolen one the city had given her. She looked very Greek and very withdrawn as she faced her guards, a foreign prisoner paying polite attention to her new jailers. "I thank you, sir, for your care in this matter," she said formally. "I am sure they are well suited to their position."

Itaz presented the first, a lancer chosen from the king's standing army. This man had the skill to be a member of the king's guard, but had been passed over because his father was an Eskati Yavana, though a landowning one who had married a Saka wife and given his son a Sakan name. "Pakores, son of Diodotos," said Itaz, leading him forward.

Pakores stepped forward again, bowed, and taking the queen's hand, pressed it to his forehead, the gesture the Yavana servants use to their masters. "Rejoice, O Queen!" he said in Greek.

Itaz tried to stop himself from grinning at the queen's look of astonishment.

"Rejoice, O Pakores," the queen replied, recovering and inclining her head in greeting.

"I do rejoice, O Queen," he said earnestly. "I am very glad of this chance to serve you."

"I thank you, sir, for your loyalty," she said, stumbling only a little. She gave Itaz a bewildered glance; he grinned again and presented the next man. This one, though a Saka noble, came from a part of the valley above the middle of the Jaxartes where the land is poor and would be completely desert if it weren't for an irrigation system constructed by King Antimachos; in that region even the councillors make offerings to Antimachos from sheer gratitude. The officer bowed very low and, after a moment's hesitation, copied Pakores and pressed the queen's hand to his forehead. "It is an honor to serve the descendant of the god Antimachos," he told her fervently.

And so it went. Each of the five expressed his delight in being chosen to serve the queen and humbly pressed her hand to his forehead; with growing confusion, she thanked them for their loyalty. When all five had been presented, Itaz added, "And for my own part as well, O Queen, I am honored to command your guard—and to serve you, as my duty requires." He had considered touching her hand to his head, as the others had, but didn't dare cross the invisible barrier between them. Instead, he went on, "If you would care to review the rest of the men, they are waiting at their barracks, and would be delighted to receive a visit from their queen. If you're free, of course"—with an apologetic glance at his father—"and if you're feeling sufficiently well."

"Thank you, Lord Itaz," said Heliokleia, meeting his eyes: the deep blue-green gaze made him dizzy. "If my lord will excuse me, I would like to review my guardsmen." She looked at Mauakes questioningly.

The king's eyelids had drooped and he was watching the scene slouched back on the couch, without expression. "Of course," he said smoothly. "I will come with you. Perhaps the officers could tell the men to prepare themselves, and you and I and Itaz will come to join them in a few minutes, eh?"

Itaz nodded and gestured for the officers to go. When the door had closed, the king sat up, slapped the gaming board so that the pieces all jumped, and demanded, "What in the name of all the gods do you think you're doing?"

"I've chosen some officers who'll be loyal to the queen," said Itaz.

"You have indeed! One half-Yavana, one half-Bactrian, an Antimachos worshipper, and a fellow who's so clearly smitten with her that he goggles like an idiot and blushes to take her hand: from the look of the first four I can guess the mind of the fifth. I chose some reliable men for that guard: where are they?"

"Father, they *are* all reliable men," said Itaz. "At least, they seem reliable to me. I only picked men who'd had experience in war, were of noble blood, and had some idea how to conduct themselves in a palace. What's wrong with them?"

Mauakes squinted at him. "What does your friend Tasius think of them?"

"I'm not obliged to consult Tasius about who I recommend to the queen as an officer in her guard."

"He will not be pleased that they are, as you put it, loyal to the queen. I had the impression, when this guard was proposed, that they were meant to be loyal to the council."

"You were angry about that," Itaz pointed out. "And I've agreed that you were right, about the alliance and the marriage both. Just the other day you said that it wasn't necessary to form a guard as a check upon your queen. So I gave up any idea of picking men loyal to the council, and I've simply chosen officers whom I thought she'd like and who'd be willing to work for her. I've told them all, too, men and officers alike, that if you'd wanted them to be her keepers, you'd have attached them to your own guard: they're to obey her. If that isn't what you wanted, I'm sorry; you'll have to tell them so."

Mauakes stared at his son for a long while in silence. Heliokleia stood where she had received the officers, before the couch where her husband sat, looking at the floor. Her cheeks were flushed pink.

"I heard a story, which I thought was absurd," said the king at last. "That you saw a vision of King Antimachos the God."

"Why is that absurd? Gods do appear to men sometimes."

Mauakes let out his breath with a hiss. "When did this happen? In Bactra, at some fire temple? While you were drunk with some of that what-do-you-call-it root?"

He winced. "It happened on the ridge road, on the way home," he said sharply. "I wasn't drunk. My horse strayed, I went after it, I . . . met a man sitting by a fire, and we talked. It was all very calm and ordinary. I thought it odd that the man had a white horse larger than mine, and that a wealthy Yavana should be sitting by a fire on his own, so far from the road, but I didn't think about it much. In the morning, though . . . he'd left no tracks. The ground was soft, and I could see where I'd been, and my horse, but of him, nothing. And of his horse, only this." He fumbled in his purse and brought out the three white hairs; again they seemed to glow softly of their own accord. Heliokleia lifted her eyes and stared at them; her lips parted, but she said nothing. "And I saw the man's face in the firelight, quite clearly. Afterward I remembered it and looked at a coin of Antimachos, and it was the same face. I didn't mean to tell anyone, but I had to borrow the coin, and it came out—and since it has come out, I won't lie about it."

There was a long, tense, cold silence. Then, "I see," said Mauakes in a particularly mild voice. "So you're now content to worship my predecessor Antimachos as well as Ahura Mazda and the Sun? I would have thought that your religion viewed him not just as a man, but as an unbelieving heretic, doomed to fall into the chasm of Hell." The mildness faltered just a little at the end, and the raw jealousy and hatred underneath showed through like a rock under a gauze scarf.

"Father, I don't know nearly as much about the gods as I did last spring," said Itaz simply. "Why should we think we understand them? We talk of 'water' and the Yavanas of 'hydor,' but we mean the same thing. Surely it must be harder to know a divinity than it is to know water."

"But my ancestor Antimachos was not a divinity," said Heliokleia suddenly, meeting Itaz' eyes again. "We may not know what water is —but we do know it isn't dust. Gods do not die. Antimachos was a man."

"So was the Buddha," returned Itaz quickly.

But she only shrugged. "And we Buddhists don't deny that. The

Buddha didn't even teach us about the gods—merely how to escape suffering."

"You don't really believe," the king asked Itaz, "that Antimachos *was* a god? If he was, why didn't he appear to me in his wrath when I chased one of his sons out of Ferghana and made a drinking cup out of the other's skull?"

Itaz hesitated. "I don't believe he was a god," he said at last, "but he was a king who held the glory of the Sun, as surely as you are—and a good man, too, who could win the loyalty even of those he conquered. And we believe that the souls of the blessed may look back toward us over the Bridge of the Divider. I had begged the gods to make my path clear to me. But the gods are very high and great, and even when they answer us, it's hard for us to understand them. So why shouldn't they use a spokesman with a human face? And why shouldn't a king who's held the Sun's glory borrow the Sun's horses to fly him back to the world? Particularly when people on earth still worship him and call him to help them, and when his house and ours are linked? Say he was a ghost, then, a spirit come in friendship to advise me. I was glad I met him, and grateful for his help."

Mauakes snorted in fury. "What you had," he told Itaz, "was a dream." His face was set in anger and contempt, but his hands were afraid: they clenched each other in his lap till the knuckles cracked in the stillness. He had not been a friend to the house of Antimachos. Desperately, he barricaded his mind against the thought of that ghost's return, telling himself that it wasn't, couldn't be, true.

Heliokleia was looking at Itaz with the delicate, self-mocking smile of amusement, the smile of Antimachos. Slowly, she put out her hand and picked up one of the white horse hairs from his; she twisted it about her fingers. "May I keep this?" she asked, not commenting on his story. He saw, quite clearly, that she did believe that he had seen only a dream, but that she liked the dream, and would remember it.

"Please do," he said, smiling at her.

Her smile vanished. She looped the single white hair around her necklace and tied the end, then turned to Mauakes. "Sir," she said politely, "if we are to review the guardsmen, we ought not keep them waiting."

Mauakes snorted again, but took her arm and led her out of the room. Itaz followed slowly. He had meant to please Heliokleia by his choice of officers, but he hadn't expected to irritate his father. And he had certainly not meant to discuss his vision on the mountainside. Once again, nothing had happened as he'd planned it.

The guardsmen cheered for the queen and beat their spears against the ground when she appeared. She thanked them for their devotion, greeted many of them by name, and made a short speech praising their fine order and their loyalty. They enjoyed it. Looking at her, Itaz saw that she enjoyed it, too. But though Mauakes smiled blandly and said nothing, it was plain to his son that he did not enjoy it, that, despite what he had said, he had not meant the guard to be loyal to the queen —or the council, or to anyone but himself. But he couldn't admit this to Itaz or to his wife, and so he pretended to accept it.

When the queen started back to her room, each of the five officers offered to provide guards from his own company; she smiled, picked the nearest one, and asked Itaz to arrange a rota. Mauakes gave her a forgiving smile and went off to meet with one of his ministers, and Itaz and the chosen guards went back to the room. Heliokleia walked with a lighter step than she had for weeks, her head up and the purple cloak fluttering from her straight shoulders. Itaz found himself smiling. Once he would have found something sinister in her pleasure at the power of commanding a guard; now he understood it. She had taught herself how to be a queen, and she didn't know how to be a mere piece of royal decoration. Her pleasure was like a carpenter's at a piece of good wood, or a weaver's at a hank of fine wool, the satisfaction of finding tools for a job. It was worth offending his father to give her that. When they were back at the room, he stopped at the door. "There was another matter, O Queen, if you have the time for it," he said.

She stopped, facing him. "What is the other matter, Lord Itaz?"

"Some time ago, my father suggested that we discuss the proposals about changes in the government put forward by the council and by the city. He said that anything we two could agree on, he would have to grant. Well—shouldn't we discuss them?"

"He said 'anything the Yavanas and their worst opponents' could agree on," corrected Heliokleia. "And it somehow seems that you are no longer an opponent, Lord Itaz."

He shrugged, still smiling. "Not to you, O Queen. But I'm still a

Saka and a councillor, and you're still the benefactress of the city. We have different views of things. If we talked together we might each discover points the other had missed, and we might come up with some ideas we could agree on and my father would like."

She looked up at him expressionlessly for a moment—then smiled. "Perhaps we would," she said. "Would you care to discuss it now?"

Tasius was not pleased when he discovered what his ally had done with the queen's guard. He appeared the following evening as Itaz was preparing to ride out of the city, and asked, in a tone of suppressed fury, if he could ride out with him, "to discuss one or two things." Itaz consented, and waited resignedly for the outburst.

It was not long in coming. "What in the name of all the gods do you think you're doing?" Tasius demanded, as Mauakes had, as soon as they were out of the palace stables. "I and my friends worked hard to win that guard! And it's pretty much all we've ever managed to get from the king, too!"

"I thought you already had some picked men out observing the Yavana tax collectors."

"The observers don't count! All they're allowed to do is report anything irregular to the council lord concerned and the king. They're toothless and dumb. But that Yavana witch has managed to convince the king to shower all sorts of honors on her friends in the city! That guard was all we had to rein her in. We all thought that with you in command of it, we'd have a real chance to pry her claws off the administration—and you've thrown it away, chosen a pack of Yavana lovers to officer it and ordered the rest to obey the queen!"

"You must not call Queen Heliokleia a 'Yavana witch,'" Itaz said icily. "Take back that name or the discussion ends now."

Tasius glared at him with a mixture of rage and disbelief. Itaz paid no attention, but instead studied the road before him. His black and his brother-in-law's bay picked their way across the market square and onto the east road.

"I take back the name, then," said Tasius at last, "though it might seem to some that the queen had cast a spell on you."

Itaz shrugged. "I was wrong about her. I've changed my mind. There's no magic in that—merely a willingness to recognize honesty when I see it."

"No magic? I've heard some very strange stories recently about you and a god called Antimachos. There've been two or three different versions of how he appeared, in a cloud of smoke or a blinding light, but they all agree that he came to tell you to give up your enmity to the queen—which you've done very thoroughly, and at some cost to the people who thought they could rely on you. And I've heard it said that some of the Buddhists work magic, and make their followers believe they see a thousand impossibilities—and the Yavanas have always been addicted to sorcery. Whatever happened to you on your way back from Bactra, I don't believe you saw the spirit of some deified dead Yavana."

Itaz sighed, controlling his temper with an effort. "Whatever I saw on my way back from Bactra—and I wish I'd been able to keep that to myself!—it merely confirmed what I'd seen anyway in Eskati, but had refused to believe. The queen is perfectly honest and straightforward. When she abjures ambition, she means it. She has gone a very long way toward adopting our customs and is doing her best to be a good queen of the Sakas, and the only thing that stops her being a better one is that she's not allowed half the scope she deserves. Far from having 'claws' in the administration, she's not even allowed to speak to an administrator. If she were given the liberty a queen of our people should expect, the people, and most of the council, would all adore her. Some of them do anyway. I think I'd have had to believe it anyway, when I got back to Eskati, but a vision made it easier for me. And, once more, if you call her a witch or imply that she got the better of me by magic again, this conversation is over."

Again Tasius glared. "Is there anything left to say?" he demanded. "You admire the Yavana, and you threw away the power of guarding her. But perhaps there's no magic. You wanted command of a troop of picked men, and, with the council's help, you got it. So you feel free to turn your back on the council. You've betrayed me and your allies. I hope your father's pleased with you."

Itaz set his teeth and glared back. "You're far too hasty with accusations of betrayal. I never swore you any oath of undying loyalty, and never promised to shut my eyes to the truth to avoid changing my mind. I agreed to a scheme, I broke it to my father and backed you on it in the council. It wasn't you who made me commander of the queen's guard: that was the queen's idea. But I haven't turned my back on the council. Would you like a seat on the Eskati city council?"

"What do you mean?" Tasius asked angrily.

"Would you like a seat on the Eskati city council, with the right to speak in its deliberations and vote for its offices, and the obligation to report its doings to the tribal council?" Tasius stared in confusion, and Itaz went on sarcastically, "Just think of all the opportunities for intrigue! The support for this or that aspiring magistrate to be traded against his backing for such-and-such a policy; the deals, the bargaining, the back-stabbing! The factions of the city council make the tribal council look tame, or so I'm told. Wouldn't you like to be on it?"

"What do you mean?" Tasius demanded again, going red.

"The queen and I have agreed that there ought to be representatives from the tribal council on the city council of Eskati, men who could put the Saka point of view if the city proposed a new tax or whatever. I said I thought you'd be a good representative. You speak Greek well. I think I may have made a mistake."

"But . . ." Tasius stared. Itaz could see him examining the idea in his mind, moving about it and prodding it, like a man looking over a horse he wants to buy, "But . . . would the king permit that?"

"I don't know. He did say that whatever the queen and I agreed on, he'd have to grant. That was before the war, of course, and before I . . . changed my mind. He may feel differently now. The queen was going to ask him, when she had the opportunity."

Tasius had decided that this horse was a bargain. No one needed to point out to him the advantages of being a crucial link between the will of the tribal council and the plans of the city; no one needed to instruct him in questions of influence or intrigue. "The queen agreed to this?" he asked incredulously.

"I told you. She wants to be a good queen, of Sakas as well as of Yavanas. We decided that one of the chief problems with the way things have been done in the past was the gulf between the two. Of course, in the past they hated us and we hated them, but now we have a common enemy and a friendly alliance; we ought to bridge the gulf.

That was one of the ways we thought we could do it. There were a few other ways we'd thought of, as well, and perhaps you have some ideas of your own—if you're willing to entrust them to a man who betrayed you and who's under the spell of a Yavana witch."

Tasius rode in silence for a moment. Then he smiled a quick, false smile. "You were right: I was too hasty," he said. "I didn't understand the situation properly. I thought you'd turned your back on us, but really you've simply found a better way of doing things; I apologize. You're quite right; we're much more likely to achieve our aims by discussion and compromise than by confronting the king. I can promise you my full support for this idea."

Itaz gave one of his father's snorts of contempt, but accepted the offer and listened without comment to Tasius' suggestions for giving the council more power in Yavana affairs.

They reached the turning that led to Itaz' small stud farm, and Tasius reined in. "I'll stop here," he said, smirking genially. "I suppose we've said all we need to—and I'm sure I'd be an unwelcome guest."

"What?" said Itaz, who had meant to continue on down the road to the fire temple; then, "Oh—yes. Another time, perhaps."

Tasius waved, turned his horse, and galloped back toward the city, looking smug. Itaz watched him go with a mixture of amusement and contempt. Then he looked back at the farm track. He had not seen Philomela since he bought her. He'd been afraid of her gratitude, distrustful of his own nature. He did not want to sleep with her again. He felt as though he were a juggler, spinning desires and obligations precariously in the air: one more complication and the whole wheel might crash into ruin. Yet the girl was his responsibility: he had bought her and sent her off to this farm, and if she were miserable on it, he would have to do something about it.

But what would he do? He was guiltily aware that he was making use of her to tell a lie without actually lying, trying to win some breathing space from his father's suspicions. But probably she did hate it, immured in the countryside on a small farm, with just the foreman and his family and slaves for company; probably she would beg him to take her back into the city and find her a husband. How long could he put her off?

Just a little while, he told himself earnestly, just until everything around him had stopped changing, and he could find a safe balance. He'd given Philomela freedom; surely she could give him six months or a year of safety? He turned his horse into the track and rode slowly, guiltily, toward the farm.

When Itaz arrived, Addac, the foreman, was stabling the eight royal and twenty-two half-royal horses with the help of the two farm slaves. He greeted his master quietly, bowed, and took the black stallion as Itaz dismounted. "How long will you stay, my lord?" he asked.

"For supper," said Itaz. The man nodded and began to unsaddle the horse. "Where's Philomela?"

Addac paused, looking unhappy, then continued unfastening the girths. "In the house, my lord," he answered.

Itaz looked at him apprehensively. "Isn't she happy here? Hasn't she settled in well?"

"Oh, yes, my lord," replied the foreman, "she's settled in very well." He handed the horse to one of the slaves to rub down. "Give him just a light feed of the mash, and not too much water," he instructed. "Lord Itaz will want him again tonight." He wiped his hands. "I'll show you in, my lord."

Philomela was in the farm kitchen, kneading bread, Addac's four-year-old daughter perched on the table beside her. Addac's mother, red and fat, was cleaning out the oven. The foreman led Itaz in, then stood morosely by the door and watched intently as Philomela started, then smiled, waving dough-covered hands.

"Lord Itaz!" she said. "Look! I'm making bread!"

"I'm making bread too," said the little girl. Her grandmother turned from the oven and beamed.

"Indeed you are," replied Philomela, rubbing the dough off her fingers. "You're a great help to me, sweetheart. Because I didn't know how, did I?"

"No," said the child importantly. "*I* knew. *You* knew how to sing, but not how to make bread."

Philomela had the dough off. She lifted the child off the table and set her down safely on the floor, kissed her head, then crossed to Itaz, beaming at him. He thought she would kiss him, but she only stopped in front of him, bouncing a little on her toes like an excited child. "Thank you so much for sending me here," she said. "Everyone is so kind, and there's so much to do, and I like all of it! Are you staying to supper? Will you stay the night?"

"I'll stay to supper," said Itaz, "but not for the night."

"Ah." Did she look disappointed, or relieved? "Two days ago I made a cake for you, in case you came. It won't be as good now as it would have been, but it has sesame, and cashews, and honey . . ."

"Can I have some?" asked the little girl, taking hold of Philomela's skirt.

"Of course, sweetheart!" said Philomela tenderly, then suddenly and unhappily remembering, "That is, if Lord Itaz says you can. It's his cake."

Itaz laughed. "She can have some. And if you make another one, don't bother saving it; if I come, I can take whatever's about."

After the meal, the foreman came out with Itaz to the stable and held a torch while a slave saddled his horse for the ride back to the palace. "The girl, uh . . ." he began as Itaz was about to mount.

"Yes?" Itaz paused. He dismissed the tired slave to his rest with a wave of the hand and took the stallion's bridle himself.

"She says that you . . . that you weren't meaning to keep her as a concubine. That you bought her out of kindness, because she was unhappy."

"That's true. I'm glad I did, too. That girl was never meant to be a whore."

"Uh." The grunt seemed to be agreement. "She says you're giving her six half-royal horses as a dowry. Uhh . . . do you want me to choose some?"

"Yes. Six good ones. But . . . not quite yet."

Addac looked alarmed. "No? So she's not to marry yet? But you don't want to stay the night?"

Itaz stared at him a moment. The foreman was a big, slow, soft-spoken man, a slave's son, ordinarily given to a ponderous calm; he was very good with horses. Now his wide face was creased with anxiety. Itaz remembered that he was a widower, his wife having died two years before. He laughed. "You don't mean to say that you want to marry her yourself!"

"Umm . . . well, my lord, my little girl has taken a great liking to her. And she loves the child. And she's a lovely girl, my lord, and as you so rightly said, never the sort to be a whore, that was clear as day from the moment she arrived. Rushes about wanting to help with everything, chatters all the time; a lovely girl. And if you don't want her, and only bought her out of kindness and piety, to save her from the brothel, well, you see . . . and the six horses, well, that's a fair dowry; my old mother says I couldn't do much better than that. And the fact of the matter is, yes, my lord, I do want to marry her. With your permission, of course."

Itaz was silent for a moment. The black horse jerked at the bridle and shifted impatiently, and he patted its shoulder absently. "I had to borrow money from my father to pay for the girl," he said at last, ashamed of himself and glad of the dim light that concealed his transparent face. "I had to let him think that I meant to keep her for myself; I can't let her marry you instantly. Wait until midsummer: then you may have her with my blessing, and the horses as well. If . . . if you can't wait for her, and she's willing to have you before then, be discreet —and I'll give you the horses at midsummer. But keep quiet about it until then, or my father will be angry with me for wasting his money."

Addac brightened. "Yes, my lord! So you're not going to, uh . . ."

"I'm not going to sleep with her, no. Our Lord the Sun, who sees all, knows that when I bought her I meant for her to marry honestly and be happy."

"Yes, my lord," said the foreman again, this time with immense satisfaction. "May the gods bless you for your goodness to her."

Itaz vaulted into the saddle and gathered up the reins. He looked down at Addac, and thought of Philomela. They would be very happy together, he saw, suddenly: they would have children and grow old in peace, plenty, and love. He had done a thing casually, mixing generosity with guilty deceit, and by some divine mystery this had come out of it. And if he did nothing else in his life, this might well be something that would make a life worth living. The gods again had been unexpectedly kind, and he was grateful. "Thank the gods, who have favored you," he told the foreman. "Pray for me." He set his heels to the stallion and sent it galloping back toward the city.

Midsummer, he reflected gratefully, was still a very long way off.

If he hadn't found firm footing in the unsteady ground between the king and queen by then, he was unlikely to find it at all.

⊐⊐⊏

Queen Heliokleia spoke to the king about the proposals she and Itaz had agreed upon that same evening. In her rooms upstairs she washed, and anointed herself with myrrh, then sat and meditated for a long time—which usually she didn't do at evening. When she at last sighed, uncurled herself and asked for a cloak, I asked her if the meditation was going well; it was the only way I could think of to ask why she'd chosen to do it then.

She smiled ruefully. "No. It is very hard. But as the saying goes, 'Say not that goodness is too hard to achieve, for drop by drop the bucket is filled to overflowing.'" She held out her hand for the cloak she'd worn that day, and I gave it to her. She stood. "I wished to discuss some things with my husband, some administrative proposals which Lord Itaz and I had agreed on," she continued, draping it over herself, tossing one end over her shoulder. "I thought I'd do that better with a clear mind." She ran both hands back from her forehead over her loose hair, pulling it away from her face, and the expression of rueful earnestness was wiped away like a letter being rubbed out by the blunt end of a stylus, leaving behind only the blank calm. I looked at her in exasperation.

"He hates that look, you know," I told her. "If it comes from the meditation, you'd do better to go riding first and speak with an unclear mind."

Some expression came back: puzzlement. "What look?"

"You have a face like marble when you go down the stairs. Like pure Anahita looking down upon men."

That brought a quick, small, tired smile. "And what should my face be like?" She straightened the draped cloak, and went on in a low voice, not looking at me, "I can't smile joyfully, like a wife who loves her husband. Duty is all I can manage, and perhaps he hates the sight of it in my face; in fact, I know he does. But what other natural feelings could I have to show, except hatred and anger? I've meditated: I don't hate him, and I'm not angry. And that is the goal I struggled to reach."

And with that she slipped out the door, barefoot and silent on the steps down to her husband's room. I felt, as so often, bewildered; but after a moment I realized that it was the closest thing I had ever had to a confidence from her.

Mauakes was already in the bedroom, sitting half-dressed upon the couch. She greeted him quietly, asked his permission to discuss the proposals, and then explained them as humbly as she could. He listened to her without expression. When she had finished he said, "You discussed all these with my son? Was that his idea?"

"Yes, sir," she replied quietly. "You had suggested we should do so, and said that you would grant any proposal we could agree upon. I believe Lord Itaz is now very eager to work for the success of your alliance, and forge new links between your people and mine."

Mauakes grunted. "Itaz is certainly very eager," he commented sourly. "But it seems to me he's eager to make use of you to get himself a very influential position. A far easier and more fruitful way than trying to persuade the council to oppose me. He's put in a few ideas that will delight the councillors and win him some backing, hasn't he? I assume those were his, and the proposals aimed at strengthening the powers of the city were yours? Or has his new enthusiasm for the divine Antimachos driven him into the arms of the Yavana city council?"

His son's vision troubled him. In his heart he believed in it, but he could not admit this, even to himself, and he escaped from his jealous fear of the smiling ghost by becoming even more suspicious of his son. Itaz, he told himself, was playing some game, hoping for some mysterious advantage by this pretended meeting with a god: he would have to be watched more closely than ever. Itaz' new involvement in affairs of state seemed to him confirmation of his suspicions.

But Heliokleia shook her head. "Sir, all either of us has done is to talk over schemes put forward by differing groups of men, find compromises between them, and suggest these to you. You alone have the right to act. Anything that delights the city or the council will be proclaimed by you alone, and it is to you that they will be grateful."

"They will know who to thank," said Mauakes harshly. "And it won't be me. Anyone with sense could manage that, and Itaz has sense, for all his air of bold thoughtlessness."

Heliokleia licked her lips and tried again to be reasonable. "Sir, it was your suggestion that your son and I should talk and see what we could agree upon. If we draw up proposals at your direction, and you choose among them, rejecting the foolish ones, modifying the rest, and enacting them through your ministers and council, why should the people thank anyone but you?"

"Uh," said Mauakes. "Don't trust Itaz. He's playing some game for power. And he had no business trying to get it through you. He shouldn't have worried you at all; you've been ill."

She was silent for a moment. The memory of Itaz seemed almost a concrete presence, waiting for her at the door. Why on earth, she wondered, did Mauakes distrust him? No king ever had a more honest and loyal son, or one that loved him better. But she could see clearly how the king viewed it: Itaz was flattering her and playing on her for a political end of his own. And almost anything she said to defend him would only fuel the suspicions. But she had to try to say something; silence, too, would inflame them. "Lord Itaz was ready to postpone any discussion of the proposals if I were unwell," she told Mauakes. "But I agreed to it at once; we both thought it would please you. And in fact," she continued, though reluctantly, "I am much better." She was; the unexpected loyalty of the guards and the work of agreeing and presenting the proposals had lifted her from her resigned despair, and with the rise in her spirits the headaches had almost disappeared. This was good—but she knew that if she was fully recovered her husband would reassert his rights in bed, and this she had been dreading. Still, it had to be faced sometime, and if Mauakes had this to satisfy him, he might be prepared to think more leniently of Itaz. It was working, too; she saw her husband's lips curl with satisfaction, and he put a hand on her thigh. "Sir," she finished, trying to smile, "I don't believe that your son had any aim in mind except to make amends for his earlier opposition to your wishes. He was trying to be helpful."

"The best help I want is for him to stop meddling," said Mauakes, losing his satisfaction. "Damn him and damn those officers he picked for you! Tell me, how long did that fellow Sarozi stay and goggle at you before his shift started this morning?"

Already the officers were becoming a source of as much anxiety as pride. The king suspected them, watched them for signs of improper desires, watched her conduct with them, asked her about them. Already she scarcely dared speak to them. "I don't know what you mean," she told him. "None of my officers 'goggle' at me. Their conduct is attentive and respectful; were it otherwise, I would reprimand them."

"Huh. That fellow Sarozi gave you flowers when he started his shift on guard. Wild roses, he said, picked in the countryside, less fair and sweet than you. Was that 'respectful'?"

She sighed, wondering which of the girls had told him this. "Yes, sir, it was. It was common palace courtesy, of the sort any queen receives half a dozen times a day, particularly if she's been ill. I've been told your first wife received the same. I'm sure they do it to show their respect for you."

He grunted, unconvinced. "Itaz should have let me choose the officers for the guard."

"He is its commander: it was his duty to choose them! And you seemed very pleased that he should be commander, when I chose him. Surely you'd rather have your son behaving like a prince and fulfilling his duties to the army and the government, than wasting himself in luxury and indolence?"

Mauakes snorted. "But by the Sun, he does that too! Two hundred drachmae he borrowed from me, to buy himself an Eskati whore. He's set her up on his farm by the lake and he rides out there every evening after putting your guard to bed."

The thought of this seemed to cheer him, however. Heliokleia accepted it in silence. After a momentary stab of loss, she felt relieved. Itaz had a mistress; he was taken, safe. For all his warm smile and the light in his eyes, he couldn't really want her; her arid virtue was secure, and she could concentrate on subduing her unruly soul in meditation with only regret, and not fear, to torment her. "Is that luxury?" she asked her husband. "He puts the guard to bed first."

Mauakes laughed. "So he does. First the guard, then the whore; can't ask better duty from any young man than to postpone the one for the other. Ah well, leave him be; I suppose he'll settle down. Is your head really better?"

"As I said," she replied, keeping carefully still to avoid giving any sign of revulsion, "I am much better."

He caught her arms and pulled her onto his lap. She tried not to notice his smell, the stink of bad teeth, old sweat and aging flesh. To like a man because he is young and strong and handsome, to despise another because he is old and smells, is to accept illusion as reality. Youth and good looks, like love, are a mirage, apparent one moment, vanishing into a desert of suffering the next. Duty is real. Her duty was to be a good wife. Recovering from her despair, she gathered up all her strength of will to fulfill that duty, to start over and obtain merit by doing the task well.

Mauakes felt at the back of her head, touching, through the thick hair, the slight ridge along the bone; she didn't flinch. "You are better, aren't you?" he said with pleasure, stroking her. "Well enough to sleep with your husband, then?"

She looked down, rigidly suppressing the shudder. "Yes."

"Very good!" he exclaimed delightedly, and began to take his clothes off. "I'll think about your plans for the city, eh? Perhaps put a few of them to the midwinter session of the tribal council, and if the council swallows them, give them to the city. But you keep quiet about it until then."

"As you wish."

"Good," he said, and turned his attention back to her. He was as tender and gentle as though she were made of the most delicate gauze, and she hated it every bit as much as she'd expected.

When she came upstairs the next morning she had the same blank, dutiful look as when she had gone down, but it did not fade even after her usual bath. She dressed and sat down to meditate, then suddenly looked up at me. I was the only attendant in the room, as the others went out to get some food after the bath. I was just putting the old cloak aside to be washed, since it was stained with sweat. "Tomyris," she said, "was your home like Eagle Crag?"

I put it down, smiling at the memory. "Very like," I said. "If anything, a bit wilder, particularly in the mountainous parts of the estate. There are fewer people in the Terek Valley."

"Were you . . . happy . . . there?"

"Yes," I said simply. "Most of the time."

She looked down, frowning. "But I suppose one could be unhappy, even in a place like that. Most of the people there, the poor, the peasants tied to their drudgery—they must be unhappy."

I was shocked, then angry. "You mean you think we treat our tenants badly?" I demanded, "Overwork them and starve them? My family is noble and honorable: we wouldn't live in pleasure ourselves if our dependants were wretched. I can promise you, we don't: they're as happy as people anywhere."

"And how happy is that?" asked the queen bitterly. I realized that she hadn't meant anything against my family, and forgot my indignation: she was just preoccupied with her own unhappiness, which she was convinced lay thick over the whole earth.

"Most people are happy, I think," I said more quietly. "Oh, everyone has things to grieve them. Things they want and can't have, things they treasure that break, beasts and cattle that are lost, people that die. But I think by and large most people like their life. As your own people say, it's sweet to see the sunlight."

She shook her head. "My own people believe that we live one short life, and afterward stay forever in shadow, gibbering ghosts on the banks of the river of oblivion. But philosophers say that we cannot escape the sunlight, that on death we are reborn, and if one life is happy, the next is sure to be full of suffering. Perhaps . . ." She looked up wearily. "Perhaps in my last life I was a man, and I raped or ill-treated a woman, and so Necessity requires that in this life I am married . . . as I am."

I was silent a moment. I'd heard of the Indian notion that the soul is born and dies many times, and I'd known that the Buddhists held it fervently, but the idea didn't interest me. I could never believe that I was ever anybody else but myself, and even if some part of me had once been part of a man, or a horse, or a goose, I'm none of those, so what did it matter? Maybe the bread roll I ate this morning was made from wheat that grew from land that was fertilized by the bodies of men dead long ago, but that doesn't make me a cannibal. I was much more interested in what the queen was permitting me to know about the deformity of her marriage, the thing that had frightened and disturbed me and which no one would talk about.

"Do you hate him?" I asked before I could think better of such a question.

She sighed. "No. But I don't understand him, and he doesn't understand me. He says he loves me. It makes me feel like a fly being wrapped up by a spider in one thread after another, so that it can't move foot or wing, and waits to be sucked dry. I don't know what he loves; it isn't me. No, I'm wrong: wrong to say that, wrong to feel that. I will try again." She crossed her legs.

"Why don't you just tell him you want more authority?" I demanded. "Why won't you fight back?"

"Authority!" she said with a weary disgust. "Fight! Tomyris, the reason I came to Ferghana was to make peace between my people and yours: if I fought for rights and authority, I'd be setting Yavanas and Sakas at each others' throats; I'd be failing in the very thing I most hoped to achieve. The only authority worth fighting for is authority over my own soul. Perhaps if I can master myself, and understand my husband, the rest will come. But what's the good of getting power over others if you lose it over yourself and your own intentions?"

I couldn't answer that—it wasn't how I thought of things at all. Heliokleia bowed her head and folded her hands in meditation, and I saw, for the first time, that her stillness wasn't statuelike, passive and helpless. It was like an archer's, who holds a bow bent on a difficult target and tries to see and think of nothing else. And suddenly everything fell into place, and I understood her. Even before she'd learned a philosophy to confirm her thoughts, she'd believed that you couldn't look for happiness in the world: the world would betray you with loss and with death. The only happiness possible was to want nothing the world could give, and instead win an absolute and ruthless dominion over your own soul. This, to her, was the central thing, the thing that mattered, and all that strength and courage and intelligence and ability were bent first on subduing the elusive and unruly self. But that dominion was precisely what Mauakes wanted as well, and his invasion of her domain was the reason he caused her so much pain, and the reason she would never love him. Because she was strong—much stronger in her will and her concentration than he was, infinitely stronger than me, and in this matter she wasn't going to yield the breadth of a hair.

I gave up arguing with her after that. But I felt, yet again, that there was worse grief to come from the marriage than anything I'd seen already, and I was afraid.

But Heliokleia turned all her formidable power of self-discipline and concentration on the goal of behaving like a good wife and good queen of the Sakas, and for a little while it almost seemed as though she could satisfy even the king. She obediently did not discuss the proposals for the reform of government with anyone else, and told Itaz only that his father had agreed to consider the proposals before the next meeting of the tribal council. After that, she tried to avoid the king's son, though his company was like fresh water to a thirsty land. She could not afford bitterness or regret. She had to master her soul's rebellion. Mauakes began to look happier.

The autumn dragged on into winter. The queen felt ill frequently and endured it stoically. Then, a few weeks before midwinter, she woke wanting to vomit and, finally, counted over the days and realized that she was pregnant, and must have been so for some time.

It was something she'd dreaded from the day she arrived in Ferghana. The Sakas would be afraid that her child, if a boy, would become the king's heir; the Bactrians would be eager for him to be; the boy himself would grow up virtually imprisoned, and herself with him, just when things were becoming a bit easier. But the despair and loathing she felt at the discovery were worse even than the miserable situation required. She did not love Mauakes, and all her efforts to renounce her disgust and revulsion had merely driven them deeper inside; now they had germinated in her womb, and Mauakes' child was growing within her. Her body was not to be her own again, even during the day; her husband had taken possession of it utterly.

Mauakes expressed a bland sympathy when she said she wasn't feeling well, and she stumbled up to her own room and was thoroughly sick.

We'd noticed, of course, in our horrible intimacy, that the queen had not had her monthly courses for some time. But since these had stopped at the accident, it didn't mean much. Inisme had been whispering for over a month, though, that it was time they started again. She'd been looking at the queen's face and hair and figure, and commenting on them as well, until I told her to be quiet. "Very well," she'd snapped, glaring at me, "but I think she's with child, and if she's sick one morning, we'll all know what it means."

Now even before the slaves had finished cleaning up the mess, we began squealing with delight, even me: "Oh, my lady, you must be with child!" "May the gods grant that it's a son!" "Lie down, and I'll fetch you some water with nard—it's a good sign if you're very sick, it means the child is strong." It never occurred to me, despite what she'd said that time in the corridor, that Heliokleia would want not to have a child. Everyone in the valley looks on barrenness as the greatness misfortune a woman can suffer, and healthy children as the greatest gift the gods bestow. Besides, I like children. When my little sister Tistrya died it was the greatest grief I'd ever known. I remembered the dream I had dreamt before leaving for Eskati, and believed suddenly that I understood it. Heliokleia would have a daughter, a slim, smiling little girl who would deliver her and the rest of us from the empty misery of our lives, as Tistrya had saved me from the dry river in the place of death. I could have wept for joy: it would all turn out well, after all.

It was no help to Heliokleia, of course. She lay down wordlessly. She wished, more than ever, that Padmini were there to be consulted. Padmini wouldn't have approved of what Heliokleia already intended, but she'd see the wisdom of it, and she'd know what to do. She knew herbs and remedies for such things.

Afterward I realized that she began hinting round the subject almost at once. "Are there things I should not eat?" she asked us as we bustled about fetching things. "I've heard there are herbs that cause miscarriage . . ."

But we didn't know anything about what herbs anyone might take to procure a miscarriage. We all helpfully recommended good foods for pregnancy—mare's milk, white bread, sesame cakes. Inisme ran to tell the king, and presently she came back with him: he was grinning.

"They say there's a reason you're not feeling well," he told her, sitting down on the couch beside her and patting her stomach. "Well . . . well." He caught her stare of bleak hatred and stopped grinning. "Aren't you pleased?" he asked.

"Why should I be?" she asked very coolly. "You don't want a child of mine. Nobody wants a child of mine. It would be better if it were never born."

"Tut tut. It may be a daughter."

"What if it isn't?"

"You don't need to worry, my dear; I'll be pleased to have him. He won't come to any harm from anyone here." The king was telling the truth: he liked children, and had been a loving father—until his sons were old enough to be a threat. Little children were safe, and he could indulge simple affections with them that overwise had no outlet. He smiled again in anticipation of a fat cheerful baby to play with, a son he had gotten on this proud descendant of Antimachos. "He'll be a loyal subject of his . . . umm, nephew, I'm sure," he told her with relish. Her bleak stare did not alter, and he patted her stomach again and said tolerantly, "Lie down for a while and you'll feel better."

He left. Heliokleia covered her head with her cloak and wept until she was sick again.

Everyone made a great fuss over her. The guards gave her presents; the king's daughter and daughter-in-law visited to organize the four of us attendants and teach us how to care for a pregnant woman. They lectured Heliokleia, too, about what to eat and what to wear and what to do and what not to do. Their goodwill, however, was already marked by apprehension, and they talked pointedly about the child Moki. Heliokleia again raised the subject of dangerous herbs and other things to avoid, but the women seemed not to understand at all. "Don't do too much riding" is all Amage would say on the subject. "That's supposed to be bad for you. And eat often, during the early months, and avoid chilling and too much heat."

"Really?" said Heliokleia. "I was thinking of riding to . . . to the lakeside, to pray to Anahita for a safe delivery."

"Oh, that should be fine," said Amage. "Why, I used to ride twice as far as that regularly when I was carrying my eldest, and I've always felt it was good for him."

Choriene just sniffed and observed that to pray to the goddess was a very proper intention. "And perhaps," she added, "you might pray for a daughter, since a son . . . might cause trouble when he's grown."

"I shall pray for a daughter," said Heliokleia miserably; and the two women approved.

CHAPTER

XV

The queen rode out to Anahita's shrine on the day after the midwinter festival. It was the first day of the winter meeting of the tribal council, and Mauakes was busy managing this. He sent Itaz, with me, Inisme, and ten of the guardsmen, to escort the queen on her pious mission. Itaz understood perfectly that his father planned to introduce the proposals for reform himself and receive all the credit for them, and wanted his unreliable son out of the way. It hurt a little, and he felt mildly and indefinably cheated, but he was resigned to it. He was, however, reluctant to go. Anahita's shrine was sited directly opposite the Mazdayist fire temple, and he had been to that temple more often than he wanted anyone to know. Nonetheless, on the appointed day he had our party ready in good time, and we set off in the bright clear winter morning.

The valley is cold in the winter. Up at the Terek end we get deep snow. Down at the other end of the valley, by the lake of Eskati, the snow is lighter and the chill is less severe: nonetheless, the lake sometimes freezes from shore to shore. We'd chosen a mild, sunny morning for the pregnant queen to ride out, though, frosty but not bitter. There was a dusting of fresh snow that glittered in the morning sun, and the breath of the horses steamed white. The queen was bundled in the purple woolen cloak and rode hunched-up in the saddle, a Saka cap pulled down over her ears—it's a foolish-looking hat, with its pointed top and its earflaps, but very warm in cold weather. Inisme and I had tried to persuade her to wear a good fur-lined Saka coat as well, rather than the Yavana cloak, but she insisted that she couldn't ride properly in the sleeves: how anyone cannot ride in sleeves and can ride in a bit of Greek drapery is beyond me. Itaz kept glancing at her as we rode. He could not help a sense of jealousy and resentment at the thought that she was carrying his father's child, but he knew nothing of what she felt; he imagined that she was pleased, and could not understand why she looked so grim and and was so silent.

We reached the temple in just under an hour, as it's quite nearby. The fire temple is the only Mazdayist temple in Ferghana: it is situated where the Jaxartes runs down into the lake. Anahita was worshipped there before the fire temple itself was built, but the Mazdayists pay great attention to the goddess, and gave her a small but elegant white temple on the lakeshore, facing Ahura Mazda's sacred fire temple by the river: it was here that we'd paused to pray when I first rode down in Eskati. That spring it had gleamed against the blue of the water; but when we rode up that winter morning, it squatted darkly against a plateau of snow-dusted ice. The fire temple itself stood in the middle of a sea of mud. The midwinter festival is the Mazdayist thanksgiving for the creation of cattle, and all the Mazdayist landowners in the region had brought their beasts to be blessed the previous day, leaving the temple yard looking like a cow pen. Heliokleia looked around the gloomy site resignedly. Embarrassed for his faith, Itaz hastily sent one of the guardsmen to fetch the priest.

"It's much more beautiful on a fine day," he told the queen apologetically, "but the interiors of both the temples are very beautiful. And the fire temple will be warm. We'll stop there first, and I'll see if the priest can bring you some warmed wine."

Heliokleia shook her head. "I'll pray to Anahita first. It's what we came for. And shouldn't I fast before making an offering?"

"We don't fast," replied Itaz. "Feasts are the gifts of Ahura Mazda, and hunger belongs only to evil, and there's enough of that without adding to it." He looked at her closely. "Do you mean to say you haven't had anything to eat this morning?"

She gave a slight inclination of her head and changed the subject. "What are those towers there?" She pointed to a row of stone and wooden platforms set on the hill above the road, on the other side of the yard from the temple. They stood very black against the sky; birds were fluttering and wheeling about the nearest.

"Funeral platforms," said Itaz shortly. Pious Mazdayists don't like to bury their dead in the ground, like the Sakas, as they say it's a pollution of earth; still worse is the Greek custom of burning them: that's a pollution of the holy fire. So, in their words, they "bury them in the sky." Which sounds very fine, until you realize that it means they chop the bodies up and expose them on a platform to be eaten by birds. Kites and vultures are messy eaters, and the ground about these platforms is littered with torn, half-devoured bodies, mixed with the droppings of the birds. The stench is appalling.

Heliokleia stared at them for another moment, then turned her attention back to the temple, as the guardsman came out with the priest.

The priest greeted the king's son respectfully and affectionately, but made no comment on his recent extreme piety, much to his relief. Heliokleia again refused the offer of a warm drink and a place by the fire, and asked to go directly to Anahita's shrine to make her offering.

The little building was cold, the sacred pond in front of it frozen solid, and we stood about in the gloom inside and shivered. The queen made a gift of money to the temple, then took off the hat and the purple cloak and knelt before Anahita's fire, and the priest marked her palms with ice from the pond, in place of water, touched her forehead, her lips, and her breast with the same, and prayed that the goddess would be gracious to her, and give her a safe delivery. She bowed her head humbly under his blessing, and prayed silently that the goddess would release her from the burden she carried, or forgive her if she took steps to release herself.

The prayers done, she pulled the cloak on again and we all went back outside, where she made her offering to Anahita—a dozen doves.

Anahita prefers offerings of birds and flowers, and there were no flowers to be had in the winter season. The priest freed the birds from their cage, one by one, tossing them up into the air; one after another they flew to the left, northward, beating dark wings irregularly along the lakeshore. That in itself was a bad omen, but it became a catastrophic one: a kite, which had been flying down from the north toward the funeral platforms, was attracted by the doves and stooped on them, striking and killing the third one.

Inisme and I, united for once, shouted together in horror; the priest exclaimed and made a gesture to avert the omen. Pakores, who was the guards officer of the party, ran along the lakeshore and drove the kite off its prey, then came back holding the dead dove in his hand. Heliokleia looked at it impassively, then put out a hand to touch it. The soft, shimmering feathers about its neck were stained with blood; the body was still warm. "What should I do with it?" she asked Pakores.

He looked from her calm white face to the dead bird, then back. He had no idea. He had wanted to reverse the omen of death, forgetting that death is inexorable. Silently, he offered the bird to the priest, who set it down on the snow beside the frozen pond.

"We must pray to the goddess again," said the priest earnestly. "Perhaps she will change her mind."

"Very well," said Heliokleia, "I will pray." She turned eastward and raised her hands in the Greek fashion. The wind off the lake pulled at the loose wisps of her hair and billowed the purple cloak dark as blood behind her. "Artemis-Anahita, Protectress, pure, full-flowing, healing," she called, her voice ringing low and clear, "if ever I prayed to you or made offerings, hear me now, and fulfill what my heart desires! Be merciful, and I will come gratefully in spring to make you thanks offerings of incense and bright flowers."

The priest nodded vigorously. "She will hear that. And I will pray too, and offer sacrifices to her and to Ahura Mazda for your child's health. Now you should come inside and rest."

Heliokleia glanced at the sky, which was clouding over. "I think, sir, we had better start back to the city," she said. "The wind is rising and there may be a storm. May the gods grant that I come again, when the weather is fairer."

No one quarreled with that, and we all remounted and started back toward the city. But the weather continued to worsen. We had scarcely passed the funeral towers when the sun vanished in a bank of heavy white cloud. The wind shifted, and came sweeping down from the steppes, blowing the loose surface snow stinging into our faces. The queen sat straight in the saddle, her cloak loose to let the wind in, hoping that the ride and the chill were doing her enough damage to fulfill the omen. As it grew colder, Inisme and I began to worry that they might.

"Please, my lady, do up your cloak," Inisme told her when we were a couple of miles from the temple, shouting to be heard over the wind. "You'll take a chill."

Heliokleia pulled at her cloak; it was promptly torn open again. Yavana drapery! I told myself, cursing it.

"We must stop," I said. "The wind is too strong, and it's going to start snowing any moment."

"I'm fine," said Heliokleia doggedly. She was feeling faint and sick, her teeth were chattering and her fingers were numb, but she welcomed the discomfort. Let the body that her husband owned suffer; let Mauakes' child slip out of the world half-formed, and his soul find another place on the wheel of rebirth.

Inisme and I shook our heads and looked at Itaz, who had slowed his horse beside the queen's to see how she was. "We ought to stop," I said. "Don't you have a farm nearby, Lord Itaz?"

Itaz hesitated awkwardly, then looked at Heliokleia's blue-lipped face and said, "Yes, just west of here. We'll stop and you can rest until the wind dies down, O Queen."

"I'm fine," protested Heliokleia again—then remembered that Itaz was supposed to be keeping his mistress on this farm. A mistress who had been a whore. There was someone who'd know, if anyone did, what drugs could be taken to procure a miscarriage. "But I wouldn't mind stopping for an hour or so."

It had begun to snow by the time we reached the farm, and the wind was still rising. No one was about in the yard. Itaz helped the queen down from her horse, then leaving the rest of the party to put the animals in the stable, led her stumbling into the house. He opened the outer door, pushed aside the skin hung beyond it and brought her into the central room, the kitchen.

I learned what they found there long afterward, from Philomela. The foreman Addac was sitting on the floor by the kitchen fire with Philomela on his lap, her arm about his shoulder and her tousled head resting on his chest, their fingers woven together. Addac's little daughter was playing with the kithara brought from the brothel, plunking its strings idly. At the gust of cold air all three looked round. Philomela blushed and jumped up; Addac sat with his legs akimbo and mouth open, staring. Heliokleia stared back, astonished.

"Lord Itaz!" exclaimed Philomela. "We didn't expect you!"

Obviously not, thought the queen. But Itaz didn't seem at all annoyed at the tender scene they had just interrupted. "This lady is the queen," he told the foreman, scowling at him. "We were caught in the snow on our way back from Anahita's shrine: find her a seat and something hot to drink at once; she's in a delicate condition. And you'll have to rearrange the horses in the stable; there are fourteen of us in the party."

"Of course, my lord," said Addac, clambering to his feet. He bobbed his head, pulled a bench over to the fire for the queen, and shouted for his mother. Philomela stared shyly for a moment, then ran to fetch a pot to heat some wine. Addac's mother came in with a rug, and Itaz went back out to the stable with the foreman to check the horses and bring in the others.

The queen stared at the girl who was busily warming the wine while the old woman built up the fire. Young, slim, pretty in a soft sort of way. Did Itaz love her? If Itaz loved her, how could she possibly, of her own free will, sit on the floor by the fire embracing the son of a slave? And why would Itaz tolerate it?

The girl poured the warmed wine into a wooden cup and brought it to the queen, smiling nervously. She bobbed her head, offering it. Heliokleia shook her head. "Are you the girl Lord Itaz bought for two hundred drachmae?" she asked.

The girl bobbed her head again, still with the nervous, appeasing smile. "Yes, O Queen," she said. "He has been very, very kind to me."

"What . . . what were you doing when I came in?"

"Oh!" the girl hesitated, then laughed shamefacedly. "Oh, I'm not really supposed to say. But I can't bear it that you should believe I'm being false to Lord Itaz, my lady, who's like a god to me. I'm going to marry Addac, the foreman here, and Lord Itaz is going to give me a dowry of six horses. Please take this, O Queen; you look very cold."

Heliokleia took the cup of wine and curled her numb fingers around it. "Lord Itaz approves of this?"

"Oh yes!" Again the nervous laugh. "He told me to find someone to marry. Most men pretend to have pious intentions when they're really full of lust; Itaz pretends to be lustful when really he's being generous and pious. He bought me out of pure kindness, because he felt sorry for me, but he had to borrow the money from his father to pay. So he pretends that he wanted me for himself, so that the king won't be angry with him for wasting the money. Really he hasn't set a finger on me since he bought me; he said he meant for me to marry honestly and have children. But he told Addac that we must be discreet until midsummer, because by then his father will think he's had his money's worth and won't mind."

"But . . . but he comes out here every evening, doesn't he?"

"Every evening? Oh no. Once every week or two. That's why we were so surprised to see him today."

"But . . ." Heliokleia began in bewilderment. The door opened again, letting in some more cold air, and Inisme and I came in, followed by the guardsmen, Itaz, and Addac, all chafing our hands and stamping our numbed feet. Philomela jumped up and rushed to warm more wine.

The queen sat silently in the crowded kitchen, sipping the wine and thinking. What the girl had said was obviously true: Itaz' behavior alone confirmed it. So why was he pointedly riding off in the direction of the farm every evening? Where was he going? And why was he misleading everyone about it?

She had a horrible suspicion that she knew why. She thrust it from her mind as impossible. Why should she believe everything revolved about herself? Itaz might have resorted to this deception simply to be able to speak with councillor friends freely, without rousing his father's constant suspicions. Or he might be playing "some game for power" as his father suspected. Or he might have another mistress elsewhere, a married woman—though she found that hard to believe of a man so enthusiastically devoted to the good religion. Whatever his reasons, it was very probable that no good would come of her prying into them. She set the cup down and sat very straight on the bench, feeling dizzy with exhaustion.

"Would you like to lie down and rest for a little while, my lady?" I asked anxiously, hurrying to her side. She was still pale as summer grass, and looked ill.

"Thank you, I would," said the queen. "Perhaps this girl—what is your name?—will show me where I can be private."

"My name's Philomela, O Queen," the girl chirped, eagerly appearing at her elbow. "I would be honored to serve you in any way I can."

Heliokleia stood, waved aside my offer of support, and allowed Philomela to show her into an adjacent room to rest. It was a fine room, its walls decorated with paintings of horses, and the woolen bedspread woven with bold zigzags of red and blue: she guessed it was for Itaz' use when he visited the farm. It backed onto the oven and was warm. The queen sat down in the bed and pulled the bedspread over her cold feet, curling up for warmth, and Philomela shyly put the rug, brought in from kitchen, over her shoulders, then prepared to go.

"Stay a moment," said Heliokleia, and Philomela obediently returned and stood before her attentively, with folded hands. "You have a Greek name. Are you a Greek?"

The girl hesitated. "Only half Greek, O Queen, though I say I'm Yavana if anyone asks. I come from Bactria. My father was a Greek soldier in Alexandria-on-the-Oxus; my mother was one of his slaves. My father sold me when I was ten. My mother used to call me Lota, but Gyllis, the brothel keeper who bought me, changed it to Philomela because the men prefer Yavana girls."

"I had heard that Lord Itaz bought you from a brothel."

"Indeed, my lady. He was very kind to me, and I am most grateful."

"Were you very unhappy there?"

"Oh yes! I hated it. And Gyllis was cruel. If anyone got pregnant, she had to drink a potion, and if that didn't work, Gyllis tried all the other remedies, even if the girl died of them. Gyllis never allowed anyone to just have the baby quietly; she said it wasn't worth her while feeding them for ten months when the men wouldn't touch them."

Heliokleia was silent a moment, imagining the misery of such a life, ashamed of her own luxury. She had meant to ask about the potions and other remedies directly, but this young girl, so indignant even at the memory of abortion, was not the professional courtesan she had imagined, who would part with the relevant information for a fee. "Did Gyllis buy many girls in Bactria?" she asked instead.

"Oh yes. She bought all her girls in Bactria; she couldn't use Yavanas from Eskati; everyone would be ashamed to sell them where they might meet them again. She goes down with a caravan every year or two, and comes back with some girls, and she teaches them flute playing or dancing before starting them to work."

"I see. Are they all slaves, sold by their parents, like you?"

"No, my lady. Some of them were stolen. Gyllis knew a man who sold lots of girls, and some of them he got illegally. But he said it was safe, he had protection."

"From my brother's minister Demochares?"

Philomela stared at her in stunned admiration. "Yes, Queen. That was what they said."

"I'd heard as much in Bactria. My brother is conducting an investigation, and would be glad to know more about this. Tell me, what was the name of this man who said he had Demochares' protection?"

"Dionysios, my lady, the son of Pantaleon of Euthydemia."

It was the sort of name she had looked for, in vain, in her own investigation a year, or a lifetime, before: the name of a middleman, one of Demochares' creatures, who might possibly be tempted or threatened into betraying his master. Now, too late for her to feel much joy about it, she had it. Joyful discovery or not, she knew what to do with the name. "Dionysios, the son of Pantaleon of Euthydemia," she repeated thoughtfully. "Thank you, Philomela. I will inform my brother."

Philomela beamed and bounced with excitement. "Thank *you*, O Queen. Oh, to think that maybe I've helped you put a stop to it! How wonderful! You're just as great a queen as everyone says, and just as gracious, even to me."

Heliokleia looked down a moment, ashamed, then resolutely continued with her main purpose. "There was a matter I wanted your help on, Philomela."

"My help?" squeaked the girl delightedly. "Anything, O Queen."

"You mentioned potions and remedies against pregnancy," said Heliokleia in a low voice. "I would like to know what they are."

The girl stared at her, the delighted excitement slowly changing to bewilderment and disbelief. "But . . . but why would you want to know that?"

The queen sighed. "You know that I expect a child?"

"Yes! All the city's talking about it; all the Yavanas have given thanks to the gods for it."

"Why should they give thanks? This child will cause them nothing but grief. If it's a boy it will cause conflict from the moment it's born, and its life will be nothing but a choice between treachery and prison. It is not to be the king's heir, and the Bactrians will firmly believe it ought to be. And the Eskati Yavanas will side with the Bactrians, while the Sakas side with the king's grandson Moki. No one wants it; it has no place in anyone's plans. It would be better by far if it were never born."

"But . . . surely, a child like that . . . descended from Antimachos on one side and the Saka lords on the other . . . how could you not want . . ."

"A child like that should be either a king or dead. My husband will not permit it to be king. I've asked you for help, Philomela."

"But it might be a girl, my lady! You prayed to Anahita; maybe she will graciously help you."

"Anahita has given me an omen of death. I hope it's true. If it isn't, I have to take steps of my own. I must not bear this child."

"But a little baby . . . oh, how awful! I never thought a queen would have to . . . I'm so sorry, my lady. Of course I'll help, but I'm so *sorry!* It must be dreadful for you."

Heliokleia did not respond. Again she felt ashamed: obviously the girl had jumped to the conclusion that this was something Mauakes had demanded, and couldn't believe that an admired Yavana princess would determine on it herself. Probably, she thought, it was a dreadful thing to do. But she saw no future for the child, and little for herself as its mother—and she believed that the soul she prevented from entering the world here would simply go somewhere else. So she asked quietly, "What is the best drug to use?"

Philomela told her of the things used in brothels to procure abortions—drinks of linseed and wormwood, pellets of ground lupin inserted in the womb; fasting, bleeding, lifting things too heavy for you. Heliokleia listened intently, and when the girl had stumbled to a halt, she asked at once about contraceptives as well—and was told of the twists of wool soaked in oil and white lead; the pastes of pomegranate peel and oak galls, the sponges of vinegar and myrtle oil. Oh yes, I know about these things. I got to know Philomela fairly well, later on, and we talked about Heliokleia and the things Heliokleia had wanted to know. The queen listened with a calm face, though hot inside with embarrassment, and struggled to commit it all to memory. Philomela was again nervously coming to a stop when there was a knock on the door.

Itaz had watched the queen go off with Philomela with some discomfort. He could not say why it made him unhappy to see the two women, the unloved one he had slept with, and the loved one he hadn't, going together into the same room—but it did. He was aware, too, that his deception must have been revealed to the queen, though nothing had been said about it, and he was anxious to speak to her, to ask her not to tell his father. When Philomela did not return immediately, he grew steadily more anxious and uncomfortable, and at last went and knocked on the door. "May I come in, O Queen?" he asked.

There was a silence, and then Heliokleia's voice said "Yes," and Itaz went into the room that had been his, and saw the queen sitting, straight and pale, her hair tousled by the wind, in his own bed. He was under no illusions; he knew this was the only suitable room for a woman of her rank to rest—but he felt as though he had been bled until he was faint. He clung to the door for a moment, then managed to choke out his excuse for interrupting: "It's snowing more than ever, O Queen, and it's lunchtime. We can have a meal in a few minutes, if that's acceptable to you—or do you wish to sleep first?"

"Thank you, Lord Itaz," said Heliokleia calmly. "I do not need to sleep. When lunch is ready, I will get up, and when we have finished, we can ride back."

Itaz noticed Philomela, crouching beside the bed; noticed that she looked upset about something. He was eager to get away from the farm himself, but the blizzard outside was growing in strength. "We may have to stay the night," he told the queen reluctantly. "You should not have to ride in this weather, not in your condition."

"It's not far to the city, is it?" asked Heliokleia. "And I do not think your father would approve if I stayed away for the night."

"No," admitted Itaz. "He wouldn't." He glanced again at Philomela and added, to her, "If the queen has finished with you, you'd better let her rest."

The girl got up hurriedly.

"Philomela has been very helpful, and I am deeply grateful to her," the queen said, giving the girl a wan smile. "She's been able to supply me with the name of a Bactrian Greek that would interest my brother."

Philomela brightened at this so much that Itaz saw they must have talked about something else afterward, and it had been that which upset her. About himself and his deception? What had they said?

"I'm very happy if I was of service to you, O Queen," said Philomela, going to the door, "And . . . and I'm very sorry." She went out.

Itaz quickly closed the door and caught her arm before she could go back into the main room. "What are you sorry about?" he demanded.

"Oh, Lord Itaz," said Philomela sadly, "I don't think the queen will have that baby."

"What! Has she hurt herself? Is she bleeding? Should I fetch a midwife?"

"Oh no! Nothing like that. She just . . . doesn't think she'll have it." The girl stared at him curiously. "I thought you didn't like her."

Itaz let go of her arm and slumped against the wall. "I changed my mind," he said, yet again. "It's true there was a very bad omen at Anahita's temple. Probably it frightened her more than she'd admit."

Philomela touched his shoulder timidly. "You're worried about her."

He nodded.

"Oh, Itaz," she whispered, "it's her, isn't it? She's the one you're in love with. I should have seen it when you came in just now; you looked like you'd seen a vision. No wonder you were so unhappy. Oh, how terrible!"

"Can't you ever keep your mouth shut?" he snarled at her. "Leave me alone."

"I'm sorry," she said again, miserably, and went back into the kitchen to help prepare the lunch. After a moment, Itaz followed her.

Heliokleia, who had got up to listen on the other side of the door when she overheard Itaz' first question, anxious that the girl might betray what she'd been asked, closed her eyes and leaned against the rough hide curtain, feeling sick with terror and exaltation together. Itaz was in love with her: enough in love that people around him had guessed it from his unhappiness; enough in love that he tried to practice deceit to prevent them from seeing it. She expected nothing but torment from it; she reminded herself of her duty; she told herself of the shame of loving a man when she carried his father's child—but the starved part of her he had woken before began to leap for joy. The one she loved, loved her, and not all her pessimism or all her philosophy could still the beat of triumphant happiness.

The snow was still swooping down when our party set off again after lunch, and the road was invisible. Itaz tried to insist that we all remain at the farm for the night, but the queen again pointed out that her husband would be furious, and the farm was no more than two miles from the city. So off we set, bundled in our coats with our hats strapped tight over our ears, silent in the howling wind. The snow was so thick that I couldn't see farther than the horse in front of me—the queen's Shadow, turned into a shadow indeed by the white drifts. Itaz trotted up and down the line, his great black steaming in the cold, checking that everyone was still there. Once the horses had been forced out of the farm, though, they were eager to return to their stalls in the city, and they hurried, sure-footed on the paved road beneath the snow, back to the snow-blurred walls of Eskati.

Heliokleia must have felt the ache in her groin the moment she got back on her horse, but she said nothing, and I thought she had bent over to keep her face out of the wind. When we at last arrived back at the palace stables, however, she stayed doubled up in the saddle, white and shivering. No one noticed at first; the horses stopped in the stable yard, stamping and steaming, and the grooms, who'd been waiting for us anxiously, ran out to tend them. I slid off Terek and patted her neck, worried chiefly about my lovely mare, who was shivering. Itaz was the first to pay attention to the queen: he dismounted and came at once to help her down. She sat hunched in the saddle for a moment, looking down into the dark narrow face turned up to hers, and noticed, re-motely, the thick snow, caught on the right side of his cap and frosting his eyebrows; the melted snow in wet pearls along the lashes of his eyes. She did not take his offered hand. "Queen Heliokleia," he said, his face changing with concern, "are you well?"

She brought her leg across the saddle and slid off the horse; as her feet touched the ground she fainted into his arms.

I heard Inisme give a sharp, birdlike cry, and I turned from fussing over my horse to see the queen slumped in Itaz' arms, and Shadow's saddle covered with blood. I stood there appalled, gaping. I couldn't even think what it meant, at first—I had no experience of childbirth, and the only thing that occurred to me was that some enemy had stabbed her. Itaz knelt down in the snow and began tearing off his coat to put under her. "Don't stand there gawking!" he shouted at all of us, furiously. "Tomyris, fetch a light! Inisme, go find a doctor! Pakores, you come here and help me carry her in!"

When Heliokleia woke again a moment later, she was lying on the ground in a circle of lamplight with Itaz' coat under her; Itaz, shiver-ing with cold, was straightening the thick leather by her head. Looking up she saw the white sky, the falling snow; her eyes, dropping from the mad whirl of the snowflakes, fell upon her horse and rested on the reddened saddle. Anahita had been merciful and kind, and had an-swered her prayer without any need of drugs. She blinked at tears of release; Itaz, seeing and misunderstanding, caught her hand. "Lie still," he urged tenderly. "Perhaps it will still be all right. I'm sorry: I knew you were worried about the child, and the weather was foul—we should have stayed at the farm."

"No," she murmured. "No, this is what I prayed for. Don't be sorry." He stared at her, aghast, and she pressed the hand that held her own. He looked away, bowing his head over her hand till she could feel the warmth of his breath on her fingers, then abruptly let go and signaled Pakores to take the other side of the coat. Between them they carried her up the stairs to the palace and set her down on her own couch. I went ahead, holding the lamp and opening doors. I felt completely numb.

King Mauakes had closed the council meeting that morning when the snow began, then gone home to pace back and forth in his bedroom, wondering what had become of his wife. At lunchtime he began to consider sending out men to search for her, and he swore to himself, cursing Itaz for heading the party, and himself for permitting it to go. He was just starting down to the stables when Inisme came running, flushed and snow-soaked, and gasped out that the queen had returned, Itaz was taking her to her room, she was miscarrying, where would she find the doctor? He sent her to fetch the doctor and ran up the stairs to her room three steps at a time.

The king found Heliokleia lying on the bed, smiling, her trousers and tunic soaked with blood. Itaz and the guardsmen were standing awkwardly over her while I and the other maids fetched water and compresses. My mind was working again, even if the only useful thing I could think of was the foaling sheds at home.

"I've sent for the doctor," Itaz told his father at once.

Mauakes glared at him and stamped over to his wife. The drunken smile remained glued to her face. Mauakes turned on Itaz. "You were in charge of the escort!" he shouted, "Why in the name of all the gods did you make her ride back in a blizzard? Why did you even let her set out?"

"Sir," said Heliokleia, propping herself up on an elbow. "Sir, it was a clear mild morning when we set out. When the storm began, Lord Itaz wished to stop for the night at a farm he owns; I was the one who insisted on returning. I believed you would be angry with me if I didn't. This is the will of the gods. Anahita gave me a clear sign of it this morning at her temple."

Mauakes stared at her, at the blood, then shook his head. He caught her hand. "I'm sorry," he said. "I'll give you another baby."

Itaz noticed how the smile twisted and vanished, and believed it, if he hadn't the first time: she had no intention of bearing his father's child. He had a sudden suspicion of what she had discussed with Philomela, and slipped out of the room, afraid that his face would show feelings he could scarcely define.

He walked down the steps to the dining room, completely at a loss what to do with himself. His sister Amage was sitting at the dining room table with her eldest son Goar, a boy of twelve; they were playing knucklebones.

"You're back!" said Amage, looking up as he came in. "Father's been frantic all afternoon."

Itaz sat down at the table heavily. "Why are you here?" he asked. Amage and Tasius had their own mansion in the city, and it was not weather for casual visits.

Amage grinned. "I wanted to talk to Father, and I was supposed to come after the council meeting. I wanted to see if Goar could have a royal horse for his next birthday." Goar smiled sheepishly. "But Father hasn't wanted to talk; too worried about the Yavana. So we've been waiting for her to get back. She's safely restored to him now, is she?"

Itaz shook his head, pulled off the heavy, snow-wet cap. Amage stared at him. "There's blood on your hands," she said in a changed voice. "What's happened?"

Itaz looked down at the dark smears on his cold-reddened hands, at his left sleeve, covered with red where he had braced it against the queen's saddle. "The queen has lost the baby," he said grimly.

"What? Just now? Merciful Anahita!"

"She should never have ridden so far, in such bad weather, in such poor health. I shouldn't have let her ride back in this snow. We stopped at my farm for lunch; I should have made her stay there."

"Merciful Anahita!" Amage said again, softly, then sighed. "Well, it's probably for the best. The child would have caused nothing but grief, and plenty of that. She knew that, and she didn't want it herself. Goar, dear, the king certainly won't talk to us now. Go tell the servants to fetch our coats, and we'll go home."

Goar glared in disappointment, then sulkily got up and went out, kicking the door shut behind him. Itaz stared at his sister for a long minute, noticing, as he never had before, a certain calculating hardness in her round face. "How do you know?" he asked.

Amage shrugged. "It was perfectly clear that she wasn't pleased to be pregnant. I don't think she would have wanted the baby even if it was to be the heir, though she would have put up with it then. As it was, she was asking me and Choriene about things that were dangerous to a pregnancy. I pretended not to know what she was after—but I knew. I told her long rides weren't good, and fasting and chills, and at once she said oh, she'd been thinking of riding out to Anahita's temple. She'd never given a moment's thought to Anahita before, you can be sure of that! I don't approve of that sort of thing, of course, but she showed good sense in thinking of it."

"Didn't you tell her she shouldn't ride out so far?"

"No. I told her a short ride like that should be fine. It should have been. If she miscarries for a ride like that, she would have miscarried anyway. You're angry about it, are you?"

Itaz looked away. "She fainted when I helped her off the horse. She was covered with blood. She might have died—she might die." He repeated it, horrified, "She might die!"

Amage let out her breath in a long snort of exasperated pity. "Do you think she wouldn't have bled in childbirth, Itaz my dear? There'd have been far more danger to her in that than in a miscarriage in the third month. You were right, her health was not good, and would certainly have grown worse if she'd carried the child to term. As it is, it's over quickly, and most likely she'll recover just as quickly. Though there's no safety anywhere when it comes to childbearing."

"Father wanted that baby."

"Father wasn't thinking. He likes babies, but he wouldn't like a son descended from the Antimachid and Eukratid dynasties as a rival for Moki. There would have been a war over that boy, Itaz; sooner or later, people would have started killing each other because of him. The more I think of it, the more sensible the queen's answer seems. And Father didn't really want anything more than another hold on the Yavana anyway. He's infatuated with her." She looked at her younger brother with narrowed eyes. "She's not a good person to be infatuated with, Itaz. She's certainly not good for Father. Oh, I don't want to criticize her: she tries very hard to be what we want, she's very dutiful and virtuous—but she's completely incapable of love. Father's tying himself into knots trying to possess something that isn't there to be possessed. He looks—and she's very beautiful; he listens—and she's eloquent and brilliant; he tries to love—and he goes galloping full tilt into a void. Loving her is like pouring water into a sieve; anyone who tries to drink from that cup is going to go thirsty. It's a good thing she isn't going to be a mother."

"Why are you saying this to me?" Itaz demanded in a low voice.

"I've seen you watching her. You look like a child, longing for the moon." Amage patted her brother's arm. "Oh, I know, I know, you're very dutiful and virtuous yourself, and you wouldn't dream of doing more than watch, and I know Father would still flay you if he realized: I won't say anything about it to anyone else. But she's no good, darling. The sooner you realize that the better."

Itaz stared at her in a long silence. Goar returned with the servants and the coats; Amage patted her brother's arm again. "Believe me," she said, "it's for the best." She got up, pulled the coat over her shoulders, and left the room.

Itaz remained sitting for a long while, thinking over the queen's life. A void, a long emptiness, without love, without children, without hope, filled only by an arid duty. He thought of what Amage had not seen—a young woman standing in a mountain pool, laughing joyfully at a fish. Where would that woman be in ten, twenty years' time? Accustomed to her loveless marriage, her barrenness, her loneliness: formal, rigid, frozen in her virtue, the lovely face lost forever behind the mask of calm? Perhaps even the gentleness might go, the sweet grace given to servants and inferiors; she would become stern, fair but severe and unbending; perhaps even sour and harsh. He understood, as Amage could not, how much was being sacrificed for virtue, and sacrificed deliberately, by a long bitter effort of the will. Was it worth it?

Surely sin wasn't happy. Anyone could see the misery and waste it caused. Surely, of all things, the most important one to cling to was virtue? So, at least, he had always believed.

But from the gods' point of view, which Antimachos had put to him, wasn't the contradiction of virtue and love, goodness and happiness, a false contradiction to begin with, the product of human error, rooted in the world's evil? How could you cut through the brute stuff of the afflicted world, and join the two streams back into one channel, so that virtue was joyous and happiness was good? Or were the Buddhists right after all? Was suffering the first and most basic truth of human life?

"I arrive in the world, I accept affliction, I am contented with death." Perhaps his own faith also believed that life was suffering. But suffering to some end, surely, not suffering pointlessly, incessantly, with no escape, and no finality even in death. If that were true, why would the gods create such a terrible world? The gods had heard him once, they had spoken—why would they abandon the woman he loved?

He did not like the conclusion to which his thoughts were leading him. He jumped up and fled them, running back down to the barracks to spend the evening drinking, in the warm mindless chattering of friends.

CHAPTER

XVI

A mage was right; the queen recovered from the miscarriage quickly. She was back on her feet the next day, and you would have thought that she had never bled in her life. She even took an interest in the deliberations of the tribal council. The lords and ladies of the council were, predictably, pleased that they were given influence among the Yavanas, and displeased that the Yavanas were given influence among them; they thanked the king for the first but, out of pity, didn't blame the queen too much for the second, and they grudgingly accepted both. The Yavanas of the city, who had less to lose, were delighted, and sent a delegation to the queen to express their gratitude and convey their condolences on her loss. She received them graciously and said the appropriate phrases, but when they promised to offer sacrifices to the gods to ensure her fertility in future, she smiled and told them she was in no hurry. That same day she sent me down to the herb shop in the city to buy pomegranate peel and myrtle oil, sponges and wool. She told me that the doctor had recommended these to stop the bleeding, and at first I believed her. But I noticed that she kept on using them even after all the bleeding had stopped, and never mentioned them to the king, and I guessed then what she'd discussed with Philomela, and what the preparations were really for. I said nothing about it, though, and the others thought the things were something to do with the Yavana passion for bathing. I'd been naive before, but I'd learned: it would do nobody any good if the queen became pregnant again. She didn't want it and only evil would come of it.

But the second time I went to fetch the preparations, while I was carrying the aromatic bundle back through the snow-wet streets of the city, I thought of my baby sister Tistrya again. She used to grin toothlessly into my face and pat me with a fat little hand; the first time I took her into the stables she howled with terror, but when I took her out she howled to go back in. No babies like that for Heliokleia; no child come to save us from the place of death. Only the dry river and the cold and the brooding menace beyond. I had to stop in the temple of the Sun and cry.

Heliokleia tried to go on as she had before, but something in the rigid self-discipline she had achieved before the pregnancy had snapped. She behaved correctly, as before; she was outwardly docile and obedient to her husband, as always. Yet something, some pliancy, was missing, and the king was no longer appeased by it. Perhaps he had, after all, understood that she loathed the idea of bearing his child; perhaps his ability to delude himself that he could turn the queen into a loving wife was waning; perhaps he was simply impatient, and the idle winter hours gave him nothing else to turn his attention to. But he understood, somehow, that all his dominion over her was a shadow, and his clumsy courtship, his presents, his attentions and his tenderness, left her farther away from him than ever. He grew restless, irritable, and demanding. He spent his days watching the queen, and woke her in the middle of the night to make love. He questioned her constantly about the conduct of her guards, of the petitioners from the city, of the servants, and particularly of her four attendants. And he lost all patience with me and wanted me dismissed.

That happened when the first thaw came, though the king had been displeased with me for some time before that; I never went down to him with any spying reports, as the others did, and on the rare occasions when I was summoned, I didn't have much to say. But when the first thaw cleared the roads Heliokleia heard of a Yavana merchant who was making an early journey to Bactra, and she wrote a letter to her brother, telling him the name of the slave trader which Philomela had given her. It was a short letter, and she wrote it quickly, after breakfast. She signed and sealed it and gave it to me to give to the merchant. I took it, slowly, and stood holding it for a minute: the parchment was smooth under my fingers and the clay of the seal was still damp and heavy. Then I bowed to the queen and went directly from the palace to the man's house.

The merchant was pleased at being asked to be a royal courier, the more so as I'd brought him a gift from the queen for his trouble. He offered me food and wine, and he put the letter in his strongbox, locked it, and promised to deliver it faithfully. I went back to the palace, feeling proud and frightened, but free at last of the shame of the other letter, the one I hadn't delivered unread. And as I'd expected and dreaded, that afternoon I received a summons from the king to attend him in his study.

I went down and stood in front of him with folded hands, and he looked at me, his round face at its most moonlike. It was a gray day in late winter; the room was cold and the light was dim. For the first time, and with a shock, I noticed that the hair around the flat face was as gray as the beard, and that there were weary hollows under the agatelike eyes.

"What did the letter say?" he asked without a word of greeting.

"I didn't read it," I said, just as bluntly.

However tired and hollow, the eyes themselves were as shrewd and penetrating as ever. "When I gave you your position," Mauakes told me softly, "I asked if you were my loyal subject. Did you lie, when you answered me?"

"No, my lord, never," I said. "I am a loyal Saka. And your wife is loyal too, and would never do anything to betray you. I'm perfectly sure of that, and I didn't need to look at her letter to know there was no harm in it."

"You cannot *know* that if you haven't *seen* it!" snapped the king. "I think I am a better judge of what I need to know about my wife's loyalty than some ignorant girl from the mountains! I am your king, and I made it clear to you long ago that I wanted to know what she says in her letters. If you refuse to obey, what are you but a miserable traitor?"

"My lord," I said, "I haven't *seen* the sun rise tomorrow, but I *know* it will—and if it doesn't, everything will be so upside down that there'll be no point in knowing anything. My lady Heliokleia has a passion for virtue and would sooner cut her own throat than fail in her duties as a queen, and if I didn't know that by now, after all these months serving her, I'd be more than ignorant; I'd be downright idiotic. I'm no traitor."

"You insolent, arrogant donkey!" the king shouted, getting to his feet. He slapped me. "You will go find the letter, and you will tell me what she said in it, today, or you can go back to your family before the week is out!"

"My lord," I said shakily, "the letter's gone already"—which wasn't quite true—"and in taking it unopened to the man who will deliver it, I was obeying the orders of the mistress you appointed me to serve. If you meant all along for me to disobey her even when she was ordering nothing treasonous, you should have told me so when you offered me the position: I would have refused it readily enough then. But I've done nothing to betray you, except to refuse to betray her. And if you send me home now . . ." I had to bite my tongue to stop myself. I'd thought he might send me home, but I'd thought he'd leave a decent interval for me to arrange some excuse. If I were dismissed suddenly, as he threatened, everyone would think it was because of some fault—stealing, or some kind of unchastity, or telling lies. I'd be disgraced. It would be hard for my parents to find me a husband. My brothers would be ashamed before the whole army. I tried not to think about it, how my honor would be injured unjustly. I stood there, trying not to beg, blinking my eyes and clenching my fists.

The king glared at me. "You heard me," he said. "I want to know what was in that letter before the sun rises tomorrow. Now get out."

I bowed and got out.

When I came upstairs, still rubbing my hot cheek where I'd been slapped and blinking with the effort not to cry, I found the others sitting about spinning or weaving—except for the queen, who was reading. Inisme glanced at me and sniffed; Jahika and Armaiti looked away nervously. Heliokleia looked up impassively, then continued reading as though she'd noticed nothing. A little while later, though, she rolled up her book and yawned. "Tomyris," she said, "I need to stretch my legs. Come walk with me down to the stables."

I picked up my coat. "I'll come too," offered Inisme, but Heliokleia smiled and shook her head.

"I'll let Tomyris explain what the grooms are doing with the horses," she said. "Just fetch my cloak for me. Thank you."

She said nothing more until we were on the steps down from the palace to the stable buildings, and certain not to be overheard. Then she asked, "Was it my husband who slapped you?"

"Yes," I replied, seeing no reason to lie about it. I was frightened by his threat, and I wanted any help the queen could give me. Shame, even wholly undeserved, is a terrible thing, and I didn't think I'd bear it with any grace. I'd complain, and rage, and grow bitter with regret.

"What did you do?" asked Heliokleia.

"It was what I didn't do," I told her.

"That letter?" she asked, and stopped on the step just below me, staring up at my face. "You mean, you didn't show it to him?"

"Of course not," I replied angrily. "It was a private letter and you'd told me to take it directly to its bearer."

"Oh, Tomyris!" she said, and her voice held such a mixture of feelings that I couldn't name any of them. "Of course I said that. But, my dear friend, I never expected you to run headlong into the king's anger rather than disobey!"

I set my teeth, suddenly furious with her. I risked my reputation to keep faith with her, and she'd expected me to betray her all along! "You think I'm a traitor?" I asked her. "Is that all you know of me? That's what he called me. But I'm no Greek: I'm a Saka noblewoman, and my honor is worth something to me, even if no one else gives a copper for it. If you expected to be betrayed, why didn't you give your damned letter to Inisme?"

"I suppose I hoped you would read it and pass on to him what it said," she replied quietly. "Inisme would have put it in his hands, and that Sakaraukai slave would read out every word to him, stuttering and slurring and looking for guilty meanings in every syllable, and the thought disgusts me. But I'm sorry! I should have known you better. Was the slap the worst, or was there more?"

I told her about the threat to dismiss me within the week unless I discovered what was in the letter. She listened in silence, standing straight and still on the wet steps in the gray light. Water from the thaw trickled down the steps at our feet, sliding shinily over the pale stone. When I'd finished she sighed and shook her head. She understood what it meant as quickly as I had. "Well, then," she said wearily, "you will have to go fetch the letter back. The merchant leaves tomorrow, doesn't he? Go now, give him my apologies, and tell him that I've remembered something I need to add to what I wrote before. Bring it back, the king can satisfy himself as to my honesty, and the letter can go in the morning."

"I'm not crawling back to the king with it!" I said vehemently. "I'm no spy, even if you're willing to be spied on!" I was still twisted inside with the humiliation of being thought a traitor by king and queen both, and as I've said, I hate defeat. I felt sick at the thought of creeping obediently back to the king after my proud stand against him; and it made me even angrier that I wanted very badly to do as I was told.

Heliokleia looked up at me for a moment seriously—then smiled, the slight, mocking Antimachid smile, but with something sad in it, infinitely older than my rage. Suddenly my anger had the feet kicked out from under it, and I stood there staring back, bewildered and a little foolish. She liked me, she'd said, back at Eagle Crag, and she'd said it even though she'd believed I was spying on her for the king— and I had spied, too. Did I have any right to be indignant, or talk proudly about the deceitfulness of the Yavanas?

"When it comes to spying, what choice do I have, or you?" she asked. "But you don't need to take the letter to the king. I'll give it to him myself. If he wishes to behave meanly, let him at least admit that he's doing it; perhaps he'll be shamed out of it. He's a proud man and hates shame almost as much as you do."

I stared at her a moment, then grabbed her hand and pressed it a moment. I had escaped lightly. "Go fetch the letter," Heliokleia ordered gently, and I ran off to retrieve it.

I had the letter back within the hour, and that evening Heliokleia gave it to her husband and told him that she'd ordered me to fetch it back, as she understood that he wished to see it. She never told me what he said to that. I gather, though, that he asked her to leave the room for a few minutes while he summoned his Sakaraukai slave, and afterward he sent the letter back to the merchant by one of his own servants. "It was not such a very confidential letter," Heliokleia told me, shrugging off my thanks. "I had expected that he'd learn what was in it one way or another."

The king didn't apologize, of course. Instead he complained to the queen of my "insolence"—I suppose with some justice—and told her that I ought to be dismissed. But the threat of sending me off himself and at once was quietly allowed to drop.

Heliokleia did not answer the charge against me at once. She did not dare say simply that she liked me; that would only inflame her husband's resentment. Instead, after a moment's thought, she said, "Sir, she has not committed any fault worthy of dismissal—and her family would be most offended if we dismissed her groundlessly. It would be a disgrace to us both if they reported us as unjust, but particularly to me, since she's my servant. She's a young woman, headstrong and passionate, and likely enough she'll soon find herself a man, marry him, and leave of her own will. Surely we can wait until then?"

And this Mauakes accepted, to the extent that he suggested to a number of eligible young men in his guards that I might be a good prospect for a match. When they began paying me attentions I was completely mystified—the queen hadn't told me what suggestion she'd made to her husband to divert his anger. But I quite enjoyed the young men's attentions, though none of them impressed me much. And the king would see them talking to me, and console himself for the fact that I was still about by telling himself that soon I'd be gone.

However, he wasn't shamed out of using spies on his wife. The episode stung, stung bitterly, since he did hate shame, but his restless exasperation couldn't let him rest. His wife neither loved nor trusted him, and the fact that she was faultlessly correct, and he was in the wrong, only made him resent her more. But since he couldn't bear to hate her, he found others to bear the resentment in her place. His next target was one of her guard officers, Sarozi.

Sarozi was a tall, bright-faced young man with a stammer and a sweet, slow smile; Havani liked him and said he was the best officer in the queen's guard, apart from its commander. That may have been prejudice: like us, Sarozi came from the Terek Valley, and we knew his family slightly. He wasn't an obvious man for anyone to resent, being quiet and tolerant, but he made the mistake of openly admiring his lady, and thus won even more of the king's displeasure than I had.

His story was much the same as mine; weeks of growing royal hostility, followed by a sudden call for immediate dismissal and disgrace. This call, though, was made to Itaz, as Sarozi's commander, and the crime that occasioned it was laughable; he'd merely made the mistake of giving the queen a present of new cheese, the first of the spring season.

"Get rid of him," Mauakes told Itaz.

"What's he done?" asked Itaz, though with a sinking feeling that he knew.

"Lusted after his mistress," snapped Mauakes. "Dismiss him from the guards."

"He hasn't done anything remotely improper!" protested Itaz. "He's a perfectly loyal and obedient man, and a fine officer. I can't dismiss him."

"Nothing improper? He looks at her as though she were a whore, and he tries to corrupt her with gifts. I want him sent packing!"

"If it's a crime to admire your wife," said Itaz through his teeth, "you'll have to punish every man who's seen her. Sarozi wouldn't dream of treating her with disrespect, and you ought to know that she'd be the first to complain of him if he did."

"I told you to dismiss him!" said Mauakes angrily—then suddenly stopped, and instantly slipped on his most moonlike look, watching his son. "Of course, you appointed him, didn't you? He owes everything to you, and the others wouldn't trust you so well if you dismissed him. A hundred picked cavalrymen loyal to you alone is a thing worth keeping, isn't it? Even at the cost of some dishonor to your father."

Itaz hunched his shoulders miserably and sighed. "Father, I can't dismiss a man who's committed no fault other than looking at the queen in a way you don't like and giving her a piece of cheese. It isn't right or fair. I'll keep an eye on him, if you like, and if he's insolent to her I'll take action."

"So he'd have to rape her before you'd take action?"

"Father, it is inconceivable that any man in that guard would assault her. Sarozi wouldn't dare to kiss her hand. He admires her, certainly, but I doubt that he even thinks of her as a woman; she's his lady and his queen and untouchable as Anahita. I'll reprimand him, if you like, but it would be against all custom and precedent to dismiss him for a thing like that, and it would disfigure you in the eyes of all the army if you did."

The king was fiercely irritated by this answer, but it was so indisputably true—dismiss a man from the guards for a piece of cheese!—that in the end he accepted it, though he held it as a grudge against his son. But the sight of Sarozi continuing to lead his troop of guards to their station at the bottom of the stairs was too much to bear. In the end, he offered Sarozi a promotion into his own royal guard to remove him from proximity to the queen. Sarozi, however, was very reluctant to place himself under the king's command, and understandably so.

"B-b-but why?" he stammered in bewilderment when Itaz told him of the king's offer. Itaz answered indirectly: Sarozi was a fine officer; the king appreciated his skill, and so gave him this opportunity for advancement.

"B-b-but the king has complained to me of my troop's turnout and my own conduct every time he's seen me," said Sarozi in astonishment. "I can't do a thing right, in his eyes: it's always 'B-back to barracks and p-polish your helmet! Wipe that smile off your face: you're on duty!' And if we ride anywhere, 'Your horse changed gaits on the wrong foot!' He has nothing for me but contempt. So why does he offer me promotion?"

Itaz gave up being discreet: they were private anyway. "The king knows you're a fine officer, but he detests your attentions to his wife," he said.

Sarozi simply gaped for a moment. "I haven't p-paid any improper attentions to the queen!" he protested at last. "I'd kill any man that did! I admire her, certainly, but if a man can't admire a b-beautiful young queen when he has the honor of serving her, then where is he?" After a moment he added, "Has *she* complained of me?"

Itaz shook his head. "A king's power is great, and must be held jealously," he said very softly. "And his jealousy is no trivial matter.

His first wish was to dismiss you. Take the promotion, man, and keep out of his way."

"I can't, if I take the promotion, can I?" returned Sarozi.

"If you take the promotion, I don't doubt he'll arrange it that you can," replied Itaz drily.

In the end Sarozi agreed. Havani, who was very sorry to see him leave the queen's guards, arranged a farewell banquet for him, to which he invited me and a few other sisters and mothers of guardsmen. At the end of the evening I found myself outside the barracks, having a long whispered conversation with Sarozi in the cold and the moonlight. It was a relief, an immense relief, to complain to someone who understood about the injustice of the king's suspicions, though afterward I doubted very much whether it was wise. But Sarozi didn't betray me.

As soon as he'd left the queen's service, Sarozi was sent off to patrol the Jaxartes, so he was, indeed, well out of the king's way. But the king's resentment, deprived of one object, was still unsatisfied, and it came crashing down on poor Pakores, the half-Yavana officer who had the effrontery to speak to the queen in her own language—and there was plenty left over for me. I grew sick of the king, sick with anger at all the trivial and stupid things he found to complain of, and I would have wished to go home and have done with him—except I wondered what would become of the queen when all her friends were gone, and all the false targets down.

But the winter wore on; the snow melted; the first blue irises appeared in the lowland plains. It was the time of the year's end and the year's beginning, the most sacred and most joyful festival of the year. At the Year's End we consecrate the night to the dead, and set out food for them at table; New Year's day is life's new beginning, and a time for feasting and exchanging gifts. The Mazdayists celebrate in the same way, and also, at Year's End, give thanks for the creation of mankind; and at New Year's, for the creation of fire, by which the world is made pure.

The king celebrated the festivals publicly, offering sacrifice to the Sun at Year's End and leaving gifts of roast meat overnight in the temple—food which was to be eaten in a public banquet next day. His wife stood beside him during the sacrifice, and said and did what was proper to the occasion, with the unfailing correctness that had become a subtle reproach and no longer satisfied him. He left out swaddling clothes and a rattle in her room, as an offering to the spirit of their unborn child, and she did not protest—but she didn't touch the things, either.

Itaz celebrated the festival eagerly, like a good Mazdayist. It was the time of renewal, and he longed to slip off the misery and confusion of the past year and begin again with purity and hope. He rode out to the fire temple on the evening of Year's End for a long service by lamplight. It was midnight when he started back, his head singing from the ritual sip of haoma, to snatch a few hours' sleep before the dawn of New Year's day. The funeral towers were silent, untroubled by the black beat of wings, and all the world was hushed, as though it held its breath. The day of mankind's creation is the night of the dead, he told himself—but the new day will be the day of fire. In the chill night of early spring, riding home under the white jewels of the stars, he believed it entirely. All doubts for the moment were lost; suffering and denial must end in joy.

He woke, light-headed and happy, and began the day with the fresh milk and new cheese traditionally eaten on the morning—white foods, for a festival of light. He put on his finest clothing, dyed with red and stitched with gold, and went to greet his family before setting off for the temple again and the year's greatest service.

Mauakes and Heliokleia were sitting in the dining room, eating the new cheese, the fresh nuts with white sugar, in heavy silence. Itaz swept in, glittering and smiling, and took his father's hand. "A joyful new year!" he said, kissing the hand, grinning into his father's unhappy eyes; then, turning to the queen, he took her hand and kissed that too. "Much joy in the new year, O Queen!"

Heliokleia looked up into his face. Her deep eyes were shadowed and her face was tense and thin. But she smiled. "Much joy in the new year to you, O Itaz." Her fingers curled a moment around his, then let go.

"I have gifts for you," he told them. "I'm off to the temple in a moment, so you can have them now. They're only small."

Mauakes snorted. Itaz grinned at him again, affectionately. On this morning even his father's temper and suspicions seemed endearing, the petty vices of a great but testy old man. He reached in his purse for the presents, which had chosen carefully the week before, and he set his father's down on the table. It was an Indian carving of an elephant about the size of a man's fist, made in ivory. "Now you have six," he told his father, "and they didn't even have to calve."

After a moment, the king laughed. He looked up at his son's open face, and his own cherished resentment melted. He picked the little elephant up and rubbed its fat back. "Comes cheaper than the other five," he observed.

"No, the other five carried a treasure that only the wealth of Bactria could afford," Itaz said, "and only a king like you could keep." The joyful freedom of a moment before was already beginning to slip from him, however. The touch of the queen's hand, the softness of her skin against his lips, like a heavy blow numbed first and ached afterward. He turned back to her with some of his usual constraint. "This is for you, O Queen." He set down on the table before her a silver brooch in the shape of a running horse.

She stared at it a moment, then looked up at him without touching it. Not quite smiling, her eyes were lit with amusement, the look of Antimachos, but gentler. It had reminded her as he'd wished, and he smiled back at her, welcoming the amusement, laughing at himself for his own earnest and heartfelt belief in a white horse and a man met camped on a mountainside.

"I have a gift for you too, Lord Itaz," she told him. "Only a small one, though." She lifted a fine silk cord from around her own neck and set the pendant it supported on the table beside the brooch. He saw that it was a coin, a silver drachma marked with the winged thunderbolt. He picked it up, felt that it was warm still from her flesh: that warmth made his hand unsteady as he turned the coin over. It was, as he'd known it would be, a coin of Antimachos the God. He looked down from the stamped face into the real one, and saw that she was smiling openly now. He touched the coin to his lips. "Thank you," he said very softly—and turned to find his father watching him with a fresh, even bleaker disapproval. "It's a coin of Antimachos'," he said after a moment, by way of explanation.

"Indeed," said Mauakes drily. "Your favorite divinity."

Itaz laughed. "No! Ahura Mazda is my favorite. And I'm off to the fire temple now. A joyful new year, Father, and good fortune attend you!" He hung the coin about his neck and strode off to fetch his horse.

Mauakes stared expressionlessly after him, then looked back at his wife. She sat very still, her cheeks flushed, smiling a little. When he had given her his own New Year's gift that morning, an expensive gold-plated belt, she had not smiled like that, though she had said the correct words of thanks.

A man who is thirsty might well suffer when he finds that his cup will hold no water; but his pain and his anger will be much worse if it seems that another man might drink from it easily. For my part, I cannot blame the king, not now, when I'm growing old myself and know a bit more of the ways of love—though at the time I thought him inexplicably cruel. He was a great king, no tyrant but a man who ruled by the Sun's glory and conferred great benefits on his people. Perhaps he should have been less jealous of power, shouldn't have married a woman so much younger than himself, or, having married her, shouldn't have wanted anything more from her than the fidelity and compliance she was willing to give. But if he'd been a man content with what he could get easily, he would never have become king of Ferghana, and the kingdom he wrested from the Yavanas of Bactria would have been swallowed up by them again. The silver brooch lay, still untouched, on the table before the queen. The king reached over, picked it up, and looked at it. It was quickly and clumsily made, Sakan handiwork rather than Yavana—but it was graceful and lively. He looked back at his wife. She had not protested, but she had stopped smiling, and her face was white again. "It's a cheap thing," the king told her. "Not good enough for you. You won't wear it."

She bowed her head a moment. "I think it's pretty, sir," she said, looking back at him, "and the thought was charming. But if you wish me not to wear it, I won't." She was watching the brooch, though, almost hungrily.

"It's a shoddy thing. I'll throw it out," Mauakes told her, and she again bowed her head and accepted it in silence.

The day was full of public banquets and celebrations, and we were
all busy—we four queen's attendants in standing still and sitting still
and occasionally pouring wine. I was very tired that evening. When
the queen had undressed, and washed, and gone downstairs, I hung the
clothes she'd wear the next day over the clothes chest, and on top of
them put the king's New Year's gift, the gold belt. It was a heavy thing
of red-dyed leather, with gold panels stitched onto it. The gold was set
with Badakshan ruby and jasper and lapis lazuli, embossed with griffins,
tigers, horses and eagles, running and flying and leaping on each other
so that the eye tired just looking at them: the gods know what it must
have cost. I patted it, then yawned and went to bed.

When I woke next morning, and after I'd dressed, I went to check
the clothes I'd laid out the night before. They were all there—but not
undisturbed. The belt, the priceless and brand-new belt, was damaged.

I couldn't believe it. I stared at the thing, then picked it up and
stared some more. Half of it was damp, the leather stained and blotched
with water; two of the gold plates were bent, and the buckle had been
crushed on one side. It looked as though someone had dropped it in the
bath and then jumped on it. "Inisme! Jahika! Armaiti!" I yelled, and
they stopped what they were doing and came to look. They were, all
of them, horrified.

"Who dropped it?" we asked each other. "Who had it last?" And I
realized, with a sick churning of the stomach, that the last person to
touch it must have been me. When I'd hung it up the night before the
slaves had already been asleep, and the other attendants had been on
their way to bed.

Any of the others might have been forgiven for the accident; I
knew, already, that I would not be. Damaging a precious thing like
that was an excuse for dismissal that everyone would accept, and the
king had been willing to dismiss me with no excuse at all. I sat down,
staring at it and licking my lips. But Inisme was unexpectedly firm and
helpful. "We will take it down and show it to the king," she said, "and
tell him exactly what happened. Perhaps one of the slaves bumped into
it in the night, or perhaps it was damaged when you hung it up, and
you were too tired to notice. It was an accident, we don't know how it
happened, and we'll all tell him so."

So we went down, Inisme and me, and knocked on the king's door. His body slave let us in.

Mauakes was dressed, apart from his boots, but Heliokleia was still in bed, a huddled shape and a tangle of blond hair under a blanket. We bowed to the king, and Inisme held out the belt.

"What's this?" asked Mauakes in surprise.

"Oh, my lord!" said Inisme unhappily. "Your present to the queen —it's been damaged somehow. We don't know how it happened, but when we went to arrange her clothes this morning, it was like this!"

Mauakes took the belt and examined the damage. When he looked up from it, he was as angry as I'd feared. "Who put this away last night?" he demanded.

"I did," I admitted miserably. "I put it over the clothes chest for the queen to wear this morning. And this morning it was still there, but like that. I was very tired last night; perhaps it was already like that, but I didn't notice."

"You! You, of course! You slovenly little vixen!" shouted the king. "You dropped it and stepped on it, and now you're lying about it to escape the punishment. You're not a fit person to attend a queen: you're an insolent, disobedient, lazy little slut, and you can go back to your family today!"

I stood very straight and stared at him. Somehow the idea didn't frighten me as much as it had the last time. It was what I'd expected, this time. At least, I thought, people will know I wasn't sent off for unchastity.

"She isn't lying," Heliokleia said suddenly and clearly. We all looked, and found that she was sitting up in bed, the blanket pulled up to her shoulders. "There's no need to dismiss her. I was the one who dropped it. I didn't realize it had been damaged when I put it back."

Her face was as calm and statuelike as ever, but it was muddy and runneled with tears. There was a twig caught in her tangled hair, and the hands locked about her knees were dirty. I had a sudden shocking feeling that the mask she'd worn since I met her, the reserved dignity she thought was a natural part of her, had broken and fallen off, but she was not yet aware of it.

"You dropped it?" said Mauakes after a moment of shocked silence as he took in her appearance. "When?"

"Last night. I couldn't sleep, so I went upstairs. I dropped the belt accidentally when I took it off the clothes chest, and in the dark I couldn't see what had become of it. I put it back over the chest and came downstairs again."

"And rubbed your face in dust?" demanded Mauakes mildly. "And cried?"

She put her hand to her face, realizing, then put it down again, becoming, despite the grubby tear streaks, even calmer and more regal. "It fell into the courtyard," she said. "I had to search for it. I couldn't see it in the dark."

"How did it 'accidentally' fall out the window?" he bellowed, appalled: he had believed he had a firm hold on his wife, that he knew most of what was in her mind—and suddenly it seemed he didn't even know where she went at night. "What were you doing with it? What were you doing, wandering about in the courtyard alone at night? Why were you crying? Was it alone?" He glared at her, breathing quickly in rage and fear. "Were you alone?"

It was the wrong time to ask insulting questions. What had happened in the privacy of the night before had left even her brutal self-discipline strained to the snapping point, and at this it broke, as it had only once before—not into rage, but into the icy self-righteous ferocity of her brother's house. She swept all of us with her eyes, and we all, even the king, looked away: there was something inhuman about that icy green gaze. "Sir," she said in a voice that cut like a winter wind off the steppes, "I am the daughter of a king. I do not lie, or break my sworn oath, or conduct myself like a common harlot. Of course I was alone. You may doubt me, sir, if you please: I cannot prevent it, and you will doubt me whatever I do. But I can swear on the altar of any god you care to name that my conduct toward you has been blameless from the hour that we met, and I don't think there is a man in this kingdom so abandoned as to bury himself in lies enough to say otherwise. Moreover, you have men guarding the house who would know if I had left or anyone else entered: you may be quite sure that I did not leave this palace. You are free to try me and divorce me for this hideous crime, this unheard-of trespass, of walking in the courtyard of my own house at night; and nobody would be better pleased than me if you did. But you will only make yourself contemptible to everyone who hears of it. As for how the belt came to fall out of the window, you would be wiser not to ask it, as the answer is not flattering to you and we have witnesses."

"Damn the witnesses!" shouted Mauakes. "Tell me what you were doing last night! Everything!"

"Very well then," she replied, biting off her words as though it disgusted her even to speak to him. "Last night, after you had woken me and finished your business with me—which the gods know disgusts me—I fell to reflecting upon your conduct toward me: your ground-less jealousies; your pointless resentment and persecution of whoever of my servants and my guards is particularly devoted to me; your ceaseless demands upon my time and my body; your restrictions upon my freedom and denial of the rights I ought to have as a queen. Reflecting upon all these things, I became angry, as I think is not unnatural. I left your bed and went upstairs to my own room, wanting to be private. There I saw the belt—a thing you had given me, as though you could buy my affection with gaudy trifles while you hoard such things as authority and freedom. And being angry, as I said, I picked it up and threw it out the window. Then, as I am committed to being your loyal queen and good wife, I regretted what I'd done. I went out, found the belt after a search, and fetched it back. Then I struggled for some time to master my resentment and accept your unreasonable and arbitrary conduct, as I always have, with loyal obedience. If I wept, for anger and for the waste of my life, it is none of your affair. I told you once that I don't need your love; I'll add now that I don't want it, or anything else that you have. The only gift you could give me that I'd receive with pleasure, would be your absence. But that, the gods know, you've never been willing to give, and I've accepted my fate, miserable as it is. I came back to your bed as before, and would have said nothing about any of this. But you demanded a full account of what I did: now you have it."

Mauakes stared at her in a stricken silence, blinking. His shoulders were hunched, and his hands hung stiff and heavy by his side. He looked old and shrunken and exhausted. He had no doubt she was telling the truth, but that truth was one that left him too stunned and injured even for anger. He was in love, with her and with the brilliant elusive shadow of Yavana rule. He had struggled to win her, to make her love him. And instead of love he had this: contempt and disgust, reined in by a proud, self-regarding virtue. It burned, like Greek fire, with a clinging, unquenchable flame. Outright hatred and open enmity would have been far easier to bear.

Heliokleia stared at him proudly and scornfully for a minute, and his eyes fell. She turned to me and Inisme. "Tomyris," she said, "put the belt away and get out my riding clothes. I will go out of the city today, to Anahita's temple: when I return we will all try to forget what has been said."

"I dismissed the girl," Mauakes croaked, not sure what he wanted to do, or whether he could do anything.

"I have not dismissed her," Heliokleia replied coolly. "She has been a willing and faithful servant to me—unlike most of her fellows."

"Tomyris," ordered Mauakes, gathering himself together, "you are to return to your family today." But he was still blinking, and his voice cracked.

"If you send her away," Heliokleia said calmly as I stood stiffly straight, though unsteady at the knees, "I will continue to give her the honors and the salary of a royal attendant, and I will tell her family that she has been the best and most loyal of all my servants: I do not dismiss her. You will only make yourself ridiculous, sending her off. But if that's what you wish—Tomyris, I am sorry, but we must obey the king. You will have to pack your things and go back to your family. I will go with you out to the city gates."

"You will not!" said Mauakes. It came out sounding more like a child's shriek of defiance than a king's command.

"Won't I?" asked Heliokleia. "What shall I do instead, then? Sing to you? Play Four Armies? Inisme, get my riding clothes ready."

"You will stay here today."

Heliokleia looked at him a moment, then turned deliberately back to Inisme and me. Inisme looked as white and frightened as I felt. "Inisme," she said, "I gave you an order. Obey it."

Inisme shot a terrified glance at the king and didn't move.

"If you disobey me," Heliokleia said quietly, "I will dismiss you."

"I do not allow you to dismiss her," said the king.

Heliokleia pulled the blankets about herself and stood up. "You are not to attend me again," she told Inisme. Antimachos the God, descended from Heaven, couldn't have sounded more lordly. "If my husband wishes to retain you as his spy, he is welcome; I will not have you as my servant." Inisme burst into tears; the queen ignored her and turned back to the king. "Now, since we have together dismissed my attendants, I will go and get dressed by myself."

Mauakes moved in front of the door. Heliokleia straightened the blankets round her shoulders and stared at him, and still he could not meet her eyes. "What do you think you're going to do?" she asked in a tone dripping with contempt. "Lock me in this room naked and feed me on bread and water, until I beg you to forgive me? Or will you just throw me against the bed and break my head again? Don't you think it's just a little tiny bit excessive? Two royal attendants dismissed and a queen imprisoned, because a belt fell into a garden? If you will move out of the way, I will go and get dressed; then I will ride with Tomyris out to the city gates, and then I will go on to pray at Anahita's temple, and beg the goddess to be gentle with me and help me to be a good wife. When I come back, we will all pretend this hasn't happened: that is the only sensible thing to do."

Mauakes stared back, his face now completely blank. "Inisme," he said, "get the queen's clothes ready, as she ordered."

"Inisme is not my attendant," said Heliokleia.

"But we will pretend it hasn't happened," Mauakes said, retreating abruptly and raggedly into his blandest manner. "No royal attendants have been dismissed, and no one has been imprisoned." He moved away from the door.

Heliokleia stared at him a moment longer, questioningly, then turned to the two of us. "Inisme—and Tomyris," she ordered, "get my riding clothes, please."

We left the room as fast as we could run.

It took me a long time to understand what had happened, that morning and the night before. I was a reluctant and terrified witness to an argument over a belt—but for Heliokleia, the belt was almost irrelevant, and the important object in the quarrel was one she never mentioned: the brooch that Itaz had given her. Though she had yielded and subdued her rebellion to a thousand greater demands, she wanted that brooch. Itaz had chosen it for her, picking it out from the stock of some merchant; she could imagine him seeing it and smiling as he thought how she would understand what it meant. She had thought of it again and again during the day of drawn-out public banquets, and the humiliations of the night.

She did not cry. She did not cry before her husband at any time; and she certainly would not cry when she'd give away so inflammatory a secret if she did. But she had no time that day for her usual self-crushing in meditation, and she didn't give up the longing for a gift she wanted from a man she loved. She dreamed of it—dreamed that the brooch leapt from Mauakes' hand and became a white horse, and she mounted it and rode from the palace down a lane of light, flying over the city to meet . . . and the king woke her. She could not sleep when he had finished with her; she stopped thinking of the brooch and thought of the man who'd given it to her. She got up, leaving her husband snoring, and looked in the king's clothes chest. The brooch was not there. He must already have disposed of it. That was probably fortunate, for he'd remember, if it were missing he'd know that she must have taken it, and what would he do if his worst suspicions were confirmed? But she couldn't go back to bed. Restlessly, she pulled a cloak over her nakedness and slipped out of the bedroom, up to her own rooms. Everyone was asleep, and the gold belt hung tauntingly across her clothes chest, a shackle ready to be fastened on in the morning. She picked it up, rolled it up, went to the window, and flung it out into the courtyard below.

At once she regretted it. He would remember that, too; he would know. She would have to fetch it back. She ran down the stairs, past the king's room, past the dining room, out into the dark courtyard. No one was about; her guard retired to their barracks at dusk, and the king's guard merely watched the entrance to the palace. The pavement was cold on her bare feet. There was no moon, and the court was nothing but gray pavement and black shrubbery: where had the thing landed? She searched for it, shivering, grubbing in the bushes with fumbling hands; in the end she felt it at the edge of the fountain and picked it up. It had unrolled when it struck, and the end was dripping wet. But there was nothing to be done: she went back upstairs with it, teeth chattering, and hung it over the clothes chest as before. Then she sat down to meditate, to escape the misery and anger. But for the first time resigned obedience seemed worse than the anger. She didn't want virtue, and she didn't want release into Nirvana: she wanted love, and a kind of life she'd never known. She sat shivering on the floor by the chest and thought of Itaz, and began to cry—silently, so as not to wake the sleepers. After a long time she went back down the stairs and crept into the king's bed, curled up under the blankets to warm her icy feet and hands, her back to the man she had married. When Inisme and I came down the stairs next morning, her mask had indeed broken—or to put it differently, it finally felt to her like a mask, a false pretense, not a true ideal, and she could not force herself into it again.

When Inisme and I had fled, Mauakes also left his room. His legs were trembling and he felt faint. He went into the dining room and sat down, trying to make sense of what his wife had said, trying to find something to do. Dissolve the queen's guard and let his own men watch her? Dismiss all the maids, and buy some Parthian eunuchs to keep her, as they keep their queens, in seclusion? He would only make himself ridiculous, and offend his own people. It was best to do as she'd said, and pretend that nothing had happened. After all, it was only a belt thrown out of a window in a fit of midnight anger.

He didn't convince himself. The queen had detested him all along. Fight as he would, defeat all his enemies, however great, achieve whatever glory he could; it wasn't enough. The mocking ghost despised him, as it had all along: and it was right. He had been tyrannical and unjust—and yet he had never wanted to be; he had tried, all along, to be kind, to make her love him. He had been forced into the wrong; she had forced him, for her own self-righteous pleasure, so that she could stand and coldly sneer at him, daring him to be even worse. There was nothing he could do. Even the one gift she'd said she wanted of him, absence, he could not give her: he loved and wanted her still. He felt sick with humiliation; his confidence in himself, in his ability to command and control his people, was shaken to the roots. He didn't want to see his ministers or the officers of his army; he felt they must be sneering at him behind his back, despising him secretly, like the queen. He was wounded and didn't know how to cry, so he sat in silence with no expression on his face.

After a while Itaz came in. The silk cord that held the coin the queen had given him was around his neck, the coin itself hidden under his tunic, worn close to the heart. He greeted his father cheerfully and called for the servants to bring him some breakfast. "You haven't eaten," he observed, seeing the clean table before his father. "Are you waiting for the queen?"

Mauakes looked at him with narrowed eyes. "Are you?"

"Well, if you want me to . . . is she coming soon?"

"No. She's going out of the city today, to pray at Anahita's temple."

"What? She didn't say anything about it to me. I'll have to arrange an escort." He rapped on the table and called to the servant who stuck his head round the door, "Tell them to forget my breakfast, and just bring some bread for me to take with me."

"You think you're going with her, do you?"

Itaz looked at his father in surprise, realizing for the first time that something was wrong. Mauakes looked back blandly. Itaz thought back over the events of the past few days, trying to think what he might have done to arouse suspicion. Surely just giving the queen a brooch wasn't enough to cause offense? It would have been discourteous not to give her something on New Year's day. "Yes, I thought I'd go with her," he said uncertainly. "I know the priests at the temple, after all; I could show her—"

"You will stay here," ordered Mauakes curtly.

Itaz blinked, then shrugged. "If you wish, Father. What do you want me to do?"

The king hesitated, then said smoothly, "I'm drilling the army today; you still have a wing to command, and I want the queen's guard to drill with it."

"But it's the day after New Year's! It's bad luck to drill now. And most of the men are still celebrating with their families!"

"Then the summons to assemble will be all the more surprising to them, won't it? It will be excellent practice against a surprise attack: we will see how they manage it."

"Yes, Father," said Itaz doubtfully—and ran a finger along the silken cord.

It was an unfortunate gesture. The king's eyes glinted and he said, "Are you still wearing that coin? Let me see it."

Puzzled and reluctant, Itaz slowly drew the cord over his head and passed the coin to his father. Mauakes looked down at the silver face, locked forever in its mocking smile. He closed his fist on it. "I do not like you worshipping this Yavana tyrant as a god," he said. He shoved the coin into his purse. "You're not to wear it."

"It's mine," said Itaz, alarmed. "I can do what I like with it. Here, give it back."

"No!" shouted Mauakes, suddenly furious again, and struck the table. "I said you're not to have it! You're ridiculous and disgusting, making a god out of a man whose son's skull served me for a drinking cup! Antimachos has been feeding maggots for fifty years, and you, pathetic little cringer, choose to worship him! It's bad enough that you come back from Parthia shaving your chin like a catamite and drugging yourself into a stupor for your foreign god, but when you pick a native god, you pick the enemy of your own house! Even the Yavanas won't be deceived into supporting you by that; they're too clever to believe that anyone could be so stupid!"

Itaz sat rigidly, staring as his father spoke. Once he would have leapt up and answered angrily and instantly, but the months had disciplined him, and he hesitated until his father spluttered to a halt. When Mauakes paused, red-faced and panting, Itaz found that his first flush of anger had already given way to bewilderment. His father had never attempted to interfere with the worship of Antimachos, valued his Parthian alliance, and made the odd donation to the fire temple: his complaints were only an excuse. "I told you what I believe about Antimachos," he answered quietly. "I don't worship him. But we are his heirs, so why shouldn't we be respectful? And the queen gave me that coin. You have no right to take it away. What's happened to make you so angry?"

Mauakes made an incoherent noise and struck the table again. A servant came in with the bread; Itaz waved him out again, got up, and went over to crouch at his father's side. "Have I done something?" he asked.

Mauakes made another noise, then to Itaz' horror, began to cry, putting his thick hands to his face and sobbing in choked snuffling grunts. "Father!" Itaz said. "What happened?"

"It's that damned woman," said Mauakes, grinding out the words. "You were right; what you said when I first agreed to marry her was right. She comes from a people who have always been our enemies, from a family without natural affection, and she'll do nothing but cause me grief. She's despised me from the day we met, and sneered at me behind my back. Nothing is good enough for her; she detests us all."

"But it's not true," said Itaz in bewilderment. "She doesn't."

"She does! She's told me so herself."

"But she doesn't—she's never sneered at you; she's always spoken of you with great respect. And she doesn't detest us. She's practically made herself a Saka for our sakes. I was wrong, I thought we'd agreed on that."

"She said that . . ." began Mauakes, then stopped, unable to repeat the humiliating words: old, ugly, stinking, contemptible, ridiculous, arbitrary, and unreasonable, don't want your love or anything else you have, only your absence. "Vicious unnatural witch!" he said despairingly.

"Heliokleia?" said Itaz, his voice sharp with disbelief.

His father looked at him. "What is she to you?"

Itaz gaped, caught off balance. "A queen," he said stumblingly. "Father, whatever she said—she didn't really mean it. She's not vicious. But she has been very unhappy, desperately unhappy. I told you I thought so before. If you would simply leave her a little more space, she would arrange her own soul to please you. She wants to be a good queen. But if you keep boxing her in and trying to drag out all the secrets of her heart, how can she—"

"Why do you defend her?" shouted Mauakes. "She wants to be a good queen, yes: she wants power. She doesn't want love, but give her power and she'll be happy. Any of them, any of her family, all they want is power: Eukratides murdered his master for it; Platon his father, Heliokles his brother. And I deny her the rights of a queen, don't I? And she thinks she can get them from you, and she's said so, hasn't she? And you've agreed. You're eager to help her! A pretty pair you make, conspiring against me!"

"How can you . . ." began Itaz, stunned by this sudden attack in the middle of his offered comfort.

"Get out of here!" roared Mauakes. "Go see to your men. If I find any proof of anything between you and the queen, you'll die for it, believe me. Get out!"

White with indignation, Itaz stood. He opened his mouth, met his father's eyes, and closed it again. He got out.

In the corridor he remembered that Mauakes still had the coin, and almost went back in to claim it. Almost. The king obviously wouldn't give it back quietly, and the image of trying to drag it from his father by force, perhaps even coming to blows, stopped him. How could he lay violent hands on any old man, let alone his own father, for the sake of a silver drachma? Robbed, insulted, and cheated even of a chance to defend himself, he turned on his heel and stalked off with a face like a thunderbolt.

In the room behind him the king put his head in his hands, feeling more lost, more confused, and lonelier than ever.

Mauakes roused out his standing army and the two royal guards and drilled them in the mud of the practice field all day. Many of the men had gone home to their family's estates for the festival season; many who'd remained in Eskati had gone off to spend the day with friends and couldn't be found. The rest were aggrieved. "It's flat contrary to custom to have anything to do with war at the New Year feast," Havani told me next evening, as though I hadn't known. "It's an ill omen for the year to come. Besides, I was going to dinner with my friend Naru. Sarozi was going to be there, too; he's back from patrol for the festival, and he said to invite you." At that I, too, regretted that the king had called a drill, even though by then I had more serious things to think about.

But all the guardsmen and soldiers had had plans for parties and visits and hunting expeditions, and they were forced instead to gallop about tilting in the mud, and, by afternoon, in the pouring rain. They were sullen, inattentive and clumsy; their officers rebuked them and they became even more sullen, and poisonously angry as well. They cursed the king under their breath. The king himself rode about the field, watching expressionlessly—except when he took a turn tilting himself. Then he charged the target with such violent ferocity that his lance splintered and he was thrown from the saddle. He got up, stiff, sore and covered in mud, and called for another lance. Itaz, watching, suddenly stopped hating him and began to feel sorry for him. If the queen had said—whatever she had said—she must have done so through unhappiness, and Mauakes was unhappy as well, trying desper-

ately to escape an inner pain by frantic actions and savage words he
didn't really believe. Amage was right. Heliokleia was not good for
him.

At last, late in the afternoon, the muddy troops rode home through
the pelting rain to their barracks, sunk in exhaustion and resentment.
Itaz went with his men to the army stables, saw that the horses were
tended, then dismissed the men, telling them jokingly that at least they
could now lord it over their fellows who'd been away. Then he went
to check his own mount, which he'd left at the royal stables, apart
from the others. When he came to the stableyard he saw that the
queen's party had just returned.

The queen had arranged her own escort that morning, assigning the
task to Pakores without any intervention from Itaz, and had ridden,
with both Inisme and me, to Anahita's temple, stopping first in the city
to buy flowers and incense to offer to the goddess. Her escort had been
disturbed by the choice of offering, remembering that she had promised these specifically to the goddess before—but no one made any
comment. She was, in fact, still so coldly furious that no one dared say
anything to her at all.

When we were out of the city, Heliokleia summoned me to ride
beside her.

"I am sorry you were put in such a difficult position this morning,"
she said.

I laughed nervously. "I felt like a pine tree squashed between two
avalanches," I admitted. "But thank you, my lady. You stood up for
me to the king himself." I had not felt sorry for the king at the time:
rather, I'd enjoyed seeing him withered by that blast of icy words. The
pity came later, with memory and understanding.

Heliokleia sighed and rode in silence for a minute, staring at her
horse's mane. "Tomyris," she said at last, looking up again, "is there
any young man about at the palace that you might wish to marry?"

I thought of Sarozi. But I scarcely knew him, and anyway, he
wasn't at the palace now. "No, my lady," I replied. "Why?"

"Because it would be best if you could find one, and leave my
service as quickly and quietly as possible. The king will not forget
what I said this morning, and he won't forgive it, or you. Your life

will be very difficult if you remain, and I can't promise that I'll be able to protect you forever."

"But, my lady, the king backed down. He admitted he was unreasonable."

"He did nothing of the sort. He agreed to pretend that nothing had occurred. He has ruled your own country since before you were born: have you ever heard of any occasion where he failed to get what he wanted, in the end?"

Stricken, I said nothing for a moment. Then I looked at the queen. "He won't get what he wants this time, though, will he?" I said very quietly. "Not from you."

"Perhaps not," she said, "but he will not give up easily. And . . . and I don't think I can go on as I have done. I tried, before, to be what he wished—but it would all be a lie now. Everything has changed. I don't know what I believe anymore. If my philosophy is true, it isn't true in the way I thought but in some other way which I don't understand, and it can't help me now. I don't know what will happen between my husband and myself. Perhaps we'll both give up the struggle in the end, but there will be a desert between us first. And perhaps one of us will die. Perhaps I will."

Her voice had fallen to a whisper as she finished, and I knew, with a sudden perfect clarity, what she foresaw, held in reserve for herself. The common resort of Greek women pushed too far—a scarf, or a belt perhaps, tied to the window and knotted around her neck, the leap into the courtyard, and darkness coming with a jerk about the throat.

"No," I said, shaken. "Don't. Don't give up hope too soon. My lady, I've told you: you could win the people over to you, you could fight him."

"And I've told you," she replied, with the Antimachid smile, "I didn't come to Ferghana to make people fight one another."

"Don't send me off," was the only answer I could think of to that. "You'll need friends. Don't ask me to run away and leave you to face his anger alone."

Heliokleia sighed. "Do you think you can help? Now? You know better than that yourself. The one thing I don't need is friends—people for him to injure in my place. Better to have no one and nothing, and be strong. Besides, I won't proceed in any way you'll approve. I shouldn't have said what I did this morning; I lost my temper. I will yield and beg his forgiveness humbly this evening, if Anahita grants me the strength. It isn't really so terrible. Many women endure far worse."

I began to cry. Heliokleia looked at me with a remote sympathy, then leaned over and patted my hand. "You see, I'm not the kind of queen you want to serve either," she said gently. "No generous, brave, and loving lady, just a cold-hearted devious Yavana. I'm sorry."

"But you could be as brave and generous as any queen that lived," I sniffed despairingly. "You could be a great queen even now, if you'd do it!"

"One great ruler in a kingdom at a time is enough," the queen replied drily. "And you already have a king."

We rode on in silence to the fire temple. It was crowded with worshippers, come to celebrate the second day of the New Year festival with bonfires and music. The pond by Anahita's temple, which had been frozen and black before, was deep and cold and blue-green, cut by the red-tipped arrows of small fish. The queen made her offering of flowers and incense and prayed to the goddess, and the priest invited her and all our party to remain for the feast and the afternoon service at the fire temple. She agreed, and asked him so many questions about his religion that he grew quite excited, hoping that she might convert.

I slipped away from the Mazdayist service while it was still at its peak, and went back down to Anahita's shrine. I wanted to pray, and I'd rather pray to Anahita and our lord the Sun than to the Wise Lord, whom I've never really understood. Anahita's priest stayed where he was, at the fire temple, but that was just as well: I wanted to be private.

Anahita's shrine was deserted, except for an old countrywoman sitting beside the sacred pond, selling flowers: yellow and purple crocus, blue iris, and a few early tulips red as blood. "Come make an offering to our lovely lady?" she coaxed, holding out the basket of flowers as I approached. "Pray to her for a good husband and fine children, and she'll answer you, indeed she will; she's a good and merciful goddess, and sure to hear a pretty young lady like yourself."

I gave a smile that probably looked as tired as Heliokleia's, and gave the old woman a couple of bronze coins stamped with a clumsy counterfeit of Heliokleia's father; it was enough for all the flowers I could carry, and I went with them into the temple.

I didn't go up to the main altar, to the statue of Anahita that looked so much like Heliokleia. I wanted to pray to the goddess I had known as I grew up, the clumsy big-eyed Saka doll image who was merciful and kind and sent the sweet waters flowing from the mountains to make the earth green. When I'd come before I'd noticed an old, neglected statue by the door, probably the one the lovely Yavana sculpture had pushed from its place, which was no longer needed but which no one quite dared to put out. It was wooden, clumsily carved so that you could see the chisel marks, and the paint had worn so thin you could see the grain of the wood under the pink cheeks and the black of the hair and eyes. But the crude face had a smile at once mysterious and kind, and she was my goddess. I placed my armful of flowers at her feet and knelt down in front of her, touching my forehead to the cold stone floor.

"Pure Anahita," I said, sitting back on my heels and turning my palms toward her, "full-flowing, healing, worthy of all praise, hear me!" And then I sat there, wondering how to go on.

I had prayed to Anahita hundreds of times before: for water and a good growing season; for the marriages and childbeds of cousins or friends; for sick children; for good fortune on a journey and an endeavor. I had prayed hardest and most painfully for what had not been granted, Tistrya's life. But now I wanted to pray for something different, and I suddenly realized that I wasn't sure myself what it was. I knew I was afraid, for my lady and for myself, and mysteriously for the whole kingdom—but I didn't know what to ask for to mend it. I could see them in my mind, the king and the queen, and the thing between them twisted and rotted, a deformity, a broken, gangrenous limb that was spreading a slow poison through both their lives, and through the lives of everyone around them, seeping into the kingdom as though it would dim the glory of the Sun itself. And yet that poisonous marriage was a compact sworn by the Sun and by Anahita, and I didn't see how I could beg the gods to break it. But what else could I pray for? For the queen to be forbearing or Mauakes to be kind? The queen was far too forbearing as it was, and Mauakes had already tried to be kind, and it had only made matters worse. And how could I pray for Heliokleia to learn love? To love the way he wanted her to, she would have to annihilate her own nature. Yet I wouldn't

have said she was cold and uncaring, not anymore. Only . . . Antimachid. I remembered the descriptions of her uncle Menander, the
king of the wheel, the saint, the rock that could not be shaken in any
wind. I knew, well enough, that my lady was tormented and wretched,
contemplating death—and yet it was true, it was perfectly true of her,
she could break Mauakes and the kingdom and her own life without
breaking herself. She needed a way out true to her own nature—but
what was that? Did it exist? Was there anything I *could* justly pray for
—and would the gods be willing to hear me and grant it if I did?

If, as the priests say, the gods always hear us, still they don't always
grant what we ask. But I thought again of the streams coming down
laughing from the mountains, and the earth growing green in the
warm sun. Surely the gods will be kind, if Necessity permits? They'd
heard Itaz, and answered him in a way he didn't expect, so why
shouldn't they hear me?

"You know why I've come," I told Anahita bluntly, looking up at
the clumsily carved, worn-through face. "Don't let my lady die. Don't
let her go on suffering pointlessly. Wash the evil away and heal us. And
you, Lord Sun, hear me and help. Why this has happened I don't
know, but you are a god, and know all things. There's nothing I can
offer you that's of any value, but the kingdom is yours, and the marriage was made in your name; it is in your hands. Hear me, and I will
praise you and make offering gladly for the rest of my life."

I touched the statue's foot, feeling for it through the moist petals of
the flowers. It was hard and wooden and it did not stir, and the shrine
was silent as stone. Angry and despairing, I touched my forehead to the
floor again and left, going back to the fire temple to attend my mistress.

It was midafternoon before we started back to the city. The rain
had started by then, and most of the other worshippers were also
returning, laughing and cursing at the wet. On the road by the funeral
towers, Heliokleia stopped. Two of the towers were occupied that day,
and the crows and vultures squatted and squabbled over them. The
queen turned her horse and rode toward them.

At the time I could only think she was riding to look at death, the
fate she foresaw for herself. But I heard once, some years ago, that this
is what the Buddha recommends as a cure for carnal longing: to visit a

charnal house and gaze upon the bodies of the dead, seeing what will become of the flesh for which you burn desperately, and I think that was in her mind as much as the other. The queen would have found it difficult to get permission to visit a charnal house: death, so we and the Mazdayists believe, is the ultimate pollution. All the escort shouted in horror when she rode toward the tower, but everyone hesitated to follow her. Even the worshippers returning along the road stopped in their places and shouted to her to keep away. I followed, in the end, but at a distance, afraid of the silent towers and the birds' great wings. But she stopped only when she was close enough to see. The ground below the tower was littered with bones and bird droppings, and the rotten-meat stink was damped down by the chill and the rain. A crow was pecking at something that had fallen off the tower to the ground, its feathers sad and ruffled by the wet. Riding closer, she saw that it was eating a child's head: the long black hair was trampled under the bird's feet. Half the face was already gone, reduced to a wet red skin on white bone, but the other half was untouched: soft cheek turned to the pouring rain, moist lips parted, the dark lashes lowered over the eye— only the eye was missing. She stared at it for a long moment; it had been the face of a girl. How had she died?

Fever or dysentery, drowning or a fall, and her parents had left her body to be buried in the sky and commended her soul to paradise. People die easily; we all die, and if we hide ourselves in the grave, clothing our shame in earth, we merely feed maggots instead of crows. Heliokleia glanced up at the birds on the tower; a vulture spread its huge white wings and shook them at her, considering whether to fly; the crow looked up from its feast with a beady black eye. The queen turned her horse and rode back, to me and to the rest of her horrified attendants, then started again toward the city without another word.

It was dark when we arrived in the palace stableyard, and the servants came out to meet us with torches, the flames hissing and spitting in the rain. Heliokleia dismounted and handed her horse to a groom, pulled up her wet cloak, and turned to go into the house— then stopped, seeing Itaz coming out of the stable toward her.

"Greetings, O Queen," said Itaz, joining her. His hair and clothing were soaked, sticking to the skin, and his trousers and boots were muddy. "May I have a word with you?"

"Of course, Lord Itaz," she said. "Shall we go into the palace, where it's dry?"

He hesitated. He meant to tell her how much his father had been distressed by their quarrel, thinking she might not otherwise understand this. He suspected that the king would be waiting for her impatiently in the palace: if they went in, the quarrel might break out again before he had any chance to intervene. "It will only take a moment," he said. "Why don't we simply go into the stables?"

"Very well. Inisme, Tomyris, don't wait. Lord Itaz?" She turned and went out of the yard, under the sheltering eaves of the stable. The guardsmen of the escort, tired and incurious, led their own mounts off to the army stables, thinking that their commander wished to discuss some guards' business with their queen, and Inisme and I led our mares to their stalls, let the grooms see to them, and started up the stairs toward the palace.

Our horses were at the front, the near end of the stables. Looking about for somewhere private, Itaz decided on the far end, where his horse and the mounts of the king were chomping their evening feed in the dark. He took one of the lanterns from the grooms and led the way to his stallion's stall, which was screened by a wall of hay shocks from the rest of the stable. He hung the light against the roof pole, and turned to the queen.

The stable was warm from the bodies of the animals, and it smelled of dung, horses, and clean straw. The lantern cast a hazy gold light in the dusty air, so that they seemed to be floating in honey. The queen stood in the golden dimness like the statue of Anahita in her temple in Bactra, her wet cloak loosened from her shoulders and her hair curving in crescent-moon wisps above her fathomless eyes. Itaz felt his heart stop. He forgot what he was going to say, and simply stood looking at her.

"What did you have to say to me, Lord Itaz?" Heliokleia asked, after a moment.

He started, then smiled ruefully at himself. "I'm sorry. Forgive me for . . . interfering, but you had a quarrel with my father this morning. I don't know what was said or why, but he was greatly distressed over it. I thought he might not say as much to you, but I thought you ought to be aware of it."

"Aware of what?" she asked after a moment, puzzled.

"That he was very distressed. He cried, O Queen, and said some wild words."

She stared in astonished bewilderment. "He *cried?*"

Itaz went on hurriedly, "Again, I don't know what was said or why, but . . . but I thought you should know he's not indifferent to your opinion of him, even if he pretends otherwise. And if you could speak to him gently . . . that is, please be gentle with him. He was hurt."

"Did he ask you to say this?"

"By the Sun, no! My father, ask me to say a thing like that, to you? Merciful Anahita!"

"No, of course not." She leaned one arm against the stall, looking down. "Probably he found some excuse to lose his temper with you, and accuse you of the gods-know-what. Plotting his downfall with me, perhaps."

Itaz winced. Heliokleia looked back up at his face and saw that she'd hit the mark, and remained for a moment, watching him—the dark, passionate face and the clear eyes; the love and concern sitting there openly for anyone to read. "But you came to say this anyway?" she asked him. "You do love him, don't you? But I asked you that before, didn't I? And you said of course."

"He's a very great king," said Itaz, "and he's so easily hurt."

That, she knew, was the crucial thing for Itaz: Mauakes was hurt, and Itaz, who was easily moved to pity, pitied him. He had no reason to love his father, but he needed no reason; he loved because it was in his nature to, as it's a horse's nature to run. She thought suddenly of the symbol of her own philosophy, the eight-spoked wheel. Each spoke was an aspect of the eightfold way, their equal length was justice—but their center, the hub from which they all depended, was loving kindness and compassion. She, who called herself a Buddhist, was less perfect in the way than this fire worshipper, committed to the burning house of the world.

"I don't love him, and I don't know how to go about trying to love him," she said wearily. "You say he's not indifferent to my opinion of him: I wish he were. Nothing I do seems to satisfy him; he must have my soul's love, and I can't give him that. Can't, not won't: it isn't

there for him. Though I admit I don't even want to please him anymore, though perhaps I should. I've struggled not to hate him, and
even that seems to have been a mistake, as now I feel nothing at the
thought of him but disgust, exhaustion, and despair. Couldn't you ask
him to leave me alone, just a little bit? If he would only give me some
space to breathe, I might feel some affection, or, like you, some pity: I
could build on that."

"I . . . tried," said Itaz, "but you know how he is. He can't stand
to be contradicted."

"I know." Her voice was becoming unsteady, just a little, so little
that perhaps nobody else would have noticed the small tremor under
the calm, but his ears were tender to the least catch of her breath. "I
can't please him and I can't argue with him. He asks, and asks, and asks,
and he gives nothing. He tests me constantly; watches me, spies on me,
persecutes me without pause. I wish he were dead—or that I were. I'm
sorry. I should not be saying this. I will speak to him gently this
evening; I meant to anyway."

"Oh," Itaz said tenderly, feeling her pain almost as his own. He
made a slight move toward her, then stopped himself.

"I shouldn't have spoken as I did this morning," she went on, after
a moment. She knew she should have gone at the last sentence, but she
couldn't, not to return to her husband. She felt the closeness to Itaz
almost a physical sensation, as though they stood together in a pool of
water and sensed each faint current when the other moved. "But I was
angry. It was a very stupid quarrel, Lord Itaz, carried to ridiculous
lengths. I threw a belt he'd given me out of the window last night in a
fit of anger, and this morning it was damaged, and he wanted to know
how, and then he wanted to know why, and so I told him, and he
didn't like the answer."

"You threw his present out the window?" asked Itaz, putting his
hand to his neck where he'd briefly worn her gift, his own quarrel with
the king suddenly making sense. "Why?"

She hesitated. "I didn't tell him the whole truth," she said with a
sudden firm clarity, meeting his eyes. "He took away the brooch you
gave me, because he could tell that I liked it more than I liked his own
gift. I was angry, and when I woke at night I was more angry, about

that and about everything else. I told him about the everything else, but not about that: it would only make things worse to mention that."

"He took away your present to me as well."

"Well, he would, wouldn't he?" she asked bitterly. "If I won't love him, I won't be allowed to love anyone else either. And I've told him I'm willing to accept even that, but it still isn't enough." She stared into his face intently for a moment; her eyelids swept over the eyes and up again, wet with the tears she never shed in her husband's presence.

"Oh my queen," he said, and again made the slight, checked movement toward her. But she answered it this time, answered it without thinking and came suddenly into his arms. He was hard and damp and smelled of wet woolens, horses, mud, and sweat, more alive than anything else on the wide earth. She leaned against him, trembling, feeling that she'd been catapulted out beyond the circle of the moon into some other world where everything was different. He could feel the shape of her body through the wet clothes, her skin, cold from the ride, and her hair smelling of sweet myrrh and incense through the scent of horses. He felt as though his body were dressed in fire. He closed his arms around her and kissed her desperately; her mouth tasted of honey and strong wine. Her arms came round him and locked convulsively; she began kissing him clumsily and hungrily, everywhere she could reach on his face. He put one hand behind her head and ran the other down her side. "Oh Heliokleia!" he whispered, thickly, and kissed her again, on the mouth, the eyes, the throat, feeling the light strong pulse against his lips. His hand explored the sweet curves of her hips, her breasts pressed against him. He ached to pull off the wet heavy clothes and touch the soft gold of her skin, holding her in the floating light forever, until the end of the world.

"My life and soul," she told him in Greek, stroking his wet hair with a starved tenderness. "You know I love you, not him. And I heard, that time we stopped at your farm, I heard the girl saying you loved me. Tell me you love me. Don't let me go. Please don't let me go."

He couldn't answer for a long ecstatic moment; his lips were buried in her, and he was beyond speech. But in the end he lifted his head and looked down into her face. She was flushed, radiant and in tears. He kissed her again, then stood holding her, shaking with desire. "I

can't," he gasped at last. "You know I can't—we can't. My
dearest . . ." He kissed her once more, but this time she pulled away.
She struggled out of his arms and backed against the horse's stall. He
almost started toward her again, but stopped, and stood empty-armed
in the lamplight, still shaking.

"I must go," she said breathlessly, and without another word she
pulled up her cloak and ran, away into the darkness beyond the small
gold circle of the lamp.

CHAPTER

XVII

Heliokleia ran out of the stables and up the steps to the palace, shaking and terrified. Itaz at least had been in love before—shallow infatuations, maybe, with pretty courtesans, but passionate enough at the time: he had known what to expect of desire. Heliokleia had only been prostituted in political matrimony. She could scarcely remember affection, and knew nothing of love; she had despised the wishes of the body, and put all her confidence in the disciplined strength of her mind. The sight of the dead had been a comfort to her: the flesh that had caused her such grief would one day be as soaked and as passionless as the rain-wet ground. When she went into the stable with Itaz it was in a mood of weary resignation—and her body had taken her mind like a dog taking its puppy in its mouth, carried it to an impossible goal, and said, "Here; *this* is where we should be," in tones that were almost irresistible. She was stunned. She felt weak, burning, and faint; she wanted to go back to Itaz; she wanted never to see Itaz again. She wished that he were dead—and she wished that her ashes could mingle with his, and join him scattered on the wind.

She stopped inside the back door of the palace, panting, out of sight of the guards. She felt that she must have been changed almost beyond recognition by what had happened to her. The body that she had despised as the gift and creature of illusion, then held in loathing and disgust as Mauakes' toy, that body had become a priceless treasure, because Itaz loved it. The world wasn't a futile and empty wasteland, but miraculously good and terrifyingly evil at the same time, higher and deeper than she'd ever imagined. And she was appalled by it and by herself.

She went unsteadily through the courtyard and up the stairs to her own room. She sat down on the couch, still trembling, then, after a moment, crossed her legs to meditate. The habit of years told her she must give up this incestuous, despicable, and hopeless desire. But when she closed her eyes and tried to detach herself from sense, all she felt was joy.

I came in with a steaming water pot for the queen's bath a few minutes later—Armaiti had gone to her family for the day, and Jahika was off at a New Year's party with some friends. I found Heliokleia sitting still and straight on the couch, legs crossed, hands folded—but flushed and rain-sprinkled as a wild tulip just opening. She didn't look herself, and I wondered if she was bracing herself for another confrontation with the king. I set the jug down hesitantly. "My lady?" I asked.

Heliokleia opened her eyes at once. "Yes?"

I couldn't think what to say, so I asked, "Did Inisme come up with you? And did you want to bathe now?"

"I would like to bathe now—but what do you mean, did Inisme come up with me? She came up with you."

I shook my head: at the foot of the stairs to the palace, Inisme had stopped, snapped her fingers, and turned back. "She left her hairbrush in her saddlepack," I told Heliokleia, "and she went back to the stable to fetch it. I thought she'd come up with you and Lord Itaz."

Still cross-legged on the couch, Heliokleia's flushed, radiant look drained away. She stared at me, and her face slowly went white, the skin seeming to collapse before my eyes into the fine thin bones. "When did Inisme go back?" she asked in a whisper.

"We hadn't even started up the steps; she just said, oh, she'd forgotten the hairbrush and went back . . . what's wrong?"

"She was spying," whispered the queen. "She must have been. And I didn't see her." She put her hands to her head with a sudden jerk, curling the fingers against her cheeks, as though she were going to tear her face in mourning—then sat with them frozen there. For a long minute she made no sound. Then, "She must be with the king now," she whispered. "Telling him what she saw." She uncurled her legs and jumped up.

By this time I was staring open-mouthed, still blank with ignorance. Something had happened in the stables, it was clear, but declarations of love between Heliokleia and Itaz never occurred to me; if I suspected anything in the cold sick confusion of the moment, it was some political scheme against the king. "I . . . I didn't think," I said, stammering. "I . . . was there anything to spy on? I thought it was only Itaz on guards' business . . ." I stopped, staring at the queen's face. The white stricken look had gone as quickly as the radiance; everything now was determination and decision.

"Stay here," the queen ordered shortly. "I'm going to see the king. And if you have any loyalty to me, don't tell anyone that you told me that Inisme wasn't here. If he thinks I came to him of my own will, it may work. Is he in his room?"

I stammered that I thought so, and she was away, running.

None of the guards had been on duty at the bottom of the stairs that day, since the queen had been out; no one spoke to Heliokleia as she ran to the door of the king's study. She knocked sharply, and the king's voice ordered curtly, "Go away!"

"It's me," she called back urgently. "Please, sir, I must speak with you."

There was a moment's pause, and then the door opened and Mauakes stood aside to let her enter.

There were two lamps burning inside, set on the shelf at either end of the row of cups. Inisme was standing by the far wall, looking frightened. The king was round-faced, bland, and unreadable.

"Inisme!" said Heliokleia in surprise. "I thought you were with Tomyris, fetching the bath water."

"I was discussing her position with her," said the king smoothly, "since you so objected to her service this morning. Was that what you wished to speak about? You seem distressed."

"No, sir. I wished to speak about your son Itaz."

The bland gray-bearded face didn't change, but she saw the edge of the rage flash briefly in his eyes, and knew that she was right: Inisme had seen something and related it to him already. She tried to give no hint that she suspected as much. "But first," she said, "I wished to ask your forgiveness."

"My forgiveness."

"Yes. I used intemperate words this morning, sir, moved by a fit of unreasoning anger. And last night I was jealous and ungrateful and damaged a beautiful gift which you had chosen for me. I have prayed to the goddess and tried to amend my heart, and I am content to yield to you, to be what you wish as much as is in my power. And so I beg you to forgive me for my pride and ingratitude."

"Uhh," said Mauakes. "Prettily said. But what did you want to say about my son?"

"Only—sir, please, let me send the girl out. We need privacy."

Mauakes raised his eyebrows, then gestured to Inisme. "Go back to the queen's rooms and wait for her," he ordered.

Inisme bowed, slipped out, and came upstairs. I was mixing the bath water, and I tried to keep on doing it when I heard her steps come haltingly into the room. When I'd muddled the hot and cold together I looked up, as naturally as I could. I'm no use at pretending, but one glance at Inisme told me I didn't need to worry: she was far too shaken herself to notice. "Whatever's the matter?" I asked, surprised enough to sound perfectly honest.

Inisme sat down on the couch Heliokleia had left only moments before. "When I went down to the stable . . ." she said in a stunned voice, then, her eyes focusing on me, she suddenly launched into a torrent of words, as she had before, either to relieve her own feelings or to involve me. "I went to see what they were talking about, Itaz and the queen. You'd call it spying and betrayal. But what I saw—that was betrayal." I gaped as much as Inisme could have wished, and she shook her head and said, "I wouldn't have believed it if I hadn't seen it. I wasn't sure whether he assaulted her, or whether she went to him willingly; I couldn't see clearly, and I couldn't hear what they were

saying. But his hands were all over her. It was an assault, I'm sure of
that now: it looked as though she was struggling, and now she's gone
to the king to tell him so herself. An assault on his stepmother! And
him such a devout man!" She began to cry. "This is not how things
should be!" she wailed. "This isn't how I thought it would be! Being a
royal attendant should be honorable, and it's all hatred and quarreling
and treachery. I wish I'd stayed at home!"

I didn't know what I felt, and I had nothing whatever to say. After
a while, staring at the steaming bath, I thought, irrelevantly, that I'd
have to fetch more hot water.

Downstairs, Heliokleia was facing the king with her mask locked
into place as never before, playing a role this time in deliberate deceit.
"Now, what is it?" asked Mauakes. "Anahita, you look ill!"

"Sir . . . I think you ought to send Itaz back to Parthia."

"What?" he asked, for the first time startled into showing some
feeling: rage, hope, and disbelief chased each other across his face.

"Yes, sir. He was . . . insolent . . . to me just now in the stables. He is a young man, of course, and has a passionate nature, but that
doesn't entirely excuse . . . insolent behavior toward your wife. I'm
sure he means no evil, sir, but . . . he needs some time to settle down,
and I don't think he will here, not as commander of my guard. If you
sent him to Parthia, where he has friends, he may learn to behave more
moderately. Perhaps . . . perhaps he could find a wife there. But I
don't think he should stay in Eskati, not just now."

"What did he do?" the king demanded harshly.

"He . . . he kissed me. We were discussing . . . something else,
and I was . . . distressed over our quarrel this morning, and perhaps
he thought this would comfort me."

"He kissed you?" The king stepped forward and grabbed her arms.
"How did he kiss you?" he demanded savagely. "On the mouth? Did
he take hold of you? Did he put his hands on you, there, and there, like
that? Did you struggle?"

She struggled loose, gasping. "Please!" she cried as he caught her
wrists to pull her back. It was too much: after the bitter night and the
shocks of the day, it was too much. Her breath caught in her throat and
she bowed her head, her chest working with sobs that were still soundless.

The king stood holding her wrists trapped, staring at her, his body brushing hers. She felt that he had an erection. The shaking worked upward, strangling her; she choked on the swallowed grief, terror, and regret, and gave a great wracked sob. The long-suppressed tears flooded hot and salty into her eyes, blinding her.

"By our Lord the Sun," said Mauakes, "he assaulted you—that's why you're so distressed. He made some pretext to talk to you, took you to the back of the stables, and assaulted you. Inisme saw it. She told me. My own son, the stinking pious hypocrite! He'll die for this."

"No!" she cried in horror, blinking up through the tears. "That is . . . sir, he's a foolish young man, no more. He was insolent and crude, but not . . . not evil. He did no harm; I . . . I put him off, and he stopped and let me go. I would be ashamed beyond measure if you killed your own son for my sake. There's a much better solution, sir: send him to Parthia."

Mauakes didn't answer, only glared at her furiously. He let go one of her hands and brushed her cheek, held the wet fingers triumphantly up in the lamplight, shining proof.

"All he did was kiss me, sir!" she protested, "When I pushed him away, he let go!"

"Inisme said you struggled to get loose," returned the king. "She saw that, she said: he embraced you and you struggled to get away, and ran. And she didn't see everything, she said."

"If she was watching, why didn't she call for help?"

"She wasn't sure that you hadn't consented, to begin with. She's a loyal servant, and wanted to tell me the whole of who was to blame."

"How could she? How could she hide herself somewhere and watch?"

The king grinned, baring his teeth. "So it was an assault; he used violence, and for all your philosophy you're in tears over it."

"No, no, it wasn't like that! He kissed me; I pushed him away and ran back to my rooms; as soon as I'd collected my wits I came straight here to you—but I don't believe Itaz meant anything by it, it was just a whim. Perhaps it was even a joke, a bad joke."

"He's been lusting after you for months," returned the king furiously. "I first saw it when he came back from Bactra, but I couldn't believe my eyes. But even before that, he was watching you. I saw him watching you and I thought it was hatred. He's been after you, hasn't he, talking to you, trying to slip up and touch you, giving you presents —the foul, unnatural liar! He offered you power, didn't he? That was what he wanted to talk about this evening, wasn't it? He knew you'd quarreled with me, and he took his chance, he thought you'd consent, and go with him for the sake of a few stewards of your own and a real command over your guard. What did he offer to give you when I was dead, eh?"

"Sir, you're making much too much of it! There wasn't any plot. He never offered me anything. And nothing happened. He kissed me, insolently, and I pushed him off."

He snorted, and she saw that he didn't believe her. Of course, he was telling himself, she doesn't want to admit to her ambitions, and she's exaggerating Itaz' innocence to protect her own.

But at least she had convinced him that he knew all there was to know about the incident, and there had been no secret plot between them, no long adulterous liaison for which both she and Itaz might have had to die. And surely he wouldn't kill his own son for a kiss?

"Sir," she whispered, "I was revolted by his insolence, but he hasn't harmed me. And . . . and he's made me like you better."

Mauakes' tight grip on her hands relaxed a little, and he looked at her searchingly. Her face was wet, shocked, and vulnerable, no longer proudly calm but human and wretched and afraid. Afraid for Itaz, not herself, but he didn't know that. "He frightened you and hurt you?" he asked, more gently then, with a return to fierceness, but this time some triumph as well. "He never expected you to come here and tell me this. He thought you were a whore he could buy with power instead of gold. That was his mistake."

"I don't think he thought at all," said Heliokleia in a small voice like a little girl. "He just . . . acted. I don't want to see him again. Please send him away from me—far away, as far as Parthia."

Mauakes let go of her hands, and held her shoulders. "He didn't think, no," he agreed at last. "He didn't think. And I will send him very far away from you. Yes. I'll do that."

She closed her eyes, shaking with relief now. The king drew her out of the study and into his bedroom, where he reasserted his sole and unquestionable domination of the body she had despised. She yielded to him in silence, her eyes still closed, struggling desperately not to imagine making love to Itaz, because any thought of him and his departure was too painful to bear.

The next day she waited for the king to summon Itaz and tell him to go back to Parthia. But Mauakes was moonlike and mild. He greeted his son at breakfast and talked to him about the army drill the day before. Heliokleia watched nervously, not daring to speak. After the meal she cornered her husband privately. "Aren't you going to send him away?" she asked.

Mauakes only gave her a forgiving look. "It takes time to arrange these things. He has been here for two years, and was expecting to stay for good. I will speak to him this morning, and send him off on an errand to the Sakaraukai, and then . . . we'll see if that's time enough to have everything prepared for his real departure."

Itaz was not surprised when his father summoned him that morning and appointed him as envoy to one of the tribes of the Sakaraukai. There was some real business to be conducted with the confederacy, questions about the Tochari that needed to be settled before the summer—and Itaz had guessed that the king would want him out of the way after the previous day's quarrel. He didn't object; he'd been reassured to see that the queen, though clearly nervous and unhappy, was back in his father's good graces. He agreed to the embassy at once, hoping that everything would have settled down by the time he returned. As he was leaving the study, however, he noticed that his father was still wearing the coin of Antimachos the God, and a rash impulse of honesty made him try to recover what was rightfully his.

"May I have my coin back?" he asked as casually as he could, pausing in the doorway.

The king's eyes glittered, and he put his hand on the silk cord. "Your coin? Why do you want it?"

"For luck. If Antimachos has any influence among the immortals, he ought to use it to promote the interests of his great-great-grandson by marriage. And even if he doesn't, the queen gave it to me."

"And that makes it valuable to you?"

Itaz smiled. "Yes. I respect your wife, Father, and your wisdom in choosing her."

"So I gather," said the king, just a little bit too softly. Itaz looked at him a moment apprehensively, bracing himself for another outburst. But none came. Mauakes pulled the coin over his head and held it dangling in the calm air a moment, watching his son with his penetrating eyes. "Here it is."

Itaz took it with a smile and put it about his own neck. "Thank you, Father. I did want to keep it." He bowed and went out, missing the look of hatred that stabbed his retreating back.

He left on the embassy early in the afternoon. When he was about to go, he went up to the queen's room to take his leave, but was told, by Inisme, that the queen was meditating and had given orders not to be disturbed. He stood a moment in the corridor, thinking of her, aching to see her. Probably, he decided, it was best not to. Desire must be starved to weaken it before they could meet again. "Give the queen my respectful greetings, then," he told Inisme. "And say I wish her good health."

Inisme nodded, and Itaz shuffled his feet a moment, then set off with a long quick stride down to the army stables, where his escort was waiting.

Inisme went slowly back into the rooms. She had had another summons to the king that morning, where I think she was told to take charge of all the queen's interviews with Itaz. The rest of us were told nothing about the incident in the stable, and I don't think Inisme dared to tell the king that she had already blurted out everything she'd seen to me.

"He wishes me to give you his respectful greetings," she told Heliokleia, who was sitting stiffly upright on the couch. "And he wishes you good health."

Heliokleia nodded calmly, then stared at Inisme with deep, considering eyes. Inisme had recovered her composure the previous evening even before the queen came back upstairs; that afternoon she was as well groomed as ever, not a hair out of place, and her face showed no triumph. "Inisme," said the queen quietly, "where were you yesterday? When you watched . . . what happened?"

"I hid behind the straw," Inisme replied without hesitation. "It wasn't a good place, because I couldn't hear, and I couldn't see everything, but it was better than nothing."

"Why did you bother?"

"The king didn't trust Lord Itaz, so I thought I should try to see what he wanted with you. It was good that I did. I never would have dreamed that he'd do that, to his own father's wife! I thought you . . . might be too ashamed even to mention it to the king. As it was, my lady, I'm very glad that what I said supported you."

"The king said that you thought I had consented, at first."

Inisme flushed slightly. "That was what it looked like, at first. I couldn't hear what you were saying, and when he first took hold of you it looked as though you were kissing him. Then I saw that you were struggling, and finally you got loose and ran off. When I told the king what I'd seen, I still wasn't sure what it meant—but when you came in looking so upset I realized you must have been fighting him all along. I told the king that, my lady. I hope you believe I wouldn't lie about you."

Heliokleia looked at her wearily, trying to imagine the scene in the stable, glimpsed, in the dim lamplight, from behind the shocks of straw. "You are the king's loyal servant, aren't you?" she asked.

"Yes, my lady," said Inisme with some vehemence. "King Mauakes holds the Sun's glory, and he freed all Ferghana from the Yavanas, and brought my own family back from poverty and exile. I am his loyal servant, as I ought to be. And I was proud to accept service in your household, since it was his. I knew that a proper queen, like you, would be willing to submit herself to her lord in everything, so I always believed you'd excuse me if I trespassed on your privacy in the cause of serving the king."

"I see," said Heliokleia quietly. "I had underestimated you."

"You thought I did it for money, like a Yavana, didn't you?" asked Inisme.

"No. I thought you did it for your family's advantage, like a Saka. But it seems you do it on principle." She looked at Inisme for a moment with the faint half-smile. " 'Dogs bark at those they don't know,' " she added in Greek.

"What was that?" asked Inisme suspiciously; her Greek was still erratic.

"A saying of one of our Yavana philosophers about how difficult it is for people to understand foreigners. Never mind."

Inisme looked at her, then shook her head. "I don't understand you at all," she complained.

"I don't understand you either," replied Heliokleia tiredly.

The door opened and Mauakes came in, looking satisfied. "He's off," he told Heliokleia. "Did he try to come here to say farewell?"

"Yes," said the queen evenly.

"Did you admit him?"

"No. I had him told that I was meditating, and he sent respectful greetings and wished me good health."

"Respectful greetings! Ha! He wouldn't know how to show respect for Anahita herself." He flung himself down on the couch. "Sing to me," he ordered.

"If you wish," answered the queen, and fetched her kithara.

She spent a great deal of time over the next few weeks singing to the king, reading, meditating, and playing Four Armies. She had nothing else to do. It was a life of paralyzing tedium, but she bore it resolutely. Whatever went on in the privacy of her thoughts she kept strictly to herself, and admitted no one to her confidence. Not even me.

I was utterly bewildered. I'd had time to think, by then, and it was now blindingly obvious that she and Itaz were in love. And I saw, perhaps more clearly than they did, that they were both bound to love honorably and at a distance; they had sworn oaths to the king, and both of them would prefer death to betrayal of that thing beyond them—God or Virtue or Nirvana—to which, in all their differences, they shared a commitment. But I could guess how the king would look at it. I wanted to help. I wanted to stand by my lady in this hour of danger, I wanted to fight for her, or carry her messages, or at least share her grief. I wanted to let her know she had at least one friend she could rely on. But she said nothing to me beyond, "Could you exercise my horse?" and "Please fetch the myrrh." She had involved me in one lie —that she had gone to the king spontaneously—which was one lie more than I'd ever backed before. But she never even told me why, or what had happened: all I knew then I learned from Inisme. I lived in a world of doubtful guesses and sudden panics over conjectures. Ignorance was torment: I couldn't sleep or eat properly for wondering when the storm would break, and I felt so desperate I wanted to smash something. But whenever I tried to speak to Heliokleia, she treated me with polite attention, like a patient adult hearing a tedious child. I was utterly wretched. I thought she blamed me for leaving Inisme to spy on her, and I conducted furious arguments with her inside my head, explaining to her how unfair she was being—but when I tried to say one of them out loud, she simply looked at me with the cool green gaze, and all my words withered. Almost, I thought then, almost I could hate her.

The king began the arrangements he had promised. He had the foreman of Itaz' farm summoned and questioned him. Addac did not keep his master's secret. He considered it creditable to free a poor girl from slavery in a brothel, and could not believe that the king would be seriously annoyed to learn that the money his son had borrowed had been spent piously rather than indulgently. Besides, Philomela was pregnant, and he wanted everyone to be clear whose the child was. "No, he never touched her," he told the king, with heavy satisfaction. "He didn't visit more often than every other week, and then left after supper. He said I could have her with his blessing, and he's providing the dowry himself. He bought her out of pure kindness and piety, but he was afraid you might think he was wasting your money. But I'm sure, O King, that you'd rather your son spent his money on piety than whores, and won't be angry."

"Mmm," said Mauakes. "Where did he go, then, if he wasn't visiting your . . . wife? He left the city more often than once every two or three weeks."

Addac nodded in even greater satisfaction at the description of Philomela as his wife. "He went to the fire temple, I'm sure. He goes there often."

"Of course," said Mauakes. "Thank you."

When Addac had gone, the king sat in silence for a long time, thinking. He could summon Ahura Mazda's priest and check whether Itaz had been there—but what would be the point? He was sure in his own mind that his son had been involved in some scheme, and had been secretly engaged on it while everyone believed he was visiting his whore. Itaz wanted his father's crown and his father's wife. All that open honesty was nothing but deceit, and all the signs of filial affection, which always moved him despite himself, were lies. Probably Itaz laughed about it with his friends, those unknown confederates with whom he plotted: "I told him the woman doesn't detest him, and he almost believed it, the old fool! And when he asked what she was to me, I said she was a queen!" The king could almost hear the roar of derisive laughter, and the jeering responses, "Well, she will be, won't she?" They despised him; they all despised him. He remembered now everything Itaz had said and done since his return from Parthia; all of it, but especially all the words of sympathy and respect, made him writhe inwardly with humiliation. He had been tricked and made a fool of. Itaz had been trying for power all along: he had tried to win the council's backing against the Yavana alliance, but when that had failed, and the queen had turned out to be beautiful, he had changed his plans, tried for a backing of Yavanas and Sakas jointly, made promises to Tasius, to the city, and no doubt to others, taken the queen's guard to be his own. And all the while he had lulled his father with lies, and laughed when he was believed. But he would learn—they would all learn, as the sons of Antimachos himself had—that King Mauakes of Ferghana was not to be despised. Heliokleia had not been seduced, and the king was deceived no longer. He smiled to himself, then summoned Itaz' friend Azilises.

When Itaz returned from his embassy, after the middle of the spring, his father went down to the army stables to greet him. The men of the escort had dismounted and were seeing to their horses when the king arrived; Itaz was giving orders to the grooms about the beasts' provisions, holding his own mount until he could take it to the royal stables. Mauakes paused by the corner of the building, studying his son —the tall, lean shape, the quick hands gesticulating at the grooms, the narrow face, stern and earnest as he delivered orders, flashing suddenly into a smile as they were accepted. The servants and guardsmen obeyed him readily and happily; they liked and admired him. The king stood very still, his throat tight with grief and an unexpected pride. He remembered Itaz as a child, pelting out to the stables behind his brothers, all sharp elbows and tumultuous enthusiasm; remembered him bringing something to show his mother, explaining it to her breathlessly. That image, forgotten for years, suddenly jumped clear in his mind: the child holding his treasure—a carving, he remembered now, done by some groom or guardsman—tracing the lines of it with eager fingers; and the tall woman, arm about her son's shoulders, laughing and exclaiming at it; the two faces, narrow, dark, shining with shared pleasure, resting close together above the crudely chiseled piece of pine. It had been a long time since he thought of his first wife; this memory must come from a time not long before she died. She was the one who'd given Itaz his height and his sharp keen face, but that restless, passionate spirit, where did that come from? From his father, untempered by the cunning and reserve, or as some whim of Heaven? Mauakes took a deep breath, half-blind with longing, love, regret— then remembered that the honesty was an illusion, a cloak pulled over intentions of incest and treachery, and that the passionate child must have died years before; perhaps his life had ended with the woman's, or in his Parthian exile. Too late to change the world.

Mauakes walked forward into the stableyard, smiling, calling his son's name. Itaz turned, smiling with pleasure, and embraced his father.

"So, you're home safely," said Mauakes. "But by the Sun, you look tired!"

"It was a long journey home," admitted Itaz. "The grazing was bad, and we had to hurry to make the supplies of fodder last. My horse is worn out. But how are you? And the queen?"

"Well, well," replied the king. "Here, let's take the beast to his own stall—you there! See to these horses!" Mauakes began walking up to the royal stables, one hand on his son's arm; Itaz followed, leading the black stallion and telling his father about the reception of the embassy.

"It seems to have gone well," agreed Mauakes when they had reached the stables and a groom had come out to take the stallion. "Is your horse favoring his off hind foot a little?"

"He had a stone in it earlier this afternoon. No damage done. But he's tired."

"So are you, by the look of you. How would you like to have a couple of weeks off to go hunting?"

Itaz smiled with surprise. "I don't need it, Father. I can rest here in Eskati."

"But I'd like you to go. I was thinking of this while you were away, and I decided you've had a hard year. A young man needs time to enjoy himself occasionally. I had an old hunting lodge repaired for you, up in the Mountains of Heaven, three or four days' ride from here, and I decided to give you a new horse."

"Father!" said Itaz, touched and astonished. He looked at the king in happy bewilderment. Mauakes must have regretted the violent language he had used in their quarrel, and must be trying to make amends. Itaz did not particularly want to go hunting, and would have preferred to rest in Eskati—but he couldn't possibly refuse his father's gifts. He tooked Mauakes' hand and kissed it. "Thank you. You were very kind to think of it."

Mauakes jerked the hand away, then made up for it by smiling. "Wait until you've seen the horse."

The horse was a red bay stallion, black maned and black tailed, the pick of the royal herd, three years old and just finished with its training. Itaz was delighted with it.

"And if you want a companion on your hunt," Mauakes went on, "I've given your friend Azilises leave from my guard."

Itaz snorted. He had gathered that Azilises was angry with him—for taking Philomela the last time they were together, and for avoiding brothels and drinking parties since. The guardsman had said nothing to him directly, but he had heard other people quoting the biting comments Azilises had made about his supposed arrogance. Still, he told himself, Azilises was very good company, usually, and had befriended him when he had first returned from Parthia, still lonely and disoriented. He'd be sorry to lose him as a friend forever: a hunting expedition with him might be entirely to the good. "Thank you," he said.

"Good," returned the king, satisfied. "Azilises has already prepared supplies, and you can leave tomorrow."

Itaz opened his hands in astonished acceptance, and agreed.

He again tried to take leave of the queen before he set out next morning, but this time was told that she had left the city for the day and ridden out to one of her nearby farms to inspect the new foals. He couldn't help his feeling of disappointment and resentment: he had missed her. "Did she know I was going today?" he asked Inisme.

She shrugged. The queen had not been told even that Itaz had returned. "I didn't know," she said. "And she didn't ask about you."

"Oh," he said, unhappy and alarmed. He remembered again the short, ecstatic moments in the stable, "Please don't let me go," and her clumsy, hungry kisses. He knew, without self-conceit and without doubt, that he could have taken her back into the hay store and had her then and there; the knowledge had been tormenting him ever since. He had refused; he had sent her back to his father. Did she hate him for that? He couldn't believe that she didn't hate the thought of treachery and incest as much as he did, that she wasn't glad he'd spared them that. But still, was she angry? Was she determined to stamp out what she felt for him, ready to use all her ferocious strength of will on that, and never see him again? Never?

"Please," he told Inisme, "convey my greetings to your mistress, and tell her I'm sorry."

"Sorry?" asked Inisme, surprised. "What for?"

"In case I've offended her. And sorry, too, that I've missed her twice; it's discourteous to run off from my place as her guards' commander without even saying goodbye. Just tell her I'm sorry."

"I'll tell her," replied Inisme, nervous and unhappy. Itaz might have noticed that the reaction was more than could be accounted for by the need to convey the message—but he was thinking only of the queen. He smiled at the maid and set out once more for the stables, where Azilises was waiting for him.

It was the next morning before Inisme relayed Itaz' message to our mistress.

"I didn't realize he was back!" exclaimed Heliokleia. "Where was he going?"

"Hunting, my lady. He said to tell you he was sorry. He made some pretext about how it was discourteous for the commander of your guard to go without taking leave of you, but I think he meant something else by it. Perhaps he really does regret assaulting you."

Heliokleia said nothing, but her face was crimson. Itaz was sorry. Why should he think he needed to be sorry? All the guilt was hers: she had thrown herself at him shamelessly. If only she could see him, privately, and explain what had happened, tell him what she had done to counter it, explain why they must not see each other again, warn him to be on his guard when he spoke to his father! But she would never be permitted to see him alone. Why had he gone hunting?

She spoke to the king about it that night when they were in bed together. Mauakes was very silent and irritable, and made love roughly; when he had finished, he lay heavily beside her, open-eyed in the darkness. It did not seem a good time to raise the subject with him, but even one of his rages would be preferable to the misery of not knowing.

"I learned today that Lord Itaz has gone hunting," she said hesitantly.

Mauakes grunted.

"I hadn't even realized he was back from his embassy," she said. "Haven't you made the arrangements for him to go to Parthia?"

The king snorted and was quiet for another long minute. "He's not going to Parthia," he said at last.

"No?" she asked. She felt a coldness in her chest and stomach, a feeling not yet identified as fear. "You said you were sending him away."

"I am." There was another long silence.

"Are you sending him back to the Sakaraukai, then?"

The king laughed harshly; the sound was wholly forced and unnatural. "I'm sending him to Hell."

"What? What do you mean?" She pulled herself onto her elbows and stared at her husband through the darkness.

"He won't come back from that hunting trip. He's going to a hunting lodge on Azes' land, in the Mountains of Heaven, three or four days' ride east. I had the lodge redecorated for him: all the new paneling is soaked in pine resin. It will light up like a torch at the least spark. This fellow Azilises, Azes' son, is ambitious—like all his clan. He's reported to me about what my son does ever since Itaz returned from Parthia. I offered him the command of your guard if he would give the incestuous hypocrite some drugged wine the evening they arrive at the lodge, then throw the lamp on the floor when he went out. He'll say that he woke to find the lodge on fire and escaped, but Itaz was drunk and slept too long; it will look like an accident."

"Oh no," cried Heliokleia in agony. "No, you can't do that, not to him! He's your own son, he loves you, you can't *want* to do that to him!"

"He's a cunning liar who's been plotting against me behind my back, who assaulted my wife in my own palace!" Mauakes returned with blind savagery. "I'd have him beheaded before my eyes, yes, and drink from his skull, if I didn't think it would cause an uproar among his supporters."

"But there wasn't any plot!" Heliokleia protested desperately. She leaned over across her husband's chest and seized his shoulders, "Please believe me, he never promised me anything; he just lost his head; he's a passionate young man, that's all, and he always talked of you with the greatest love and loyalty of any man in your kingdom! When he took me into the stables, he wanted to tell me that you were distressed over our quarrel, and beg me to apologize to you; I don't believe he meant to do anything wrong! And he sent me a message saying he was very sorry. Please, please, he shouldn't *die* for that!"

"Huh!" Mauakes said contemptuously. He rolled over, throwing her hands off, and got up on his elbows. "There was a plot, all right. I don't think he got too far with it, though; I haven't been able to find out who his allies are—though I suspect some of them, the gods know I do. He borrowed my money to set up that whore as a blind; I found out from his servants at that farm that he never touched her after buying her. He rode out of the city every evening—*every evening!*—and he didn't go see the girl. He was plotting, all right. If you'd agreed to go with him, you'd have been a part of it, have no doubt about that."

"I don't believe it," she said. She was shaking. "He's your son, he was always loyal to you."

"He was a filthy liar!" snarled Mauakes. "He put on a holy face and pretended to be devout, but secretly he was full of lust and ambition. He lied to me a hundred times over, and he fooled you completely. He was burning for you so much he couldn't contain himself, and he made the mistake of moving too soon, and trying to take you by force. But I've no doubt he wanted my crown as well. Let him burn; he'll burn now forever."

She put her hands to her face and lay still. Let him burn. She saw him lying in the hunting lodge, and the flames eating the walls; waking, drugged and confused, stumbling up, falling, screaming, burning alive. "No!" she cried aloud. "Oh, in the name of all the gods, no!"

"What is it to you if he dies?" the king demanded, grabbing her hands and pulling them away from her face. "Were you a part of it after all?"

"Would I have to be in love with him to want him not to be burned alive?" she whispered vehemently. "Is that the only reason you can think of that I'd protest at you murdering your own son? Do you really believe he's the sort of man I would condemn to die in agony, because of one kiss?"

Mauakes lay perfectly still for a moment, half on top of her with her wrists gripped in his hands. "No," he said at last, very quietly. He let her go. "No. But it won't hurt him. I found a strong drug for the wine; he won't wake. The smoke will have choked him before he burns, and he won't feel a thing. It has to be done."

"Please! Send a messenger after him; call them back and send him somewhere else!"

"No. He tricked me and laughed at me and thought he'd take what's mine, and he'll die for it. Anyway, it's already too late. It's a three- or four-day ride to the hunting lodge, and they've been gone two days already. Azilises wanted to get it done with as soon as possible: he's sure to do it the evening they arrive."

The queen lay very still for a long time. Then she said thickly, "Sir, he was a Mazdayist, even if he fell from the goodness of his faith. Let me go to the fire temple tomorrow and make offerings to the god he worshipped for his soul's welfare."

Mauakes was quiet again. He shook his head, then rubbed his face with one hand. He sat up and pressed both hands to his eyes, then suddenly gave one of his choked, snuffling, ugly sobs. "I loved him!" he said, not to her but to some invisible accuser. "The all-seeing Sun knows it, I loved him, the filthy liar! Yes, go to the temple tomorrow, pray to his god to forgive him and admit him to their paradise; I'll give you gold to pay for the sacrifices. Go tomorrow. But keep quiet about why you want to make offerings to his god; I don't want his accomplices alerted."

"Sir, I will," she said, and for the first and last time, kissed her husband unasked, with a tender gentleness that was almost like love.

The queen set out for the temple at first light next morning, with
Inisme and ten of her guard commanded by Pakores. I wanted to come
too—I could sense that something was up, though I didn't know what
—but Heliokleia refused to bring me. "Stay here and look for a husband," she told me. So I was reduced to watching resentfully in the
stableyard at dawn next morning as the party set out. Heliokleia wore
the purple woolen cloak over the white and gold riding clothes; she
wore her crown and her necklace and earrings, the repaired gold belt
and gold brooches on her shoulders; her fingers glittered with rings.
She looked at Sakan, as gaudy, and as royal as she had ever looked in
her life, and she sat straight and proud on the tall gray mare. She didn't
want or need anybody, I told myself bitterly. My ardent offer of
loyalty and faithful friendship was as unwelcome as the king's of love.
I was just an embarrassment to her. She'd go her own way and die
alone in her virtue—and to Hell with it and her! I'd take her advice
and go find someone to marry, someone ordinary, to whom it mattered
whether I loved them or not. I turned away and went back into the
palace, my eyes stinging with tears of shame, loss, and futile anger.

Mauakes, who also watched her set out, also looked at her with
bitterness, but it was a bitter satisfaction. His son might be lost, but at
long last he had won the Yavana woman absolutely. He waved to her
as she rode out into the city, and she turned in the saddle and waved
solemnly back.

When the party arrived at the fire temple it was still only an hour
or so after sunrise, and the lake shone in the light of a brilliant spring
morning. The squabbling of the carrion eaters on the funeral towers
was almost drowned by the calling of the ducks and cranes along the
shore, and the earth was green and bright with flowers. Heliokleia
reined in her mare before the temple, instructed the others to find
somewhere to leave the horses, and asked Pakores to go into the fire
temple and fetch the priest. "I wish to make a small offering to Anahita
first," she told them all. "Inisme, wait here for me a moment, and
arrange the offerings"—she had brought some incense to add to what
the priest would give to Ahura Mazda, and it was loaded on a pack
horse. Inisme nodded and, dismounting, led the pack horse over to the
temple steps and began to unload it. Heliokleia took a small jar of
frankincense from her and rode down to Anahita's shrine.

The priest came from the temple, beaming with excitement and convinced that he must have converted the foreign queen, for her to appear so suddenly wanting to offer lavish sacrifices to his god; the guardsmen unsaddled their horses and tethered them under the trees behind the temple; Inisme arranged the incense in neat piles on the temple porch: frankincense and nard, sandalwood and cassia. When she finished the queen wasn't yet back from the shrine. Pakores discussed with the priest the way the sacrifice would be conducted, and where: Inisme gave him the incense. The priest called his servant to put the incense ready beside the fire, and the servant stowed it safely. Still the queen had not come back. Inisme went down to see what was keeping her.

Anahita's temple was closed and locked. Obviously the priest wasn't there. Inisme went back to the fire temple and reported it; Ahura Mazda's priest went to look for his colleague, and soon found him tending the garden around the shrine, tipping green weed from the pond onto his compost heap. Anahita's priest had seen nothing of the queen.

Pakores became alarmed, and Inisme was frightened. They searched the temple precincts: Heliokleia was nowhere to be found. "Perhaps she fell into the lake," said Inisme faintly.

"Why would she do that?" demanded Pakores.

"Perhaps when she came to the shrine and found that the priest wasn't there, she decided to pick a flower while she waited for him to come back. Maybe she waded out to pick a lotus—that's a sacred flower to her. Is it . . . is it deep?"

They ran down to the lake; there was no sign of her. The priest sent all his servants out to look for her, while Pakores and three other guardsmen stripped down to their tunics and waded into the lake, peering fearfully into the cold water, diving for loose branches and outcroppings of rock. The rest of the escort saddled their horses again and rode out, searching and calling, looking along the edges of the lake.

After a while, one of the priest's servants returned and reported that a tenant farmer nearby had seen the queen galloping away from the lakeshore, going east. Pakores staggered out of the lake, drenched and shivering, and pulled his cloak over his wet shoulders. "Is he sure it was the queen?" he demanded.

"You couldn't mistake her for anyone else, not the way she was dressed," said the servant.

"Going east? Why would she . . . oh!" said Inisme, going white.

"But why would she ride off eastward?" Pakores asked in bewilderment.

"I . . . I don't know," gasped Inisme, refusing to believe that she did. "We must follow her and bring her back."

Pakores pulled on his trousers, shoved his wet feet into his boots, and went to his horse without another word. The whole party galloped to speak to the tenant farmer; he confirmed sullenly that he had seen the queen, "About an hour after sunrise." It was now almost noon. After a moment's fearful hesitation, Pakores ordered Inisme and one of the men to return to the city and inform the king, while he and the rest of the guardsmen set out in the direction the queen had taken.

Inisme and the guard arrived back at the palace early in the afternoon, only to discover that the king was not there. To sit alone with his thoughts during that long day was more than even he could bear, and he'd taken some of his guards officers out to the practice fields for a polo match. There, in the midafternoon, Inisme found him, and there she told him what had happened.

He understood instantly, but said nothing. He slid off his horse as though he had been stunned, and sat down, on the cold mud of the field, staring blankly up into the hard blue sky beyond the mountains.

"My lord!" said one of his officers. "Are you hurt?"

"They have betrayed me," Mauakes said thickly.

Everyone clustered around at that, exclaiming, "Who has betrayed you?" "What's happened?" "What does he mean?"

Mauakes looked up and around at them with a sick white face. "Antimachos," he whispered, "he's done this. He has his revenge at last."

No one could possibly know what he was talking about, but silence fell like a sword stroke, and the whole party stood frozen, the hairs on their necks crawling with something like recognition. Like a ridge of rock under the waters of a stream, the gods stirred the current of the waking world. "Are you loyal?" whispered Mauakes in real doubt. "Any of you?"

The silence crushed him for a moment longer; then Inisme knelt beside him. "Sir," she said, "you are our king: we would die for you." And the officers, beginning with their captain Spalagdama, found their tongues and joined in furious protestations of loyalty.

"My wife told me that my son had assaulted her," the king said, the words slurred with pain. "She knew that she had been seen with him, so she lied to save herself. She begged me to send him away, but I meant to have him killed. And she discovered that, and couldn't bear the loss of him, and she has gone to help him. Lying, unnatural, poisonous, Eukratid whore! She's gone to Itaz. They've broken every oath they've ever sworn, both of them! Dishonored!" He shoved his hands into the mud, then smeared them down his face. "That's what they've done to me."

There was a long, stunned silence. Then Spalagdama said—in a tentative, uncertain tone, because, like the others, he was almost as shocked by the king's admission that he had planned to have his son murdered, as by the report of incestuous adultery and treason—"Then they must die, my lord."

Mauakes looked up, to him and through him, his face shrunken and gray under the mud. "They will die," he said, his voice suddenly becoming recognizable again. "Go back to the city as fast as you can and tell my guard to ready their horses. I will follow, and we will ride today."

Spalagdama bowed and rode back to the city as fast as his horse could gallop. The king followed slowly, like a wounded man. But when he arrived at the palace, and saw his whole guard busy arming and saddling, he took charge of it with all his usual forcefulness and clear-sightedness. If there had been a plot, it would have failed. He told half the men to unsaddle again, posting them instead as a garrison at the palace. He made arrangements to confine the queen's guard to their barracks, requiring them to surrender their weapons to his own men. He put the standing army on alert and set it to watch the city. And he ordered that all the queen's servants—including even Inisme—should be shut in her rooms, kept prisoner by the garrison, to await his return.

I was sitting in the queen's room, reading one of her books, when

Inisme stumbled in escorted by four nervous guardsmen. Her face and their uncertainty told me what had happened even though I couldn't guess it; when we were locked in the room, all four attendants and the slaves, and Inisme whispered her story to us, it seemed to me as though it was something I had heard long, long before.

"What will happen to us?" wailed Jahika when Inisme had finished.

It was the old slave Parendi who answered, and answered after a long silence. "Nothing," she said. "We knew nothing about it. They all know that. She never told us anything at all."

Armaiti looked at me, and I shook my head. "I didn't know anything either," I said slowly. "You know that. She's scarcely spoken to me for weeks."

And suddenly I saw the tenderness, the affection, behind the exclusion that had hurt so much. It was like that moment by the lake at Eagle Crag, when I saw that the darkness I had feared behind the mask was all in my own mind. She'd kept faith, all along; she had simply refused to let me suffer for her. In her own way, she'd kept faith even with the king. If Mauakes had not attempted murder, there would have been no adultery. I am convinced of that. She was far too strong and far too proud to put herself in the wrong. Perhaps the situation was like a catapult: the springs twisted tighter and tighter about the bowlike arms, the string drawn back until it creaks and the whole machine sits tense with menace. But if no one looses the trigger, the springs stretch and slacken gradually, the string frays, and the power dissolves slowly into tired failure. Mauakes let the bolt of disaster—the thing threatened by the omens from the start—fly free. And yet, as I look back, that disaster seems the best outcome. The worst Hell would have been for all three to go on, in sterile festering misery, blighting their own lives and the lives of all around them, until one or another died of natural causes. We make rules for ourselves in our mortal kingdoms, saying what is right and what is wrong, and these we live by, distrusting the rules of others who differ from us in custom. Custom, as the Greek poet says, is king; without custom no woman could raise her children and no man farm the earth; without custom we would be voiceless, bereft of speech and ignorant as beasts. But sometimes the gods strike us suddenly, showing us another world, visiting us with disaster or with love, and we see suddenly that custom is not fixed in the world's nature: beyond custom is the god, and beyond law our own natures fumble with truth, blindly and alone. This, I think, is what the philosopher meant when he declared, "All things here are steered by the thunderbolt."

I put away the book I'd been clutching, and going to the perfume chest, I picked up some incense and burned it to Anahita and to all the gods, begging them to grant my lady a safe arrival, and a safe escape from the net that was being drawn up behind her.

It was dark before the king set out, and since he could not rely on getting fresh mounts for a hundred and fifty men, they did not go far that night. Heliokleia was far, far ahead of them.

CHAPTER

XVIII

Heliokleia had ridden directly past Anahita's shrine without stopping that morning, and set off along a farm track eastward at a gallop. Itaz had left for the hunting lodge two days before, and it was a three- or four-day ride—ordinarily. But a person who could get fresh horses, and was prepared to ride hard, might do it in less time. If Itaz had been in no hurry, she just might be able to catch up with him. She had known what she would do the moment the king refused to send a messenger. It had leapt into her head all at once, tiny and complete, like a city seen from a height, and she had lain still beside her husband considering it. If she gave up her crown and her position, broke her oath of marriage, disregarded the expectations of her brother's house, the detached virtue of her faith, and her hope of release in another life —then she had a bare chance of saving the life of the man she loved, though no guarantee of escaping with him from her husband's rage. She told herself it was insanity, and she already knew that she would do it.

Heliokleia galloped eastward along the farm track for about an hour, then turned Shadow by an irrigation ditch and rode, trotting and walking, down to the main road east. She had put on all her jewelry that morning, thinking that she might need money, but as she rode she took off the crown and the necklace and put them into the saddlebag, which already contained all the gold Mauakes had given her to pay for the offerings at the temple. She was already some miles east of Eskati when she rejoined the main road. The people she met stared at her, seeing the purple cloak and royal horse and doubting their eyes, but she didn't give them so much as a glance and touched her mare to a canter, knowing that her very confidence would reassure them. By the time her escort had traced her to the road and discovered which way she had gone, it was already late afternoon, and she was far away.

Shadow was a fine horse, and had been spoiling for exercise that morning: the queen rode her hard until the sun was low. But even royal horses can't gallop forever, and when the sun flooded up the mouth of the valley behind her, the mare was stumbling with exhaustion. The queen rode boldly into the town of Seven Pines, more than thirty miles from Eskati, stopped the mare by the local lord's house and knocked. His servants called him to the door, and he recognized her. He was deeply shocked to find her unattended, and he ordered his people to look after her horse while he invited her into his house to rest.

"I thank you, sir, but no," she replied firmly. "My husband would be displeased. Sir, I must ask a favor of you. I have a friend who is near death. I have come from Eskati so fast my escort has been left behind, though I hope they will catch up with me before nightfall. Could you lend me a fresh horse, and provide fresh horses also for my three followers when they arrive here, as they soon should? I wish to see my friend alive, and must hurry."

"Where is your friend?" asked the lord, reassured. He believed her story at once: her horse was very fine, and might well have outraced the inferior mounts of an escort. "I can provide men to ride with you."

She smiled. "My friend is at the lord Azes' estates, in the mountains: I expect he has sent men out to meet me and guide me. There is no need to bother your people, and my own escort would be angry if you took their place. Just give me a fresh horse; I will ride more slowly, and my own people will catch up with me."

He did as she asked and gave her the best horse in his stable, and after a moment's thought, some bread and wine to eat as she rode. She thanked him and gave him a piece of gold, "As a token of my gratitude for the trouble you've taken." She rode out of the town at a walk, then touched the horse to a gallop as soon as she was out of sight.

The local lord prepared three fresh horses for the escort, then waited impatiently for them to appear. When they didn't, and it was dark, he sent men down the road to search for them, and more men after the queen to warn her that her followers had been delayed: neither party encountered anyone. The king's messengers didn't arrive until the middle of the following morning.

There was a half moon that night, and Heliokleia galloped on, pressing the horse hard, afraid that her deception wasn't as successful as it had appeared. The land was quiet, gray in the moonlight, and the peaks of the mountains glowed white. She slowed to a walk, ate the bread and drank the wine, then spurred her mount to a gallop again. How far had she come? She wished she knew the valley better. How could she find the hunting lodge when she reached Azes' land? She would have to ask—well, if she went fast enough, she would arrive before any messenger from the king, and Azes himself would probably take her there. She leaned over the horse's neck and crooned to it, urging it onward.

The moon set, and the horse refused to gallop; when she kicked it, it merely trotted a few steps, then slowed again, hanging its head. It was drenched with sweat and foam dripped from its mouth. The queen led it over to a clump of trees by a roadside spring and tried to take its saddle off. It was dark, and she had never unsaddled a horse: always before that had been done by grooms. She fumbled with the buckle for a while and finally gave up. The horse was thirsty, but she knew enough not to let it drink until she had walked it up and down to cool it off. She wasn't sure how much to walk it, however, and she staggered back and forth with the tired animal stumbling after her for a long time. At last she allowed it drink—and let it take too much. Finally she tied it to a tree and lay down to rest for an hour before the morning.

She couldn't sleep. The hunting lodge was a three- or four-day ride; Itaz had been gone three days now. Suppose it was already too late?

She told herself that he wouldn't hurry; he'd just returned from a long journey, and he wouldn't want to press the pace. Probably he would arrive about the middle of the fourth day, stable his horse, look about, then have a meal and drink with his friend. Azilises wouldn't carry out the plan before nightfall, if what the king had told her was true: he would have to pretend to everyone that he too had been asleep when the house caught fire, and he could hardly do that in broad daylight. She must arrive before nightfall the next day, but if she did that, it should be enough.

At the first red of dawn she untied her borrowed horse and climbed back into its saddle. The horse shied, laid its ears back, and fought her, snorting and stamping, but she drove it back onto the road. As the light grew, she saw that the saddle had rubbed it raw about the belly and across its withers. It walked with its head drooping, shivering as the girth caught its sores, stiff and bloated with too little rest and too much water, and it was unable to do more than walk. She patted it guiltily, and stopped at the nearest sizable farm.

She interrupted the farmer at his breakfast, told him, as she'd told the lord of Seven Pines, that she was riding to see a friend who was near death, and asked him to return the horse to Seven Pines and sell her a fresh mount. He did not recognize her, so was not shocked to see her unescorted, and readily agreed, knowing that he could charge her a high price. She paid gold for a bad-tempered nag, which the farmer saddled for her, slinging her own saddlebags across its back. "A fine horse," he told her, patting the beast, which bared its teeth at him. "Can run all day without damage, and not too slow either; just be sure you thrash her if she acts up, and she'll serve you well." He handed her a riding whip, gave her directions to Lord Azes' lands, and she set out again.

The previous day and night had brought her just short of sixty miles from Eskati, an ordinary two-day journey. Now she had a day for a day's journey: surely, she told herself, she could do that! She kicked the nag to a gallop: it ran with a bone-shaking jolt, but it was fast.

Around noon she reached the Dry Fork, as they call the place; the land is poor, watered by Antimachos' dikes. Lord Azes' land is some distance upstream on a mountain torrent that joins the Jaxartes at this point. Heliokleia's heart rose: she had made good time. She checked with a farm woman who was doing her washing in the stream that this was indeed the correct turn, then touched her tired horse to a trot, off the main road and up the track toward the mountains.

She had gone about a mile when the horse began to limp. If she'd been a Saka, she'd have dismounted quickly, checked its hooves, taken the stone from the near fore, and gone on—but she wasn't a Saka. She'd learned to ride less than a year before, and had never looked after her mounts herself. She rode on without noticing for some time, but when the limp became so pronounced that the horse no longer set the foot on the ground, she at last realized what had happened. She dismounted. The horse stood on three legs, resting only the tip of the near fore on the ground, and laid back its ears at her. She remembered that the animals did sometimes get stones in their hooves, and looping the reins over her arm, she knelt and checked the turned-up foot. The stone was plain to be seen, but when she touched it the horse kicked and shied; the foot was raw and inflamed. Heliokleia tried again, and the horse almost pulled her over, then tried to bite her. Shaking with exhaustion, she tied the animal to a tree, put a handful of grass in front of it, knelt between it and freedom, and tried again, speaking to it soothingly. The horse kicked again, then stood snorting and trembling. Her hurried fingers could get no purchase on the stone; she remembered that her guards used a knife to pry them out. She rummaged through the saddlebags; she had no knife. The end of her gold necklace, though, was stiff and narrow, and might work. She took it out and knelt beside the horse again, putting the forefoot on her knee. The horse bared its teeth warningly. She tapped the hoof, as she'd seen the guardsmen do, then dug at the stone with the end of the necklace.

Several things happened at once: the stone jumped out; the necklace slipped from her hand; and the horse reared, squealing shrilly in pain. Its hooves tore the air above Heliokleia's head, and she had just time to put up her arms to protect herself when the injured forefoot cracked against her left arm and knocked her onto her face. The loosely knotted reins were torn from the tree branch, and the horse shied and galloped away down the road, open saddlebags flapping behind the empty saddle.

Heliokleia jumped up and ran onto the road in time to see the horse disappearing round a bend, going back the way she had come. She ran after it a little way, but the animal was headed back to its familiar stall, and at the sight of her broke into a jolting run until she was well behind. If she followed it all day she might catch it—but time hung like a mountain over her head; she was buried under time, and crushed. She stood in the middle of the stony track in the spring sunlight, arms hanging limply by her side, and watched the horse trot away, carrying all the money she had brought so carefully to pay for her journey.

After a few minutes she put her hands to her face. The arm the horse had kicked ached brutally. How far was it? She had made good time so far; perhaps, perhaps, the lodge was near, and if she hurried, she might yet be in time? She began to walk back up the track, holding her hurt arm and crying silently.

When she reached the place where she'd tied her horse she saw something gold glinting in the grass and she remembered the necklace. Did she dare use it to buy another horse? People would be suspicious of it when it was offered by a woman on foot: they might stop her and send to their lord to see if she was a thief. Still, the necklace might still be useful for something. She stopped, picked it up, and for lack of a better way to carry it, fastened it around her neck, then began to walk quickly up the mountainside, clutching the necklace with her injured arm. It was about the middle of the afternoon.

She was not used to walking far, and her feet were dressed for riding in loose boots of soft leather, white with elaborate gold laces, sharp heels, and soles no thicker than a pancake. The track was stony and dry, and within two miles every step was painful to her bruised feet. She stumbled on, trying to detach herself from sense. After another mile she saw a herdswoman with a flock of goats staring at her. She called to her, saying that her horse had bolted, and promising a reward if the woman could find her another—but the woman merely stared at her, then began to drive the goats away. The queen pressed on, disheartened, struggling, blind with weariness, up the steep slopes, mile after painful mile.

At dusk she met a man and a boy, driving cows home to be milked, and again she called and asked for a new horse. They stared at her in wordless suspicion and made a gesture to avert evil: beautiful, going on foot in her royal riding clothes and purple cloak, pale and fair-haired, she seemed so impossible that they did not believe she was a real woman, but a demon sent to tempt them.

"I have a friend at a hunting lodge of Lord Azes," she said desperately. "He's near death, I must reach him tonight. My horse has bolted; in the name of all the gods, please, I will give you this"—lifting the gold necklace—"if you can bring me a horse."

"You mean the hunting lodge the king had repaired for his son?" the boy chirped up, while his father made the gesture against the evil eye again. "You've come the wrong way for that; it's back about three miles to a track by a split oak, then twelve miles straight up the mountain. You'll never come there tonight, even with the fastest horse in Ferghana." His father clouted him, and the boy rubbed his ear.

"Please," said Heliokleia in a cracked voice, "give me a horse. There's a man's life at stake."

"Don't speak to her," the man snarled to his son; and he began to drive the cows onward as fast as he could.

The queen turned and stumbled back down the track, sobbing. Everything she had done, and all for nothing. The king's men would find her in the morning, she would be disgraced and punished, and Itaz would be dead. But perhaps her count of the days was wrong; perhaps Itaz had stopped on the way, perhaps Azilises had found he couldn't do it, or couldn't do it at once. She could not give up, not now; she must go on to the end, even if that end was the smoking ruins of a mountain hunting lodge in the cold light of morning.

Her fingers twisted in the gold necklace and caught in something fine, curled about the gold. She looked down and saw the single white horse hair that Itaz had given her when he came back from Bactra, gleaming in the last light. She pulled it free and held it up to the final pink smear that was fading in the west. She had never believed in Itaz' vision, and she didn't believe now—but she was desperate and weak with exhaustion and would try anything. "If it's true," she said aloud, "then send the horse here now, Grandfather Antimachos, and you, Lord Sun; send him to take me to Itaz in time!"

Nothing happened. Bitterly, she fastened the hair again to the necklace—it was the only thing Itaz had given her she had left to keep —and staggered on.

Three miles down the track; three slow, agonizing miles. The sun set, and the waxing moon cast a soft light over the empty fields and dark road. She was not afraid, walking alone in the strange land: her heart was so stunned that she would have welcomed death. Limping down the path she saw the split oak she had been expecting for the last mile and a half; something white was waiting beside it. As she stumbled nearer she saw that it was a horse.

She stopped dead. The white horse moved out of the shadow of the oak tree, and its coat glowed in the moonlight. It came up to her and nuzzled her shoulder; its breath was warm, and it smelled of sunlit meadows. Hushed and frightened, she stroked its neck, the coat silk-soft over the steel of the muscles. As though it were a signal, the horse knelt, and slowly now, as though in a dream, Heliokleia climbed onto its back.

There was no need to guide it. The white stallion turned into the track of its own accord, and began to canter up it, moving as easily as water. The canter became a gallop, and then something else; there was no jolt of hoof upon stony ground, but each step poured like music into the air: the queen looked down and saw the track falling away below, the trees twisting in the moonlight. The mountain peaks sang joyously into the sky. She clung to the stallion's mane, and his ears pricked forward, nostrils flaring as he ran along the wind. There was a moment that seemed to last forever, when the mountains bent over to the stars and the whole sky rang with light—then the trees rushed near, and the flight became a gallop, the gallop a canter, and the horse stopped lightly before a hunting lodge, dark in a moonlit forest clearing. Heliokleia slid from the horse's back. She no longer felt weary, and the pain was gone from her arm. "Thank you," she told the horse, whispering, unable to comprehend the wonder of it; and the stallion bowed its head.

She turned back to the lodge and saw that it was not completely dark, after all. Light shone in a window, red light. Fire. She ran toward it.

The door was unlocked and opened at her touch; inside, the house was full of smoke. Coughing, she beat at it and ran into a central room. The walls were covered with flame. She ran through one open door: a latrine. She ran out, into another: the red light showed her a man's shape, lying asleep upon a low couch. She ran to him and grabbed his tunic. "Itaz!" she shouted. "Itaz! Wake up!"

He stirred, opened his eyes, and smiled at her—then closed them again and went back to sleep. She slapped him. "Wake up!" she shouted. "There's fire!" She dragged him off the bed; he fell onto the floor and opened his eyes again, frowning in puzzlement. She pulled at him. "Come on, please!" she said. "Please!"

"It's you," he said in pleased puzzlement. "What are you doing here?"

"Come on!" she screamed. The flames were reaching the bedroom now. She pulled at him, dragging his arm across her shoulders.

"For you—anything," he said, smiling stupidly, and climbed to his feet. They stumbled out of the room.

In the main room, the roof was alight, and burning fragments crumbled down onto the floor: the door she'd left open was visible as a black shape in a wall of fire. She pulled Itaz through it; behind them, the roof collapsed and the blaze leaped savagely upward.

She guided Itaz across the clearing and seated him on a pile of leaves under a rhododendron. He leaned over, shaking his head in drugged confusion. She looked back at the house. It was blazing furiously now, and from the stone stable building behind it she could hear the terrified whinnying of a horse. They would need a horse. She ran across to the stable and found the bay tethered in his stall, rearing and snorting in terror. The roof above the stable was tile, and didn't burn, but it smoked in the heat, and the walls were cracking. She threw her cloak over the bay's head, and when he was still, managed to untie him and lead him out. Then she calmed the horse and led it over to the rhododendrons.

The night air seemed to have woken Itaz from his drugged sleepiness. When she appeared with his bay stallion, he looked up quickly, then stared at her. She tethered the horse to a branch and crouched down beside him; he put out his hand and touched her face. "Am I dreaming?" he asked.

"No."

He looked at the burning house. "I seem to be awake—but how . . ."

"Your father told Azilises to give you some drugged wine and set fire to the house. I arrived only just in time to pull you out."

"Azilises? I came here with Azilises. Where is he?"

"I don't know. He must have left just before I arrived."

He stared at her again, then again tentatively touched her face. His own face was invisible in the shadow. "It isn't a dream, is it?" he said quietly.

"No," she replied again. "It's true."

The hand pulled away from her and clenched into a fist. He shook his head, then looked again at the burning house. "Why would my father want me killed?" he cried loudly, his voice ringing over the hiss and crackle of the flames.

"Because we were seen, that time in the stables," she answered in an urgent whisper. "Inisme saw us."

He stared again, then jumped up, caught her hand, and pulled her out into the firelight. "She saw us? She told him?" he asked, watching her face.

She nodded. "I found out as soon as I was back in the palace," she whispered, "so I went to your father and told him you'd been insolent. I thought that if he knew how I loved you, it would make him hate you even more. I thought he would accept it if I said you'd just lost your head and been insolent, that he wouldn't look for any plot between us, and would simply send you away. But I was upset, I told the wrong lie, and I told it badly. I'm sorry! He decided that you were in the middle of some scheme to get me and his crown both, and had tried to rape me when I didn't go along with it. I tried to tell him that it wasn't true, and in the end he told me he would just send you back to Parthia, but he didn't. He found out that you hadn't been sleeping with that girl at your farm, and he took that as proof you'd been deceiving him, and had formed some conspiracy against him. He said he would send you to Hell, but he wanted it to look like an accident, to avoid any trouble with your supporters."

"And he got Azilises to . . ." Itaz asked in anguish. Azilises had been at his most witty and entertaining during the journey to the lodge, but that night at supper he'd been quiet, nervous and unhappy.

"I'm tired, and I ache from riding," was all he'd say. But he'd provided a flask of vintage wine, and pressed it on his friend before going to bed.

"He promised to make Azilises commander of my guard in your place."

Itaz looked away in misery and confusion.

"So I came to warn you," said Heliokleia breathlessly. "He told me, when you'd been gone two days he told me, and I rode—oh, by the gods! I lied to him, and slipped away, and I've come so far, so fast! My horse bolted, with the crown and all the money I'd brought, and I had to go on, on foot. I thought I would be too late; yesterday evening I was sure I would be too late." She caught his arms, feeling the muscle through the crumpled tunic, the warmth, bewildered, miserable and alive. "I thank all the gods!" she said fervently.

He stood still a moment in astonishment, then caught her shoulders and stared disbelievingly into her face. "You came openly?" he asked.

"I slipped away from my escort and rode like a madwoman. I changed horses twice. They'll know where I'm going, and they'll follow; they'll talk to the people who gave me the horses. I think we may have a day's lead, but not more than that. We can't stay here."

"He'll kill both of us if he catches us now! He'll be sure we're guilty of adultery and treachery both, and he'd kill us for the adultery alone. With you here, with me, he won't need to make anything look like an accident. He'll rouse the whole valley to hunt us down! Why did you come?"

"There was no one I could send. I couldn't leave you to die."

"But I'll almost certainly die anyway, and in disgrace, too: everyone will say I was a liar and adulterer all along! Yes, and you'll die too! He'll have you strangled for this and impaled outside the city gates! You've ruined yourself and me! Why did you come?"

She took a deep breath. "Better to die for what I love than to go on living the way I was. And we might escape: it was impossible to get here in time, but I did, and we're both alive. Even if we die, though, if I die with you, I'm content." She laid her hand on his face. "The world isn't what I thought it was. Perhaps some things in it are good enough that any amount of suffering is worthwhile to attain them."

He stared at her again. "I couldn't live with myself," he had told Antimachos, "if I won happiness only through my father's ruin; I'd end up hating the woman and myself." And perhaps, if he'd plotted against his father, or seduced his father's wife, that might have been true. But his father had condemned him to death and Heliokleia had come through ruin and exhaustion, probably only to die at his side. He put his arms around her and kissed her. She wrapped herself around him, pressing herself against him, and began to shake with tears. He pulled her back under the rhododendrons, then spread the purple cloak on the dry leaves and laid her down. She unfastened the gold belt and tossed it aside, still crying. He kissed the tears, stroking her face gently; she pulled off her trousers, and he helped her off with her tunic; then she helped him with his. Naked, they looked at each other, bodies dappled with the leaf shadows cast by the light of the dying fire. It seemed to her that all her life she had been plodding resolutely across a barren desert toward this instant. Now the river came flooding into the dry scrub, and the steppes grew suddenly green with spring. She lifted her arms and pulled him down onto herself, and her limbs flowered, like the dry wastelands, with precious incense.

They made love, quickly and passionately, then pulled the cloak round themselves against the chill, huddled into the dry leaves, and made love again, slowly and tenderly; then fell asleep wrapped in each other's arms. They woke to a morning white with mist, stiff and cold. Itaz sat up, confused, shivering at the chill air, then looked down at Heliokleia curled in the leaves beside him, still asleep. The memory of the night came back clear as though it were newly etched in stone. He looked at her in silence. For her sake his father had tried to kill him; for her sake he would be under sentence of death, and could hope at most for exile and poverty for the rest of his life.

For his sake she had thrown away a world. He stroked her hair gently and she smiled, knowing him even in her sleep, and moved nearer. Looking down at her, Itaz felt again that he was divided from himself; that he was a new man, unknown to himself, no longer fixed to home and birth and condition, but rootless and free: it was as though he had just been born. He owned nothing but love, and that alone still defined him.

He lay down beside her and kissed her, and she woke and moved
again into his arms. They made love again in the hollow of the leaves,
with the birds calling tentatively around them in the white day.

When they had finished, Itaz was the first to move. He sat up,
looked about and saw his new horse, still tethered to the branch. He
reached around for his clothes, then got up, shivering, brushed the bits
of leaf and dirt from his skin, and dressed hurriedly. "You said they
won't be more than a day's ride behind us," he said.

She nodded, reaching for her own trousers. "I left my escort at the
fire temple. I don't know how long it took them to realize where I'd
gone, but it must have taken them some time. Then they would have
had to send back to the city to ask the king what to do. He must have
understood immediately where I was going, and probably set out after
me as soon as his horses were ready. But he couldn't have started out
much sooner than the afternoon of the day I did. I rode most of last
night—I mean, night before last—and I don't think he would have
been able to do that; there wouldn't be the horses ready for all his men,
though he may have sent a few on ahead to seize us. But I think he'll
be a day's ride behind."

"Azilises may come back this morning, though, to see whether he
was successful," Itaz commented distastefully. "We'd better leave as
soon as we can. Do we have any food?"

Heliokleia shook her head. She had not eaten the previous day, and
she became aware that she was very hungry.

"And you said you lost your money when your horse bolted."

She nodded. "Most of it. I have a little silver in my purse, and
some jewelry."

"We may need that if we get away. There was some food in the
stables, and I had some money . . ." He trailed off, looking at the
hunting lodge. The building itself was burned to the ground, a pile of
blackened beams in the center of the clearing, but the stable walls still
stood, though the roof had fallen in. He crossed to it with his quick
stride, picked his way into the rubble, and began tossing the roof tiles
aside. Heliokleia came and helped him.

There was some dried meat left in strips under one beam, and some
loaves of bread, dusty and smoke-blackened but edible, next to the
wall. They breakfasted on these and washed them down with a drink

of water from the spring. Itaz dug out his mount's saddle, saddle blanket, and bridle, found his hunting bow in its case with his arrows, then located a sack of grain, which he carried back to his hungry horse. While the animal ate, he kicked through the ashes of the bedroom, looking for the silver, without success. His sword lay in the place where he'd hung it, at the head of the bed, but the bedstead and the wooden sheath block were burned to ash, and the sword itself was twisted and useless, the handle burned away. He had no spare clothes, and no coat. "It's a good thing I was too tired to undress last night," he commented, looking down at the crumpled tunic and trousers."

"It pays to sleep in your boots," agreed Heliokleia, straight-faced.

He kissed her, then saddled the horse while she packed some of the food in the saddlebags. He hung the bow case in front of the saddle, helped Heliokleia up into it, and jumped up behind her. It was not a comfortable way to ride; there was no space for his legs between saddle and saddlebags. He climbed into the saddle and pulled Heliokleia onto his lap, and they started down the track.

"Where do we go?" asked Heliokleia.

"Away from here, first," Itaz replied. "We can think about anything further than that as we go."

She was quiet for a minute, thinking. "We could pretend we were a merchant and his wife," she said at last. "We could say we were going to join a caravan at the south road, cross the valley and look for a real caravan, and then go through Bactria into India."

"Oh, excellent!" he said sarcastically. "Why would we be riding a royal stallion—pillion? Why wouldn't we have any merchandise? No one would believe us for an instant, even if they didn't recognize us, and plenty of them would. Particularly you; anyone who's seen you will remember you."

"I could change the clothes, and you could change the horse."

"They'll remember you, not the clothes. Even if you were ugly, they'd remember your hair and eyes. Fair Yavana women aren't common enough to pass unnoticed, and you're so beautiful everyone looks at you twice."

She gave the Antimachid smile. "You would think so," she observed.

"It's true! We can't be inconspicuous. You're known, I'm known.

And my father will rouse the whole valley, shouting that his wife has run off with his own son! It will be treachery to help us, and there will probably be a reward for anyone who catches us. We could never get past Eskati unremarked."

"Even if we traveled at night?"

"We would still need food. And fodder for the horse. And we don't have much money, and if we try to exchange jewels for it, we'll be even more conspicuous. And even if we could get out, and get to India, what would we do there? Would your uncle protect us?"

She was quiet for a moment, then shivered. "No. He would hand us back to my brother. Adultery is an evil, and he wouldn't support me in it."

"And your brother would . . ."

"Keep me in his house in disgrace for the rest of my life, and hand you back to your father. We can't rely on help from anyone."

They rode on in silence. There was a sound of horses' hooves approaching through the mist below them, and Itaz jumped off the horse and led it quickly into the undergrowth. He held it, stroking its nose and whispering to it to keep it quiet, as four or five horses clopped past them up the track.

"There goes Azilises, probably with his father," whispered Itaz as the sound vanished. "He'll realize that I've gone."

"Will he look that closely in the ash?"

"He'll look for the horse in the stable."

"He won't know, though, that you know about the drugged wine. He'll think you must have woken and run out of the house after he left, and he'll expect you to go to his father's fortress. You'd be safe there. His father isn't part of the plan. Maybe you could go there and borrow another horse and some supplies."

"Don't be ridiculous! You couldn't go there, and where would you wait? What if my father has sent some fast messengers posting ahead of him? I'd be seized on the spot. And even if he hasn't, I can't just say, 'Greetings, lend me another horse and a pack animal laden with food and don't send anyone with me when I go!' "

"Don't just criticize! If you don't like my ideas, think of some of your own!"

Itaz jumped back on the horse and started it down the path again, moodily silent. The mist was beginning to lift.

"I'm sorry," said Heliokleia after a little while.

He pulled her against himself and kissed her. "I can't think of anything. We have food to last today and perhaps tomorrow. We can ride till then."

"Ride which way?"

"West, of course. It's the only way out of the valley."

Heliokleia was silent for a few minutes, staring ahead into the fog. Then she shivered. "There's the Terek Pass," she said in a whisper.

"It's closed," returned Itaz. "No one has gone that way and returned since King Alexander's days."

"I've heard the story," Heliokleia said sharply. "But even if it's true, and not the crude rumor of avalanches, or a tiger dead long ago —no one has been there for years uncounted. The guardian may be asleep, or dead. Or he may not trouble those who go there and don't intend to return."

"No," Itaz whispered, his eyes beginning to light up, "he might not." He had never lived in the Terek Valley: to him the thing in the pass was only a story. And the fear of swords makes most people forget their fear of demons. "The people on the other side are Sakas, so it's said, but they don't know or care anything about my father. We could go there. We could sell your jewels, and I could find service as a mercenary in some city. As a king's son, I might be given a captaincy. We could make a life there. And no one would expect us to go that way. They wouldn't be watching for us."

"How far is it?" she asked eagerly.

"A week's ride? Ten days? We have to cross the Naryn and swing round and up the Terek Valley."

"Could we do it? All your objections about going by Eskati would still hold true: we'll still need food, and fodder for the horse, and we'll still be noticed."

"If we stay in the mountains we won't meet many people, and we should be able to live off the land. The grazing is good this time of year, and game is plentiful. I have my bow, and if we catch nothing, we can use your silver. There's a chance, my life: when my father doesn't find us here, he'll look for us westward. We have one horse between us, and we can't go fast—but if we go east, where no one's been alerted and no one is looking for us, then we have a chance!"

"East, then!" said the queen eagerly. "And may the gods favor us!"

Itaz remembered that they were adulterers and perjurers both, and not those the gods were inclined to favor. The guardian of the pass might well snatch them both. He closed his eyes, silently praying to Ahura Mazda to understand and to forgive.

They didn't go down to the main road, but followed tracks along the mountainside, winding in and out of forest and across open hillsides inhabited only by a few goats. It was a cold damp day, and they were high enough in the mountains that Itaz shivered in his tunic. Around lunchtime they stopped at a hovel where they bought some goat's milk and a sheepskin coat from a nervous and hostile shepherdess. Heliokleia paid for it with some of her silver. "We can afford one old coat," she told Itaz when he protested. "And you need it."

Itaz pulled the coat on. It was well used, dirty, and too small, but better than nothing. They drank the milk, got back on the horse, and rode on. The shepherdess looked after them with suspicious eyes, and they rode directly south until they were out of her sight, knowing that she would report them to her lord.

Late in the afternoon they started a bevy of pheasants from shelter in the scrub, and Itaz managed to get an arrow to his bow in time to shoot one; that evening they cooked it on a spit over a campfire, then ate it with some of the bread, leaning against each other and staring into the embers. "Are you sorry you came?" asked Itaz, stroking Heliokleia's hair.

"No," she answered without hesitation. She leaned her head back to look up into his eyes. "Are you sorry I came?"

"Oh, no!" he said, kissing her and fondling her breasts. "I've never been so happy." She gave a shiver of joy and pulled closer to him, and he held her in a perfect and tranquil delight. It was perfectly true, he realized, that he had never been so happy. Yet he had sworn to his father, by Ahura Mazda and by the Sun, that he would never betray him, and he had broken his oath: he ought to feel ashamed. His father had tried to murder him: he ought to feel appalled. A friend had betrayed him: he ought to feel grieved. He faced exile and death: he ought to be afraid. Instead, he was blissfully happy. All his life he had struggled to please his father, please his Parthian hosts, please the gods. Now he had failed. But in failure, he had found something else, a treasure buried in the ruins, and everything around and within him seemed to be at rest. He could neither justify nor even explain his happiness, his sense of the goodness and beauty of life, but he couldn't regret the betrayal that had been forced on him. He remembered again what Antimachos had said about the difference between human and divine outlooks. He laughed. "You clever Yavanas!" he said softly.

"Me and who else?" asked Heliokleia, smiling at him.

"Your ancestor Antimachos—or whoever it was I spoke to on that mountain. He said our whole predicament was the result of human perversity, and I think he was right."

To his surprise, she didn't smile tolerantly, but sat up straight, looking serious. "There was something I hadn't told you," she said, and described the moonlight encounter with the white horse. "Perhaps I dreamed it," she finished. "I was desperate with fear, and so tired I didn't know where I was. I might well have dreamed it." She brought out the necklace and looked for the white horsehair she had tied in it— but it was gone.

Itaz frowned. He took out the two hairs he had kept—he had twined them about the Antimachos coin—then shook his head. She might have dreamed it—but he didn't believe she had. "The gods may favor us, after all!" he whispered in awe.

"I pray they do!" she said vehemently. "If any of them will bring us safely through that pass, I'll worship him until the end of my life."

"Me too," said Itaz—then taking his hand off the coin and putting it back on the breast, added, "We ought to rest—and I for one won't be able to without something else first."

Her eyes began to smile again. "And what would that be?"

"Ah! What would you do if I said 'a drink of water'?"

She picked herself up on her knees and kissed him passionately, unfastening his coat as she did so. She pulled the coat off and ran her hands under his tunic up his chest; it took his breath away completely. "What about the drink of water now?" she whispered, smiling at him, the girl he had seen at Eagle Crag come back again. "Are you going to get up and get it?"

He had no inclination to do so.

They slept in the bushes again, on top of the saddle blanket with the purple cloak spread over them both, woke in the morning, and rode on. They continued for several days without seeing anyone but the occasional herders with their flocks. Game was plentiful, there was plenty of grazing for the horse, and the weather was fair. Blissfully happy, they almost forgot the unseen pursuit, boiling in the valley to their right.

In the afternoon of the sixth day after leaving the hunting lodge, they reached the valley of the Naryn River, which joins the Jaxartes from the northeast as the Terek from the southeast. They were reluctant to descend to it, painfully aware that in the more densely populated river valley it would be far harder to escape notice—but the valley had to be crossed if they were to reach the Mountains of the Sun and the Terek Pass. They rested for a few hours, then rode down into the valley at evening, and continued across it until late into the night, covering as much ground as they could under cover of darkness—but the horse had hard work, carrying two, and had to be rested before the morning. And the next morning they had to buy fodder for it, and food for themselves, as the supply of bread was long gone, and they were keeping the dried meat for the pass. At the farm where they bought the things, people stared at them and muttered; laborers going down to the fields stopped to gape at them as they rode by, and they knew, as they pressed on, that people must be running to some lord to ask who and what they were. But no one stopped them, no hoofbeats followed in quick pursuit, and if the messages reached anyone who took them seriously, they didn't do so in time.

They reached the other side of the valley by dusk, and settled with relief beside another campfire in the foothills. The mountains about the Terek Pass were, at that time, the least populous part of all Ferghana. "We've done it!" Itaz declared jubilantly. "No one was watching for us; maybe they hadn't even heard that we'd fled. We've caught my father out. And no one will catch us now! We're almost there!"

"We've *almost* done it," corrected Heliokleia. "It won't be done until we're on the other side of that pass."

They saw no one through the whole of the next day, but rode up along the flanks of the mountains, going due south through a wilderness of juniper, and pine, dark rhododendron and feather-leaved ephedras. The mountain spring, later than that in the valley, was at its height: birds sang, and the earth was purple with crocuses and blue with iris. Game was plentiful again, and easily caught: Itaz shot a wild sheep, and they had meat to roast then and some to save for the day that followed. "Tomorrow we should reach the pass," said Itaz. "And may the gods grant we get through safely!"

But the next day was one of delays—a track that stranded them at a cliff face, a stream that forced them halfway into the valley again before they found a ford, and finally, as they scrambled up the Terek Valley itself into the high mountains, snow. The snows stay late on the Mountains of the Sun, and cling to the pass itself all year round. When they camped that night, they were still below the treeline and some miles from the pass. They built a fire of driftwood on the gravel beside the river, where the snow had melted, and huddled between it and the horse all night for protection from the cold.

The following morning dawned clear and radiant, the sun white in a sky full of eagles. They gave the tired horse the last of the fodder they'd purchased, ate the last of the wild sheep, then mounted and set off up the river.

It was heavy going. The snow was soon deep, and they had to dismount and lead the horse through the drifts, shivering and stumbling in the cold. At noon their hands and feet were numb and lips blue with the chill. They were above the treeline and near the pass itself by then and there was nothing to use to build a fire. But they paused to catch their breath, and sat in the shelter of a drift, holding each other closely for warmth.

Suddenly the horse lifted its head, its nostrils flaring, and laid its ears back. And they felt in that instant the thing we in the Terek Valley always felt beside that river: the sense of something alive, high up beyond them, looking out with a profound, unspeaking malice. Itaz jumped to his feet, looking back, looking round bare stone and deep snow and silence. He looked down at Heliokleia. She took his hand and pulled herself to her feet. They looked at each other, telling themselves silently that it was nerves, it was the tension of being so near to escape. But they didn't dare say this aloud, instinctively afraid of the emptiness of words in that silence. Without speaking, they caught the horse's bridle and pressed on.

They hadn't gone far when the river with its deep drifts twisted off to their left, and looking up the slope directly before them they saw the ridges of rock falling to a place where the sky brightened, unlocked from the mountains behind it: the pass itself. They looked at each other again, then joined hands and began to climb the slope.

The going was much easier: the wind had swept most of the snow clear, leaving only an inch or two of fine ice that crunched underfoot. It was a still, sunny day, windless, and the air was almost warm. It was utterly silent, apart from the crunching of the snow beneath their feet. No wind hummed in the rocks, and no eagles turned in the flat blue panel of the sky. Fair and calm—but the silence seemed to grow heavier as they climbed, until their footsteps boomed in their ears, and under the rasp of breath they could hear the beating of their hearts. It was hard to move; their feet seemed to stick to the ground. The horse was trembling and sweating, and started at nothing, the corners of its eyes showing white with fear. Itaz held it tightly, afraid that it would bolt.

They reached the top of the slope at last, and paused, panting. Ahead the pass lay open before them, its floor of snow and wind-cleared gravel, and its walls of sheer stone, bordered by fallen boulders and scree. It was empty of everything but sunlight and silence. Beyond, a long way beyond, folds of red mountain fell away: the other side, the east, the unknown world.

They looked at each other with shining eyes, then turned to look back one last time into the blue-green haze of the valley below them.

Spread out down the slope and strung along the river was a line of armored horsemen. In the middle, just turning his golden bay onto the slope behind them, was a short stout shape in gilded armor: over the distance between them Itaz felt the shock of his father's eyes. Someone, somewhere, had told Mauakes enough for him to guess where they meant to go, and he had caught them at the very doorway into freedom. Itaz gave an inarticulate cry of horror and turned back to his stallion. Heliokleia was already scrambling into the saddle; he jumped up behind her and urged the horse forward into the pass, taking his bow from its case and stringing it as he went.

The floor of the pass was level, but uneven, and the horse was tired and hungry. For all its fear and their urging it could not go fast. Itaz

leaned forward, holding Heliokleia close with one arm, the other gripping his bow, waiting. It came, before too long, the sound he was
dreading: a soft whistle in the air. An arrow fell in the gravel behind
them, then another. Shouts rang out; more arrows flew. Then the horse
reared and screamed with pain, landed staggering, galloped a few steps,
tossing and curvetting; there was an audible thud as another arrow
struck it—and it fell. Itaz grabbed Heliokleia and rolled free; there was
another whistle, and an arrow stood trembling in the scree beside him.

Itaz slapped Heliokleia down behind the horse, which was lying
still now, dead, one arrow protruding from its rump and another from
its side. He pulled his bowcase from its place on the horse's withers, set
an arrow to his bow, and stared grimly at the men who were galloping
toward him. They were armored, but the scale armor blankets had been
taken from the horses, presumably because they were too burdensome
in the steep pass. He rose to his knees and shot: one horse fell. He seized
another arrow and shot again. There were shouts; the other riders
turned their horses and rode back, shooting over their shoulders as they
went; they reined in just out of bow shot and waited at the other end
of the pass. Heliokleia grabbed Itaz' arm and pointed at a block of
stone behind them surrounded by scree and half-melted snow. He nodded, and they left the horse and ran over to it. The boulder's top was
propped against the cliff, and there was a hollow in the loose stones
beneath it. There they knelt. Itaz peered out from under the protection
of the rock and saw that the king's guards were riding back.

Silently, methodically, he set another arrow to the bow and shot:
another horse fell. He shot again, killing another mount, then waited,
his bow bent and the arrow's feathers sharp against his cheek, until he
could see the riders' faces. One of them was Azilises. He set his teeth
and let go of the string: the arrow flew straight and caught his betrayer
in the eye. Azilises fell and his horse plunged on; Itaz shot again at the
man who tried to catch its bridle, and hit him on his unprotected knee;
he shot again, injuring another horse. The riders turned back, shooting
arrows that buried themselves in the gravel. Itaz ran out toward the
horse; Heliokleia slid out and began drawing arrows from the gravel in
silence. But another troop of guardsmen came galloping down toward
them, shooting at Itaz when he was halfway to the horse; he dodged

back to the boulder and crouched behind it to shoot again and again. Heliokleia handed him some more arrows.

The troop of guardsmen turned back; their own arrows bounced uselessly off the stone, and they regrouped out of bow shot to talk about it. Azilises' horse stood in the middle of the pass, reins dangling and head drooping in confusion.

"We won't be able to catch it," said Heliokleia quietly, one hand on Itaz' arm. He glanced aside at her, then stared again at the horsemen at the other end of the pass. "We have to try. If we could get out of the pass . . ."

"They'd follow us. There's no reason for them to stop this side of the mountains."

He glanced at her again. "Do you want to surrender, then?" he asked.

"No," she said quietly. "I said I'd be content to die with you. I regret nothing. May your god grant you his paradise, Itaz my life."

He set the bow down and caught her hands, gazing into her earnest face. He kissed her. "I've had paradise here," he told her. "The god won't give me another one in death."

Her mouth curled in the Antimachid smile. "I seem to remember you questioning whether we know everything there is to know about a god."

"Perhaps," he replied. He stared at her a moment longer, memorizing her face—the skin flushed with the cold, the tangled, dirty hair, the brilliant eyes fixed so tenderly on his own. "Do you still hope for release?" he asked her.

"Release into what? I don't know nearly as much about it as I used to. I am ignorant of what my life is now, let alone death. Perhaps the gods are merciful. All I know is that I love you, and I regret nothing."

They kissed again, a long kiss full of promises. Then Itaz looked out from under the block of stone, and saw that another group of horsemen was riding toward them, at a walk this time. One of them was in gilded armor. "My father wants to talk," he observed. "We don't surrender?"

"No."

The king's party stopped beside Itaz' horse, and the king looked about for them. Itaz stood, holding the bow in his hands, with an arrow on the string, and his father turned his horse toward him, and stopped it, dead still. He was close enough that his face was clearly visible under the gilded helmet, and he glared at Itaz with bitter, accusing eyes, eyes that knew everything and despised it. Itaz had a sudden strange sense that he had lived this scene before, and he dropped the arrow from the bow, feeling a fear unlike any he had known.

"Father," he said.

"Lying hypocrite!" returned Mauakes savagely. "Where is she?"

Heliokleia stood as well. The king looked at her with contempt. "You whore," he said, and to Itaz, "Did you know she accused you of rape?"

"I know what she accused me of, and why," Itaz replied. "Why did you want to talk to us?"

"If you come quietly, and name your accomplices, I'll send the whore back to Bactra," Mauakes told him. "You'll get an honorable execution, but she'll live. That's the only offer I'll make, and it's more than you deserve."

Itaz glanced at Heliokleia; she shook her head. "No," she said quietly, then raising her voice and addressing Mauakes, "No. I'm sorry."

Itaz turned back to his father. "No. She doesn't want to go—and I don't have any accomplices. I never meant you any harm. I loved where I shouldn't, but I wouldn't have betrayed you. Apart from one kiss in a stable, there was nothing disgraceful between me and your queen. Father, please believe me."

In answer, Mauakes drew his sword. The look of contempt was frozen in place, but under it Itaz saw the pain, the agony of shame, loss, humiliation and loneliness that the king could not admit to. Itaz glanced at Heliokleia, at his dropped arrow, then remained standing absolutely still. "I won't fight you," he said. "I always loved you, and I never wanted your ruin. End it as you wish."

Mauakes' eyes burned into his own, and the king drove the golden bay closer, lifting the sword. In the cold, the snow under his feet, Itaz remembered suddenly where he had seen all this before, and he cried out even as the noise broke sudden and horrifying across the pass. There were screams of terror. Mauakes turned, his mouth falling open

in a soundless shout, and the thing that guarded the pass flung itself
through the ranks of his men and caught him in its coils.

Itaz screamed and dived for his arrow. The guardsmen scattered,
whirling on their horses, and shot at the thing. The arrows, theirs and
Itaz', slid from it unnoticed. Mauakes hacked at the coils with his
sword, then screamed as the steel shattered in his hand; the scream was
choked into a shriek, and then the king and his horse had vanished in
the tangle of coils, teeth, claws, and eyes. A tail lashed at a man on
horseback and swept him against a rock; his skull broke open and
spilled blood upon the snow. The coils and claws uncurled, and
Mauakes' arm flew through the air and landed on the slope just below
the boulder. Then the body appeared, torn open. The thing twisted
through the ranks of the guards like a driving whip through a flock of
chickens, tossing men and horses dead and disemboweled in every
direction. The guardsmen turned their horses and fled, galloping madly
out of the pass, weeping and shouting as they went. Heliokleia backed
under the boulder, staring and shaking, whispering "Merciful
Anahita!" over and over again. Itaz looked for another arrow and
couldn't find one; he was crying so hard he could barely see. He
dropped to his stomach, watching. The thing tore a guardsman apart
and swallowed the head, then looked about itself. It seemed to be
scaled in shadows, and the air around it blurred like the air above an
oven. It was the size of an elephant, but longer, fanged, stinking. A
second head protruded from its shoulder, grinning red-eyed, and its tail
was toothed; it was a deformed confusion of shapes jammed into one,
and horribly real. It twisted on itself like smoke, shimmering darkly,
writhing across the pass, then went back to the king's body and sniffed
at it. Itaz scrabbled in the gravel and found another arrow, one arrow,
the last. He began to kneel to set it to the string. Heliokleia caught his
arm.

"You can't kill it that way!" she whispered. "You saw: arrows and
iron slide off it like dust. It hasn't seen us; if we keep still, maybe it
won't."

"Do we let it *eat* him?" demanded Itaz, also in a whisper.

"He won't feel it! And I don't want to die that way!"

The thing left the king and began to eat his horse. It picked up its stinking head, mouth dripping blood, and looked directly at them with a horribly conscious malevolence.

Itaz set the arrow to the bowstring again. "It's playing with us. It's not a beast, or any natural creature: it knows we're here and it's waiting for us. We can sit here till we freeze to death, or we can come out. We might as well end it quickly."

Heliokleia bowed her head, her hands clutching each other. Her shoulders shook, but she did not cry. "Very well," she whispered thickly. "Death is death, however we come to it. I will try to be brave. May the gods have mercy on us!"

Itaz rose to his knees. His hands were shaking so much he could not shoot. He waited. The thing was eating the horse again, and paid no attention to him. There was a rustle of gravel behind him and he glanced back quickly, sick with terror—and saw a horse, a white horse standing motionless on the snow at the foot of the cliff. He let out his breath in a long gasp and knelt motionless, not daring to move. It was a dream, he told himself: all of it was a dream.

The air smelled of carrion and sunlit snow together, and his hands were red with cold. If it were a dream, it was one from which he could not awaken. Slowly, afraid to breathe, he crawled away from the boulder toward the stallion, then stood, extended his hand to it. The horse came over, walking so lightly it left no tracks upon the snow, and bowed its shining neck to touch his hand: its breath was warm. Heliokleia had climbed to her feet, leaning with her back against the boulder, and was staring at it in tears.

Itaz patted the horse unsteadily. It knelt in the snow and waited for him. He swallowed, then climbed onto its back, the bow in his hand and the arrow across his knees. The horse turned and leapt over the boulder into the air; it seemed to stand unmoving on the sun's rays, half-dissolved into the white light. The thing below looked up, saw him, and gave a bellow of rage and astonishment so loud that snow slipped from the peaks, rumbling down the further slopes in a torrent of rock and ice. The white horse leapt again, one step carrying it to the other side of the pass, and the thing twisted about and followed it. In the center of the pass the monster jumped into the air, reaching with its claws, and fell down again to the earth with a jolt that shook stone; it bellowed once more. The air around it shook with horror. Itaz set the arrow to his bowstring and turned the stallion with his legs; he could feel the sunlight like a wind on his face. The monster leapt again, reaching upward: its claws tore the air beside his knee, and he could feel the heat of its breath. Landing heavily, it faced him and bellowed again. Itaz shot the arrow down the red throat into the hot darkness within.

The monstrous bellow became a vomit of blood and half-eaten flesh, the roar gargling over it. The thing leapt again, tore at the air with its claws, then bit the earth, rolling over and over, its coils twisting. The ground beneath it churned like mud under a horse's hoof, stone covered its scales, and it lashed itself into the rock like a snake into the dust. The snow melted about it, and it blended into the bare bones of the earth, twisted, faded, sank, and was gone.

The white horse descended and struck the stone with its hoof. There was a flash of light, and the rock lay smooth as before, marked only by a single hoofprint, like the lock upon a door. The stallion turned and cantered easily across the pass. Heliokleia stood waiting by the boulder. Itaz slid off the stallion and into her arms. When they had kissed and embraced and gasped each other's name, they turned and found that the horse was gone.

Mauakes' body still lay, torn and dismembered, where the thing had dropped it. Itaz went over and knelt beside it. His father's face was covered with blood, the mouth still open in that final scream; his remaining hand was locked on the hilt of his broken sword. Itaz picked up a handful of snow, washed the blood from the face, and closed the staring eyes.

Heliokleia came and stood silently beside him, looking down at the body. Itaz' father, whom Itaz had loved. He looked smaller in death; the blood that had been washed off the flat cheeks still stained the gray beard and hair. The face was furrowed in pain, and the curling folds seemed familiar to it, revealing something she had never before noticed: the pain wasn't new. Not only the violence of death, but older pains, a thousand betrayals, deaths, disappointments, and failures, had shaped those lines. Yet to her that face had been, from the moment she arrived in the valley, the mask of authority and domination, to be endured with discipline and disgust. Now, suddenly and too late, she saw the face under the mask. For a terrible moment she had a vision of her own face scarred by thirty years of discipline and misery, and saw how much she was like him—and the pity she had never been able to feel flooded her, too late. She knelt in the snow beside Itaz.

They heard the crunch of a horse's hooves behind them, and they looked up quickly—but it was Azilises' horse, which had vanished at the appearance of the nightmare, and now had turned back in the direction of its home. It was reassured to see humans, and came over to nuzzle Itaz' shoulder. Itaz caught its bridle and stood up, still looking soberly at his father's body.

"He loved us," Heliokleia said, wonderingly, all at once believing it.

Itaz nodded. "He did," he agreed simply. "But he was . . . clumsy . . . with love, and didn't know how to live with it."

Heliokleia leaned toward the body. "I'm sorry," she told it. "I could never give what you wanted—and in the end I betrayed you. Forgive me!" Words, empty words, spoken to one who could not hear. Blinking at tears, she looked up at Itaz. "Should we bury him?" she asked hesitantly. "I don't want to leave him lying here like carrion."

Itaz stared down at them, his father and his father's widow. "He should be buried in Eskati," he said slowly. "And we could take him there. The guardsmen won't hurt us now. We don't need to run anymore."

He trudged back to the boulder and fetched his father's arm from the place where it had been hurled, and set the limb in the torn sleeve. Together they rolled the body in its cloak, and fastened the blood-stained bundle with belts taken from the corpses of Azilises and the dead guardsmen. "We can come back for them," said Itaz, looking with regret at the body of the man he'd killed.

They slung the king's body across the horse and, walking one on each side of the animal, led it back the way they'd come, down the slope to the Terek River.

The king's guards were waiting by the river, talking among themselves in terror and uncertainty. Sarozi was with them—more because the king hadn't trusted him in Eskati than because he wanted him on the journey—and he told me about it afterward. Loyalty to King Mauakes, and their pride in their own honor and courage, had brought them to the pass: now the king was dead and they had run away. No one wanted to go back up the slope; they were afraid even to stay where they were. But they were ashamed to go back to the city and confess that they, the king's guard, had abandoned their lord, and left his body unburied and his death unavenged. Spalagdama, the second in command, suggested that they go down below the treeline and offer sacrifices to the Sun, then return at dawn next day to face the monster. "But the Sun won't help us!" objected one of the guardsmen. "That thing is no creature of his. You saw it!" "The Sun is lord of all the world!" protested Spalagdama. "It's blasphemous to say that the Terek Pass is outside his power!" "But that thing must be as ancient as the Sun himself," the man answered. Couldn't you feel it?" "When the world began," another whispered, "it must have been there, and it has hated the Sun and his creatures ever since: it's not a mortal being at all, but a chimera or dragon from the darkness before time." "It is a creature of Nemesis," said another, "and that goddess accepts no sacrifices, and cannot be placated with offerings." And they began to argue over what it was, and what god they could call upon to defeat it.

Then Sarozi, who'd been looking nervously at the long slope, cried out, and they all turned and saw Itaz and Heliokleia descending toward them, and fell silent, staring in disbelief. "We'd seen the horror take the king and half a dozen others," he told me afterward. "We'd *seen* it. Nothing mortal could fight that thing. Nothing, we'd thought, could escape it. When we saw Lord Itaz and the queen coming toward us, leading the horse, we thought it was some demon trick to destroy us; if one man of us had stirred, the whole troop would have been off and away down the valley as fast as we could gallop. But we were all so stunned and sickened we couldn't even move. No one raised a bow.

"When they came closer, I saw that they weren't some illusion, but real: their hands were red with the cold, and the queen's teeth were chattering. And we saw the bundle wrapped in the king's cloak on the horse's back, and the blood on it, and we guessed what they were bringing down. We couldn't believe that they'd got away, still less that they'd brought the king back, and we simply stood there, staring. It was so quiet you could hear the horse's hooves crunching in the snow, and the river rushing behind us. Lord Itaz and the queen led the horse right into the middle of us, then stopped. Itaz put his hand on the horse's body and announced, 'The thing that guarded the pass is dead, by the help of our Lord the Sun,' in a voice like a god's. 'Here is my father, whom I never meant to betray. I wish to return to Eskati and bury him.'

"We all looked at each other, then glanced back up at the pass: we still couldn't believe it. Itaz could see we didn't, because he repeated what he'd said. 'The pass is clear. The guardian is dead, and the Sun's horse has put his foot upon its tomb: I can show you the mark on the stone.'

"We didn't know what to say. We'd come to that place to kill those two, and now our king was dead and they had come back from the pit of Hell and told us the devil that kept it was gone. We were all silent. In the end, the queen said, 'There are other bodies up there, the bodies of your comrades. Do you want to leave them unburied? If you like, we will go up to the pass with you, and you will see for yourselves that there is nothing there but the dead.' And she looked at us, with her eyes like the eyes of a god, and at that, somehow, we believed them. We all stirred, and then suddenly Spalagdama pushed his way up from the back and dropped to his knees before Itaz. 'Our king is dead,' he said. 'The Sun has given you his glory. Be king for us, Lord Itaz.' And the rest of us shouted, as though someone had taken a spell off our tongues, and we crowded round, yelling, 'Be king, Lord Itaz, be king!'

"Itaz was thoroughly astonished; you could see this was the last thing he'd expected. He started to protest, telling us that he'd never take the place of his brother Goar's son.

" 'He's a child, and we need a king now!' said Spalagdama. 'The Sun has favored you, who can doubt now that your father condemned you unjustly? Let Goar's son be king when he's grown, but you be king for us today!'

"Itaz looked at Heliokleia; she said nothing. He shook his head. 'It's for the tribal council to decide who will be king,' he told Spalagdama. 'For our part, we must return to Eskati and bury my father. Find me a horse, and one for the queen, and I will take you up to fetch the dead who remain.' "

But, said Sarozi, they all knew from that moment that Itaz would be king, and rule jointly with Heliokleia. Sarozi gave the queen his own horse, and the whole party rode up to the pass, and found it, as had been promised, empty except for the dead and one hoofprint etched upon the bare mountain stone. They fetched the dead and started down into the valley again in the last of the sunlight.

It was twelve days later when they arrived in Eskati. The story of what had happened in the pass had traveled before them, at first as a wild rumor, then, when Itaz and Heliokleia sent messengers in advance to order the arrangements for the king's funeral, as solid fact. I didn't hear the rumor, as we were released from the queen's quarters only when the messenger arrived: the man the king had placed in charge of the garrison took his orders seriously. If it had been up to him, I think we would still have been squabbling in the queen's room when she came back, Inisme, Jahika, Armaiti, the four slaves, and me—but when the certain news came that the king was dead, Kanit took charge of the city. And Kanit released us all from our confinement, and told us to prepare our mistress' reception.

So when the queen came riding back into the city, I was waiting, with the others, on the temple terrace, as I had been when I first saw her. The city was crowded again—from the moment the rumors began, people had come flooding in from all over the valley. More had joined the king's party on its way from the pass, so that when Itaz and Heliokleia rode through the gates, they were followed by a huge multitude of councillors and cowherds, warriors and shepherdesses, come to say farewell to Mauakes and to honor the new king. But it was Itaz and Heliokleia who rode in first, going side by side in front of Mauakes' body—placed now on a long wagon picked up along the way. The garrison made an aisle for them through the crowd as they came into the market square, as they had at the wedding a year before, but there were no songs, only a heavy, solemn silence. The two rode very straight and slow, not looking at each other. But when they stopped before the temple and dismounted, their hands touched briefly as they turned together toward the wagon, and I saw the utter trust and confidence between them, and knew that I wasn't wrong: she was still going to be the queen, and this time she was going to be happy. I ran forward, jumped down from the terrace, and took her horse's bridle. She turned, startled, then smiled and kissed my cheek. "Tomyris," she said, and her voice was rough with joy.

"Welcome home," I told her, grinning and crying together. "Welcome home."

What happened after, everyone knows. When Mauakes had been decently buried, there was a great meeting of the tribal council to decide who should rule the kingdom. Some argued that the valley should abandon the house of Mauakes: Itaz, they said, was an oath breaker and an adulterer, and Goar's son was a child. The council, they said, should rule Ferghana as it had long ago. But even those who suggested this did so without conviction: our age is one of kings, and in it a council swims against the current. Tasius suggested a regency for Goar's son, with himself as regent. "Do you want the Yavana to be queen again?" he asked the councillors. "Will you bow to an adulteress from the house of Antimachos, and lose the favor of our lord the Sun?" But the eyes of the councillors were on Itaz even as his brother-in-law was speaking. Here was a man who had ridden one of the Sun's own horses: who could doubt that the Sun favored him? And if Itaz and Heliokleia were oath breakers, Mauakes had broken his oath first. He had not kept his wife in honor, as he had sworn at their wedding; he had injured and imprisoned her; and he had tried to have his son murdered. So the Sun's glory had departed from him in the Terek Pass, and had passed to Itaz. And they would bow to the house of Antimachos, and gladly: they wished now to be reconciled with that shadow, ghost or god, and enjoy peace. When Spalagdama proposed that Itaz should be king, most of the councillors rose in favor, and the rest yielded to their will. So Itaz was made king, in the Sun's name, and he married Heliokleia on the day he took the crown.

They ruled jointly, and ruled with such wisdom in peace, and such courage and authority in war, that people said the golden age had returned. It was a golden age for me, certainly. The palace women's quarters were filled with a constant stream of people: administrators and ambassadors; petitioners, counterpetitioners, and lawyers; tribal councillors and city councillors (always arguing with each other); dike builders, well diggers, and architects; poets and painters, sculptors and philosophers. I had great authority with them all, being a favorite of the queen, and later of the queen's daughter Theodota, whom I instructed in riding. When I married—I married Sarozi, of course—

Heliokleia gave me a dozen mares of the royal breed, as well as a dozen geldings and a bit of land; she and Itaz also allotted us our own room in the palace. It had been a part of the king's room, but Itaz wouldn't sleep in his father's place, and rearranged the upper area of the palace instead, so that his room adjoined his wife's. Sarozi and I were very pleased with our little room on the courtyard, though it was a bit cramped when the children came, and we found excuses to go off to our lands in the Terek Valley as often as we could. But we were certainly very happy. You couldn't be unhappy in Eskati while Itaz and Heliokleia reigned: there was a kind of gladness and good nature among the inhabitants of the palace that spread outward to light the whole city in its glow. The city council rejoiced in its restored rights, the tribal council in its new prosperity, and when we looked about Ferghana, it seemed that the valley would outshine the glories of Bactria. As for the king and queen, they were so happy you could have lit a fire from the warmth between them.

A golden age, but a short one. Itaz and Heliokleia ruled for only seven years. They had one child, their daughter, my lady Theodota. The queen was pregnant for the second time when the Tochari invaded again in strength. The enemy made only a light assault on Ferghana this time, but they took everything else up to the Oxus River: all the grazing lands of the Sakaraukai, and all of Sogdia. The Sogdians and the Sakaraukai fled in every direction, but particularly southward— south into Bactria. The Yavana kingdom fell to them; King Heliokles the Just, and Heliokles the Victorious his son, fell together defending Bactra; the city was sacked, and its people killed or enslaved. The Sakaraukai and the Tochari after them press on, past us now, going south. India will go the way of Bactria, I think, if not in my lifetime then before my children are old. Menander might have held it, but Menander is dead, and his son Straton is no "king of the wheel."

King Itaz led the defense of Ferghana against the Tochari, then took his standing army, his guard, and volunteers from among the councillors and rode to the help of our Bactrian allies. But when he left the valley, the Tochari heard of it, and his force was attacked and surrounded before it reached the Oxus. The Ferghanans used the elephants to fight their way free, but the king was mortally wounded in the battle, and died during the retreat home.

When the news was brought to the queen, the shock brought on labor prematurely. It was a bloody and exhausting business, and ended with a stillborn son and the queen too weary from grief and loss of blood to rouse herself again. She turned her face away from us all and died, clutching in her hand a silver brooch, wrapped with a single white horse hair—the brooch which Itaz had given her, the replacement for the one that was lost.

Itaz was buried in the sky, according to the custom of his faith and his own wish. Heliokleia's body was burned, and the ashes interred in a stone tomb in the market square, before the temple. But some people have sworn to me that, on the night she was buried, a white horse came running from the north, from the fire temple, making no sound as it ran, and that Itaz was riding it. It stopped at the tomb, so they say, and Heliokleia ran out, whole and laughing, and leapt upon its back. And the two riders embraced, while the horse flew into the sky and ran up the wind and away, over the Bridge of the Divider to the House of Song. That is what I've been told. But I kept watch at that tomb most of the night and saw nothing, and people often say what they wish were true—though it could be true, nonetheless. A year or so ago I dreamed a dream like the one I had before I first came to Eskati: the dry river, the silence, and my dead sister crying out to me. I'd understood long before what the river was—the healing power of the gods, clearing the ancient hatred from the pass and renewing our lives—but I never understood what Tistrya had to do with it all. This time, though, the dream continued.

I embraced Tistrya, laughing, with the river singing behind me, and I said, "Tistrya, darling, why have you come here? Why you?" She answered, grinning, "Because I love you. Did you think death stops that? It doesn't end things, you know. It's only from this side of the bridge that the division looks sheer. If you climb high enough, the steep hill becomes part of the valley, and the valley seems a plain." "How high have you climbed, then?" I asked, and Tistrya, still smiling, waved her hand at the sky: far away I saw the star she was named for, the brilliant silver-green star that the Greeks call Sirius, shining beyond the blue of heaven. "Beyond that," she said.

When I woke, the star Tistrya was shining outside my window, and I stood for a while with the night wind on my face, looking at it.

From there this whole world must seem no larger than a speck of dust, and perhaps even the difference between life and death is imperceptible. I am growing old now, and that thought was comforting.

When Itaz and Heliokleia died, the succession passed to the king's nephew Mauakes, son of Goar, who, at fifteen, was this time considered old enough to rule, though only with a panel of advisors. When Heliokleia's daughter came of age, King Mauakes married her, and so they rule jointly, and on the whole, rule well. The valley has prospered, and through the Terek Pass we have begun a trade with the Silk Country. And as I said, King Mauakes and Queen Theodota have just commanded a fire altar to be built by Heliokleia's tomb, for all the valley is convinced that she was a kind of god.

She wasn't a god. She was a kind and generous lady, a wise and just queen, a devout philosopher, and in the end, a loving wife and delighted mother. She was, perhaps, a queen "of the wheel," and a rock unshaken by any wind—and she was my friend. But water is not dust, and what a god is like is beyond our imagining. Still, as the Yavana poet says:

> *Divinity has many forms*
> *Gods bring unlikely things to pass*
> *The likely outcome twists and turns*
> *God takes the unexpected way at last.*

EPILOGUE

There is really no need for anything more, but in reviews of some of my other books I have been mistakenly accused of anachronism, and I thought that this time I had better list a few sources for details which may seem improbable. Yes, the Hellenistic Greeks did use naphtha (W. W. Tarn, *Hellenistic Military and Naval Developments*—or better, read Polybius), and catapults were used in some of the circumstances I have described (E. W. Marsden, *Greek and Roman Artillery*). Elephants, even in very small numbers, were used to devastating effect against untrained cavalry (e.g., Seleukos' "Elephant Victory" over the Galatians: for discussion see H. H. Scullard, *The Elephant in the Greek and Roman World*). Despite everything that's said in basic textbooks about the impossibility of heavy cavalry without stirrups, it was not only possible, but used from the Assyrians onward; more pertinently, it was employed by the settled steppe dwellers on the Iranian borders and by the Parthians (M. A. R. Colledge, *The Parthians,* T. Sulimirski, *The Sarmatians, Cambridge History of Iran,* vols. II and III). The prominence

447

of women in Saka society is not a feminist invention (Sulimirski again, plus Herodotos IV and VII), and for that matter, Hellenistic Greek queens did not follow the Athenian ideal of the retiring housewife (any Hellenistic history—or look up Arsinoë, Berenice or a Cleopatra in the Oxford Classical Dictionary). For a general discussion of the Bactrian Greeks, the classic source is W. W. Tarn's *The Greeks in Bactria and India,* together with A. K. Narain's *The Indo-Greeks* (the two disagree on just about everything). But G. Woodcock's *The Greeks in India* is much more readable, and has nice pictures.

On quotations: "the philosopher" quoted is Herakleitos—fragments lvi and cxix; "Against Necessity . . ." is Simonides, fragment 542, "Dione's daughter, Love" is from Euripides' *Helen* 1098–1106; and "Some say the infantry . . ." is a loose, and filled-in, translation of Sappho fragment 16; "Divinity has many forms" is the close of Euripides' *Helen, Medea, Bacchae,* and, I think, one or two other plays, all are my own translations. The Mazdayist quotations are from the *Avesta,* in the translation by Spiegel and Bleeck, (London, 1864), corrected in some cases by comparison with R. C. Zaehner's *The Dawn and Twilight of Zoroastrianism.* I haven't quoted any Buddhist texts directly, only paraphrased bits of the first sermon and the fire sermon. Many of the religious assumptions of the characters are based as much on Greek philosophical ideas as on the developed religions.

Finally, the Buddhism and Mazdayism represented in this book are an attempt to reconstruct the beliefs of the time, as they would have been held by people living at the fringes of early forms of both, in a polytheistic society, and are unlike the "classic" picture of either faith, and certainly unlike anything one would find today. If I offend by my portrayals, it is by mistake, not intent, and I offer to the reader my sincere apologies.